AND INTO THE FIRE

ROBERT GLEASON

A TOM DOHERTY ASSOCIATES BOOK
NEW YORK

AND INTO THE FIRE

I want to thank my publisher for permission to quote the Sister Cassandra lyrics from my novel *End of Days* and for permission to adapt three pages from that novel, the scene in which Sister Cassandra sings "Hiroshima Girl."

A Forge Book
Published by Tom Doherty Associates
175 Fifth Avenue
New York, NY 10010

www.tor-forge.com

Forge® is a registered trademark of Macmillan Publishing Group, LLC.

The Library of Congress Cataloging-in-Publication Data is available upon request.

ISBN 978-0-7653-7916-0 (hardcover)
ISBN 978-0-7653-9702-7 (e-book)

Our books may be purchased in bulk for promotional, educational, or business use. Please contact your local bookseller or the Macmillan Corporate and Premium Sales Department at 1-800-221-7945, extension 5442, or by e-mail at MacmillanSpecialMarkets@macmillan.com.

First Edition: June 2017

Printed in the United States of America

0 9 8 7 6 5 4 3 2 1

FOR LINDA QUINTON

SPECIAL THANKS

To Sister Megan Rice, the bravest, most decent person
I have ever known.

ACKNOWLEDGMENTS

To Sessalee Hensley and Christine Jaeger for all their help and support.

To Tom Doherty, to whom I owe so much.

To Susan, again and always.

To George Noory and Lisa Lyon for always being there.

To Elayne Becker and Eric Raab, editors extraordinaire.
Your guidance was inspired.

To Jerry Gibbs for over five decades of incomparable friendship.

To Maribel and Roberto Gutierrez—I will never forget.

To Herb Alexander, 1910–1988—You were one of a kind.

[Y]et they repented not of the works of their hands, that they should not worship devils, and idols of gold, and silver, and brass, and stone, and of wood.... Neither repented they of their murders, nor of their fornication, nor of their thefts.

—Revelation 9:20–21

Here lived stupid vulgar sons of bitches who thought they could hire DEATH as a company cop.

—William S. Burroughs, *The Wild Boys: A Book of the Dead*

The darkness drops again . . .

—William Butler Yeats, "The Second Coming"

We're all mad here.

—Lewis Carroll, The Cheshire Cat in *Alice in Wonderland*

PART I

Swift is the reckoning of Allah.

—The Koran

1

"If the wretched of earth wish finer apparel, they should work harder."

—Prince Shaiq ibn Ishaq

Shaiq ibn Ishaq—Saudi Arabia's ambassador to the United States—entered the office of Lieutenant General Jari ibn Hamza. As head of Pakistan's Inter-Services Intelligence (ISI), the general was a man of simple tastes, stringent self-abnegation, and dogged devotion to Allah and country. In keeping with the general's strict Wahhabist upbringing, the walls were devoid of mirrors, artwork, even Islamic icons. Nor in the general's office would music of any kind ever be heard. Even Jari's decor reflected this moral severity—nothing but dark wood, black leather, and polished brass.

Moral severity was not a trait Shaiq aspired to, and the general always annoyed him. In fact, self-sacrifice did not even exist in Shaiq's lexicon. His was a world of sumptuous opulence and unstinting pleasure.

Still, men like Jari had their uses, and Shaiq allowed him a small, patronizing smile.

Coming out from behind his massive mahogany desk, Jari looked at the ambassador and nodded.

"*Alhamdulillah*," he said simply. Praise be to Allah.

"*Ashokrulillah*," Shaiq responded quietly, quickly. Thanks to Allah.

Seating Shaiq on a padded leather armchair, the general took the leather couch next to him. One of his assistants immediately brought them a silver coffee service and placed it on the mahogany coffee table between the two men.

A man of great power and even greater wealth, Shaiq was accustomed to servile obsequiousness. The general, on the other hand, had never made an attempt to hide his feelings. Among other things, the ambassador was, once again, late—almost forty-five minutes late. Shaiq never arrived at scheduled meetings on time, and Jari viewed such chronic procrastination as a personal insult and an indisputable sign of weakness. The general despised weakness of any kind.

Jari was the antithesis of weak. He dressed simply—combat fatigues, black jump boots, and a black beret. He adhered to an exacting code—part Bedouin, part military, part Wahhabist tradition. His was a way of life that prized the demanding desert virtues of moderation and modesty, of hard work and harsh discipline, of commitment to Allah and rigorous self-denial. It required of him an unwavering willingness to endure danger, sacrifice, and hardship. He lived by that code and presumed one day to die by it.

He wasn't sure what drove the wealthy Saudi sitting next to him. From Jari's point of view, his mustache was too impeccably trimmed, his hair too elaborately coiffed. He was too handsome, too smooth, too charming for Jari to ever trust him.

Nor did the general approve of Shaiq's attire. Most officials favored traditional Arab garb. They covered their heads with the keffiyeh and their bodies with the long, white *thawb,* or robe. Or in his case a military uniform. Shaiq instead wore a Brioni suit—pure Escorial jet black. Jari recognized it because once an enterprising American reporter named Julie ("Jules") Meredith had photographed Shaiq wearing the exact same attire, then published a story in *The New York Journal-World* on his sartorial self-indulgence. The reporter identified each article of clothing and each piece of jewelry. She had then added up the dollar value of Shaiq's ensemble. The total came to over $871,000. When Jules Meredith told the prince the cost of his couture, then asked if such extravagance was not unseemly in the face of so much poverty in the Islamic world, Shaiq was disdainfully defiant.

"I see myself as an exemplar of excellence, a role model for the masses, a standard of conduct and behavior, which, if they were wise, they would strive to emulate. I therefore do not hold myself to your bourgeois rules and protocols."

"But should you flaunt your wealth so blatantly when your people live lives of such deprivation?" Jules Meredith asked.

"If the wretched of earth wish finer apparel, they should work harder."

"Is that how you came to own a limo plated in twenty-four-karat gold? Hard work and rugged individualism?"

"I own three. Why? Is something wrong with that?"

"Isn't such ostentation in poor taste?"

"Not at all. I deserve no less."

The ambassador then treated the reporter to his most scintillating smile and gales of derisive laughter.

Still the article had smarted. The ambassador had once told General Jari it had inspired him to buy a plurality interest in *The New York Journal-*

World. At the very least, he could exert some control over "that Meredith bitch," as he had referred to her.

"If I have my way," Shaiq had later told the general, "I'll make her life a living hell."

Reaching across the table for the coffee service, the suit's silk sleeve slid up Shaiq's wrist, and Jari glimpsed the platinum Rolex Oyster Perpetual with emerald-cut diamonds beneath the French cuff. Its gold links glittered with nine-carat diamonds.

How many child-slaves died in Sierra Leone's bloody mines, harvesting those stones? Jari wondered. *How many underage sweatshop laborers did it take to stitch those clothes?*

Now Shaiq was pouring coffee out of the sterling silver carafe into a white china cup, to which he added cream and four teaspoons of sugar. Putting it to his mouth, he winced. Unable to imbibe the strong bitter Pakistani brew, he added more cream and sugar.

Jari cringed.

The man drinks his coffee like a . . . girl.

The general finally forced himself to make eye contact. He was sorry he had. The aquiline nose, regal as Caesar's, was framed by eyes so brilliantly blue Jari wondered who his real father was—or whether the effete Shaiq wore tinted contacts. Jari doubted Shaiq was of Arab extraction. Shaiq's skin was too pale, soft, and smooth—as unlined as a baby's. His high, wide cheekbones were a worthy testament to the high-priced cosmetic surgeons who had labored so assiduously to make him look like a Western film star. In Jari's eyes, Shaiq was a disgrace to *Dar al-Islam.*

"Cell phones?" Jari asked.

"Thanks for reminding me, old friend," Shaiq said with a pleasant smile. "I forgot."

Pulling out his Samsung Galaxy 5000, he was unable to find either the sim card or the battery, let alone remove them.

Jari removed the Samsung from Shaiq's fumbling hands. He quickly unclamped and unscrewed the inside lid, then extracted the battery and sim card for him.

"As you know," Jari said, "America's intelligence and law enforcement agencies can activate these smartphones and convert them to microphones. They've been monitoring any conversation they choose, and this is definitely one they would seek to audit."

The Saudi minister gave him a dazzlingly capped grin and three soft claps. "Bravo, *mon général.*"

Again, Jari inwardly cringed.

Still Shaiq was indispensable to the general's plans. The former minister of Saudi intelligence, current ambassador to Washington, and the Saudi king's envoy to the United States government, Shaiq was the most politically powerful man in the kingdom, as well as its wealthiest. He was also Pakistan's most important personal ally and its most loyal fundraiser. In the United States he was just as formidable. He owned almost half of *The New York Journal-World*—the most prestigious newspaper on the face of the earth, in print and on the Internet—and large pieces of two major cable news networks. His critics complained he'd bought off and silenced the American news media.

Those were the only reasons Jari tolerated him. He had the cash and the clout Jari needed so critically.

"You want to know what progress we've made?" Jari asked, knowing exactly why Shaiq had called him.

"Precisely so."

"I will not give you the exact details, but Operation Flaming Sword is about to begin."

Shaiq nodded.

"Our commanders have chosen their teams, and they are in place."

"And you are absolutely sure this is necessary?"

"Your profits continue to fall, no? The West has come to rely on their own shale oil, on their natural gas deposits, on their wind and solar farms. Without their hydrocarbon imports, your country faces ruin. Since you and your royal family are our preeminent benefactors, we face ruin. They spurn us all with impunity; we cannot allow this to continue."

"Still, Operation Flaming Sword carries with it unprecedented risks," Shaiq noted.

"The permanent loss of the West's petrodollars poses even graver dangers to us both," the general said. "Do you have any idea what would happen if you continue down this road to ruin, if word of your ultimate insolvency becomes known? Our people will rise up en masse. Your cities will burn, your streets run red with blood. We must make the Americans curse the day they started their renewable energy industries. They think global warming scorches their cities and farmlands?" Jari said, rising angrily in his chair. "We will show them real heat, and they will, once again, turn to us."

"Just as they did after we flattened their World Trade Centers," Shaiq said, "and they sent their armies into Iraq."

"Our people will cringe and cower in terror at the threat of U.S. nukes incinerating Mecca, Medina, and Riyadh," the general said.

"And we will send the price of oil into the stratosphere," Shaiq said.

"They will once again view our help in the War on Terror as indispensable," the general said, "and come to us with their checkbooks open."

Jari's desk phone buzzed. He took the call, nodded once, and said, "Good."

"I gather your new financial installment has arrived," Shaiq said.

The general smiled and pressed a button. A dark bearded man in a white floor-sweeping *thawb* and a matching keffiyeh headdress entered. Four bearded men, similarly dressed, followed him. They each dragged behind them eight enormous steamer trunks—made of teak and steel and equipped with rear wheels—by leather handles. The trunks' edges were trimmed with an eighteen-karat-gold plate, inlaid with diamonds and pearls. Their gold-plated, titanium latches were secured with matching titanium padlocks.

As was typical of Shaiq, he had brought the money to Jari in the most expensive packaging money could buy.

"As requested," Shaiq said, giving him a polite bow, "you now have $500 million in used, unmarked, pressure-packed, nonsequential $100 bills. No wire transfers or bank withdrawals large enough to attract undue attention." He placed the keys on the general's desk. "The quintessence of black money."

"*Alhamdulillah.*" All praise and thanks to Allah.

Gazing fondly at the trunk, Shaiq smiled. "Do you know the English poet Milton? He has a line: 'It is better to reign in hell than to serve in heaven.' Do you think it will come to that? For us?"

"If it does," the general said, "then *inshallah*." Allah's will.

Looking suddenly at his watch, Shaiq said, "General, as much as I love our little conversations, I must hurry to my plane. I'm expected in New York."

"The City of . . . Sodom," Jari said with a faint smile.

"For business," Shaiq said, "not pleasure. *The New York Journal-World* is having a revenue-raising ball, and it certainly needs some additional revenue. Since I am their second-largest stockholder, I must attend."

As Shaiq left, the general leaned back in his desk chair and stretched long and hard. He wondered if the rumors he'd heard about Shaiq were true. Underage girls? Sadomasochistic trysts? Erotic asphyxiation? Who knew? But did the Brioni-suited degenerate really understand what he was getting into? No, the general had not conveyed to him the full violent scope of the nuclear attacks, nor would Shaiq have understood their inevitable apocalyptic consequences. Shaiq saw the nuclear strikes as a series of acts so unimaginably catastrophic that no one would dare counterattack. An all-out nuclear war would be so bad for business it would ultimately be unthinkable, and the West would eventually cave. The nations of earth would demand that the nuclear horror come to an end.

In Jari's worldview, however, nothing "came to an end"—not until one

side or the other was obliterated. The age-old blood-mandate to retaliate to-
tally was sacred and absolute: it could only be satisfied by the utter destruction of the foe—in this case the infidel foe.

Shaiq, Jari believed, could not grasp any of this, nor could he ever fully
embrace the coming clash of civilizations. The man's entire being was shel-
tered and held together by filthy lucre. Avarice defined him. He was nothing
but money, the illusion of power and empty words.

Well, in this case, Jari thought to himself, Shaiq's talk would soon be
translated into action. . . .

Shaiq, you'll get a bigger bang for your buck than you ever imagined.

For the first time that evening, the general's smile was sincere.

2

"During one New Year's celebration the Saudi monarchy decapitated forty-seven people in thirteen cities in a single day."
—Jules Meredith

After CIA Director William Conrad finished his morning briefing, he and President George Caldwell retreated to the president's private study. Taking off his light gray sport coat and laying it on a nearby couch, the president eased himself into a dark overstuffed chair. Conrad kept his own suit coat on. Catching a glimpse of himself and the president in a wall mirror, Conrad didn't like what he saw. Three and a half years in office had aged them considerably and expanded the president's paunch. They each looked closer to their late sixties than their late fifties, which was the range of their actual ages. Moreover, the president looked pissed.

He picked up a copy of *The New York Journal-World* off the coffee table in front of them and handed it to Conrad.

"Seen the Jules Meredith piece on the Saudis?" the president asked. "The paper put it above the fold."

"Prince Shaiq is going to be madder than hell," his CIA director said.

"The Meredith woman comes close to referring to him by name."

"If he weren't the co-owner of her paper," Conrad said, "she probably would have."

"Instead she referred to him as 'a high-ranking Saudi official and a well-known financial magnate.'"

"I'm surprised she didn't call him 'the Prince of Darkness.'"

"She called him and his relatives everything else," the president said. "Listen to this." He read part of the article aloud:

The Saudis underwrote Pakistan's proliferation of nuclear weapons technology, including that equipment and expertise needed to manufacture fissile nuclear bomb-fuel. They bankrolled Pakistan's nuclear weapons program and its director, A. Q. Khan, often described as "the Father of Pakistan's atom bomb." Khan eventually became the world's most prolific purveyor of black-market nuclear weapons technology in history, offering it to rogue states everywhere—Libya, Iran, Iraq, North Korea, Syria, even, some believe, Pakistan's arch-enemy, India, earning him the nickname "the Johnny Appleseed of Nuclear Proliferation."

Another fact of Saudi life, which was seldom publicized in America's mainstream media, is its religiously inspired savagery. Long before ISIS was born, Saudi Arabia's state religion, Wahhabism, had institutionalized all of their worst abuses—the demonization of art, science, mathematics, archeology, music, journalism, democracy, women and all non-Wahhabist peoples. While the American media pillories ISIS for its barbaric brand of justice—its amputation of heads, hands, feet, even eyes; its stonings; its interminable floggings, during which they administer as many as a thousand lashes; its subjugation and sequestration of women—Saudi Arabia routinely brutalizes its people in the same ugly way, publicly, in plain sight.

Riyadh's Deera Square is known in the Kingdom as "Chop Chop Square" for its endless beheadings and amputations. Sometimes after a person has his head cut off, the Saudis crucify the body, placing the head in a plastic bag and hoisting it over the body where it appears to float, almost preternaturally abeyant. They display these crucified headless corpses in public for as long as four days. Recently, the Saudi secret police arrested Ali Mohammed al-Nimr, the nephew of Sheikh Nimr al-Nimr, a renowned Shiite cleric, whom the Saudi authorities had recently killed. After torturing and beheading him, his body was crucified and publicly displayed. His crime was attending a peaceful prodemocracy rally.

During one New Year's celebration the Saudi monarchy decapitated forty-seven people in thirteen cities in a single day. After those horrific executions the Algerian journalist Kamel Daoud made the inevitable connection, calling Saudi Arabia "an ISIS that has made it."

Yet the U.S. media was and still is embarrassingly silent about this incessant procession of atrocities that Saudis call a judicial system.

The current administration has also turned a blind eye to these horrors. Treating the Saudis as allies, all but drowning them in oil money, Pentagon's central goal is to maximize high-tech arms sales to the Kingdom. The standard rationalization has always been that since they have vast oil deposits, the U.S. has to curry favor with them regardless of their support of terrorism; hence, we arm them to the teeth. Saddam Hussein, however, also had prodigious oil reserves, and we executed him. The more direct explanation is that the Saudis know how to play the United States. They understand that the weakness of America's Power Elite is *money and that they have always had a small, fanatical army of Saudi billionaires eager to invest in firms friendly to U.S. politicians and in the campaigns of the politicians themselves—often secretly via partisan think tanks and unregulated trade organizations.*

Nor was the Obama administration immune to Saudi influence and entreaties. He and his people attempted to sell the Saudis nuclear power plants, which would have been a never-ending nightmare of apocalyptic proportions.

Meanwhile, the Saudis continue to bankroll those terrorist groups seeking an apocalyptic war with the West, most notably with the United States, a nuclear Armageddon in which they dementedly believe they shall prevail.

"Isn't there any way to shut her up?" the president asked.

"Of course there are ways," Conrad said, "but you've ruled them out."

"We may have to revisit those options."

"There was a time," Conrad said, "that had she pulled shit like this, the Agency would have had her hit."

"Too bad we can't order drone strikes in the U.S.," the president said with a mirthless laugh.

"Next time she's in the Mideast," Conrad said, "we'll consider it."

"If she interviews a terrorist," the president said, "we can call one in."

"We'll say she was collateral damage."

"The price she paid for hanging out with our enemies."

Conrad leaned back and let out a long, slow sigh. "We can always dream."

3

"I'm sure the electric cattle prod had nothing to do with it."
—Hamzi Udeen

Hasad ibn Ghazi stared down from the hill at the sprawling nuclear complex below. His face was darkened with synthetic, nonflammable skin-paint, and he wore a black watch cap along with matching fatigues and boots. The full moon and the surrounding desert sands were so luminous he could study the nuclear site with 8×30 Steiner military binoculars. He did not need infrared field glasses.

"You sure you'll be able to find the central storage site?" Hamzi Udeen asked. Hamzi was wearing the same apparel, his face also darkened. "There must be at least fifty buildings down there."

The light-green, steel-reinforced concrete buildings were remarkably similar in appearance.

"I've been through the satellite photos, base map, and photos of the facility so many times I could find the locations we need underwater, on Sodium Pentothal, in my sleep," Hasad said.

Hamzi looked at him skeptically. "So walk me through the plan again?"

"After going through the main gate," Hasad recited tonelessly, still staring through the binoculars, "the first building on the right is the Visitors Center. We go there for ID tags. Then we drive past the High-Flux Isotope Reactor Building, then the Electron Linear Accelerator Site, followed by the particle accelerators, the various bomb-assembling buildings—trigger assemblies, lenses, tampers, casings complexes."

"And then we come to the uranium processing facility?" Hamzi asked.

"You *have* been paying attention," Hasad said.

"*Inshallah.* But with only satellite photos of the buildings' roofs, how will we recognize those buildings in the truck at ground level?"

"I only have to recognize one," Hasad said.

"I have no sense of direction," Hamzi said, shaking his head. "I could get lost in my coffin."

"Fuck this one up, and you *will* be getting lost in your coffin."

"And Mahmud al-Tabari will escort us inside?"

4

"As long as I don't have to talk to them."
—Jules Meredith

Julie ("Jules") Meredith—Middle East correspondent for *The New York Journal-World*—entered the revolving doors of the Imperial Hotel. Strolling through the lobby toward the Empire Ballroom with long purposeful strides, she caught a glimpse of herself in a large wall mirror: her tight, black silk gown, cut three inches above her knees; her matching sling-back pumps with six-inch heels; her thick waist-length mane of dark hair contrasting her surprisingly pale skin; the hawkish glint in her wide-set eyes—raptor's eyes, as her old friend, Elena Moreno, had called them. No wonder most people were wary of her.

A luxurious New York hostelry, the Imperial Hotel was famous for its immaculate white marble façade; its opulent lobby with its alabaster walls lavishly festooned with oil paintings portraying illustrious personages from America's past—Washington, Lincoln, Theodore Roosevelt, FDR, JFK, and RFK—its swank red velvet couches and chairs; its stained-glass windows, illuminating more famous figures from American history; the Big Apple Bar, a great old-school, dark-wood watering hole, boasting a celebrity clientele, nonpareil and par excellence, a Who's Who that tonight was in evidence everywhere; and, of course, the legendary Empire Ballroom.

Whenever Jules entered the Empire, she was in awe: Sixty feet wide and twice as long, its gold walls gleamed, as if they were twenty-four karat, and its oak floors were burnished to a mirror gloss. Overhead, the forty-foot-high hemispheric ceiling boasted a dozen spherical chandeliers, each ten feet in diameter, festooned with what seemed to be thousands of crystal prisms, each of which reflected and refracted any and all light, illuminating the spectacle below.

As she strolled across the floor, Jules noted the circular ceiling murals strategically placed between the chandeliers—eight painted panels depicting New York City's history:

- Henry Hudson, cruising down his eponymous Hudson River, at the helm of the *Halve Maen* (Half Moon), his sails swollen with the wind. Entering New York Harbor in 1609, Hudson on the foredeck—with slate-gray hair, beard, and mustache. Dressed in a long black coat, he was pointing at Lower Manhattan, claiming it for his employer—the Dutch East India Company—as well as the country that owned it, the Netherlands.

- Peter Minuit in a long brown heavy coat with matching pants and boots, a wide white collar spread over the top of his coat, and a black hat with a broad brim. Meeting with a half dozen feathered, hair-braided, blanket-draped Indians, he was putatively purchasing the Island of Manhattan for twenty-six dollars' worth of beads and wampum.
- The Battle of Long Island—which was actually fought in Brooklyn—with flags flapping, banners flying, bayonets bloodied, muskets smoking, and flintlocks blazing.
- The New York City slave revolts replete with their gallows hangings, firing squads, violent insurrection, and mass graves.
- The Civil War waterfront draft riots with mobs of angry resisters, thronging the streets of lower Manhattan, brandishing torches and axe handles.
- The Triangle Shirtwaist Factory inferno with its women employees leaning out the upper-story windows, screaming, sobbing, their hair on fire and clothes smoldering.
- Then up to Harlem: black singers, dancers, and musicians, in tuxes and evening clothes, entertaining the Cotton Club's handsomely dressed, elegantly turned-out, exorbitantly wealthy white patrons.
- Inebriated GIs mobbing Times Square—celebrating the end of WWII—including white uniformed sailors, who hug, dip, and smooch pretty young women.
- And, of course, no self-respecting New York mural would be complete without those two infamous airliners smashing into the flame-shooting and smoke-shrouded World Trade Centers.

Jules searched the room for a bar. Thankfully, her drinker's divination—her own instinctive dowser's wand—quickly guided her to one. She tried to savor—not shoot—her first double shot of eighteen-year-old Macallan single-malt but was only half-successful. A second double in hand, she was ready to work the room. This was *The New York Journal-World*'s annual advertisers' ball, and the event teemed with ad execs and the corporate heads these people shilled for. Her employers wanted her to mingle, chat them up and be friendly. As the paper's chief investigative reporter in the

Mideast and a highly regarded presence on the TV news shows, as well as radio and in print, she was much in demand. The paper wanted her here to glad hand the rich, impress the mighty, and show the flag to one and all.

Hank Prewitt, their tall, brown-headed, freckle-faced fashion editor, bumped into her first. He, too, had a large glass of straight whiskey.

"Why are all these tuxedos so tedious?" he asked. "Everything's black, black, black. Black coats, black socks, black shoes, black ties contrasted by those maddeningly moronic white shirts." The paper's resident fashionista, Hank wore a purple satin tux, purple suede shoes, a purple ruffled shirt, and a light purple bow tie. He gestured to the room with a long contemptuous flourish of his whiskey glass.

"Almost as boring as the people wearing them," Jules said to him under her breath.

"Another whiskey'll help," Prewitt said, tossing back the rest of his glass.

Jules nodded. "Maybe if we get the blind staggers, people will leave us alone."

"Never happen," Helen Myer, the paper's publisher, said, joining them. Dressed in a long, flowing red gown, her long blond hair was artfully colored and painstakingly fluffed. Even at the age of sixty-nine, she kept her figure, and her skin was remarkably wrinkle-free. Her lipstick, as always, was a scintillating scarlet, her blue eyes possessed by a perpetually wicked glint.

She took Jules by the arm. "Come, my dear, we have captains of industry here with money pits for pockets. Before the night's over, I want every man-jack of them bent over the bar, belly down, their emptied-out pockets ripped from their pants, their wallets, shoes, and money belts turned inside out and upside down, their credit cards maxed from here to Alpha Centauri. Get out your blackjack. We must knock them out and pump them dry."

"As long as I don't have to talk to them," Jules said.

"But they are just dying to talk to you," John Jennings—*The New York Journal-World*'s managing editor and Jules's immediate boss—said, interrupting them.

John was five five, gray thinning hair and gray eyes, sharp features and a sharper tongue. Like Jules, he disdained glad-handing parties and formal events. His nickname was the Pit Bull—the Pit for short—though no one called him that to his face. Almost everyone on the paper feared him, except Jules, who actually liked him.

She had reason to. Once at a corporate meeting, when the CFO complained that Jules—while filing her stories and her expense accounts—had violated proper procedures and corporate protocol, the Pit Bull stood up and shouted:

"That little girl risks her fucking ass for those goddamn stories, pays your salaries and half this paper's bills and has more balls than all the men sitting in this room put together. Protocol doesn't apply to Jules Meredith. You don't like it, fine. But if anyone here wants to mess with her, you're gonna have to come through me."

Jennings had never found a taker.

"They want to talk to Jules about—" Helen said.

"The Mideast," Prewitt said happily.

As if on cue, the CEO of Raven Enterprises International, the biggest oil-gas construction firm in the world—particularly in the Mideast—was standing beside Jules. He had augmented his black tux with a matching Plainsman hat, hand-tooled cowboy boots (which added another two inches onto his already imposing six feet, four inches of height), and a national championship bull-riding belt buckle. He had a desert tan, gray eyes, and a gunmetal-gray ponytail held in place with a silver and turquoise leather band. He gave Jules a wide ingratiating grin.

"Ain't you the little lady wrote that op-ed piece about oil men like me underwriting all them Mideast ISIS killers?"

"The same," Helen said, grinning.

"In the flesh," Prewitt said, beaming.

And so it begins, Jules muttered silently to herself.

5

"It'll be years before anyone realizes the HEU bomb-fuel rings are gone."

—Dr. Mahmud al-Tabari, Deputy Director of the Pakistan Atomic Energy Commission

A black van with tinted windows headed downhill toward the Munir Ahmad Khan (MAK) highly enriched uranium (HEU) plant. Named after the first chairman of the Pakistan Atomic Energy Commission (PAEC), the MAK was the crowning diadem in Pakistan's nuclear program. It housed the high-speed centrifuges that purified the HEU to 93 percent uranium, thus producing the most dangerous substance on earth. Its fissile bomb-fuel was so explosive that if one grapefruit-sized chunk of this HEU were dropped onto a comparable chunk from a height of six feet and hit it square, the collision could produce 50 percent of the Hiroshima yield. If the fissile HEU were placed in a piece of old cannon barrel—an old American Civil War cannon barrel would do—with the ends tamped off, and one chunk, backed with extra-high explosive, was blasted into the second chunk of HEU at the other end of the barrel, the bomb might produce the Hiroshima yield.

Inside the van Hasad and his team sat in silence, while Hasad studied the complex. Spread out over a dozen acres, it consisted of four dozen concrete-block warehouse-looking buildings. Each one was over half the size of a football field but a dozen stories high, all of them painted light industrial green.

Once more he was amazed at how many buildings and how much equipment it took to manufacture just a few hundred rings of bomb-grade HEU.

Nor was the irony lost on Hasad that Pakistan—one of the unhealthiest, most illiterate, and most impoverished nations on earth, a country with 60 percent of its population earning less than two dollars per day—now had the world's fifth most powerful nuclear weapons program.

Hasad drove the van into the MAK's main parking lot. He had with him a crew of six bearded Pakistani men, five of them dressed as he was, in dark, conservatively cut business suits. The sixth man—and the only one who refused to wear Western attire—was Dr. Mahmud al-Tabari, the deputy director of the PAEC. A stern-looking man with a nut-brown complexion, grim eyes, deeply etched crow's-feet, gray hair, and beard, he wore the long traditional white robe and keffiyeh. He shared the front seat with Hasad.

Climbing down from the APC, Hasad led his team to a small cement-block office building painted the ubiquitous light green. Inside the office, a bearded man in a white *thawb* and eyeglasses sat in a room behind a Plexiglas window mounted on a four-foot-high wall. A plaque on his desk read GHUNAYN AL-GHAZI. Mahmud collected the documents from each of the men, then took Hasad with him into the back room.

"These are my nuclear weapons lab inspectors, Ghunayn," Mahmud explained, introducing his associates to the man. "We always come unannounced in order to check facilities for security breaches. Today, I am assisting them. Our activities are classified, and we report directly to the president of Pakistan. Any attempt to obstruct us or communicate details of our visit to the outside will constitute a violation of the country's national security statutes. Such violations can carry sentences of up to thirty years in prison. You will help us in any and every way."

"Understood," the man said, approving the doctored documents. He quickly filled out the facility's IDs, which he inserted into clear plastic holders with safety pins attached.

"Excellent," Hasad whispered to Mahmud after they left his office. He quickly distributed the plant IDs to the men.

From the Visitors Center, Hasad and Mahmud led them back into the parking lot and the APC. Hasad then drove them to the first ring of six fifteen-foot-high chain-link cyclone fences mounted with coiled barbwire. Three soldiers manned the gated checkpoint. Back at the Visitors Center, Mahmud had ordered Ghunayn to call them on their handheld Multiband Inter/Intra Team Transceivers and instruct the soldiers at all six checkpoints to stand down. Swinging open the fence gates, the sentries waved them through.

When they reached the MAK's main building, they turned right.

Hamzi, who was sitting in the back, began identifying the buildings as if he were a tour guide and they were tourist attractions:

"The High-Flux Isotope Reactor Building, now the Electron Linear Accelerator Site, followed by the particle accelerators. Those are the various bomb-assembling buildings—trigger assemblies, lenses, tampers, casings complexes. So that must be the Uranium Processing Facility? Followed by the National Enrichment Site, the HEU production plant."

"And finally, nuclear nirvana," Hasad announced, "the Highly Enriched

Uranium Storage Facility. It sits on a reinforced thirty-foot concrete mass attached to the bedrock with high-tensile steel rods, the same kind used to secure skyscrapers. Approximately three hundred by five hundred feet, designed to withstand flood, earthquake, tornados with up to 200 mph gusts, extra-high explosives, and airplane crashes."

"But can it withstand us?" Hamzi said.

Hasad turned on his tactical communications equipment, inserted a molded earpiece into his right ear, and whispered into his wrist mike, "Tactical communications is online. All units, do you hear me?"

Each member of the team whispered back their call signs into their wrist mikes:

"Tact 1 here," Hasad said.

"Tact 2 here."

"Tact 3 here."

"Tact 4 here."

"Tact 5 here."

"Tact 6 here."

"Tact 7 here."

"*Maa shaa Allah*," Hasad said. As Allah wills it.

The seven men jogged up the cement steps to the big green cement-block building that was the HEU facility and opened the large glass front door.

"This is probably the toughest glass door in the world," Hasad said to Hamzi, who merely grunted.

The lobby was fifty by seventy-five feet. The ceiling was at least twenty feet high, and when Hasad turned around, he saw that the room's rear wall was covered with two dozen rack-mounted monitors. Overhead surveillance cameras were everywhere, recording the building's activities both inside and around its exterior. Three horseshoe desks faced the front of the room. Bearded men in white coveralls studied the computer monitors set up before them.

The plant supervisor, also in white coveralls and wire-rimmed glasses, came up to Mahmud.

"Welcome to the MAK, Director. I understand you're here for an impromptu inspection."

"Yes. As you know, this test has to be done without interference or outside influence. We don't want anyone to say later you had time to conceal trouble spots and security breaches."

"That would never happen, Director."

"Just so you know, you are not to interfere. I know my way around. I can reach you on my cell if I need help."

The plant supervisor took Mahmud, Hasad, and the others to a locker room and handed each of the team white coveralls and white lab coats, which they quickly put on.

Mahmud then took them to a maintenance room. For some reason, the MAK had never installed surveillance cams in their maintenance rooms and storage closets. They were almost the only rooms that had no surveillance cameras.

In the far corner was a rusty two-hundred-liter drum. After prying the lid off with a crowbar, Hasad removed and handed each of them a Heckler & Koch MP7 Personal Defense Weapon with a forty-round magazine, chambered for the HK 4.6×30mm armor-piercing cartridge. Slipping the MP7's sling-loop around a shoulder, they each put their loose-fitting lab coats back on, covering up their weapons. Hasad then handed each of them a 9mm Glock with a thirty-round magazine and clip-on holsters, which they attached inside their pants in the small of their backs under their white coats. He then gave them each shoulder bags containing additional equipment, including coils of rope.

The seven men broke up into two groups, one led by Hamzi, the other Mahmud and Hasad. Hamzi's group first went to the loading dock and the shipping room. Searching through boxes, shipping containers, and side rooms, they pretended to look for signs of smuggling operations.

Hasad sent his men to cordon off the hallways leading to the storage vault area. When they reached the corridor in front of the vault, Hasad keyed his cell phone to the hallway surveillance camera. He then froze it. Using the stepladder, he mounted a spy-cam, then hooked it up to the vault's security feed, where it would record and transmit footage of the hallway to the security monitors. After twenty minutes it would begin transmitting the prerecorded twenty-minute clip, which it had just recorded. The plant's surveillance monitors would play that same twenty minutes of continuously looped footage, which Hasad's spy-cam had shot, over and over and over again.

Next Mahmud inserted the magnetic key into the storage vault's lock and opened the HEU tubular storage vault. The vault's surveillance cam was mounted in the near-ceiling corner. Once inside, Hasad positioned himself, Mahmud, and Hamzi directly underneath it, where they were out of the camera's range. Hasad climbed up on Mahmud's and Hamzi's shoulders, eased himself up under the vault's surveillance cam, and rigged the spy-cam next to it. Turning off the room's surveillance camera, he hooked its digital transmission system up to his own spy-cams. He then pointed the camera away from the door so he could leave and reenter the vault unobserved. In twenty minutes or so, his camera would transmit a continuous loop of the clip, which it had just recorded, to the plant's security monitors over and over and over again.

Heading back to the maintenance room, Hasad entered and grabbed a stepladder. He placed it on the big steel dolly along with a dozen old five-gallon paint cans, each one of which contained a stainless steel drum. He covered everything on the dolly with a tarp, smeared with dried black paint and grease. He whispered into his wrist mike, "Tact 1 to Tact 2. Have the surrogates. Will meet you at home base." He dragged the dolly down the hall and toward the tubular nuclear storage vault.

His men were already at the HEU vault, while the rest of them manned the rope cordons. Hamzi and Mahmud were among those waiting for him.

Mahmud once more inserted a magnetic key into the lock slot and pulled it out, and the heavy ten-inch-thick stainless steel door opened.

The interior of the vault was forty feet by forty feet with fourteen-foot-high ceilings. The walls and floor were thirty feet thick and composed of concrete. One hundred square holes—twenty-five feet deep and a foot on edge—were bored into the walls. Mahmud opened one of them up with the plastic magnetic key. Inside was a twenty-foot-long tray, holding twelve cylindrical drums, each a foot long and a foot in diameter. The trays rested on rollers. Hasad knew that each of the industrial canisters held a lead-lined steel tube that contained a hollow right-circle casting of 93 percent HEU. Each of these right-circle castings was nine and a half inches in diameter and had a hole, three and a half inches in diameter, through its approximate center. These steel tubes and their HEU castings were stored, one tube each, in the ten stainless steel canisters. Each canister and its contents weighed forty-four pounds. The entire vault—all one hundred tube-holes—contained fifty thousand pounds of HEU, enough for a thousand Hiroshima-style bombs. The bomb-fuel's design life was over a hundred years.

Mahmud pulled the steel tray out a full foot and the men began lifting the fake cans off the dollies and resting them on the floor. Then Hamzi took the cans of HEU out of the tray one by one and loaded them onto the now-empty dollies.

Nine more would follow.

They then began placing the counterfeit cans filled with forty-pound, lead-lined steel tubes on the pullout tray that had just held the HEU drums.

"It'll be years before anyone realizes the HEU bomb-fuel rings are gone," Mahmud observed absently.

6

"Three years without petrodollars...Saudi Arabia would be Somalia."

—Jules Meredith

The Big Apple Bar at 2:00 A.M. One of Jules's favorites haunts, it was all dark wood, dark leather, and darkly lit. The cocktail-party-cum-banquet was thankfully over. Jules, Prewitt, Helen Myer, and John Jennings were sitting in the corner semi-circular booth having a last round.

Jennings and Helen sat on the outside, Jules and Prewitt in the middle. Coat and black tie off, white shirtsleeves rolled up, Jennings looked around the room at the other bitter-enders—the drunken ad execs, corporate moguls, and, of course, newspaper people.

"Fuck me dead," Jennings said, staring around the bar.

"What a dump," Helen said.

"What are we doing here at 2:00 A.M.?" Jennings asked.

"Drinking," Helen said.

Jules nodded her agreement. "I personally think the whole world ought to be dark, drunk, and indoors." With that she raised her hand and ordered another single malt.

"Kid," Helen said, "I don't get you. You claim to hate the outdoors, but you've spent the last decade and a half in Mideast war zones, covering combat."

"Quite a bit of it was urban counterinsurgency warfare. I slept in Marriotts a lot of the time and drank in the lobby bars."

"Third World urban warfare?" Jennings asked. "Sounds like some nasty shit, you ask me."

"Speaking of nasty shit," Helen said with a diabolical grin, "your latest column on the Saudi royals is generating some very unusual hate-tweets. Did our guests give you a lot of crap tonight?"

"Till I thought I'd puke," Jules said.

Her three friends roared with laughter.

Ignoring their derision, Jules surveyed the still-crowded bar and spotted Shaiq ibn Ishaq. "There he is," she said, "the richest man on earth."

"In a premier Kito tux, no less," Prewitt, their *très chic* fashion editor, observed. "The most expensive bespoke tuxedo made."

"Doesn't matter," Jules said. "You can't shine shit."

"Shhhhh," Helen said, "he's headed this way."

The tall, elegant, mustached tycoon approached their table. He bore an amazing resemblance to Omar Sharif, so much so that Jules's private nickname for him was "Sharif."

"May I?" he said, indicating he'd like to sit.

"Since you own half the paper's stock, how can I say no?" Helen said, giving him her sweetest smile.

"Sure you want to rub shoulders with the hoi polloi?" Jennings asked.

"If the hoi polloi were as beautiful as Ms. Meredith here, I would consort with them eternally," Shaiq said.

"And that's what brings you to our table?" Helen asked.

"Yes, as well as Ms. Meredith's piece on petrodollar terrorism."

"I wondered when we'd get to that," Jennings muttered under his breath. He turned to Jules and smiled.

"The article," Shaiq said, "in which you say too many of the Mideast's petrodollars—particularly those of our wealthy Saudis—end up in the pockets of terrorists."

"I was only quoting former government officials and other experts," Jules said. "Brookings, for example, proved that Saudi oil money had also bankrolled and has continued to bankroll Pakistan's atom bomb program. Hillary Clinton said in a Wikileaked memo that members of your royal family are the number-one financiers of the world's major al Qaeda–style terrorist groups. As you know, that includes ISIS."

"It's not that easy to get money out of our country," Shaiq said.

"Sure it is, Shaiq," Jules countered. "Your relatives donate it to fake humanitarian charities, who then funnel it through Qatar to Kuwait, where the governments refuse to monitor such transactions, and into the coffers of ISIS."

"You believe that?" the ambassador asked.

"Reporters have no beliefs," Jennings interjected, "only sources."

"So you have no personal opinions at all on the subject?" the ambassador asked.

Jules met his cold stare with studied calm. "General Sherman defeated the Plains Indians not on the battlefield, but by depriving them of their sustenance—in that case their bison. By 1900, North America had fewer than a thousand bison. I believe we should deprive Mideast terrorists of their buffalo—of their petrodollars."

"And if you did that, as you wrote in your piece, my country would turn into Somalia?" Shaiq asked.

"I wrote: 'After three years without petrodollars, Iran would be Afghanistan; Saudi Arabia would be Somalia; and Saddam, if he were still alive, would be invading his neighbors on a dromedary with a scimitar.'"

"You don't seem to have a very high regard for our Peaceable Kingdom, Ms. Meredith."

Jules was about to say, *Quit stoning eight-year-old girls, and I'll think about it,* but Helen squeezed her knee under the table—hard enough to hurt.

"You have to forgive our good friend," Helen said to Shaiq. "Jules is brilliant but headstrong. How that piece got onto the op-ed page is beyond me. It should have been killed in the cradle. Let me take you up to the bar. They have a really good Paradis Cognac from the House of Hennessy. I think you'll like it. It was Kim Jong Il's favorite brand. He reputedly spent $1 million a year on it. I also want to talk to you about you personally doing an article for our Sunday magazine on the new Saudi Arabia."

"And your role in turning the Kingdom into a Brave New World of change and opportunity," Jennings said.

"Perhaps a special section—complete with investment opportunities and the revolutionary changes we have made in our culture and customs," Shaiq said, warming to the concept.

"A marvelous idea, Mr. Ambassador," Helen said. "We could use you as a managing editor."

"You'd have everything shipshape, no time at all," Jennings said.

"Maybe I could even whip Jules into shape," Shaiq said. "I'd certainly like to try."

He was smiling at them, but when he turned to Jules, she saw the smile did not reach the eyes.

While Helen dragged the ambassador toward the bar, Jules rose from the booth while muttering to Jennings, "That sonofabitch isn't getting away that easily."

Jennings grabbed her arm and pulled her back into her seat. "Sit down."

"Why should I? What are we—an investigative newspaper or a Saudi *Der Stürmer*?"

"Wonderful," Jennings said, shaking his head sadly. "We have more investigative reporters covering the world, including those endless Mideast conflicts, than any paper on earth. We cover the stories nobody has the balls to touch, then fight the lawsuits and prosecutions as a consequence. But in your eyes we're nothing but *Der Stürmer*—an infamous Nazi shit rag."

"But we aren't following the Saudi story all the way, and we never—ever—follow their money. We don't want to know the financial facts."

"What do you want, Jules?" Jennings asked with a heavy sigh.

"I got a guy on the inside in Pakistan—all the way on the inside. He's into everything and everyone—ISI, ISIS, the Saudi royals. The top guys, terrorist leaders, the shot-callers. He knows where every body's buried, where every nickel comes from, where it's going, and how it's going to be spent. This guy's in the middle of everything."

"And you think you and this guy can bring down Shaiq?" Jennings asked.

Jules nodded. "He can bury him. We can try the motherfucker on U.S. soil—right here on U.S soil."

"He owns half our paper," Jennings said.

Jules stared at him, mute.

"Suppose you brought down the paper with your story," Jennings said. "Is the story worth all of our jobs?"

"My guy says these people are planning horrible assaults on the U.S.," Jules said. "If we can stop that, it's worth all our jobs."

"Maybe," Jennings said, "but you have to get me the smoking-gun evidence first. You don't have that, though, and you can't get it, can you?"

"Maybe not," Jules said. "But I can get you enough shit to expose Shaiq and maybe even haul him into court."

"Never happen," Jennings said. "He's wired too tight. Right now he owns the White House, half of Congress, all the lobbyists, and our paper."

"I'm not letting this slide," Jules said.

"You have to, Jules," Jennings said. "This one's a bridge too far. I can't cover for you this time. You'll come back bloodied."

The waiter brought them fresh unrequested drinks and Jennings clinked Jules's glass.

"How'd you feel when Shaiq said he'd like to whip you into shape?" Jennings asked.

"It made my flesh crawl."

"Just watch your six. He's mean enough to kill a rock."

"Tell him to watch out for me."

"Really?" Jennings said. "How many billions are you worth?"

Jules leaned forward till she and Jennings were eye to eye. "Doesn't matter. I got the power of the press behind me, bucko, and I'm busting that bitch down to sucking eggs."

7

Hasad drove the big enclosed two-ton pickup truck with the PAEC logo on the sides up the highway toward Islamabad. Mahmud sat next to him; the other team members sat in the truck on the canisters of HEU.

"I can't believe we pulled it off," Hasad said.

Mahmud frowned elaborately, which only heightened Hasad's jubilation.

"Look on the bright side, my friend," Hasad said. "Everyone loves heist films, and we just pulled off the heist of the century. Of the millennium. Hollywood will make movies about us. We'll be superstars!"

"Yes? And how would that movie end?" Mahmud asked gloomily. "Hellfire and apocalypse?"

"*Allahu A'lam,*" Hasad said with a wry smile. Allah knows best.

"Do not mock the one true God," Mahmud said.

"Who's mocking Him?" Hasad asked. "Are you not doing all this in Allah's name?"

"*Laa,*" Mahmud said. "*Astugh-fer-Allah.*" Yes, may He forgive me.

"Then why so glum?" Hasad asked.

Mahmud let out a long heavy sigh. "You know what really gets me?"

"How easy it was?" Hasad asked.

"The facility was hardly secured at all," Mahmud said, nodding.

No, it hadn't been difficult. After they had loaded the cans onto the two dollies and thrown the tarps over them, they'd simply reloaded the tray with the phony, weighted cans containing the counterfeit rings and closed the storage hole. Hasad and his crew then dragged the real HEU cans out to the loading dock. Hasad backed a PAEC truck up to the dock, attached a ramp, and they pulled the dollies onto the truck bed.

At one point, a burly, bearded dock foreman in gray dirty coveralls wanted to know who they were. Mahmud had flashed his ID at the man. Under his name, the guard at the Visitors Center had mistakenly typed "Director of the Pakistani Atomic Energy Commission."

The foreman stared at him, unsure.

"Just wrapping up," Mahmud said.

Standing in front of the foreman, Mahmud then keyed the plant supervisor's personal number into his cell phone. When the supervisor came on, Mahmud put him on speakerphone and said:

"The inspection's over. You will be notified of our findings in a month. I remind you that this operation is classified. Revealing anything about this operation carries a prison sentence of up to thirty years at Dadu Prison in Sindh."

Overhearing the conversation, the dock foreman's face whitened. He did not know whom he feared more: Mahmud or his supervisor.

He decided it was Mahmud.

When the men climbed into the truck and took off, Hasad watched the foreman in his side mirror heave a desperate sigh of relief.

Hasad pulled off the highway onto a dry, deserted road. After a couple miles, he turned left, then another left. Next he cut across open country for a half mile. Parking behind a hill and a thick stand of desert poplar, which gave the truck ample cover, the entire team climbed down from the truck.

"What are we doing?" Mahmud said.

"We're going to bury the HEU drums."

He and Hamzi began lining cans up on the end of the truck bed. Afterward, Hasad jumped down and grabbed a can off the edge of the truck bed. The other men followed suit, the stronger men grabbing two.

Hasad then led them a hundred or so feet to the base of a hill.

"You can put down the cans," Hasad said.

He then led them to two dug holes, six feet by six feet and four feet deep, a shovel sticking in each of the two piles of excavated dirt.

"We have to put five cans into one hole," Hasad said, "five into the other, spreading them out. The HEU gives off alpha particles, which, if they hit a fellow HEU ring, can cause it to go critical. If they're too close for too long, you can get a chain reaction. So put a lot of dirt between the cans."

"Whatever you say," Hamzi said. "I just want to get rid of this shit."

Hasad quietly swung his silenced MP7 crosswise out from under his suit coat, pushed the lever to full auto, and emptied the forty-round magazine into the men, sparing only Mahmud and Hamzi. He then went from man to man putting a single round into their heads with his pistol.

"Don't worry, my friends," Hasad said to Mahmud and Hamzi, smiling. "I trust you. Without you, there wouldn't have been any operation. And Hamzi, you will be needed for other operations. Now let's get these canisters and bodies into those holes over there."

"The HEU cans won't go critical in a single hole?"

"They didn't go critical in that tube vault, and they were squeezed into those holes like sardines."

"But—"

"I lied, Mahmud. Let's start with the bodies."

While Mahmud grabbed a corpse under the armpits and dragged him toward the first hole, Hasad slipped an encrypted satellite phone out of his pocket and took two quick photos, one of the HEU cans, one of the five dead men, their bloody bodies skewed at grotesque angles. Speed-dialing a number—which connected him to an automatic rerouter in Dubai, then another in Islamabad—he transmitted the photos to his case officer, who was an ISI colonel. The transmission was end-to-end encrypted, so even if an intelligence service intercepted it, all they would get would be undecipherable nonsense symbols and syllables. Within seconds, a text appeared on his screen.

Done.

Hasad routed another number, by way of Mexico City, to his banker in the Caymans, transmitting the text:

The item?

Twenty long seconds later another text appeared on his screen.

Twenty eagles have landed.

So that was that—$20 million. Half of what was owed him. Where was the other half? What the hell was General Jari doing?

You better watch yourself, General. For $20 million I'll nuke you.

Keeping his face and attitude impassive, Hasad grabbed a shovel and joined Mahmud and Hamzi in covering up the cans and the bodies.

An hour later they had buried the men and the cans and were back in the truck and on the highway.

Almost immediately sirens were wailing, lights flashing behind them.

In his side mirror, Hasad saw a caravan of police cars and military vehicles coming at them at high speed.

"They're coming for us!" Mahmud said, his face frantic.

"Not to worry," Hasad said. "Check your side mirror."

A dozen police vehicles were turning off onto a side road leading up to the A. Q. Khan Nuclear Power Plant, which was located twenty miles up the road from the MAK HEU processing plant. The MAK was where they had pulled off their bomb-fuel heist.

At the far end of the side road, Mahmud could now see the distant specter of levitating fireballs and billowing smoke.

"Someone's blown the A. Q. Khan Nuclear Power Plant to hell and gone," Hasad said.

"But why?" Mahmud asked, his voice rising.

"Maybe they don't like nuclear power," Hasad joked.

"But what happened?" Mahmud was now close to hysteria.

"I personally think," Hasad said with an insolent grin, "a bunch of tree-hugging Greenpeacers burned it to the ground."

"I'm the deputy director of Pakistan's Atomic Energy Commission," Mahmud shouted. "I have a right to know."

"I don't know," Hasad said, "but I think it has something to do with four Humvees, a chain gun, twenty drums of Semtex, and a whole shitload of TOW missiles."

Hasad pulled over so they could watch the black flaming smoke rise high above what was once the A. Q. Khan Nuclear Power Plant.

PART II

The blood-dimmed tide is loosed. . . .

—William Butler Yeats, "The Second Coming"

1

The A. Q. Khan Nuclear Power Plant was now one colossal conflagration.

Elena Moreno, head of the CIA's Pakistan desk, was already seated in the Langley conference room. Simply attired in a gray suit and white blouse, she studied her colleagues as they entered. They seated themselves, one by one, in their leather padded, swivel recliner armchairs. In their private lives, they had all, except General Hagberg, been titans of industry. Consequently, their wardrobe reflected their wealth, status, and power. An old friend—a high-priced couturier—had taught Elena to recognize expensive men's apparel. President George Caldwell was decked out in a blue pin-striped Armani; CIA Director William Conrad favored a tan Dior Homme; and NSA Director Charles Carmony entered in what appeared to be a five-figure bespoke silk suit, custom tailored on Savile Row. A gold, diamond-studded Bvlgari glittered on Carmony's wrist. Conrad sported a Movado Sapphire, Caldwell a TAG Heuer. None of their white silk shirts retailed for under a grand, which she also estimated to be the bottom-line price point on their solid-color silk neckwear. She couldn't see the men's shoes, but she knew from experience they were Gucci, Zegna, Ralph Lauren, or Dior.

The secretary of defense, General David "Hurricane" Hagberg, was the exception, contenting himself with an army uniform.

From Elena's point of view, they were all overpaid corporate confidence men with thinning hair and expanding waistlines, lobbyists in officials' clothing, shilling for Wall Street predators, health care con artists, oil industry behemoths, and arms-dealing death pimps. These kinds of people had been responsible for the endless wars in Southeast Asia and the Mideast and were frying the planet alive in a horrendous carbon-fueled climate change holocaust, all the while claiming fealty to God, flag, hostile takeovers, and the American Way. Elena Moreno doubted if any of the men had ever done an honest day's work in their lives or—except for the general—had ever heard a shot fired in anger. They hadn't grown up, as she had, in a wind-scoured West Texas three-room desert shack, living with her old man on little more than fried dough, spit-roasted javelina, mesquite beans, and mule piss drunk out of cow tracks.

Privately she disparaged her colleagues as "mean-spirited, money-fucking whores."

"Refreshments anyone?" President Caldwell asked, treating them all to his best campaign-rally smile.

Elena studiously ignored the silver platters of pastries, bagels, croissants, and assorted donuts, all of which her colleagues were eagerly hoeing into. She also ignored the sugar and Splenda dishes, the sterling silver cream pitchers, glass carafes of iced orange juice, and bottles of Perrier alongside the silver ice bucket and crystal goblets. Instead she helped herself to one of the sterling silver Thermoses and filled her black White House coffee mug, emblazoned with the presidential shield.

"Elena," President Caldwell said, calling the meeting to order, "you may begin."

She jumped right in. "As you may know, terrorist attacks in Pakistan are escalating. A month ago we reported that a dozen Tehrik-e-Taliban Pakistan—otherwise known as the TTP—entered and blew up parts of a Wah Cantonment facility, a nuclear ordnance plant. They killed fifty-nine people and wounded seventy. We now believe those TTP terrorists were operating in conjunction with the Islamic State of Iraq and the Levant, which we refer to as ISIS. Later the same organizations, again in combination, attacked Pakistan's Kamra air base—a nuclear weapons storage facility. In one of their most daring and meticulously organized raids, these black-clad terrorists stormed and occupied the Masroor nuclear weapons storage site near Karachi. They not only knew the locations of the base's surveillance cameras, they also knew how to neutralize them. In this operation, fifteen attackers killed eighteen military personnel and wounded sixteen. They also set fire to several state-of-the-art warplanes with rocket-propelled grenades. (Note to reader: The previous attacks are based on real nuclear terrorist strikes in Pakistan over the last ten years.)

"ISIS is now the best organized and most heavily funded group we have ever encountered. Thanks to a recent infusion of Saudi petrodollars, we estimate its current worth at $1 billion, and we have evidence that it sent key advisors, soldiers, weapons, and money to Pakistan's TTP. E-mail intercepts and NSA chatter report that this new terrorist amalgam is bent on acquiring several Hiroshima-style terrorist nukes and detonating them in the U.S. This new coalition is so sophisticated and well financed that such reports can no longer be dismissed or ignored."

"If ISIS is so dangerous and fanatical," NSA Director Carmony said, shaking his head, "TTP would be scared to death of them. ISIS would swallow them up whole."

"A good point," CIA Director Conrad said. "ISIS is quite capable of murdering the TTP leadership and taking over the organization themselves."

"Understood," Elena said, "but the TTP had never seen that much hard currency before, and in the end, my sources believe, they could not say no to the money—over $1 billion in cash and gold bullion along with matching funds from a group of Saudi princes, all of it to be devoted to nuclear assaults on the U.S. We are told the payment was only recently received."

"In other words, ISIS, Pakistan's ISI, and the Saudis have gone into the nuclear terrorism business," General Hagberg said.

"Yes, and the first shot over the bow has sounded—a warm-up exercise, a practice drill, foreshadowing of terrorist attacks to come. This one, as you have just heard, took place in Pakistan." Her phone vibrated. Glancing at it, Elena said, "Our digital people have cut the video together. Here it is."

Elena began streaming it from her computer onto the one-hundred-inch flat-screen TV that hung on the wall.

"This assault ended forty-five minutes ago," Elena said. "It includes satellite and ground-level footage. A lot of it also came from the terrorists themselves via YouTube. This attack is on the A. Q. Khan Nuclear Power Plant just east of Jalalabad along the banks of the Indus River.

"Here is satellite footage of the ISIS/TTP terrorists in four U.S. Humvees— which they took off the American-equipped Iraqi Army—coming up the road to the A. Q. Khan Nuclear Plant. Every inch of these Humvees is shielded with thick, heavy, Frag Kit 6 antiexplosive armor."

"We gave those guys nothing but the best," General Hagberg said bitterly.

"Here you see them at the main gate," Elena continued. "There, the guards—dressed in Afghan National Army desert fatigues—are checking their documents, license plates, and vehicle tags. Notice here, however, the team leader—wearing the uniform of a Pakistani army colonel—steps out of the vehicle. According to plant protocol, one of the guards should be telling him and his men to surrender their ordnance, saying they'll be held at the security center for safekeeping. You see the colonel here, nodding his head, seeming to acquiesce, but instead he draws a silenced semiautomatic pistol holstered to his thigh and shoots all four guards in the head. The colonel climbs back into the lead Humvee, and they crash through the sally port, smashing the gates of the two other wire-topped cyclone fences. Their arrival is dramatic enough to alert the other guards, who are now coming at them in five of the Pakistan Army's finest Talha armored personnel carriers, or APCs. All-terrain, twelve and a half tons, with a thirteen-man crew and a 12.7mm machine gun on the roof, it's a good machine." Elena froze the frame and went in tight. "You'll see each APC has vehicle armor. They're ready for war. But can a Talha APC stand up to four fully tricked-out ISIS/ TTP Humvees?" Elena asked. Cutting back to the Humvees, she resumed the action. "Note the rooftop ordnance on Humvee number one."

"A 25mm Bushmaster chain gun," General Hagberg said. "Each bullet is an inch in diameter—twice the size of the Pakistani gun—and fires almost three and a half rounds per second. It chambers those rounds via a high-speed electric motor with a roller chain driving the bolt back and forth. It can kill anything two miles away and more."

"What other ordnance are we looking at, General, on the other three Humvees?" Elena said.

"On top of the Humvees, we have tube-launched, optically tracked, wire-guided missiles—BGM-71 TOWs—the finest tank killers ever made, capable of penetrating two feet of titanium," the general recited mechanically.

The eight fighting vehicles began fanning out.

"Now the Humvees' CROWS firing systems are swinging the long Bushmaster barrels around. The Humvee-mounted TOWs are lining up and—and—and—"

One minute—and more than 150 rounds later—five Talhas exploded into smoking red-orange fireballs, which quickly merged into a single scintillating globe of incandescent flame. The blazing sphere ascended over the wreckage like a gaudy god rising up out of hell.

"Notice those guys never used their TOWs," Elena said.

"They knew they had them with that chain gun," General Hagberg said. "Still that's some ballsy tank warfare they just showed us."

"Maybe they were saving the TOWs for something more important," Elena said cryptically.

Whatever the case, the opposition was in retreat. Over two dozen soldiers, several jeep-like Nanjing troop carriers, and a half dozen other High Mobility Vehicles were scattering in all directions, most of them racing toward the gate.

The chain gun effortlessly ate them up, disintegrating everything and everyone in its line of sight.

Now the camera cut to the Humvees.

"Humvee number one is heading for the main gate to do recon and surveillance," Elena said. "His three partners have also taken off in the direction of the aboveground storage containers to the right of the main reactor building.

"Look at those silo-type storage containers—thirty of them," Elena said.

"Every one of them is heavily encased in concrete and steel. Each of those dry silos is twenty-five feet high and a dozen feet across and is packed to the max with thirty-seven spent fuel assemblies. Circulating air continuously cools the rods. And now you see our High Mobility Multipurpose Wheeled Vehicles—the three other M1117 Humvees—approaching the long row of storage containers, halting perhaps one hundred yards in front of them.

"Uh-oh," Elena said. "Two bogeys on your five o'clock, and they're coming in fast."

"Those choppers look familiar?" President Caldwell asked.

"They should. They're ours—Bell AH-1 Cobras," General Hagberg said. "We've been selling them to Pakistan for years."

Elena froze the frame. "See the soldier in the grayish U.S.-made multicams leaning out the window of that Humvee?"

"That's a Crye Precision–made, desert-hued, multienvironment camouflage outfit, to be exact," Hagberg said.

"Now look at the weapon on his shoulder—a surface-to-air missile, or SAM for short," Elena said. "This one's an FIM-92 Stinger. ISIS took a whole brigade's worth of equipment off the Iraqi Army. Thank God the Pakistan Air Force is about to fix those ISIS/TTP bastards. Look at those Cobras zero in on that stolen Humvee, guns blazing. It's only about two hundred yards away. No way the Stinger can stop it now, can it? Uh, well, maybe. A SAM can travel at almost Mach 2. All it has to do is find the Cobra's heat signature and lock on it. All the Stinger needs is a . . . nanosecond."

Elena unfroze the frame, and two huge consecutive explosions shook the invisible camera operator as two massively swelling fireballs filled the screen for over half a minute.

The satellite cam cut to an overhead of two of the Humvees with the TOW launchers on their roofs. They were taking aim on two rows of fifteen vertical dry nuclear waste silos each. The first TOW missile blew a huge smoking pit into the spent fuel silo about two feet from the right edge. A second missile took out most of the silo's right side. A split second later, the next TOW blew a gaping hole in the one next to it.

They all watched in silence as the Humvees went right down the line, then back again on the other side of the waste containers, blasting over and over and over what was left of the remaining silos into nothingness. The men even hammered the ones that were already blown to pieces, as if delivering a nuclear coup de grace—until, in the end, the blasted silos caught fire, spewing radioactive flames and smoke.

The room was silent.

"What in God's name was that?" General Hagberg finally shouted in shock and disbelief. "They must have hot-loaded those TOW warheads with Semtex."

Whatever the case, his colleagues remained silent, and the attack continued. The sat-cam cut to the third vehicle. Surveilling the road just outside the main gate, the Humvee was now receiving incoming machine-gun fire. The clip cut to footage of another approaching Pakistani Talha APC, this one with a long-barreled machine gun mounted on its roof.

"That's a .50 caliber M2," Elena said, "sometimes known as Ma Deuce. Its range is over two thousand yards, which is approximately how far away it is now."

A satellite photo zeroed in on the armored vehicle with the M2, then cut back to the Humvee.

"Inside the Humvee, the remote-operated CROWS weapons system is swinging its big gun toward the incoming fire," Elena said.

The heavy chain gun atop the Humvee's roof sighted in on the M2 and its Talha APC over a mile away. The digitized video cut to a burgeoning reddish-yellow fireball rising up toward the recon satellite.

"That's what a chain gun'll do to Ma Deuce," General Hagberg said.

Then the satellite cut to the aboveground nuclear waste silos.

"All thirty silos are now on fire," Elena said. "The spent rods will burn and smolder for decades to come. Everything touched by its ashes and fallout will die."

There was more stunned silence.

"We got the following footage off a jihadi Web site," Elena finally said.

A terrorist camera had been filming from one of the other three Humvees' POV. They were pulling up to an industrial-green concrete building. They began blowing the building to pieces with TOW missiles. Within a minute, it was a demolished wreck.

"What the hell is that?" NSA Director Carmony asked.

"The Pool House," General Hagberg said.

"What's that mean?" President Caldwell asked.

"Most spent waste is stored in massive rectangular pools forty-five feet high," Elena said. "They contain as many as two thousand spent fuel assemblies. One pool has more spent fuel than that entire dry silo field."

"In other words," General Hagberg said, "these guys are about to do some very serious damage."

"They're going to make what their buddies did to those dry silos look like Sunday-go-to-meeting," Elena said.

Then the terrorists dismounted—a half dozen men exiting the Humvee. Elena froze the frame.

"Notice the garb and the gear," Elena said, zooming in. "Crye Precision multicams with the Iraqi desert pattern, matching tact vests, MOLLE Rucksacks, Dragon Skin body armor, and MICH headgear—that is, Modular Integrated Communications Helmets—all covered with that very fetching Iraqi desert camouflage pattern."

"They are dressed to kill," General Hagberg said.

"Indeed," Elena said. "Just look at the ordnance."

She scanned to their weaponry and went in tight.

"HK416s all with sixteen-and-a-half-inch barrels, Aimpoint CompM4 red dot sights, vertical foregrips," General Hagberg said. "Note the .45 magnum Desert Eagles on their hips—the most powerful semiautomatic pistol made."

"What's the automatic weapon that one guy has?" Elena asked. "The guy off to the side."

"He's carrying an M249 machine gun. Fucker weighs in at over twenty-two pounds," General Hagberg said. "He must think he's Rambo."

At that moment, the terrorist glanced over his shoulder and the camera caught his long hair and bearded face. Elena froze the frame and went in tight.

"He even looks like Stallone," Conrad said.

Elena unfroze the frame, and the six soldiers disappeared into the building.

"Lord knows," Conrad said, "what they plan on doing now."

"One thing we know," Elena said, "is where those six men are headed."

"Which is *where*?" General Hagberg asked.

"The main operations unit," Elena said. "Or whatever's left of it."

The men stared at her in silence. "What's in it?" Carmony asked.

"The nuclear control room," she said.

A terrorist standing behind the men with a camera mounted on his helmet was carefully documenting their entrance into the Reactor Building. After transmitting to their AV units, he himself entered.

Their own NSA editor cut to satellite footage of the two Humvees that had destroyed the spent fuel silos. Driving away from the fiery, smoke-shrouded remains of the silos, they quickly separated, each entering the complex of power plant buildings from a different direction, on a different street.

Elena cut to a four-way split screen, three of the four rectangular frames depicting the progress of the three different Humvees through the complex. The fourth frame contained sat footage of all four going from street to street. Turning left here, right there.

"Notice how methodical each of the Humvees is in its route. The one in the top left frame—he's swinging past the Boiler Building, turning at the pump station. The Humvee in the frame next to him now—he's got his itinerary mapped out. A lot of work went into this. These boys know exactly where they're going. Someone briefed them really well—excellent recon and prep." Elena froze all four frames. "Note the frame to your upper right. One of the men is rolling a medium-sized drum in the alleyway between those two buildings." She unfroze the four frames. "They're all doing the same. They're deploying a bunch of mystery drums at strategic locations all around the nuclear site."

For several minutes, they studied the satellite footage of the two Humvees' movements.

"I counted twenty of those canisters," General Hagberg finally said.

"Now for the pièce de résistance," Elena said. "Note the top left frame. A Humvee is turning at the Pump House and heading straight toward the No. 1 Unit Reactor Containment Building. Two more are joining him. Guess what they plan to do? Figured it out yet, General? I know you did. Give the four-star a big fat cigar. Hell, give all the boys in the room a round of applause. Our friends in the Humvees are going for the three remaining containment units."

"Wow," was all General Hagberg could muster.

"You got it, General," Elena said. "The A. Q. Khan Nuclear Power Plant is in for the biggest nuclear hummer of its life."

"So there's no escape for any of them," Carmony said softly.

"Never was," Elena said. "They've been dead men walking ever since they blew up that first waste silo."

When the Humvees finished their runs, they came to a stop alongside each other. The Humvees' heavy loads of Semtex blew first, followed a split second later by the twenty Semtex drums situated throughout the plant. Again, the fireballs quickly merged into a single scarlet-streaked, rapidly expanding, flame-shooting dirigible of radioactive fire.

The A. Q. Khan Nuclear Power Plant was now one colossal conflagration.

PART III

Truth is hell seen too late.

—Thomas Hobbes

1

"I'd kick his ass so hard he'd choke on his colon."
—Elena Moreno

Jules Meredith sat in a booth at Ye Auld Sod. She was in D.C., mostly to see her oldest, closest friend, Elena Moreno. An Irish bar in one of D.C.'s poorer neighborhoods, Jules figured she could meet Elena and not have to worry about any officials, political operators, or reporters recognizing them.

Jules had been sitting there ten minutes, studying the bar's customers. A lower-middle-class shot-and-beer bar crowd, they were ethnically mixed but with relatively few women. For the most part, they were unshaven men in work clothes and work boots, many of them drunk and loud. A local hangout where everyone knew everyone.

Elena's entrance was dramatic. She had changed out of her work suit into a black skirt, a matching blouse with the top three buttons open, and ebony high-heeled pumps. She was strolling through the bar like she owned it, coming straight at Jules with a long-legged, hip-swinging walk. As Elena got closer, she shook her long hair out of her face—"hair black and shiny as a raven's wing" was how a mutual friend had once described it. Elena's face also showed a hint of Mexican blood—her skin smooth and tight, cheekbones high and wide, eyes twinkling with mean merriment . . . a face Jules had known for over twenty-five years.

Jules, who was occasionally on television, dressed more discreetly—in jeans, a T-shirt, a baseball cap pulled low over her eyes, and wraparound sunglasses.

The jukebox blasted the bar with the Stones's "You Can't Always Get What You Want," and the way the men stared at Elena, the lyrics seemed to reflect their feelings.

"What are we doing in this hellhole?" Elena asked.

"Scoring crack," Jules said. "Want some?"

"I want a drink."

Elena poured herself a pint of Guinness from the booth pitcher and threw back a Jameson shot. Four more were lined up.

"Bad day at the office?"

"The briefing from hell."

"Can you talk about it?"

"More of that Pakistan nuclear shit."

"Who was there?" Julie asked.

"The president, the CIA director, the defense secretary, NSA—the most boring group of dead people I ever met."

"What do they think of you?"

"After the meeting, the president called me into the Oval Office for a private talk. He says I'm a compulsive depressive, that I always see the glass as half empty and it's hurting my credibility with his people."

"What did you say?"

"That the glass is half-full all right—half-full of bomb-grade HEU."

"He must have loved that."

"He just stared at me."

"The truth is always dark," Jules said.

"He can't handle dark."

"So what did you say?"

"I told him we're doing everything wrong in Pakistan. We've been chasing the drain so long we have almost no options left—no good ones, that's for sure. We've armed all the bad guys, bankrolled their backers, and now the vultures are coming home to roost."

"How'd he respond?"

"He almost pitched an embolism."

"Come on," Jules said, grinning, "you can tell me. What did our cretin in chief really say?"

"Off the record?"

"Have we ever been on?"

Elena took a long breath. " 'We have wars,' he said, 'in Iraq, Afghanistan, Syria. Hell, half the Mideast is in flames. Russia is still trying to destabilize and take over the Ukraine. Now you want me to do what? Invade Pakistan?' "

"Which was not your suggestion."

"Not at all."

"So when he's stuck, he makes up false assertions and imputes them to those he disagrees with."

"He's always been stupid and weak," Elena said.

"Like he was spayed *and* neutered."

"At birth," Elena added.

For a long moment, they stared into their drinks, silent.

"Unfortunately, the problem is worse than he can imagine," Elena said, shaking her head sadly. "Pakistan wants us to think their country's coming apart at the seams and that these attacks are an ISIS/TTP attempt to topple the government in Islamabad. They want to convince us that is their sole focus, and that there's no way this nuclear consortium will attack the U.S. homeland."

"And Caldwell is buying that shit?" Jules asked.

"It's worse than that," Elena said. "He said he's more afraid of me than those guys. He warned me to watch my step, that I'm pissing people off."

"You know more about Pakistani terrorists than anyone alive," Jules said. "You speak their languages, their dialects. Fifteen years undercover in Islamabad and Karachi—you barely got out of there with your life. Now you run the Agency's Pakistan desk, and they won't listen to you?"

"It's not that they won't, they can't."

"Why?"

"The truth hurts."

"What did Hobbes say?" It was one of Elena's favorite quotes.

"'Hell is truth seen too late.' And I told them hell is now coming to the homeland—nuclear attacks worse than anything we've war-gamed—and they're coming soon. I told them we have to go full red alert—pack the National Guard into the airports, seaports, borders, everything. Have the state guards patrol our nuclear power plants and weapons labs—any and all things nuclear. And we also have to warn the public."

"Then they asked you for your evidence," Jules said, "which meant divulging your source."

"And I reminded them he was my source solely and exclusively, and I wouldn't risk having his name leaked."

"Our moron in chief must have been tossing hats in the air at that one."

"He said I had his personal guarantee that the informant's identity would not go beyond those men I'd just met with."

Jules exploded with laughter. Elena had to wait for her to calm down before she could continue.

"And you said?" Jules asked, barely able to contain her mirth.

"I told him, with all due respect, he couldn't guarantee anyone's complete silence. I'd seen gentlemen, including the ones in that room, leak countless classified reports, especially when their tenure in office was near its end. I then reminded him that half the people in his cabinet were about to return to the private sector. In a few months, they'll be history. They could leak with impunity, then head out, memoirs in hand, on their speaking tours. I also pointed out that Woodward was writing a book about the administration, interviewing the entire National Security apparatus, including everyone in that room. I said my story was so juicy and the chances of someone in that room leaking it was close to one hundred percent."

"And the president said?" Jules asked.

"If I could not produce the informant, then I had no source, no evidence, no practicable plan. All I had were hunches and intuition."

"He didn't say 'woman's intuition,' I hope."

"I'd have shoved both his Gucci loafers *and* that fucking Testoni briefcase up his bitch-ass."

"Could you pull your source out of Pakistan, bring him to the States, and have him explain how bad it is over there?"

Elena stared at Jules a long moment, silent. "Yeah, maybe if I could find him. He's disappeared though—no address, no GPS, no cell phone. He's in so deep I have no one in Pakistan who can reach him, either. His only contact is me."

"He's really as good as you say he is?"

"You know the ISIS and Pakistani Taliban merger?"

"I heard rumors."

"Take them to Morgan Stanley."

"And your source knows this . . . *how*?"

"He's the guy who brokered the deal."

Jules stared at her friend, stunned. "What was your last word from him?" she finally asked.

"He said things were hot—hotter than hot."

"What happens if ISIS/TTP stops buying his cover?"

"They'll hang him by the hocks over a slow-burning fire and hook electrodes to his genitals. When they've wrung him dry, they'll drop him in a hole, fill it with cement, and weld the trapdoor shut."

"You got eighteen years with the Agency—two more and you have your pension," Jules said. "Then no more of this shit. Focus on that. Focus on what's important."

"This is important," Elena said.

"Can you tell the president things have gone to hell and your guy's gone to ground?"

"He'll repeat that I have no source, only 'intuition.'"

"God is he stupid," Jules said.

"I've known dumpsters that weren't as dumb as him."

"The CIA director, Conrad, can you turn to him?"

"You gotta be kidding."

Jules nodded knowingly. "He's got a thing for you."

"All he does is stare at my tits."

"That's only 'cause he's afraid to grab your ass."

"I'd kick his ass so hard he'd choke on his colon."

"He got drunk at a Christmas party and told a reporter you have the face of an angel, the soul of a cash register, and a body that would make the Pope throw Mother Teresa out a Vatican window."

"How do you know that?"

"*Le reporter, c'est moi.*"

"Some crew I'm working with," Elena said, shaking her head.

"Some crew indeed. But that doesn't mean you're out of options, does it?"

"I contacted a guy last night."

She had contacted a guy. It took her half the night—sitting on her bed, staring at the computer, contriving a hundred different reasons not to do it.

In the end, however, she had no choice.

He said he'd always be there if she needed him, and she'd sworn she'd never call the chit in.

But she did it: she punched in his code, then his call numbers. . . .

I figured you'd have something going down," Jules said.

"Given that clown I'm dealing with, I better have an ace to play."

"What can I do to help?"

"You wrote an article on the Hudson River Nuclear Power Station, the HRNPS, a year or two ago?"

"About how poorly protected it was," Jules said.

"Do a piece on how terrorists—using the attack on the Pakistani nuclear power plant as a paradigm—could hit the HRNPS and burn it to the ground."

"But without tanks and chain guns," Jules said.

"Exactly," Elena said.

"I researched that plant so thoroughly I could write the piece tonight," Jules said. "It'll almost write itself."

"ISIS claims they want an all-out global war with the West, fought in the Mideast," Elena said. "What better way to start one than to incinerate U.S. nuclear sites and set off terrorist nukes in U.S. cities?"

"Think the article would help?" Jules asked.

"The idiots I work with are immune to reason," Elena said. "Maybe if you inflame the public opinion, they'll listen."

"Consider it done—but right now I'm starting to wonder about the clowns in here."

"They're a little low down even for us."

"Don't look, but that pimp dude over there can't take his eyes off you."

"Time to shake and bake."

Throwing back their drinks, they waved for the waitress, who was no-where in sight. However, the pimp dude was, and he was coming over to them, giving them a cold shoulder-pumping stroll. He had a long, black leather trench coat, matching leather pants, a long black ponytail, and boots that featured jingling silver rowels. He wore sunglasses and favored an ebony walking stick with a brass tiger's head for a handle. The tiger's jaws were wide open as if in midgrowl.

"You some fine-looking ladies," he said. He fixed his gaze on Elena. "And, ah baby, I know you feelin' me. I seen you walkin' in here, swingin' your thang like it was a diamond mine, all the time it sayin' to me, 'You gotta teach me, Doctor D., how to turn this fine, funky butt into mucho bucks. Gimme a chance to make sumthin' of myself, to star in your stable, to be the star I know I can be!'"

Elena was just getting up. "Hit it, Clarence Thomas. We're out of here."

He gave Elena a long slow smile, but then grabbed a fistful of her hair, giving it a hard yank. Ignoring the pain, Elena gripped his lower forearm with her left hand and got his hand in her right fist. He pulled even harder on her hair, and the agony was excruciating. Still, she slipped her left forearm under his wrist. Taking hold of her right elbow and cross-hawking his hand, she bent it back. Instead of giving up, though, he snaked an ivory-handled stiletto out of his boot with his other hand. Seeing the blade flash out of the handle, Elena reflexively broke his wrist—the sound sharp as a rifle crack. Howling in agony, he collapsed to the floor. Jules quickly relieved him of his shank, stuffing it in her purse.

"Time to rock on out of here," Jules said, dropping three fifties on the table.

The women headed for the front door, the stunned crowd parting before them.

2

"I'd say he's a man not unfamiliar with violence."
—Jules Meredith

Hasad sat at his Islamabad apartment desk. Elena's e-mail from the night before was on his computer.

She had finally written him back.

The e-mail evoked memories of her, Jules, and the nine months he'd spent at a university in Texas—the only period in a lifetime of unremitting violence and inexorable death that he'd experienced something resembling love.

The memories came flooding back. . . .

He'd first met Elena fifteen years ago when he'd spent two semesters at a large Texas university. Even then, his ISI Pakistani handlers planned to eventually use him on undercover ops in the U.S., and they wanted him to speak English with an American accent. Unfortunately, however, his college experience wasn't all fun and games. The first few months, he was friendless. The school had never been ethnically enlightened, but to make matters worse, he had started classes a few days after 9/11. He frequently overheard ugly remarks regarding his Arab heritage.

So his first several weeks had been lonely and dull. His English wasn't that good, and he was struggling to understand American customs and idioms.

His loneliness, however, was about to come to an end. He was taking a Great Books class, and the first six weeks they focused on the ancient Greeks. Homer's Odyssey, *Thucydides'* History of the Peloponnesian War, *and Aeschylus'* Agamemnon *obsessed him. So did a pretty young freshman named Elena Moreno. Observing his rapt fascination with these ancient authors, she intuited that he was struggling with his English. She liked his soft eyes, quiet voice, and quick smile. That he was always well dressed and clean shaven and his short hair immaculately trimmed also impressed her. She decided to help him. Soon she and her friend, Jules Meredith, were studying with him every night at the library, walking him through the more difficult passages. Afterward, they would go to a bar called Red's for pitchers of beer.*

His command of the English language improved rapidly, and his obsession with the ancient Greeks would last a lifetime.

Elena and Jules lived in an apartment complex on the edge of town, where, on the weekends, the college football players partied. On Friday and Saturday nights, the football players would rampage through the complex, sometimes kicking down the front doors to get in. Stealing whatever beer and liquor they wanted, they occasionally groped and mauled the women. The men who resisted them were unceremoniously gang-stomped. The alumni in those days were so powerful they could usually hush it up.

One weekend night, a couple of the players—led by a 350-pound, six-foot-seven-inch tackle—broke through the locked door of Elena and Jules's apartment. When Hasad blocked them from entering the kitchen, where the women kept their beer, the tackle had called him a "camel-fucker" and knocked him down. Hasad bore the abuse stoically, his face empty of expression.

Then the tackle and a tall, three-hundred-pound center spotted Jules and Elena. The women fought them off. Elena raked one across the face and Jules kicked her assailant in the groin, all of which only infuriated them. They dragged the women into the bedroom.

The two women kept their flashlights and batteries in a chest of drawers in the vestibule. Hasad took off his shoes and socks. Putting three D batteries in each sock, he entered the bedroom.

A third football player was standing in the doorway, waiting his turn to rape the women. His back was to Hasad, who swung a sock full of D's at the back of the man's head. Hitting him off a pivot, getting every ounce of his two hundred pounds behind the blow, he fractured the man's skull and dropped him to the floor, unconscious.

The tackle was mauling Elena on the first twin bed. Cracking the man's skull, Hasad then rolled him over, straightened out his arm, and pulverized his elbow.

The man's screams drew the center off Jules. Shouting at Hasad that he would "fucking kill him," he swung his legs off the bed, at which point Hasad shattered his right kneecap—before the man's foot could even hit the floor. As the man grabbed his knee and screamed, Hasad hit a second time, smashing the metacarpal bones in his hand. A blow to the temple silenced his screams.

The men's injuries were so severe that they lost their football scholarships as well as their almost certain NFL bonuses and contracts. Elena and Jules pursued them legally, and though the men never did time, their sexual assault charges became part of their permanent college record.

Hasad was attracted to both women, but he was drifting toward Elena. Something about him bothered Jules, and he sensed it. She had observed him once while he was shaving in their bathroom with his shirt off. The two women had known he was muscular. Under his shirt, Elena and Jules could discern the block-like shoulders, the thick biceps and distended pecs. But with the shirt off, Jules now saw his body was also a complex of intricately turned-out cicatrices. They were almost too numerous, too encyclopedic to absorb at a glance. A few stood out though. One ancient, healed-over bullet hole had punctured his upper chest just below the clavicle and exited the posterior shoulder in a big, ugly, rather spectacular reddish-pink starburst. One barely turned-away knife thrust had left a long, jagged, alabaster trail of keloid traversing his torso from his right shoulder to his left hip. A matrix of scar tissue above his right eye showed how close he'd come to losing half his vision. On his back, he bore the broad white stripes of what he later described to the women as "an Afghani hellhole-prison."

Elena, however, had also wandered into the bathroom a moment after Jules, and when she observed the old wounds, she was not dismayed at all. Crossing her arms on her chest, she said, "Hasad, how the hell did you get all that?"

He said nothing and focused instead on his shave.

"Care to guess?" Elena asked Jules.

"I'd say he's a man not unfamiliar with violence," Jules observed.

"Yeah," Elena added, "and one who's had more than a nodding acquaintance with death."

Ignoring them both, Hasad continued shaving.

Both women were right, of course. He had seen more than his share of violent death—so much so that no PTSD study could ever convey how deeply the violence had marked him. Nor was his past open to discussion. The two friends quickly learned it was a locked box without combination or key.

Still, he had risked his life for them, and he was exciting. They went with him to target ranges and martial arts dojos where he taught them the finer points of small arms and hand-to-hand combat. The three of them gradually became closer, but still he would never discuss his past or how he came to know so much about the profession of arms.

Elena respected his privacy, sensed that there were things in his life that might not stand scrutiny. Nonetheless, he knew she was curious. His last night in America, she, Jules, and Hasad stayed up until dawn. He told them of his life in Iraq and Pakistan, his childhood, what he had done, and what he would do on return. He told them of the bombs he'd built, planted, detonated; his years as a sniper and an assassin; the jobs he'd been sent on and the men he'd killed.

Elena later found an envelope under some underwear in a dresser drawer. It contained a cryptic poem he had written to her.

But then he'd written her other cryptic poems as well.
It was part of his charm.

The golden vessel.
The rainbow's run.
Oh, glittering jewel
In my lotus heart.
Ithaca, Athena,
My Odyssey's end.

I am there.
Now.
For all tomorrows.

The following year, Elena changed her major from English to Arab studies, acquiring an in-depth knowledge of that region and its religions. In the course of her education, she also discovered she had a gift for languages and became amazingly fluent in Arabic, Farsi, and Urdu.

Jules always believed that Hasad had inspired her friend's obsessive interest in the Mideast, which, along with her passion for martial arts, had prompted her decision to seek a career at the CIA.

That career had soared.

Afterward, Hasad returned to Pakistan and did not maintain contact with Elena and Jules. Given his life, close friendship—let alone love—was a luxury he could not afford. People died around Hasad. He did not want to see the only two people that he'd ever cared for become casualties of his irredeemable wars.

Still, he wanted Elena to be able to find him if she needed him. Over the years, he sent her terse, abstruse notes—always under a pseudonym and on a different clandestine server.

Each e-mail contained his new address.

Elena had respected his privacy and never approached him.

Until last night.

She e-mailed him, and her message had hit a nerve. Through Pakistan's ISI grapevine, he knew she was in the CIA, and so he was even more concerned for her safety.

Her message was simple:

I'm frightened. Something is going terribly wrong. One of my men is missing, and I fear we're under attack. Am I crazy? What should I do?

Now he was even more worried about her—particularly given his latest job for the ISI and ISIS, the nuclear bomb-fuel heist he'd just pulled off. He was having second thoughts about it. Previously, he hadn't worried—partly because he believed the people he'd trained and commanded were too mind-numbingly dumb to execute multiple nuclear commando strikes. Even after he had provided them with the nuclear bomb-fuel on a silver platter, he didn't think they could assemble two Hiroshima-style bombs, transport them to their targets, and set them off.

He had been wrong. He had arrogantly believed that only someone as capable as himself could carry out the attacks, so he had helped that coven of psychopaths develop two nukes. But now Pakistan's ISI was not only help-ing to carry it out, they were dragging him back into it. They even wanted him to go to HRNPS to direct the attack on that New York nuclear power plant and then visit another site where he was to personally *set off* one of their nukes.

There was a time he wouldn't have cared. All he had ever questioned was the amount of his remuneration—was it enough? He'd never considered the consequences or the morality of his actions. In his world, such concerns were as useless as prayer, as meaningless as the Martian moons. He'd lived his life on the straight razor's edge and the hair trigger's trembling touch. He'd had no time for fine moral distinctions. He hadn't felt the pull of con-science in so long he doubted now that he'd ever had one. Perhaps, as his sister once told him, he had no soul to lose.

Perhaps.

But then he got the message from the Moreno woman, and suddenly he was awash in emotions he hadn't felt in decades, in feelings he'd forgotten he had ever known, something approximating . . . *love.*

He stared at his computer and her e-mail. He had to answer her. He had to advise her.

He suddenly knew there was a way he could help Elena, punish those who had so horribly betrayed him, and perhaps even mitigate the nuclear horror to come.

Hasad began typing a response to his old friend.

3

The blast ... would ... render an area the size of Pennsylvania uninhabitable.

I t was 3:37 A.M. and Elena was in bed with her laptop reading Jules's piece on melting down the Hudson River Nuclear Power Station. Jules knew her stuff. The piece was a virtual instruction guide on how to destroy a nuclear power plant. Jules had falsified a few details so the article could not be used for those purposes, but it was still scary enough to fry your hair.

I recently wrote a column on the Saudis' well-known financing of terrorist organizations, such as the TTP, which is currently launching assaults on Pakistan's nuclear facilities. Why couldn't such groups launch similar attacks on U.S. nuclear sites? The terrorists wouldn't find it that difficult to melt down a nuclear power plant. First of all, our nuclear power plants are ill-secured. The U.S. military does not protect U.S. nuclear sites. Instead, privatized rent-a-cops with dubious training and expertise guard these facilities. Nor does the government force them to defend U.S. nuclear plants against sophisticated, well-armed, 9/11-style terrorist groups numbering a dozen or more men. U.S. rent-a-cops only train to protect our sites against three or four poorly armed, ill-organized men.

Compared to attacking Pakistan's nuclear sites, attacking U.S. nuclear plants would be a day at the beach. An eighty-two-year-old nun with a heart condition, Sister Megan Rice, proved this when she breached the fence of the Y-12 National Security Complex with bolt cutters and wandered around in the open, utterly undetected, for several hours. Furthermore, the terrorists wouldn't have to come in disguised as nuns but as lab techs and security guards, even possessing counterfeit IDs. That's the modus operandi for the nuclear terrorists who attack Pakistan's nuclear sites.

Nor is melting down the plant technologically difficult. Fukushima proved that. The tsunami didn't have to destroy the reactors to destroy the facility. It did something simpler and more insidious. It wiped out the cooling system. After that, the coolant boiled away the spent fuel and the HEU reactor fuel caught fire.

Which is precisely what the terrorists would have to do to melt down a U.S. nuclear plant.

With our nuclear power plants, however, the attackers could substitute C-4 explosive and shaped charges for the tsunami. They could also detonate the backup equipment—the two low-head safety injection pumps, which are used for residual heat removal, the two low-head recirculation pumps, the two head safety injection pumps, the emergency feedwater pumps, and the diesel-powered auxiliary pumps. Then they could blow holes in the bottoms of the 8,000-gallon boric acid makeup tanks, the emergency 600,000-gallon condensate storage tank, the 390,000-gallon refueling water storage tank, and the big 1,500,000-gallon city water storage tank, probably with rocket-propelled grenades (RPGs).

Most of Hudson River Nuclear Power Station's (HRNPS's) spent fuel is stored in two huge pools. One of these is in an elevated silo on a platform. It is over forty feet high and several stories above the ground. The other pool is sunk into the ground. These two high-density spent fuel pools are huge rectangular basins approximately forty-five feet deep. The pool walls are made of reinforced concrete with stainless steel liners. They store tens of thousands of spent fuel rods—there are almost two tons alone at HRNPS.

The terrorists could use shaped charges to shatter the spent rods, driving them into contact with one another, and those thousands of tons of waste will go critical. The blast would burn off the spent rod's one-millimeter protective covering, boil the water away, and expose the spent rods to air. When the nuclear waste interacted with the air, those rods would turn to flame and render an area the size of Pennsylvania uninhabitable, killing twenty million people minimum. The damage of an attack on HRNPS would dwarf that of Chernobyl, which stored relatively little spent fuel and which was largely a fuel rod meltdown, not a spent fuel conflagration.

A small percentage of America's nuclear waste is stored in dry, silo-sized casks, and while some experts view those containers as safer than pools, they are also vulnerable to organized assaults.

They are easily blasted to pieces with shaped charges, after which the rods would automatically catch fire and chain-react.

Even worse, suppose this assault was not just an isolated mission but the beginning of a series of global nuclear power plant strikes. These attacks would be unimaginably catastrophic. The United States alone has thirty million spent fuel rods stored in seventy-seven sites throughout the country. This waste is the most lethal substance on earth. To stand next to nuclear waste is to die. Moreover, plant owners have increased their waste's lethality by extending their uranium-235's burning time, allowing plant officials to operate their reactor-generators longer and thereby generate more bottom-line profit per rod. This extra burning makes the protective cladding on the fuel rods brittle and thinner, and it accelerates hydrogen buildup within the cladding. Remember that zirconium cladding is less than one millimeter thick.

Moreover, nuclear power plants have been systematically making their waste even more lethal by extending reactor cycles from twelve months to twenty-four months. The increases allow the firms to produce more electricity per rod. However, the quantity and the concentrated lethality of the nuclear waste the plants are currently turning out is radically increased and far greater than that contained in the HEU reactor fuel rods.

A typical nuclear power station needs five billion gallons of water a day to function, and a lot of it goes into cooling the fuel rods. Blow the pumps and the water stops circulating. Pretty soon, it boils away. When the fuel temperature reaches 800 degrees Celsius, the zirconium cladding covering the fuel rods burns, generating massive quantities of hydrogen, which is extremely explosive. At 2,865 degrees Celsius, the air-exposed fuel melts, and you officially have a melted-down reactor. When this happens to the reactors' fuel rods, which are under huge white hemispheric domes made of thick concrete and steel, everything will go. Those domes will turn into horrific hydrogen-filled hell-furnaces, and all that concrete and steel will blow sky-high.

The power companies are making it easier for our terrorists to set off spent fuel chain reactions and the hydrogen explosions that these chain reactions will produce. The companies are jamming the spent fuel rods into cooling ponds that are already filled to overflowing.

Consequently, there is no reason why the terrorists will not hit us. America's ill-secured nuclear targets, such as New York City's own HRNPS, are just too tempting. America now has five to ten times as much spent fuel stored around nuclear power sites as the HEU it keeps in its reactors. Nationwide, U.S. reactors create two thousand metric tons of new waste per year, even as the available storage room dwindles into nothingness. How can America's enemies ignore such tremendous nuclear terror opportunities?

Especially when financed by all those Saudi petrodollars.

Wow, Elena thought. *Lord knows what Jules's bosses will say when they read that one.*

The paper was co-owned by one of the richest Saudis on earth.

4

For that much money the op must be very bad indeed.
—Adara Nasira

Adara was lying on her apartment couch in Islamabad, contemplating for a much-needed vacation, when her encrypted scrambler sat-phone buzzed. She hated getting calls on it. Not that anyone would be listening in on it. All its calls were packet switched, satellite bounced, and encrypted on both ends. Furthermore, only one man called her on that phone—her boss—but his calls were always disturbing. Still, as much as she disliked receiving his calls, not taking them—even postponing one—was never wise. Hasad demanded promptness from those under him.

"I'm supervising a debriefing on the Pakistan-Afghan border outside of Peshawar," he said with abrupt directness. "I want you on the next plane to Peshawar. You're helping out."

No small talk. No "congratulations on your last job." No "thanks so much for killing that fucker." No "job well done."

Just more orders.

Peremptory orders.

"You're assigned to it. I'm e-mailing you the instructions and what other information you'll need on our dedicated line and server. The paycheck will be exorbitant even by your standards—enough to retire on."

"I just finished that assignment in Syria," Adara said. "I got it done, but a lot of shit went wrong. I wanted to take some time off."

"This op isn't optional nor is fucking it up or bugging out. You're taking it and seeing it through to the end. It could also involve leaving the country for some time. Perhaps permanently. Pack enough to leave for a long time on a moment's notice."

"Suppose I say I like it here in Pakistan?"

Hasads laughter unnerved Adara. He laughed at very little.

"I'm told travel broadens the mind," Hasad said, "so consider this part of your ongoing education."

"And if I say no?"

"You do not want to contemplate the consequences."

Adara knew Hasad with painful intimacy. He was financially generous but quick to take offense. Those who crossed Hasad paid an agonizing, often lethal price.

It would be worse in her case. For two years, she and Hasad had been lovers. She thought it had gone well. They had a lot in common. They'd both spent a lot of time in America, had seen a lot of the world, and were relatively sophisticated compared to the other people they worked with. They also both viewed the world realistically—without ideology, theology, or preconceptions. To the extent they each had any morality at all, it was purely situational. Expediency was everything.

Still, he had broken it off two days ago.

He said he was back in touch with another woman with whom he'd had an affair twenty years ago, and he was serious about her. He needed time to think. He was thinking about reuniting with her.

Hasad getting serious about any woman? It didn't ring true. In fact, it sounded patently false. He wasn't capable of developing feelings for anyone.

Not that she was sorry he'd broken it off. True, he was good in bed. In fact, he was the hottest lover she'd ever had—and she'd had more than her share—but he was always, always terrifying. Part of her was glad it was over.

But the whole thing left her uneasy. She knew Hasad. The bit about the other woman could well be a cover story. Hasad could also be nursing some paranoid grudge against her, biding his time, waiting for the right moment to get even, when she would least expect it and he could inflict the most pain.

She definitely did not want to be on his shit list. She had seen Hasad do some things to people—terrible things.

No, Adara did not wish to contemplate the consequences of turning him down.

"Whatever you say, boss. I'm there."

"The instructions are on your laptop—the one with the line and server. I've deposited $1 million in your numbered account."

Oh, shit. For that much money the op must be very bad indeed.

"Copy that," Adara said, her hands starting to shake.

"Just don't fuck up," Hasad said.

PART IV

I first heard the song in Hiroshima
With firestorms blazing high.
Heard it again in Vietnam,
While death rained from the sky.
In the black smoke of the Baghdad
Countless thousands died.
In Auschwitz, in slave ships,
I heard their screams and cries.

I heard the song in Attica
Where I saw my brothers die.
I heard the song in the crack house
With my sisters oh so high.
I heard the song in the death house,
Where they take that lightnin' ride.
Heard the song just one time more:
Sang the whole damn world done died.

I heard the song.
I heard the song.
Oh God, I heard the song.
Sang the whole world's burning,
The whole world's burning,
Gonna burn your world down.

—Sister Cassandra, "I Heard the Song"

1

"They'll want your head on a stake."
—Jules Meredith

When Jules reached the McDonald's in Rockville, Maryland, it was 10:43 P.M. and three-fourths empty. She had just finished a two-hour workout when she'd gotten Elena's text on her burner phone, so she still had on her running sweats, baseball cap, and sunglasses. The McDonald's was far enough outside of D.C. and in a poor enough neighborhood to ensure the absence of familiar faces. Elena waited for her in a corner table nursing a coffee. She had just returned from the White House and was still in her black pin-striped three-piece business suit. She'd taken off her heels, though, and wore black running shoes. Jules bought a large black coffee at the counter and joined Elena at the table. Her friend seemed agitated.

"You look like you ran into a ghost," Jules said.

"I have—that friend we used to have in college," Elena said, "the Middle Eastern exchange student. You remember him."

"Of course. The mercenary. Saved our asses once. Hell of a guy. Whatever happened to him?"

"He went back to Iraq, then Pakistan," Elena said. "We stayed in touch in a strange sort of way. Every year or two he'd send me a new encrypted e-mail address and password."

"Why?"

"Before he left, he sent me a note saying that he always wanted me to have his contact info in case I ever needed him."

"But you never contacted him?"

"Never," Elena said. "I picked up bits and pieces. He'd been recruited by one of Pakistan ISI's Special Forces units and had served in Kashmir. Next, the ISI had him doing special ops on the Afghan border. In his line of work, he can't afford lovers—not even friends. My joining the Agency made friendship even more impossible."

"Still, he always saw that you had an e-mail address?"

"He was concerned that one of us might need him," Elena said.

"He was like that," Jules said. "Loyal."

"I could obviously never tell the Agency about him."

"They'd have pressured you to turn him?"

"Which would have been impossible. He was too smart. Any game I'd have run on him, he'd have run right back up my butt."

"Remember the gun ranges and martial arts classes? He was a tough guy."

"Remember when he put those three linemen in the hospital?"

"How could I forget?" Jules said, nodding.

"Those monsters could have killed him."

"He did it for you. You two had a special connection."

"It was like we knew each other in another life," Elena said, shaking her head. "Ever feel that way about anyone?"

"Like you were shaken out of the same tree twenty thousand years ago? Fought the same mastodons and saber-toothed cats? Made love on the African savannah under southern stars?"

"Turned out by the same evil preacher-man?" Elena gave her friend a wicked grin.

Jules leaned toward Elena, giving her her own evil smile. "There couldn't have been two."

They laughed, and for a while they were quiet.

Elena finally said, "The last thing he told me was, 'You'll be able to find me. Always. And if you ever need me, I'll be there.'"

"But he has to know you're with the Agency. You've run the Pakistani desk for the last five years."

"Yes, but he never said anything about that," Elena said.

"I think our Pakistani James Bond still has a thing for you," Jules said.

"Could be," Elena said.

"And you've never questioned him, not even once?"

"Last night," Elena said. "I told him I believed something bad was about to happen and that I was afraid. I also asked him what I should do about Rashid."

"You told him about our informant who disappeared in Pakistan?"

Elena nodded.

"Did Hasad get back to you?" Jules asked.

"Remember he used to write me poems in college? They were impressionistic, sometimes anagrammatic."

"They didn't make much sense," Jules said.

"He wrote me another one." She showed her friend a printout of the poem.

Remember Henry Hudson
And the power of the stars?
Where's our more perfect union?
It's one disastrous state of affairs,
New York, New York?
It's a hell of a tomb,
While somewhere out there,
The west will writhe in flames.

A bad moon's on the rise, kid.
A pair of setting suns
Will sink you forever.
My advice? Haul ass.
Get the fuck out of Dodge.

Remember me when the lights go out . . .

P.S. About the other guy, I've put someone on his case.

"Sounds pretty paranoid," Jules said.

"He has reason to be paranoid. I run the CIA's Pakistan desk, and he's doing wetwork for ISI."

"Any idea what the poem means?"

"Of course. I'm a trained intelligence expert," Elena said. "Any child could decipher it."

"Looks like gibberish to this child," Jules said.

"What does Henry Hudson make you think of?"

"He discovered and navigated the Hudson River," Jules said.

"Bingo," Elena said. "And 'the power of the stars'?"

"Thermonuclear reactors mimic the inner workings of stars."

"Any chain reactions on the Hudson River you can think of?" Elena asked.

"The Hudson River Nuclear Power Station?" Jules suggested. "The HRNPS?"

"What about 'more perfect union'?" Elena asked.

"I don't know," Jules said. "Does that have something to do with 'a disastrous state'?"

"'The disastrous state of the union,'" Elena speculated.

"Or the state of the union is disastrous," Jules said.

"What's happening in a couple of days?" Elena said. "The State of the Union address."

"And he says it'll be disastrous?" Jules asked.

"But what about 'New York, New York is a hell of a tomb'?" Elena asked.

"Adios Big Apple," Jules said.

"'A pair of setting suns/Will sink you forever'?" Elena asked.

"As you just implied, a thermonuclear weapon but a miniature man-made sun?" Jules said.

"Detonating on the earth," Elena added.

"HRNPS, New York City, the State of the Union, and somewhere out west," Jules said.

"A nuke will detonate out west, too," Elena said. "'The west will writhe in flames.'"

"It's a warning," Jules said. "He wants us to get the hell away from HRPNS, New York City, Washington, D.C., and way out west."

"Wherever that is," Elena said.

"Maybe Hasad doesn't know," Jules said.

"Apparently not," Elena agreed.

"So what's going to happen?"

"The balloon's about to go up," Elena said.

Jules stared at her in blank astonishment.

"You taking this to the director?" Jules asked.

"And the president," Elena said. "Tomorrow. I scheduled the meeting."

"You'll be in big-time trouble if you tell them," Jules said. "You concealed information about a former Islamist terrorist boyfriend. You signed numerous legal documents promising not to do that. You repeatedly perjured yourself about not knowing anyone like him before and during the time you worked at the Agency."

"You print any of this, Jules, you'll be in the deep shit, too."

Jules shut her eyes. "Any chance your employers'll view Hasad's poem as a serious threat assessment?" Jules asked quietly.

"The odds of that approach nullity."

"Still, you have to tell them?" Jules asked.

"No other way."

"And they'll want your head on a stake."

"My world and welcome to it. You wouldn't want to be me."

The two friends stared at each other a long moment in silence.

"We could take Hasad's advice," Jules said.

"Which was?" Elena asked.

"Get the hell out of Dodge. Just forget about the whole thing."

"And let 'a pair of setting suns sink the U.S. forever'?" Elena asked.

"So what are you going to do?" Jules asked.

"Look for a bullet to bite on?" Elena asked.

"Or I could buy us a few drinks at that bar next door," Jules said.

"Good idea," Elena said.

The two friends headed for the TGI Friday's across the side parking lot.

2

"You are in a universe of pain."
—Adara Nasira

The unconscious, naked man hung from a ceiling crossbeam by his manacled wrists. A bucket of warm liquid hurled in his face woke him.

Rashid's eyes blinked open, and he wearily reexamined his surroundings. The dirty-gray room was part of a concrete blockhouse—twelve by eighteen feet, a ten-foot ceiling, a dirty industrial sink in the corner, three chairs, a metal table, and two other inhabitants. A dark-looking man in work boots, Western jeans, no shirt, a beard, and long hair was staring at him. Rashid remembered him from his last few sessions. They called him Ali, and he was bad news.

Five feet from him, slightly to his right side, a woman sat in a chair. Dressed in black Levis, a Rolling Stones T-shirt, and black boots, she was smoking an unfiltered Gaulois Bleu. She stared at Rashid, eyes black and hard as onyx, unfeeling as the abyss.

She's new.

What does that mean?

What is she doing here?

Across the room, six or seven feet away, hung a large tarnished wall mirror. His captors apparently wanted Rashid to look at himself, probably hoping it would frighten him into a full confession. He had to admit what he saw—through a single bloodshot eye—was hardly inspiring. His body was covered with whip welts and burn marks. He'd lost most of his body fat. All that was left was skin and muscle stretched tightly over bone, everything about him hard planes and sharp angles.

The man walked up to him.

"Who are you?" Rashid asked him, his vision, once more, blurring, shifting in and out of focus.

"Let me introduce myself," his interlocutor said. "Again."

His dirty work boot buried itself in Rashid's groin. The blinding pain knocked Rashid unconscious.

He awoke to another bucket of foul-smelling liquid.

"What's that?" he asked, spitting some of it out of his mouth.

"Camel piss," the torturer said.

"In case you see us as gratuitously cruel," the woman said, "the urine does serve a purpose."

"No shit?" Rashid said.

"It is an excellent conductor of electricity," she said.

Glancing at the table, Rashid spotted the old hand-crank field telephone with some wires dangling from its front screws. The wires had clamps on them.

Uh-oh.

This is new.

"Where'd you say I am?" Rashid asked again, confused.

"The hole that empties into hell," the woman said, taking a long pull on her cigarette.

"I don't see any holes," Rashid said, glancing around the room.

The bearded man reared back and kicked him in the stomach so hard he fainted again. When he came to and his breath returned, his vision was spinning.

"Oh, yeah," Rashid said, slurring his words. "I see now. You're right. It's a great big black fucking hole. There, right in front of me. Middle of the room. Can't see how I missed it."

"Let me try," the woman said, pushing the man aside and approaching Rashid. "Why did you return to Pakistan?"

"I wanted to buy a pachyderm ranch."

"But there are no pachyderms in Pakistan," the woman said.

"I was misinformed."

The man stepped forward and hit him with a left hook that almost dislocated his jaw.

"How stupid are you?" the woman shouted at Ali. "You don't hit him in the mouth. He needs his mouth to talk."

She had a point. It took him several minutes before he could move his jaw well enough to enunciate words.

"Again," the woman asked, "why did you betray the ISI? To whom were you sending those e-mails?"

"I lied about the pachyderm ranch," Rashid said feebly. "I admit it. It was a mistake."

"Why are you here then?" the woman asked.

"I came here to invest in a rat factory."

"A rat factory?" the woman asked.

"Haven't you heard?" Rashid said. "Apple's trained rats to assemble iPhones, and now they want to build rat factories all over Pakistan. I want in on the ground floor because Pakistan's got some really great rats. You can't tell me there aren't any rats in Pakistan. Pakistan's nothing but rats. Some of the fattest, strongest, smartest rats on earth come from Pakistan, and—"

The man delivered a blow just under his heart. A stunning shock exploded in his chest, a thunderbolt of pure, incandescent agony. A massive sun, bright as a nuclear fireball seen close-up, blinded his vision. It exploded into thousands of stars, each of those slowly going out, slowly, slowly, one at a time, until there was only a single sun left. When it was gone, he was gone as well.

Another bucket of camel piss and again he was unfortunately awake.

The woman got up from her chair, walked over to him, and gently massaged his cheek. This close she was blindingly, achingly beautiful. At her touch, he almost cried.

"My friend," she said, "I've tortured many men, and in the end they all accept the truth of their lives—that everything they fought so hard to conceal from me was a fool's errand. Their loves and hates, joys and sorrows, agonies and ecstasies were all part of the same fraudulent fantasy, the mistaken belief that their secrets mattered, that they had once been someone who mattered, that they had had a body, a soul, that they had actually . . . *lived*. But none of that counts. In the end, it all comes to the same thing: the dream dies, the vision fades, the dreamer dims and vanishes, ephemeral as a snowflake on the scorching desert sand. So why hold out? It's all for nothing. It's all part of the same vain folly. It never meant anything at all." Then, to his surprise, she kissed him on the lips. "Give it up. Why did you return to Pakistan? To work as a CIA double agent?"

His voice was starting to wheeze and crack, but he still got it out.

"I came for your Indian food."

"But this isn't India," the woman said.

"Doesn't matter," Rashid said. "Your stuff's way better than the shit I get in Delhi or Calcutta. Ever had the curried goat in Karachi? Tandoori in Islamabad?" He somehow managed to close his eyes and smack his lips. "They're to die for. I could live on that shit."

This time when the bearded man went to work on him, it seemed like the beating would never stop, and only the woman's intervention brought it to an end.

"Your file says you graduated from the Kakul Army Academy at Abbottabad," the woman said, her voice distant and tinny in his ears. "That's Pakistan's premier military school. What did they teach you there? Hold tight against pain? Never give up? It sounded brave and noble back then, but, Rashid, you're no longer at the academy. Those teachings can only hurt you in your current state."

More camel piss, more punches, more temple bells chiming in his ears.

"Where am I?" the hanging man asked, coming to again, his voice raspy and ragged.

"You are in a universe of pain—lost amid the pathos of dead dreams and past things," the woman said. "A world in which you have nothing left to lose and nothing left to love."

The hanging man stared at her empty-eyed, silent.

"Rashid," the woman said, "you must understand you have no choice. We have techniques that can make the deaf hear, the blind see, the dead walk, and most important, the dumb speak—speak, sing, roar, shriek, giggle, thunder, chortle, whisper, banter, chatter, tintinnabulate, and sob. It's only a matter of time."

"Did you ever think of bribing me?" His voice was a reedy whisper.

"It is possible," she said, glancing at her partner. "I can call our bankers in Islamabad. How much would you want?"

"A hundred trillion dollars."

"Why did I think you'd say that?" she said, suddenly smiling.

She walked over to the desk and began unspooling the red copper wire attached to the hand crank phone's side. She checked the connections, then led the wire over to Rashid.

"The Koran tells us that a woman should never touch a man's genitals. I think the one and only God would grant me special dispensation to do so, since I only seek to torture a man to death for His sake."

She coiled the copper wire around his member, his testicles, and his ears. Strolling back to the field phone, she said merrily:

"Do I hear a phone ringing?"

She turned the crank, and the phone started to ring.

Rashid bounced on his chains like a yo-yo. His screams singsonged up and down with every bounce and jounce . . . till he passed out.

When he came to, he could barely talk or see.

"Wow," the woman said, "when I hear apes ululate like that they're usually throwing shit with one hand and masturbating with the other."

"Or doing it with both hands *and* both feet," Ali said grinning.

Then both of them exploded into laughter.

After which she began to turn the hand crank again.

PART V

When the stars shall fall...
When Heaven shall be stripped away,
When Hell shall be made to blaze,
Then every soul shall know what it hath wrought.

—The Koran LXXXI, xxxii, 1–5

1

"So there's no honor among genocidal maniacs?"

—Hasad ibn Ghazi

asad climbed the long switchback trail up the rocky hill toward the safe house. It was near the Afghan border. Vast expanses of arid wilderness stretched in all directions, uninterrupted by dwellings or towns. The turquoise sky was cloudless and clear with dim black mountains lining the horizon's rim. The sun burned overhead at its zenith, blindingly bright as a welding torch.

Soldiers idled outside the stone house, smoking cigarettes. One of them went in to announce Hasad's arrival. Lieutenant General Jari ibn Hamza, who was dressed in desert camouflage and whom he'd met before, came out to meet him. Shaiq ibn Ishaq—former Saudi intelligence minister, current U.S ambassador and oil mogul—accompanied him. He was wearing a powder-blue summer-weight suit, and Hasad recognized him from the media photos and interviews. The third one—the army colonel—he did not recognize, and he was the one who bothered Hasad. The other two he dismissed as functionaries and bureaucrats. The general might have lived by the gun once but not for decades. His reflexes, any indifference to pain and death that he might once have had, were terminally blunted by easy living. The colonel, though, was a different story. His head was hairless and hard. A lifetime of soldiering in the raw Pakistani wind and the scorching desert sun had tanned him dark as an old hide. His eyes were fixed on Hasad, sizing him up, taking his inventory, eyes flat and emotionless, eyes that neither asked nor gave. The colonel's right thumb was hooked casually inside his belt buckle near a Russian-made 9mm Makarov. Impervious to the fine desert sand of this world, it was the best pistol ever made for desert fighting. The colonel holstered it crossways on his left hip so he could pull it out quickly not only while standing but also while sitting down. Hasad knew instinctively that the colonel's right hand would never be far from that gun, that the hammer would be back and safety would be on for quick firing— what the Americans called "cocked and locked." One quick thumb flick, the safety would be off, and it would be full rock and roll. If the colonel drew it, someone would die.

The other two men might playact at being tough. The general might have even been tough once. The colonel, however, was the genuine article. Nothing showed in his cold eyes except maybe a faint glimmer of amusement. The colonel, he would have to watch.

If this meeting went south, Hasad would kill him first.

"Let's walk," General Jari said.

They headed up another goat path about two hundred yards up the mountain, stopping at a cluster of small boulders.

"You came up $20 million short," Hasad said.

"Circumstances changed," Shaiq said. "We now need you to lead the attack in the U.S."

"That wasn't part of our agreement," Hasad said.

"You really think we give a shit about agreements?" the general said, smiling.

"I give a shit," Hasad said, "and I want my money."

"My friend, the Koran does not countenance greed," Shaiq said with patronizing irony.

"Too bad you didn't hire a more devout killer," Hasad said.

"Look on the bright side," the general said. "Help us out, adapt to our new circumstances, and you will have wealth beyond measure, as well as Allah's blessings."

"You must have other men available," Hasad said.

"None as good as you," Shaiq said.

"Bullshit," Hasad said.

"I wish it were so," the general said, shaking his head sadly. "But good help is so hard to find."

"Good health, too," Shaiq said. "Anything can happen to a man these days."

"'Allah has not promised us tomorrow,'" General Jari said, quoting an old Arabian proverb.

"But you promised me another $20 million," Hasad said, "and I never agreed to setting off any nukes."

"It's a long trek back down that hill." Shaiq pointed to the goat trail, leading back down to the safe house.

"You might not make it," the general said. "Your sister might not either."

His sister had died three months ago of stomach cancer in Malta and he'd scattered her ashes at sea. Nor had he been that close to her.

But they did not know *that*.

And they'd just threatened him *and her*.

That he would never let slide.

"One more job," Shaiq said. "That's all we ask."

"Accompany the men and materiel across the ocean," the general said. "Get it all to the safe house. Work with the men there. Instruct them, give them their orders, explain the plans, then carry out the D.C. operation. That's the only strike you'll have to handle personally."

"I wasn't supposed to handle any of the nukings personally," Hasad said. "That was the contract."

"That *was* the contract," the colonel said.

"And you are?" Hasad finally asked.

"The illustrious Colonel Abdul al-Hakeem," General Jari said, introducing them.

"I know the name," Hasad said. "I've heard of you."

"And I you," the colonel said.

"Then you know in my world a deal is a deal," Hasad said.

"Unfortunately for you," the colonel said, "you're in my world now."

"Look on the bright side," Shaiq said, giving Hasad an ingratiating smile, attempting to defuse the argument. "This way you get all that money and a free ocean voyage to boot."

"An ocean voyage that will do you good," the general said.

"Sure," Hasad said softly, "across the 'wide water, inescapable.'"

"What's that?" the general asked. The allusion confused all three of the men.

"Literature," Hasad said. "You wouldn't understand."

"Perhaps, but nonetheless there'll be a $20 million bonus on top of the agreed-on $20 million," Shaiq said. "I personally guarantee it."

"Your word of honor?" Hasad asked with bitter disdain.

"But of course," Shaiq said, smiling brightly.

"The money's nothing to him," the general said. "A gratuity."

"I spill that much," Shaiq agreed.

Hasad stared at them a long moment. "So there's no honor among genocidal maniacs?" he finally said.

"I'm so glad you understand," Shaiq said.

The Saudi ambassador then treated Hasad to his most obscenely conceited, supremely condescending smile.

The smile of a man holding an ace-high straight, wired.

A lockup hand.

"You're so good at what you do," the colonel said. "How could we let you walk away?"

"Think of it this way," Shaiq said cheerfully. "Do this, and you'll never have to look at us again."

"Yes, I will," Hasad said.

"Really?" the general said, smiling. "When?"

"When I see your souls in hell."

Hasad started back down the hill.

2

The chickens came home to roost.

Rashid al-Rahman lay naked, bound, and gagged on the floor of a windowless confinement cell in his Pakistani safe house. Enclosed on all sides by cement-block walls, his cubbyhole was pitch-black and no bigger than a closet—so small he didn't have enough room to stretch out. Not that he could have had he wanted to. His ankles were lashed flush against his wrists, which were cuffed behind his back.

His only bathroom facility was the floor.

How the hell did I get here? he thought forlornly, looking back on the events of the last several months.

He blamed it all on that psychopath, Hasad. That's where it all started. Pakistan's ISI—its central intelligence service—was arranging an alliance between ISIS and the Tehrik-e-Taliban Pakistan, the dreaded TTP, and Hasad hired Rashid to help. A terrorist group even more savagely sophisticated than ISIS, it was far more dangerous than the Islamic State because of its access to Pakistan's nuclear weapons industry. A massive government-run enterprise, Pakistan's nuclear program employed over eighty thousand scientists, engineers, and technicians, all of whom had access to the fissile bomb-fuel storage facilities. Many of them were willing or could be forced to help the TTP steal enough fissile bomb-fuel to cobble together several simple but devastating Hiroshima-style nukes.

Yes, Hasad was at the root of his troubles. As soon as General Jari and his buddy Shaiq had turned to Hasad for help, he had handed them off onto Rashid, putting him into the middle of this mess.

But why did he listen to Hasad? Why did he accept the op? Even as Hasad was explaining it to him, Rashid knew he was fucked. Still, he had never known how to say no to Hasad. Not simply because he feared the violence of Hasad's vindictiveness—though that was always a factor when anyone worked for him—this time he felt he owed the man. The year before he'd accepted another mission from Jari—one that Hasad had warned him off of. Still, Rashid had desperately needed the money, and Hasad had nothing for him at the time.

Rashid was to rescue an American embassy worker imprisoned in a Taliban camp in a desert pit-cage. Nine feet deep and four feet across with a steel grid for a trapdoor, it was the most barbaric prison cell Rashid had ever seen—so barbaric its previous resident had not survived his stay. In fact, the man's rat-gnawed corpse was still in the pit with the American.

Even worse, when he and his team reached the camp, Rashid learned they'd been informed on. His men were killed on the spot, and he was thrown in the hole with the cadaver, the barely breathing American, and the ravenous rat pack. The Taliban was now seeking to ransom him as well, naively believing that someone might care whether Rashid lived or died. The hard truth was that no one did.

Except—to Rashid's eternal surprise—Hasad.

Just as Rashid had given himself up for dead and was about to succumb from the interminable beatings, dysentery, inanition, and dehydration, Hasad and his extraction team stormed the camp, killed the tribesmen guarding him, and dragged him and the American out of the pit-cage.

So he owed Hasad his life. Even before Hasad's men could take the American to Maroof International Hospital in Islamabad, Hasad was personally checking Rashid into its ER, holding his hand the entire time.

He paid for everything.

Rashid was grateful but puzzled. This wasn't the Hasad he'd known for the last decade, the man who didn't do favors and who viewed employees as utterly disposable—replaceable as used tissues.

Even more bizarre was that Rashid had felt indebted to him—a feeling he'd never felt for anyone.

Not friends, not family.

So when Hasad had ordered him to arrange for the meeting between Jari, the TTP, and Pakistan's ISIS contingent, Rashid accepted—even though it violated every survival instinct vibrating in his brain and body. Still, he'd met with the participants on and off for three months and, per Hasad's instructions, brokered their accord.

Rashid had helped finalize a plan to detonate three terrorist nukes on U.S. soil.

It had to be the lowest point in Rashid's already abysmally low career.

He had now officially become a nuclear terrorist.

At which point General Jari accused him of betraying them all to the outside world.

Jari's charge was not completely unfounded—if one considered Hasad part of the outside world. In accordance with Hasad's orders, Rashid had sent him nightly reports on the negotiations. Why, Rashid did not know.

He'd only asked Hasad one time why he wanted those reports. Hasad had answered, "Who says I want them? Who says they're for me?"

Then that last night, the chickens came home to roost. After the terrorists' last meeting, Jari's men broke into Rashid's room, seized Rashid's computer, and methodically tracked down those nightly reports in his server's trash bin. So while Rashid's transmissions were scrambled and encrypted end-to-end, then sat-bounced all over hell's creation—until God Himself could not have determined the final recipient of the e-mails—the ISI, nonetheless, had found his e-mails and had him cold.

Rashid knew better than to give up Hasad. He would do things to him that would make the ISI's pain-racked ministrations look like a mosque prayer vigil.

Which was why Pakistani intelligence had sent for "the Cleric"—the most feared interrogator in all of South Asia and the Mideast.

Locked, bound up, and gagged in his stinking, coal-black cell, Rashid could only imagine what lay in store for him the next day.

He shuddered at the thought.

To even contemplate it was to peer into the darkest pit of hell.

3

"What goes around, comes around."
—Elena Moreno

Hasad sat in a jump seat in the forward section of an ancient, reconditioned C-130 cargo plane, which the Pakistan Air Force had purchased from the U.S. in the '60s. Its four Allison T56-A-15 turboprops produced a nonstop rumbling roar. It shook, bounced, and chugged badly, and while Hasad was not normally a nervous flier, this rickety relic was getting to him.

Surrounded by wooden crates and steel shipping containers filled with various kinds of ordnance—semiautomatic pistols, machine guns and ammunition—he was the only passenger in the hold. Jammed tightly in the compartment between the closely packed crates and containers, he was becoming uncomfortably claustrophobic.

But he was alone with his thoughts, and for that he was grateful. He had a lot on his mind, and he appreciated the solitude. For the first time in a long time, he was unsure of what to do. Pakistan's ISI was flying him to Dubai, where he would catch a berth on a container ship, transporting his men and their supplies to Baltimore Harbor in Maryland. From there, he would take them to a safe house in Virginia.

The mission angered him, and he was especially furious with Shaiq and the general. They had played him false, holding out on his final payment and issuing threats. He would see to it that they came to grief with him over that.

Still, he had a nagging sense that he could turn this whole thing to his advantage. For some time, he'd wanted to see Elena again.

He'd spotted her by accident two years earlier. He was having a cup of coffee at a café in Islamabad, and she was seated at a table with a Pakistani deputy foreign minister, presumably discussing business. Instead of the traditional burqa or chador, she was dressed in a long tan skirt, a beige blouse, and a headscarf, but her face was clearly visible. He'd have recognized her anywhere. Hasad, on the other hand, wore a long, white Arab robe with a keffiyeh, a thick dark beard, a ponytail, and sunglasses. He could have been anybody.

When he first glimpsed her, he could not believe the wave of feeling that swept over him. It took every ounce of self-control not to stare gape-jawed at her. He hadn't felt like that since he'd left her twenty years ago. He knew then and there in that café that he had to have her back—no matter what it took. That she ran the CIA's Pakistan desk was of no consequence. He had to have her back even if he was flogged, castrated, dismembered, and beheaded for it. For reasons he honestly did not understand, getting her back was suddenly the most important thing in the world. In a life of incessant savagery, mayhem, and fear, she had been his only positive constant—the only thing of any value, the only person he'd ever felt truly close to. He did not want to spend the rest of his life alone. He wanted her at his side. It was as if he was her and she was him, as if they were the same person. In his entire wretched life, she was the only person he'd ever loved.

And if that wasn't enough, he was sick to death of the profession of arms—this life of bloodshed, violence, and slaughter. Didn't he deserve some peace?

Probably not—not after the things he'd done and seen.

So he'd initially thought to buy his way back into her affections. He'd dragged Rashid into his new assignment—brokering a deal between the TTP and ISIS—and had forced him to e-mail his reports on the deliberations. He'd then forwarded them to Elena, allegedly from Rashid's server. She was a CIA agent, and if giving her priceless intel about an alliance between the two most dangerous terrorist groups on earth didn't get her attention and affection, nothing would.

Furthermore, he had no use for Pakistani intelligence, the TTP, ISIS, or the murderous cretins he worked for. Nor did he hate Americans. He despised many of their country's policies and politicians, but he genuinely liked the Americans he'd known individually. Deep down inside, he wanted Jari and Shaiq's plans to fail.

Yes, he could turn this mission to his advantage.

Whatever happened, this would be his last op. Why not play it out, see where it led? Maybe it would somehow help him win back Elena. He'd also be giving America's leaders exactly what they were begging for. After seven decades of selling the most destructive nuclear arms technology imaginable to the world's most unstable nations, their political elite needed to get a taste of what they were so recklessly purveying.

Elena used to tell him, "You choose your dues. What you put out, you get back. What goes around, comes around. 'As ye sow, so shall ye reap.'" Well, the bloody nuclear instructions, which America had so assiduously taught the earth's worst despots and fanatics, would now "return to plague the inventor." Five hundred years ago, Shakespeare had imparted that brutal truth to audiences in Elizabethan England, and if they could benefit from his hard-won wisdom, the U.S. could, too.

And along the way, he planned to educate Shaiq and Jari on the real meaning of revenge. Why not? What had any of them ever done right in their sordid lives anyway, himself included? Nothing. Why bother to do the right thing now?

And anyway this could be fun.

For the first time in a long time, Hasad smiled.

4

"He's all the worst passages in the Koran rolled up into one."
—Adara Nasira

Another bucket of camel piss hit Rashid in the face, and he came to. He was sorry he had. He was back in the torture chamber. Still strung up by the wrists to the overhead beam, his shoulder, elbow, and wrist joints throbbed unbearably. The big gorilla they called Ali was yelling at him, but all he could hear was a dull, gale-force roar, blowing between his ears.

Ali got close to him and shouted in his face: "Can you hear me?"

Actually, Rashid did hear his screams now, so he nodded weakly.

"Then listen to this." He hit him in the stomach with a hard looping right.

Rashid gasped, rasped, and again passed out.

Another bucket of camel urine, and again Rashid came to. Ali grabbed him by the hair, lifting his head up.

"I don't see how you can stand to touch him," the woman said, her face wrinkled in disgust. She was seated in the corner, smoking, her face grimacing from the room's stink. Otherwise, all Rashid saw of her was a red blur, his eyes bloodshot from the incessant blows.

"I don't either," a new man added as he entered their small one-room building and closed the door. He was dressed in white clerical robes, wore wire-rimmed glasses, and sported curly white hair and beard. He carried a large black doctor's bag.

"I think the stink's harder on you and me than it is on Ali," the woman said to him. "Camel piss doesn't really bother him."

"He is part camel," the cleric said.

"More," the woman said.

The cleric dumped his bag on the wall table. "What is the prisoner's name?" he asked Ali.

"Asshole," Ali said.

"A good Islamic name." The cleric walked up to Rashid and smiled.

"Do you know who our new friend is?" the woman asked Rashid. When Rashid failed to respond, she said: "He is a doctor."

"I could use a doctor." Rashid groaned, his voice thick with pain.

"Me, in particular," the cleric said. "I'm both a medical doctor and a doctor of divinity. You know in my postgraduate work I specialized in pain therapy? Well, not so much the therapy part—more the application of it. When someone informed Pakistani intelligence—its dreaded ISI—of my exceptional talent, they quickly recruited me."

"Which just proves what I've always believed," the woman said. "Great torturers are born, not made."

"It was ever thus," the doctor said.

"He has a God-given gift for death as well," the woman told Rashid.

The cleric nodded his agreement. "I like to think of myself as 'Death's Second Self.'"

"But in the service of Allah," the woman said.

"His left hand, so to speak," the doctor said.

"Unfortunately, our friend, Rashid, is not devout," the woman said.

"But you are of the true faith, no?" the doctor asked. "You do pray to the one and only God, Allah, eight times a day?"

"More," the hanging man whispered.

"And what do you pray for?" the cleric asked.

"That you'll shut the fuck up."

An old-fashioned aluminum coffee pot on the stove began to percolate. The cleric poured himself a mugful and put it to his lips.

"This stuff's good, strong but boiling hot," the cleric said, wincing from the heat.

He emptied his mug onto Rashid's exposed genitals.

His screams shook the room, reverberated into the relativities of time, then rang, roared, and chimed through the echo chambers of hell.

"I'm sick to death of his endless whining and sniveling," the woman said. Walking up to Rashid, she grabbed his chin and shook it. "Can't you be a little more stoic about all this? Stiff upper lip and all that?"

"You are so right!" the cleric shouted. "Stoicism is exactly what he needs. The great philosopher, Epictetus, would have much to teach him."

"Enlighten him," the woman said.

"Epictetus understood only that the ignorant seek the outside world for benefit," the cleric explained, "while the wise simply let events happen."

"Rightly so," the woman said.

"We are all characters in a play the One True God has written," the cleric said, "and we must act our parts."

The hanging man stared at the woman, incredulous. "Who'd you say this guy was?" He nodded toward the doctor.

"Oh, he's all the worst passages in the Koran," the woman said, "rolled up into one."

"But the question," the doctor said, "is who are you? What do you want?"

"You're kidding," Rashid whispered weakly.

"Seriously," the woman said. "We want to know."

"Money?" Rashid asked, somehow managing a shrug.

"Excellent answer," the woman said.

"Anything else?" the doctor asked.

"Sex?"

"So you wish great wealth and beautiful women?" the doctor said.

"I'm not quite ready to die," Rashid said.

"Ah, but if you ask me, the fear of death is at the root of all your troubles—that and your dread of the unknown. You must accept the path of stoic resignation. You must see death as your wisest advisor, and welcome her as a trusted friend. One day, you will leave this world, and when you do, it must be with thanksgiving in your heart and joy in your soul. Allah lent you your life, and it's His to reclaim whenever He wishes. So let Him have that which He will take back anyway. We must all make room for others, not crowd the house of the world. To be truly free, one must embrace death, take it as a lover."

"Where'd you find him?" Rashid asked the woman, nodding toward the doctor. "Idiots 'R' Us?"

"Ah," the doctor said, "you joke. I like that. But I know you. I see into your soul."

"And I'm sure you're the better for it," Rashid said, groaning.

"Perhaps," the cleric said. "But I fear the next few hours will not go well for you."

"You mean I'm not going to enjoy our little slumber party?"

"He means you're not going to survive it," the woman said.

"You are about to soar on the wings of the night," the cleric said.

"A thousand times in a thousand different ways," the woman said.

Rashid's vision was starting to sharpen, and he could see the woman more clearly now. She was at the far end of the room, laughing, putting on red lipstick, of all things. She had changed her clothes and was now undoing the top two buttons on her black silk blouse, taking off her baseball cap, and letting her hair down.

"Damn, it's hot," she said.

She began walking toward him. Her thick, waist-length mane of raven hair was cascading over her shoulders and down her back, her hips swinging arrogantly, like a runway model's. Her wide generous lips were

now scintillatingly scarlet, her concupiscent décolletage startlingly sensuous. Stopping a dozen feet from him, she did a quick flirtatious pirouette—
apparently so he could see her black jeans stretched tight across her impu-
dently elevated derriere and observe the pruriently pointed, six-inch heels
of her thigh-high jet-black boots. Pausing to look over her shoulder at
him, she gave him the most malevolent smile he'd ever seen.

Walking up to him, she cupped his face in her hands. "Doctor, you asked
before whether our friend was religious, whether he believed in anything?
I've read his file. He believes he has to screw anything that's female and
breathing, anything with a pulse." She was now nose-to-nose with him, her
eyes fixed on his. Her hand began caressing the inside of his thighs.

"You'd give anything to have a woman again," she said, "wouldn't you?"

She kissed him, kissed him again, long, deep, luxurious kisses, her left
hand across the back of his head, pulling his mouth brutally against her
own, her tongue probing and teasing his, rimming his teeth and lips, then
plunging deeper and deeper, in and out, in and out—a sensuous simulacrum
of strenuous intercourse. Suddenly her right hand reached down low again
and grabbed him with all her might, iron tight, tighter than tight, harder
and harder, till he couldn't breathe.

A crashing tsunamic of ecstasy hit him like an express train, crushed him
like a power-vise, smashed him like a collapsing bridge. She was no longer a
woman but a force of nature—a level-50 earthquake, an asteroid strike, a
supernova blasting its blazing core into the infinite void.

He blacked out, and when he came to, the woman was still nose-to-nose
with him, grinning mischievously, her eyes glinting with sin and wicked-
ness, a gaze bottomless as hell's abyss. She was laughing at his helplessness
and pain.

They were all laughing at him.

"You're monsters" was all he could get out.

"Of mythic proportions," the woman said.

Still laughing, the doctor walked over to the wall table and opened the
black doctor's bag he'd placed there. He took out a blowtorch, a pair of tin
snips, pliers, and forceps. He put the blowtorch on the table, turned it on,
and lit it. After pulling on gray, padded, thermal-lined gloves, he began heat-
ing the shears, pliers, and forceps in the torch's brilliant bluish flame. They
soon turned incandescently crimson.

"Remember that spasm of ecstasy, boy," the woman said. "It's going to be
your last—unless, that is, you give us what we want."

With the glowing pliers in one hand and the red-hot, smoking shears in
the other, the doctor walked toward the hanging man.

5

"Maybe a little nuclear terrorism can divert our howling masses from their revenge."
—Shaiq ibn Ishaq

Lying on the black silk sheets of his massive circular bed, Shaiq stared up at the ceiling mirror, then glanced over at the floor-to-ceiling wall mirrors. His sultry, sloe-eyed mistress, Malika, brushed her long black hair out of her face and began snorting a sixth line of cocaine off his stomach with a rolled-up James Madison $5000 bill. She then looked up dreamily at him with a drug-addled smile and began moving lower, lower, lower.

Until—

Until—

Until—

Looking up, Malika saw the pressure in Shaiq mounting, becoming unbearable in its intensity. His pupils were dilating, his eyes rolling back, and his jaw trembling in and out. Without pausing, without missing a beat, she grabbed an amyl nitrite ampule off his chest and cracked it with one hand under his nose. The drug rush triggered a tidal wave of excitation, until, culminating in a crescendo of savagely sensual passion, it all but blasted the back of his head off.

Somewhere in the dim abyss of his brain, a voice whispered to Shaiq:

Too much pleasure kills.

So be it, his reptilian brain stem hissed back.

Slowly, he opened his eyes. Life haltingly returned to his body and limbs. His mistress was climbing up his supine body. Wiping her mouth, she kissed him long and hard on the lips, then rolled onto her side, her face buried in his neck.

"For a moment I thought you were going to die," Malika said.

"Part of me did," Shaiq said, "but I needed it. All that pent-up stress needed a release."

"Why are you so tense?"

She was such a hopeless moron there was no harm in ventilating. Her coke-cooked brain understood nothing and remembered less.

"I met with our clerics again. Talk about submongoloid idiots! They believe all that shit about stoning women and exterminating the infidel. They don't understand why we aren't pouring 150 percent of our petrodollars into ISIS and al Qaeda. They actually threatened me, saying if I did not increase our arms and funding for our foreign mujahedin, they would order them back into the Kingdom to teach the royal family the true faith at the point of a sword. They said that to me: 'at the point of a sword.'"

"I assume they will skim most of the money for themselves."

Maybe she isn't that dumb after all.

"At least. Still, it doesn't pay to underestimate them. They mean what they say and settle scores. If they don't get their Operation Flaming Sword soon, they'll declare a nationwide strike, incite a revolution at home, storm the palace gates, and bring the country to its knees."

"What do you plan on doing, my love?" Malika asked.

"My brothers and I all have our exit plans in place. We've been anticipating this moment for decades. All over the Mediterranean, the Caribbean, and the Brazilian coasts, we have walled villas replete with armed mercenaries to protect us and burgeoning black-hole bank accounts to underwrite our comfort. The world is freeing itself from hydrocarbon energy, and oil prices are plummeting. We have been lying about our infinite oil reserves forever. They are drying up with shocking rapidity, and we will soon go broke. We will no longer be able to buy off our eternally proliferating populace with free food, free housing, and free health care. Moreover, it will occur far sooner than Western experts realize."

"What will happen then?" Malika asked.

"A shit storm of apocalyptic proportions. Blood will flow in Riyadh's streets, and it will be worse in Pakistan. There, climate change is drying up the biggest rivers, devastating their croplands. Without our petrodollars and with nothing to eat, that country will come apart. The same thing will happen here. Our people will rise up and burn our nation down to the scorching desert sand. The Kingdom will cease to exist. We will again be reduced to Bedouinism. Since the only people here and in Pakistan—who are sincere, who believe in what they do—are the terrorists, they will end up with Pakistan's nukes. That's part of why we're launching this new operation. If we instill enough nuclear fear in people, maybe they will be too frightened to rise up against us. If we can no longer provide for our people's or the Pakistani people's welfare, maybe a little nuclear terrorism can divert our howling masses from their revenge."

"You have a lot on your plate, my prince."

"Yes, and I also have to contend with D.C. Not only the president and his horde of morons, but now some CIA bitch is making waves. She actually has evidence that Flaming Sword is about to go down. I'm worried that a couple of Caldwell's people might be listening to her. She could even go to the press."

"What can she do?"

"I think she's feeding intel to Jules Meredith, the reporter. To read Meredith's articles, you'd think she has a pipeline into Riyadh, ISIS, and Pakistan's ISI. Her analysis of the coming nuclear attacks is right on the money, that's for sure. If she digs any deeper, she could very well find the smoking-gun evidence necessary to blow the whistle on all of our operations. I don't want SEAL Team Six coming after me the way they went after bin Laden."

"So what will you do?" She was finishing up her seventh line, her nose and mouth crusted with the alabaster drug, her eyes wild with desire.

"Cancel her ticket for good. After Flaming Sword commences, I'll also have our Pakistani terrorist cells blow up pipelines and refineries all over the Mideast, then set the oil fields ablaze. I'll incite a Middle Eastern civil war that will make the violence in Syria, Libya, and Iraq look like the holy hajj. The petrol shortage will send OPEC oil prices up to $1000 a barrel. Our only hope for survival is to so terrify Washington and the Arab street that the U.S. throws money at us hand over fist, out of blind fright, and our populace is too paralyzed with horror to rise up."

"*Alhamdulillah,*" Malika said. Praise be to Allah.

"At least, it'll make the clerics happy."

"And you'll stay in power for decades to come," Malika said.

"*Alhamdulillah,*" Shaiq said. Praise be to Allah.

She didn't seem to be listening, though. Instead, she was crawling to the bed's edge and taking the sterling silver dish of cocaine off the bedside table along with a spoon and her rolled-up $5000 bill. Bringing them over, she meticulously laid out six more lines of coke on his belly with a teaspoon. She then gave him the dish and the rolled-up bill. He helped himself to five hard snorts.

"Malika?" he said.

But she could no longer hear—hear him, hear anyone, hear anything.

Instead she had retrieved the rolled-up bill and was snorting those six lines off his belly.

Then six more.

Then another six.

Then another.

Until she was, once again, drifting down over his navel, his abdomen, his hips, his thighs, until she was—

Until—
Until—
Until—
His last semi-intelligible thought was, *God, is she good.* . . .

PART VI

And the Books of the Damned were opened. . . .

—Daniel 7:10

1

"Rashid's either dead or dying in some Pakistani hellhole."
—Elena Moreno

Elena Moreno entered the Agency conference room in McLean. President George Caldwell, CIA Director Bill Conrad, and the secretary of defense, General David "Hurricane" Hagberg, were there ahead of her. This was a bad sign. They were never there early. Even worse, they each had copies of her report in front of them and were reading them. She had been convinced they'd never read her reports.

The president looked up. Without even saying hi, he started in on her.

"You say here that you have evidence that ISIS and Pakistan's terrorist group, TTP, have joined forces and are mounting three nuclear strikes against the U.S."

"My informant was at the meeting," Elena said. "He then met with a top Saudi official and personally arranged for him to transfer $500 million to Lieutenant General Jari ibn Hamza, the head of Pakistan's ISI. The money was collected by the Saudi prince, Shaiq ibn Ishaq—pressure-packed bundles of $100 bills, crammed into eight custom-built, outsize steamer trunks. Jari was to then give the trunks to Colonel Abdul al-Hakeem, a notorious ISI special operations officer, who is using the funds to bankroll an operation code named Flaming Sword. I can tell you my informant's name now for the simple reason that I believe he's dead or dying in an ISI torture chamber. Also I believe it was a nom de guerre that he used only with me. To me, he was Rashid al-Waqidi."

"That's the most preposterous story I've ever heard," CIA Director Conrad said.

"It's easy enough to confirm," Elena said. "Even a man as wealthy as Shaiq ibn Ishaq can't launder or conceal financial transactions of that magnitude."

"Let's say we find that Shaiq made $500 million worth of cash transfers," President Caldwell said. "Even if he gave the money to ISIS and TTP, that doesn't prove anyone plans on nuking the U.S."

"What other single terrorist operation would cost over $1 billion?" Elena asked. "What terrorist weapon system is worth ten figures? Only nukes. Multiple nukes purchased for multiple strikes."

"If Rashid's intel is so important, why have you kept us in the dark about him for so long?" Director Conrad asked.

"You know why?" Elena asked. "Two years ago I had a confidential informant named Mustafa ibn Miammar who warned me of a TTP attack on the U.S. embassy in Islamabad. If they successfully took that facility over, they would have gotten the name of every undercover agent we had working in Pakistan. All our operational intel was on those embassy hard drives. We reinforced embassy security, based on his report, but within a week Mustafa was tortured to death, his body dumped in front of the embassy."

"And you inferred from that incident," President Caldwell said, "that someone in the administration leaked Mustafa's name. It could have been pure coincidence. The ISI could have been onto him for months."

"If that's your call, Mr. President, I accept it. But you weren't running Mustafa and you aren't running Rashid. I was, and now I have to do everything in my power to keep my other informants alive."

"Had you told us earlier, we might have been able to mount an operation and extract him," Director Conrad said.

"Wasn't possible," Elena said. "Rashid was in too deep—into ISI, TTP, LeT, even ISIS. Still, I could always reach him. Not anymore. He's either dead or dying in some Pakistani hellhole."

"But you have no real evidence for any of your theorizing," Conrad said. "All you have is an informant we've never vetted and who's disappeared."

"I have one other piece of intel."

Elena dropped the poem on the conference table.

"I have another contact—a paramilitary I haven't spoken to in fifteen years. He changed his name a number of times, went into clandestine operations for both Pakistan's ISI and Saudi intelligence, doing the special ops they were afraid to get into. In doing so, he became utterly untraceable. Then suddenly, out of the blue, he sent me a warning." She handed out copies of Hasad's e-mail to the men at the table.

Remember Henry Hudson
And the power of the stars?
Where's our more perfect union?
It's one disastrous state of affairs,

New York, New York?
It's a hell of a tomb,

While somewhere out there,
The west will writhe in flames.

A bad moon's on the rise, kid.
A pair of setting suns
Will sink you forever.
My advice? Haul ass.
Get the fuck out of Dodge.

Remember me when the lights go out . . .

"Why the oblique phraseology?" General Hagberg asked.

"My contact," Elena said, "thinks the NSA has everyone wiretapped and monitored—even us."

"Thank you, Edward Snowden," the president said.

"What's your interpretation of the poem, Elena?" General Hagberg asked.

Elena gave it her best shot: "Henry Hudson refers to the discoverer of the Hudson River. The power of the stars is nuclear, and there's a nuclear power plant north of New York City on the Hudson River. The Army of the Potomac was part of the Union Army during the Civil War. The Union's disastrous state of affairs means the State of the Union address will end in disaster. 'New York's tomb' means New York is going to die. A pair of setting suns? Nukes are man-made miniature stars detonated on the earth. He suggests a similar nuclear cataclysm will take place out west, and his advice is to get out of town. Flee the nuclear holocausts to come."

"All right," the president said, "let me get this straight. You believe that ISI-backed ISIS terrorists are going to melt down the Hudson River Nuclear Power Station and then nuke my State of the Union address?"

"As well as some undisclosed location out west," Elena said.

"That's insane," Conrad said.

"It's only prudent to assume they are coming," Elena said evenly. "Rashid warned us. Now this man, too, and both men were on the inside."

"And who is this man," Conrad asked, "this new informant, whom you give so much credence to but whose existence you have heretofore concealed from us for God knows how long?"

Elena crafted her answer with studied precision, omitting everything she thought she could get away with.

"He's someone I knew once. Unfortunately, he went to ground fifteen years ago and has been unresponsive ever since. He only contacted me with this intelligence during the last twenty-four hours. He obviously fears these nuclear attacks as much as I do."

"Okay," Conrad said, staring at the ceiling, "now you're blindsiding us with a complete stranger, whom you haven't spoken to in fifteen years but whom you absolutely, unequivocally trust. Why is he so credible? I want everything on him: How long you have known him. Who he is. What he does. Name, background, bio, how he fits into this grand conspiracy of yours. And most important, what else are you hiding from us?"

"And I believe giving out that information will put him in mortal peril," Elena said. "Given the stakes, that risk is unacceptable."

"So you're concealing his identity from us just as you concealed Rashid's?" the CIA director asked.

"If I'd concealed Mustafa's identity, Mr. Director, I believe he'd be alive today. I could not expose Rashid to the same risk, nor will I jeopardize this new asset."

"In short," Director Conrad said, "you're in charge now. You think you run the CIA. You think you have my job."

"No, but I am in charge of this asset, and I'm not putting his life in unnecessary danger," Elena said. "The stakes are too high. The stakes are nuclear."

"You've deduced all this intelligence from one preposterous piece of doggerel," Director Conrad asked, barely able to contain his anger, "and now you expect us to make far-reaching national security decisions based on your absurd inferences?"

"I only present my findings, Mr. Director," Elena said. "I leave policy decisions to the president. But if I'm right and you fail to act, hell will follow."

"I've tolerated you for a long time, Elena," the president said, leaning back, crossing his arms and fixing Elena with a sad stare. "You know Pakistan better than anyone in this country. You know it from the inside. Hell, the TTP kidnapped and held you hostage for nearly five weeks. But if you don't trust us, I don't see how we can trust you."

"You're exactly right, Mr. President," Conrad said. "She's jumped the reservation. She's no longer part of the team."

"It's almost as if you've gone rogue, Elena," the president said wearily.

"Also, Mr. President," Conrad said, "I personally would like to see her relieved of all duties and put on a leave of absence. As you know, that's been my position for a long time."

"Sir," Defense Secretary Hagberg said, "I have to register my dissent. I've known Elena for fifteen years and have followed her work closely. I also fear

Pakistan as well as our so-called Saudi allies. That whole region is on the verge of violent revolution. Elena's conclusions—farfetched as they may seem—have a perverse logic to them."

President Caldwell was silent a long minute. Emitting a slow sigh, he said, "As much as it pains me, I have to agree with Director Conrad. Elena, I've lost all trust and confidence in you. Please turn in all your computers, flash drives, backups, everything in your office. Bill, arrange for security to clean out her office, take her ID, badge, key, pull her security clearance, and escort her from the building. Elena, I think you need several months off while we give your tenure an extremely thorough, top-to-bottom review. Most of all, I want to know who wrote that fucking poem, and everything else you've been concealing from us. If you don't cooperate with us, I swear to God I'll imprison you under the Patriot Act."

The president and Conrad left.

Before she could gather her things and stand, three large, dark-suited security officers entered the room, relieved her of her credentials, and escorted her from the building.

2

"You mean you're not going to electrocute my genitals?"
—Rashid al-Rahman

When Rashid came to, he was flat on his back on a thin mattress in a small, dimly lit space. His mouth was duct taped, his wrists bound crosswise with zip ties. His ankles and knees were also restrained. An IV was in his arm. The woman was sitting next to him on the floor, her back against the wall. She was still dressed in black Levis and a black blouse. Her boots were off, however, and she was wearing black Nikes. She was absorbed in a book.

Rashid grunted. She leaned over and removed the duct tape gag.

"Any good?" Rashid asked, nodding toward the book.

"Su-per-la-tive," the woman said dryly, pronouncing each syllable with contemptuous emphasis.

"What's it about?"

Putting the book down, she gave him a slow, disdainful stare, then averted her eyes.

"You wouldn't be interested," she finally said.

"Why?"

"It's full of long sentences and big words."

"Who's the author? The Marquis de Sade?"

She silently returned to her reading.

Rashid looked away from her and studied their surroundings. The room was about twenty feet long, eight feet high, and eight feet across. He could see now that the walls of the room were paneled with noise dampening tiles and acoustic foam. Someone had soundproofed it to the max.

At one end was a small portable toilet, a minifridge, a case of Cabernet Sauvignon, bottled water, and boxes of groceries with loaves of French bread sticking out the top. Another box was filled with Meals Ready to Eat. He saw a half-empty bottle of red wine beside his bed.

When he looked up at her, she was staring at him. She slowly lay down next to him. He noticed she had a flat, spring-loaded, leather-encased sap stuffed crosswise in her belt. He suddenly felt very tired, his body and head achingly sore. He also felt drugged. He shut his eyes and let his head sink into the pillow. . . .

*T*hen he remembered what had happened.
The white-robed cleric was walking toward him with the red-hot metal shears and pliers, grinning. The big ape called Ali was standing directly in front of him, laughing maniacally in his face. The woman was still sitting at the rear of the room. Taking a 9mm Makarov out of the shoulder bag lying next to her chair, she put the edge of her hand to her mouth and winked at him. Giving Rashid a cryptic smile, she screwed in a GEMTECH GM-9 silencer. She quickly stood, walked up to the doctor, and, from four feet away, shot him in the back of the head. Ali was turning to face her, but she was too quick for him. Before he could complete the pivot, she was at his side, putting a round in his temple. After he hit the floor, she followed up with an insurance tap to the forehead. The three shots, even in the closed confines of the cement-block room, were little more than a tap-tap-tap.
Still smiling, she walked up to Rashid again, once more kissed him on the lips, and cut him down.
The moment he hit the ground, he passed out. . . .

*W*hen he came to a second time, she was leaning over him, one palm over his mouth. She motioned him to be quiet. Pulling off the second strip of duct tape, she pressed the neck of a plastic water bottle against his lips.

"Drink it slowly," she whispered.

"I'd rather have beer," he said softly but took three slow sips.

"I have a twelve-pack in the minifridge. For the moment, though, you need some Sustacal." She opened a can and gave it to him. "After you're able to eat a couple of MREs, you can have that beer."

"You mean you're not going to electrocute my genitals?"

"No, I've been ordered to nurse you back to health."

"In order to torture me again?"

"Rashid, we're both in a shipping container on a truck, headed toward a U.S. cargo ship, which will take us to the United States. The Inner Harbor of Baltimore to be precise. I'm taking you to safety."

Rashid's head lay back on the pillow.

What the hell is happening?

Again, he passed out.

PART VII

Let them see what is on the end of that long newspaper spoon.

—William S. Burroughs

1

"I'm going to drag their dirty laundry out into the street."
—Elena Moreno

Jules and Elena sat at the Rockville McDonald's, silently staring at their large cups of black coffee. The more famous of the two, Jules wore a baseball cap and sunglasses. Elena, who'd come straight from the White House, was still in her black, pin-striped pants suit and heels. They had also been careful to avoid tails.

"Sometimes you just have to go with it," Jules finally said, "come back at them another time."

"There won't be another time," Elena said.

Jules nodded her grudging agreement. "If it goes down like you say, Caldwell and his gang could turn these attacks into a power grab."

"They'll say they need the extra authority to protect us from terrorists," Elena said. Turning toward the window, she stared out at the Maryland countryside. Rain was cascading down in slanted, layered sheets out of a blue-black sky.

"Sometimes you have to swallow the hurt and move on," Jules said.

"Never happen," Elena said, her eyes still fixed on the rain hammering the window like double-ought buck.

"The shit you know is so heavily classified, you breathe it to anyone outside the Agency, you're going away for good. The Patriot Act has provisions written specifically for people like you."

Elena turned her head and looked back at her, her eyes hard and flat as the rain-splattered window glass.

My God, Elena's going to do it.

She's going to take her findings to the press.

Jules put her hand on her arm. "They will shred your birth certificate and burn off your fingerprints. It'll be like you never were."

"And when I do nothing and the nukes go off, how do I live with that?"

"We'll both take time off," Jules said. "Go to the Bahamas. Any place except Ground Zero, USA."

"Really?" Elena said. "I know those assholes. They've talked about what they would do in a situation like this. After we get nuked, they'll retaliate with nukes. Pakistan and everyone else will do the same, and the whole Mideast—maybe half the free world—goes up in nuclear flames."

"It's everything ISIS and al Qaeda have always wanted," Jules said. "Turn 1.8 million Muslims worldwide into violent, infidel-hating fanatics."

"And once again, we march to their drums," Elena said.

"And the president can't see it coming?" Jules said.

"He's got his nose buried so far up Shaiq ibn Ishaq's ass, he can't see his own dick."

"He's not very smart, is he?" Jules asked.

"None of those boys are going to split the atom."

"They're all smart enough to think you're a threat."

"I got a news flash for you, Jules," Elena said, leaning toward her friend. "I am a threat."

"You want to fight a war you can't win?" Jules asked.

"I don't care," Elena said. "They dealt the play, and I'm seeing it through— to the end."

"Why?" Jules asked. "To what good purpose?"

"It's what I do," Elena said.

"What is it you do, anyway? I'd really like to know."

"I serve a vast, vulgar, meretricious dream."

"Which is?"

"To save planet earth from nuclear psychopaths like Caldwell, his Saudi patrons, and their Pakistani mad-dog killers."

Jules shook her head slowly. "I can't top that."

"I only speak the truth," Elena said.

"Yeah," Jules said, "but Caldwell and his crew don't traffic in the truth."

"Which is why they won't see me coming," Elena said.

"They won't guess what's jumping out of *my* jack-in-the-box either," Jules said, suddenly grinning.

"What do you mean *your* jack-in-the-box?"

"You expect me to miss out on the biggest story of the century? I could be a nuclear Woodward and Bernstein."

"This will not end well," Elena said, shutting her eyes.

"They're covering up what could be the biggest, baddest terrorist attack in history," Jules said, "and we're going to have them cold. When we're done, they'll be the ones stacking time."

"I did warn them of the coming nuclear strike," Elena said, "and they're ignoring it. I'll give you that much, and when they come after us, I'm not going to shut up and play nice. I'm going to drag their dirty laundry out into the street."

"True," Jules said, "and then they'll destroy you, say you doctored documents, withheld evidence."

"They'll probably claim I colluded with the terrorists, which is why I knew so much."

"You did conceal the identity of two known terrorists," Jules said.

"Then why are you jumping into the same trick bag?"

"Because you have such a winning personality?" Jules asked.

"It'd be easier," Elena said, "if we just cleaned out the White House with Uzis."

"If you shot those assholes," Jules said, shaking her head, "the shit'd run out of them like the Johnstown Flood."

"It's enough to make you want to quit show business," Elena said gloomily, staring at her reflection in the window.

"You can't run away from yourself," Jules said.

"Then fuck 'em all but six," Elena said, smiling, "and save them for pallbearers."

"That kind of language will give you cavities," Jules said.

"Look at it as my year of living dangerously," Elena said.

"Our year."

"You're in?" Elena said. "Really?"

"I couldn't let you have all the fun." Jules handed her friend a padded manila envelope. "I'm way ahead of you. There's a flash drive containing a copy of the article I stayed up all night writing and addresses for all the top print editors as well. By contract, I have to show it to *The New York Journal-World.* When they turn it down, one of us has to make sure it gets to the Huffington Post, *The Washington Post,* Salon.com, Slate.com, *Mother Jones,* Naomi Klein, *The Nation.* Anyone and everyone. We'll post it on blogs and Web sites."

"They'll come after us with flags flying and guns blazing, " Elena said.

"They may already be after us, which is why I gave you an extra copy."

"We'll have to get it out fast."

"And get away fast," Jules said.

"Not a problem. Just have your go-to-hell bags ready to go. I'll set it up."

"We're good?"

"We're solid," Elena said, giving her a high five.

2

"You could make a glass eye weep and turn out a nun."
—Rashid al-Rahman

When Rashid came to, he was still strapped down on his mattress, his hands fastened together with zip ties, his mouth taped. The woman was sitting next to him on the floor of the shipping container, reading a book. This time he could see the cover—*House of the Dead* by Dostoyevsky. He groaned. Putting an index finger to her lips and whispering "shush," she pulled off the tape.

"What happened?"

"You lay down with the devil, and you woke up in hell."

"And you're Dante's Virgil?" he asked, squinting at her. "My guide through the Underworld?"

"My name's Adara, and, yes, you can think of me as your spirit guide."

"Which means?"

"I'm the girl who shows up with the twelve-pack after everything's closed."

"But you were one of my torturers."

"As Dylan says, 'People are crazy, times have changed.'"

"So why are you helping me now?"

"My employer appealed to my better instincts," Adara said.

"How?"

"He offered me money," Adara said.

"There are other things more important than money."

"Like?" Her face was filled with skepticism and contempt.

"Like sex?"

"Ever try spending head?"

"I hear money is the root of all evil."

"In my world it is a many-splendored thing."

"That's all? He bought you?"

"He also promised to kill me if I refused."

"And he scares you?" Rashid asked.

"He's war, plague, famine, earthquake," Adara said. "He's more trouble than Jehovah gave the Jews."

"So why does he want us?" Rashid asked.

"He knows our work. We both lived in the U.S. for several years and speak the language fluently. We know our way around Americans."

"Suppose I said no?"

"Oh, he's the last person in the world you want to fuck with."

"What about you?"

"I'm the next to last."

Rashid stared at his rescuer a long moment. "You really are beautiful."

"But mean—don't forget it," Adara said.

"You don't hold with 'Love your neighbor' and the Sermon on the Mount?"

"In my world," Adara said, "your neighbor is cursed, the meek are fucked, and peacemakers burn in hellfire everlasting."

"What about the poor in spirit?" he asked, baiting her.

Adara shrugged. "I never invest in other people's misery."

"I could learn to love you?"

"You ever love a woman—ever?" she asked, her expression dubious.

Rashid nodded. "Sure. When I was young. Her name was Aisha."

"Why did you love her?"

"She was the first woman I didn't have to pay for."

"And that's how you define love?" Adara asked, her eyes narrowing.

"Yes. Back then." He looked at her intently. "But what about *you*? You ever love anyone?"

Adara smiled pleasantly. "Yeah. Me."

"Why?"

"I'm really good at my job."

"Which included killing those people back in the safe house?"

"I'm told," the woman said, "I have the moral compass of an iron maiden."

"You don't strike me as all that bad," Rashid said.

"I'm also told I have the soul of a sledgehammer, the heart of a whore, and the business ethics of a tiger shark."

"Now who would say that?" Rashid asked with mock disbelief.

"My friends."

"What do your enemies say?"

"That I'm Hitler times ISIS multiplied by metastatic cancer."

"They don't know you like I do," Rashid said with a wry smile.

"And what do you know about me?"

"I'm told we're all children of God."

"Not anymore. God's gone."

"Really?" Rashid asked. "Where did He go?"

"The Big Bang blasted His ass into another dimension."

"You mean He's not here anymore?"

"He has left the building."

"So where does that leave us?"

"If there's no God," Adara mused, "then everything is permitted."

"I'm told without God, there is no hope."

"Ah, there is infinite hope," she said, shaking her head, "but not for us."

"Do you like living like this—on the edge?" Rashid asked.

"It's the only place to win."

"And you expect to win?"

"I'm not sure this time," she said, suddenly serious. "This one will be bad, a leap into the abyss."

"So you're afraid?"

"Never." She suddenly smiled. "I was born in the abyss."

"I don't think I'm going to like this picture."

"You'll hate every frame."

"Then what's in it for me?"

"Nothing—except the alternative is unthinkable."

"I need more incentive than that."

"If we survive, we'll both make a shitload of money."

"Suppose the job violates my moral principles?"

"When money contends with morality," she said, laughing, "the battle is always nolo contendere."

"I'm going to hate myself in the morning."

"Buck up. We'll do some good."

"Like what?"

"We're going to lock the lid on Pandora's box and weld it shut."

"And my role in this little love fest?"

"You're the indispensable man."

"The graveyards are full of indispensable men."

"My boss wants you on board, and he's a man you don't disappoint."

"He's persuasive?" Rashid asked facetiously.

"He could make rocks sob, mountains dance, the dead cry out from terror and from truth."

Rashid looked away and shut his eyes. "I don't know."

"You have a day to decide. When we land, I have to know which side of the door you're on. But once you walk through it, there's no going back."

"And if I do join up?"

The woman stood up. Her high-waisted black trousers were tight in the legs and thighs, sharply delineating her arching derriere. Her black, low-cut blouse invitingly revealed the sensual curvature of her cleavage. Her ebony riding boots featured four-inch heels and were polished to a mirror gloss. She stretched and yawned.

God, she was *beautiful.*

A wave of lust rushed through him like a hard, hot wind.

"What do you think?" she asked.

"That you could make a glass eye weep and turn out a nun."

"You do have gonads for brains."

"Even so, the dying man wants a last fuck."

"Now there's an invitation to the dance," she said, grinning derisively.

"Buy the ticket, take the ride."

"We do this, you're on board?"

"Uh-huh." His voice was now thick with lust.

"You know what you're doing?"

"I know I want to fuck you like there's no tomorrow."

"You may not have a tomorrow."

"All the more reason."

"It will cost you."

"I'll take out a home equity loan."

"I warned you. I'm mean."

"Before this is over, you'll learn to love me."

"Like the axe loves the turkey—the hammer, the nail."

She stared at him a long, hard minute, unsmiling, her face empty of emotion. That's what got to him. Her eyes, Rashid would later remember, were flat as a diamondback's, deader than prayer, empty as the intergalactic void, absent of any emotion as two broken windows in an abandoned, gutted house.

"It's your funeral," she said.

He nodded feebly.

She began pulling off her black thigh-high boots.

3

"Let's go play Thelma and Louise."
—Elena Moreno

This time Elena and Jules were at a Baltimore McDonald's.

"Did the paper go for your article?" Elena asked.

"They slammed it down so hard it bounced," Jules said.

"It was the story of the century."

"Of the millennium. They don't care though."

"What happened to 'publish and be damned'?"

"I got damned instead."

"To what?" Elena asked.

"I think they want me in shackles and leg irons."

"Oh my God," Elena said. "They threw the Patriot Act in your face."

"Like it was chiseled in stone on Mt. Sinai," Jules said.

"They're stuck on stupid."

"They're no ordinary cowards," Jules said. "I'll give you that. They went around me and showed our story to your boss, Conrad."

"Who immediately fingered me as your source," Elena said robotically, staring at the ceiling.

"It had to be you. You were the only one in possession of the facts."

Elena leaned across the table, put her hand on her friend's arm, and smiled. "That meeting must have been terrible."

"You don't know the half of it."

When Jules Meredith, in a black three-piece suit, entered the New York Journal-World's fourteenth-floor conference room, John Jennings and Helen Myer were waiting for her at the table. Jennings was in shirtsleeves, and Helen wore a simple but elegant blue dress. Neither of them was smiling.

They were holding copies of the article—based on Elena's intelligence findings—that Jules had written.

"I don't know what to say," Jennings had said. "We told you to stop dredging up this Saudi stuff. It's old hat. Everyone knows they have rogue billionaires who contribute to terrorist-front charities."

"This time they're financing something big, something horrific," Jules said, "and it's coming here."

"Who says?" Helen Myer asked. "If your CIA source is so good, why's the Agency discounting the threat?"

Jules struggled to keep her composure.

How did Helen know the Agency was dismissing Elena's findings?

"You're wasting your time and our money," Helen said.

Jules stiffened. The tiger in her gut was pacing its cage, on the verge of break-ing through the bars. She struggled to hold it in.

"How do you know they aren't responding to the threat?" Jules asked. "I stipu-lated this material was 'eyes only.' You two weren't supposed to show it to anyone."

Her two bosses exchanged quick glances.

"Material this sensitive," Jennings said, "has to be checked out."

"If we printed it and were wrong, or if it contained classified information, we could all end up in jail," Helen said.

"The Agency and the White House are in criminal denial over this impend-ing attack, Helen," Jules said. "That's the point of the article. Someone's put the fix in over there, and we all know who that person is. Newspapers exist to expose such conflicts of interest, such negligence. We're here to wake people up and tell them the truth, not lull our leaders and people into apathy."

"You have no smoking-gun evidence," Helen said, "and we can't go forward without hard proof."

"The CIA agent quotes two deeply placed, high-level informants in this piece," Jules said. "The agent quotes them verbatim. The informants say the attacks are going down. They're risking their lives to protect us."

"Director Conrad and the president say your agent is talking out her ass," John said. "They even implied your obsession with the Saudis has driven you to fabricating those quotes."

Jennings said "her." So he and Helen had shown her piece not only to the Agency but to the president, and the two men had inferred Jules's source was a woman.

The source was Elena.

You gave them a chance," Elena said.

"They pay my salary. I owed them a look."

"And in return, they threatened you."

"They're just scared," Jules said. "I'm not."

"Then let's do it," Elena said.

"You sure?" Jules asked. "It'll go harder for you. Look what happened to Snowden."

"He wasn't trying to stop multiple nuclear attacks."

Jules opened her brand-new Lenovo computer and turned it on. "Don't worry," Jules said. "I disconnected the GPS."

Jules's cover e-mail was already written and addressed to contacts at twenty major media outlets, including four blogs and three Web sites.

"Someone will print this piece," Jules said.

"Maybe all of them."

Jules hit Send.

"I knew in my bones," Elena said, "it would come to this. These people are just too fucking bad."

"I have my go-to-hell bag packed," Jules said. "You have our fake ID kits?"

"I've had them ready for months. Several each. I've also got us a clean car," Elena said, "fake credit cards, bogus passports, phony driver's licenses and registrations—all of them matching our new IDs."

"Clothes? Hair dye?"

"For both of us."

"You sure," Jules asked, "you disconnected your GPSes? In your phones, computers, car, the works?"

"Yep."

"How much cash could you scrape up?"

"Seventy-five k," Elena said.

"Ninety-five here."

"Small bills?"

"Copy that," Jules said.

"Luckily I have firearms."

"We'll need them."

"The car's in the mall parking lot across the street," Elena said.

"Mexico or Canada?"

"We'll blend in easier up in the States. I have a friend we're meeting with who'll help us out."

"Can we trust him?" Jules asked.

"I trust him."

"Good enough."

"Let's go play Thelma and Louise."

PART VIII

Behold, I come as a thief....

—Revelation 16:15

1

"Reach too high, you fall too far."
—CIA Director William Conrad

CIA Director William Conrad and President Caldwell sat in their shirt-sleeves in the Oval Office on heavy stuffed chairs. They were drinking Highland Park twenty-five-year-old single malt scotch neat from rocks glasses. The bottle was on the circular teak end table between them.

"How much do you think the reporter knows?" Caldwell asked Conrad.

"Based on what *The New York Journal-World* leaked to us, I'd say Elena told their reporter quite a bit."

"What we saw in the article, what we squashed, is bad enough," Caldwell said.

"We certainly rubbed Elena's nose in it. Any chance she or this Jules Meredith woman will still publish it?" Conrad asked Caldwell.

"Depends how obsessed they are," the president said.

"They have to know we'd lock them up pretty near forever," Conrad said. "Jennings and Helen Myer told us they'd made it clear to Meredith. I don't take them for a couple of traitors. They've been team players their whole lives."

"Bill," President Caldwell asked anxiously, "is there any chance that the women are right and that ISI/ISIS are plotting nuclear attacks on the U.S.? Look what they did to that Pakistani nuclear plant. Shouldn't we put the country on a wartime footing? Order the National Guard to occupy our nuclear facilities and seal off the border?"

"George, you campaigned on a promise that you'd kick Islamist terrorism's ass, and for three straight years, you've told the public you're doing precisely that. The threat to the homeland was gone. Now, just before an election, you want to say you're both a liar and incompetent?"

"But what if they *are* planning an attack?" the president asked. "Hypo-thetically?"

"We polled that, remember?" Conrad said. "The secret study? What would be the public's reaction when word got out that the president hadn't defeated the terrorists and the country was in for major attacks?"

President Caldwell nodded. "It was a disaster. An admission like that would cost us the November election and drag the whole party down with us. We'd lose both houses."

"Then the next administration could have a special prosecutor determine how you could be 180 degrees wrong—how you could fuck up your assessments so disastrously and cost so many Americans their lives."

"Hell, that's what I'd do to them," the president agreed. He paused and stared out the window at the South Lawn. "Is there any chance that she's right . . . about several imminent nuclear attacks on the U.S.?"

"Let's assume a worst-case scenario—that she's figured out something that the CIA, NSA, the Director of National Intelligence, the Office of Intelligence and Counterintelligence, the Office of Intelligence and Analysis, the Office of Terrorism and Financial Intelligence, the Defense Intelligence Agency, the National Reconnaissance Office, U.S. Cyber Command, the FBI, NATO, and Interpol combined have all overlooked. Let's assume Elena Moreno is smarter than all of us put together. That still doesn't negate the fact that Meredith is capable of exposing our offshore business transactions with Shaiq. As you know, I'm in on some of those deals myself. She implies as much in her article, if people can read between the lines. She's a genius when it comes to getting financial dirt on people, and, George, you've been concealing assets and income from the IRS for eighteen years. She's close to uncovering those accounts, if she hasn't uncovered them already. Give her the rest of the year, and she'll find them. She's just too damn good at this shit. And anyway," Conrad said, "if Pakistani terrorists did nuke us, as horrendous as those strikes would be, you and I could ride that out."

"Assuming we weren't at Ground Zero," the president said.

"Granted, but if we weren't killed, we could come out stronger politically."

"Nine eleven did enhance George W.'s position," the president said.

"Gave him his second term and the Patriot Act."

"Remember those apartment building bombings in Russia in '99—in Moscow, Buynaksk, and Volgodonsk?" Caldwell asked. "They so terrified the Duma that it gave Putin dictatorial power."

"We still believe Putin staged those bombings himself so he could scare the country into letting him usurp that power," Conrad said. "That's the Agency's official classified assessment."

"Well," Caldwell said, laughing, "it worked."

"Can't argue with success," Conrad said. "You know a so-called terrorist attack worked for Hitler, too. Look at what the Reichstag fire did for him."

"It made *der Führer* the absolute dictator of Germany," Caldwell said.

"A nuclear terrorist attack against the U.S. would do something very similar for us," Conrad said.

"We could come out on top, couldn't we?" Caldwell agreed.

"We ought to have 'a New Presidential Powers Act' locked and cocked, in the can," Conrad said. "We can ramrod it through Congress the next day—hell, the same day—while the country is in the grip of stark terror, blind panic, and mass hysteria."

"Just think of what we could do without all that checks-and-balances, separation-of-powers bullshit," Caldwell said, his tone heated.

"There'd be a new sheriff in town," Conrad said, nodding.

"I can finally tell Congress and the court to go fuck themselves," Caldwell said.

"Our way or the highway," Conrad said.

"Leave them with their hearts broken and their throats smokin'," Caldwell said with a smile.

"I'm not sure I even see a downside to it," Conrad said. "Except for the casualties, of course."

"Worst case for us is that we would survive it legally, politically," President Caldwell said analytically. "We win that second term, and I seriously increase my political power. But the important thing is we'd survive this present crisis. What we can't survive is Elena and Jules Meredith exposing our financial dealings, specifically those dealings with Shaiq ibn Ishaq."

"I wish we'd never met that cocksucker," Conrad said.

"Ah hell," Caldwell said fatalistically, "getting involved with him was unavoidable. At the time, I was facing utter financial ruin, and those offshore partnerships with him seemed like a good deal for you, too."

"We were also facing financial fraud—the kind they lock people up for," Conrad started.

"Until Shaiq paid certain people off," the president added.

"We wouldn't be here without him. Those partnerships he brought us gave us a chance for you to pay off our creditors, put away some real money—offshore, tax-free—and even bankroll your run for the presidency."

"So we have no choice. If they try to go public, we hit them with everything we have," the president said.

"Maybe we should go after them with everything we have . . . *now*," Conrad said.

"You aren't suggesting . . . ?" the president asked.

"It may be our only chance," Conrad said.

"Then she's going down?" the president asked.

"Both of them. It's our best shot."

"Then we have to move now."

"I have a team in place."

"Then it's lock and load?"

"Loaded for bear."

"The poor babies."

"Reach too high, you fall too far."

"I don't know," Caldwell said.

Conrad stared at him. "What's wrong, George? You never had anyone hit before?"

"Not really."

"It's always unpleasant, but in this case—if it makes you feel any better—you never had a choice."

"But they're women," the president said.

"More's the pity, but they did it to themselves."

"I don't know. What exactly did they do?"

"They flew too close to the sun," Conrad said.

President Caldwell poured himself another glass of Highland Park 25, finishing the bottle. He drank it straight down. Conrad went to the corner bar. He selected and brought back another bottle of the Highland Park 25. He poured them each half a glass neat.

"We take care of those two first," Conrad said, "then I'll get you everything on any potential terrorist nukes."

"Elena Moreno would have been our best source in that regard," the president said.

"I know, but we clean up our own mess first. Whatever happens afterward happens."

"You're right. Has to be done. Still, they didn't deserve *this*." The president helped himself to a large swallow.

"They knew the deal when they signed up," Conrad said. "They wanted to run with the big dogs? Fine, but big dogs also bite."

2

_____

"What did you expect? Hearts and flowers?"
—Adara Nasira

Hasad drove the white Ryder Navistar 9400 truck with the Cat engine, air brakes, and ten-speed transmission off I-81 and onto SR 254. He was pulling a forty-eight-foot semitrailer. According to the map, they were fifty miles outside of Staunton, Virginia, in one of the least populated counties east of the Mississippi. The GPS directed him to one turnoff after another over several circuitous mountain roads until they reached a small hollow with an old farmhouse and a large red barn off to the side.

He drove behind the barn, got out, and opened the semitrailer's rear door. Inside was a forty-foot shipping container. He took out a key and unlocked the container's padlock. Pulling open the door, he looked inside.

A man and a woman had been keeping house there for over almost two weeks. Their waste bins and port-a-potties were full, and the shipping container was overflowing with empty beer cans and wine and whiskey bottles as well as food wrappers. Unused to the light of day, both of them were blinking. The man and the woman were both dressed in black Levis and tank tops. Like Hasad's, the man's body was covered with long-forgotten, long-healed bullet wounds and knife scars. This was a man schooled in the profession of arms.

"Looks like you two had a nice trip," Hasad said to Adara, shaking her hand.

She nodded, silent.

"I had a sneaking suspicion you might be running things," Rashid said, blinking. "Can you tell me what's happening?"

"You two are getting out of here," Hasad said, "and you don't have much time."

"We really need a shower and clean clothes," Rashid said.

"You need to get as far away from this place as you can by nightfall. See that van over there?" In the field behind them was parked a black RAM Pro-Master 2500 van with heavily tinted, one-way windows. "Under the van's rear floor in a hidden compartment, there's a 12-gauge pump, two H&K

9mm NATO submachine guns, and two 9mm Glocks—all with extra ammo. You also have an envelope with written instructions, new IDs, credit cards, and $90,000 in money belts. You each have offshore accounts in the Caymans, which my Swiss banker will replenish periodically. I will get you even larger amounts later. You have knapsacks with new clothes, toiletries, cold sandwiches, Cokes in a thermal bag, and a Thermos of coffee. You also have a full tank. Don't drink alcohol. Don't speed. You can pull over for gas but otherwise don't stop until you meet Elena and Jules at this location." He handed them photos of the two women, an address, a city map with an X marked on the location of the meet, and Elena's cell phone number. "You have five hours to get there. They're on the run, and you two are going to help them."

"Then what?" Adara asked.

"The women will give you the details," Hasad said.

"And when we're all finished?" Rashid asked.

"You go to ground, stay clear of the law for a few years, and you'll be relocated—set up anywhere you want."

"Who's behind all this?" Rashid asked.

"No questions," Hasad said.

He stared at Adara a long hard moment.

She met his gaze, her eyes expressionless. She and Hasad had been lovers, known each other, and now there was nothing to say.

"I still don't—" Rashid started to say.

"Then there it is. Go with God."

The man turned his back on them and returned to the farmhouse.

"He's a cold motherfucker," Rashid said to no one in particular.

"What did you expect?" Adara asked. "Hearts and flowers?"

"After what we've been through, he should have said something more."

"He did," Adara said. "You just weren't listening. We have a van, IDs, weapons, money, a full tank. The licenses and registration are good. That's all that counts. They'll come up clean if a cop runs them through his computer. When this is over, we'll get set up in foreign countries."

"But what's the job supposed to be about?" Rashid asked.

"Our survival, which means we focus on the business at hand. Which means we get in the car and drive as safely as we know how. We don't do anything to make the cops stop us. We have ordnance in that van that could get us decades in prison. We get through this, we play our cards right, and we'll both live like kings and queens in an island paradise."

3

"Killing two decadent Western women...will present no challenge at all."
—Colonel Abdul al-Hakeem, Pakistani Special Operations Commander

Shaiq ibn Ishaq and Lieutenant General Jari ibn Hamza were in the general's office. The ISI special operations colonel, whom Shaiq had met before in the Afghan mountains with Hasad, was there. The man made him nervous. Still, Jari had said—indeed had insisted—that Colonel Abdul al-Hakeem was the only man for the job. That Jari, who'd spent his entire life in the most violently dangerous special operations imaginable, held this mysterious "colonel" in such esteem was impressive, if disconcerting.

They sat at the conference table. Shaiq showed the colonel photos of the two women, Jules Meredith and Elena Moreno. "You know what we want done?"

"Yes, but you also told me the president and his CIA director claimed they would handle it," the colonel asked.

"They're too indecisive, too hesitant," Shaiq said. "They'll find some way to fuck it up."

"You're saying that the president and his men are stupid little girls?" the colonel asked.

Jari nodded. "They lack the necessary resolve."

"I can't stress enough," Shaiq said, "how important this is. I read an unpublished article that Jules Meredith wrote for *The New York Journal-World*. It's based on secret interviews with the CIA's Elena Moreno, head of their Pakistan desk. The newspaper and the White House are trying to suppress the story, but it will undoubtedly get leaked. Even worse, what I saw was only the iceberg's tiniest tip. I'm convinced that those two women can get enough dirt on Caldwell, Conrad, and me to take us—and no telling who else— down. If they don't have the dirt to do it now, it won't take them long to get it. So everything depends on removing them from this equation."

"I've known men like this American president," the colonel said meditatively, "and I understand completely. When a man is trapped in a pit with pit vipers, he must become a pit viper himself and strike like a pit viper to survive. But this man, Caldwell, cannot accept that. He still believes he can flutter like a butterfly and warble like a lark in this new pit viper world."

"We cannot trust them to eliminate the threat these two women pose," the general said.

"Their culture is weak when it comes to women," the colonel explained.

"Which our culture, thankfully, is not," Shaiq said.

"A great Western thinker, named Nietzsche," General Jari observed, "once wrote that in all dealings with women one must bring the whip."

"*Subhan Allah!*" the colonel shouted, laughing and slapping his thigh. Glory be to Allah. "This Nietzsche, was he of the faith?"

"No," the general said. "He did not believe in any God."

"That is too bad," the colonel said. "He would have made an excellent jihadist."

"Seriously," the general asked, "can you handle these two women?"

"But of course," the colonel said cheerfully. "You will supply my adjutant with everything you know about their current activities, photos of them, their comings and goings. We will follow them for a day or two, then handle the situation."

"I feel so much better," Shaiq said.

"We're about to commence Operation Flaming Sword," the colonel said, "and that's a complex operation. Killing two decadent Western women, however, will present no challenge at all."

4

"Close enough for rock and roll."
—Adara Nasira

After purchasing additional clothing and supplies, Adara and Rashid came out of the Walmart, which was across the street from their meeting place with the two women in the big mall. They were dressed in dark, loose-fitting bush jackets and black baseball caps. Rashid's cap featured a Baltimore Orioles logo, Adara's that of the Nationals. They headed over to a McDonald's for coffee and cheeseburgers to go. At 10:00 P.M., the Walmart's and the mall's parking lots were down to fifty or sixty cars.

As they climbed into their van, Adara asked him, "See anything unusual?"

"The two black SUVs at the edge of the parking lot."

"I know," she said.

"They've been parked ever since we got here, and they aren't empty."

"How do you know there are people in them?" Adara asked.

"Someone's been emptying a urine bottle alongside the van, and there are dozens of cigarette butts on both sides of it."

"They gave us night scopes and silencers," Adara said. "How good are you with that MP7?"

"I assume the enemy has vests, and we want head shots?"

"Definitely."

"I'm good for at least two hundred yards," Rashid said.

"That's pretty damn good."

"We're also firing UBR 4.6mm expanding bullets," Rashid said, "which fragment on impact. That radically increases the size of the wound cavity. It's almost impossible to miss a vital organ."

"Close enough for rock and roll. See that semi next to the Safeway? The driver's taken off somewhere, and it's been parked there for hours. The light above it is out. Get on top of it and you'll have a perfect angle as they exit the van. When you see them pull out their guns, you can pick them off."

"Where will you be?" Rashid asked.

"We have a van in back of the Walmart," Adara said. "We each have a set of keys. Then I'm going back to the McDonald's and having a coffee there. We're supposed to meet in the parking lot in front of it. When the two women pull into that lot and get out, the shooters will exit the black SUVs. You'll hit them from their rear flank. My guess is they'll have a half dozen or so in each van. When the action starts, I'll hit them from their front, off to the side just a little."

"We trap them in a cross fire, hopefully without hitting ourselves."

"You and I are taking on two vans filled with a dozen or more killers," Adara reminded him.

"Yes, but we'll each have a half dozen thirty-round magazines," Rashid said. "We'll have surprise on our side, and we'll make our shots count."

"I'll have a better angle on the driver's side of the two vans," Adara said. "You take the passenger's side."

"Got it."

Putting the MP7 submachine gun into a knapsack along with extra magazines, Rashid headed for the Walmart. Adara started toward the McDonald's. They ate their cheeseburgers on the way.

5

The president's hands were befouled by Saudi blood money.
—Hasad ibn Ghazi

Hasad went inside and sat by himself at the kitchen table with a bottle of Jack Daniel's and a bottle of Bud.

And thought about Jules and Elena.

He knew they were in a whole world of trouble. Elena had always been shockingly smart. Hell, she had somehow divined Shaiq's plan to nuke three U.S. cities. She hadn't connected all the dots, but it would not take her long. That the Agency was harassing her for knowing too much came to him as no surprise. Political hacks had always run that show, not real intelligence pros. That Shaiq had showered Caldwell with so much largesse that he couldn't see straight was also to be expected. Blinded by hubris and greed, the president's hands were befouled by Saudi blood money, the president had no choice but to destroy Elena the Whistleblower and Jules the Muckraker. Shaiq was making idiots of all of them.

We just can't let that happen, can we? Hasad said to himself. *No, not to my little girls.*

So he'd done everything he could for his two old friends. He'd lined up the best pair of operatives he could find and sent them to protect Elena and Jules. It had worked out well so far. The whole operation had cost Hasad nearly $7 million, but that was a small fraction of his net worth—in fact, a small fraction of this op, a mission that was also his last job.

That the two women and his operatives would now be committed to stopping his nuclear assault on America didn't bother him in the least. His heart was not in this final op. Part of him wanted it to fail.

Still, the money had been so prodigious that had he passed it up, his loyalty to jihad would have been called into doubt. In his line of work, losing the trust of one's superiors could have catastrophic consequences. So, at first, he had felt obligated to finish what he had started. You take their shilling, you do their bidding—the code of the profession.

But then they welched, threatened his sister and himself, and were now going after Jules and Elena.

No more.

He owed his employers nothing.

Especially that fucker, Shaiq.

He planned on getting him in his sights before this was over.

Hasad poured himself another double shot of JD.

6

Tortured by a gaggle of demented sadists...
—Rashid al-Rahman

ashid al-Rahman lay prone on top of the big semitrailer. The MP7's wire-stock was braced against his shoulder, its scope pressed on his right eye. He studied the parking lot and particularly the black van though its lens.

What the fuck am I doing here?

He always asked himself that question when he was involved with Hasad. A mutual acquaintance had first introduced them, and Rashid had had misgivings about him even then. He'd heard rumors about the man's ruthlessness, and something about Hasad's eyes put him off. They scared him—and nothing scared Rashid. He asked his associate what he knew about the man.

"He's the best friend and the worst enemy you could ever have. He'll also make you more money in a year than you could make anywhere else in a decade."

The money had turned Rashid's head, and he had made a small fortune during his eight years in Hasad's employ.

Rashid had also experienced more violence and terror in those eight years than he would have known in a full century of any other mercenary work. Even worse, the money had never stuck.

Why is that? Rashid now wondered.

It probably had something to do with the tsunami of hard liquor, the legions of fast women, and the horde of slow horses he'd gone through. Throw in a nose for coke, a weakness for bad cards and cold dice—all of it aggravated by a life spent living on "the edge"—and he could see, in retrospect, his entire sordid history.

But even given all that, why had he hooked up with someone as terrifying as Hasad? It wasn't that Hasad was a loyal, stand-up employer. Rashid had never known that side of the man until recently—the Hasad who was reputedly such a great friend. For the most part, all he'd seen of him was the brutal, relentless enemy whose genius for retribution seemed to be limitless.

But once more, here he was working for him—something he'd promised himself he'd never do again—and, as usual, the hounds of hell were at his back. First he'd been captured and tortured by a gaggle of demented sadists; now he was on top of a semitrailer in a dark, high-end shopping mall in Washington, D.C., with the most seasoned killers in the FBI, CIA, and Pakistan's ISI closing in on him.

Why? Is it all due to my greed?

No, Adara had him right. He had always been hell-bent on fucking any woman with a pulse, anything female and breathing . . . which also explained where most of his money had gone.

Which also explained why he was lying here on the semitrailer in a dark parking lot like a piece of bait.

And all because of that bitch, Adara. She'd torture you half to death one minute, then fuck your brains out the next. But, God, she was hot. Just thinking about her—up here on this semitrailer—got him aroused.

What's wrong with me, anyway?

Pretty much everything.

Facing almost certain death, all Rashid could think of was his . . . lust.

Come on, he thought to himself, *you have to concentrate on the job at hand—something other than money and pussy.*

He finally returned his focus to the parking lot in front of him and the black van filled with killers.

7

"We gotta get out of this place."
—The Animals

lena Moreno pulled their Chevy SUV into the McDonald's parking lot
and came to a stop. Across the parking lot was a Walmart. Next door was
a huge sprawling mall filled with ultrachic stores.

"I'm hungry," Jules said, reaching for the door.

"Wait. I don't like the Cadillac Escalade and the big black Ford van parked
about forty feet apart in the mall lot."

"I don't like not eating for hours," Jules said, pulling on the handle. "No
way anyone could be following us. Our car's clean, our hair is cut and colored,
we have great fake IDs and sunglassese. They're just cars, Elena."

She exited the Chevy.

The doors of both vans immediately opened, and five men in baseball
caps, black T-shirts, and matching pants began piling out, armed with automatic weapons held next to their thighs. The other vehicle disgorged six
similarly clad men.

Eleven men in all.

"Or maybe not," Jules said, climbing back in.

One of the men exiting the Cadillac wore a black New York Giants cap.
He took a round in the forehead just under the cap's bill, slamming him onto
his back and knocking the cap from his head. Then the next round hit the
second man behind the head, driving him forward and onto his face. The
third shot hit a man on the van's other side just under his right eye, and
when the fifth man turned toward the car, looking for cover, he instead took
a bullet in the side of the neck, whipping him the rest of the way around, a
full 180 degrees, blood geysering around the lot as he spun. A sixth shot—the
coup de grace—caught him in the back of the head just as he was starting to
collapse.

Simultaneously, the six men leaving the black Ford van dropped the moment they got free of the vehicle, the shots also flash- and noise-suppressed.

All the shots were surprisingly silent. The men simply fell where they
stood, on the spot, just like that—dead before they hit the ground.

All head shots.

Whoever the shooters are, Elena thought, *they're good.*

On the sidewalk and in the big parking lot, only a handful of people were heading toward their cars, and they were now hitting the cement, rolling under vehicles, diving out of sight. One man directly in front of them lost it. Falling to his knees, he shouted, "Please God, I know I'm a sinner, but don't let them kill me."

A nearby woman dropped her grocery bags, clutched her chest, and started shrieking and screeching over and over like an insane owl.

A blind priest's seeing-eye German shepherd panicked and bolted, leaving his master alone, helpless. Wandering the lot, his hands in front of him, the bewildered priest stumbled between the parked cars, yelling, "What's wrong? What's happening?"

Elena opened the door, leaned sideways, and stuck her head out. She spotted one of the shooters. He was on the roof of a semitrailer parked in an alley beside the Walmart. He was giving her a thumbs-up.

" 'We gotta get out of this place,' " Jules said under her breath.

" 'If it's the last thing we ever do,' " Elena said, finishing the old Animals's song lyric.

People throughout the mall and the McDonald's were having the same thought. Almost every car in both lots started up and was rushing toward exits—more than fifty cars and trucks, all at once.

The two women weren't getting out of that lot anytime soon.

And then Elena saw a tall woman approach their car, her dark ponytail hanging out the back of her black Washington Nationals baseball cap. She was wearing a dark bush jacket. It did not require much imagination to infer she had a weapon under her coat.

"Your ride's been compromised," Adara said to the two women. "Grab only what you have to have and follow me. We have a van behind the Walmart."

"Who are you?" Jules asked.

"Your only chance to get out of this alive."

"She's right," Elena said to Jules. "Grab money, medications, guns. Anything you can't buy."

They crammed everything they could carry into two knapsacks and one duffel bag. Throwing them over their shoulders, they followed the woman toward the alley alongside the Walmart.

8

"Hit me, I'll kill you."
—Hasad ibn Ghazi

Eight semitrailers full of shipping containers were off-loaded at the Virginia farm.

Later that afternoon, Hasad then assembled the new arrivals—eighteen long-haired, bearded young men—in the big farmhouse. Colonel Hakeem had smuggled them into the country in those containers. Hasad had bought the young jihadists a large assortment of shorts, T-shirts, hoodies, underwear, and gym shoes—typical American clothes—which they'd put on after they cleaned up. Hasad was dressed the same. He burned all their old clothes in an incinerator behind the house.

Earlier, he'd bought food, plastic eating utensils, and paper plates and cups at a supermarket. For tonight's meal, Hasad had assigned three of the men to boil the hot dogs and fry the hamburgers on the kitchen stove and to lay out the buns, condiments, and the potato and macaroni salads. He wanted them to eat like Americans and to start getting used to the food. They drank Coke with their meals. He had cans of coffee and a stovetop aluminum coffee pot for those who wanted it bad enough to make it.

Tomorrow, he'd have them cut their hair short and shave off their beards.

They ate around a big maple dining-room table or the kitchen table. Several of them sat in the living room and ate with their plates on their laps. Someone had already made coffee, and several of them drank it out of Styrofoam cups.

Looking around, Hasad was not pleased. The general had forced this job on him against his will, and he did not know these men. He hadn't recruited or trained them. Still, he was stuck with them.

He'd been assigned two men as adjutants—Hamzi, whom he'd worked with before, and Jamil. In fact, Jamil was heading the operation out west, and Hasad had almost nothing to do with that mission. Also, after Hasad got the nuclear power plant job in shape and prepped the men, he would be heading down to Washington, D.C., to handle that op by himself.

He was missing one thing. While he was training these men for the jobs, he needed a third man to assist him. For the most part, they were wiry little guys with furtive angry eyes and fidgety gestures. He needed a drill sergeant, a disciplinarian, someone to crack the whip over them and keep them in line. While Hamzi was running the show at the Hudson River Nuclear Power Station, he'd need someone like that.

Only one man stood out. Taller than the others, he was six two, maybe 230, more muscular. He had a closely shaved beard, short hair, and army tattoos. Sitting at the dining-room table, he ate slowly, deliberately keeping his face down, with one arm around his plate.

He'd no doubt learned the "arm around his plate" etiquette in prison.

When he did look up, he met Hasad's gaze steadily, his own eyes revealing no trace of feeling or fear.

Hasad liked him, and he didn't like many people.

He gestured with his head for the man to come to him. Picking up his coffee cup, the man walked over. Hasad took him to a corner of the living room, where they could speak privately.

"Have you had any military training?" Hasad asked.

"I was a sergeant in the Pakistan Army."

"Why did you leave?"

"I hit an officer."

"Why?"

"We were in Kashmir, and the idiot tried to order us into an ambush."

"Did you do time?"

"Six months' hard labor."

"That all?"

"I was proven right, so they went easy. They cashiered me though."

"Did you like the army?"

"Best time of my life."

"Kill anyone?"

"Yes."

"How many?"

"I did a lot of sniping, worked a lot of night ambushes, so I can't be completely sure. Over a hundred, I'd guess."

"What's your name?"

"Fahad."

"You speak English."

"Fluently. I spent five years in the U.S. working for U.S. contractors."

"Good. My first lieutenant, Hamzi, spent time in the U.S. and speaks English, too."

"So he's fluent?"

"Very fluent. He studied chemistry at Columbia for four years. You two will work out fine. You're Sergeant Fahad now—my second-in-command."

"Anything else?"

"Hit me, I'll kill you."

9

"We're in for it now."
—Jules Meredith

Jules, Elena, and their two new friends jogged slowly through the dark alleyway next to the Walmart.

"Nice to meet you two," Rashid said as they headed up the alley, "even if it is during a near-death-encounter."

"Nice to meet you," Jules said, "and thanks for saving our lives."

"All in a day's work," Rashid said.

They stopped at the edge of the building, and Elena looked around the corner.

"Our SUV is parked thirty yards away at the back of the lot. There's also a dumpster by the building about twenty yards from our ride. I need to check it out. There might be more men behind it."

"That sounds a little paranoid," Jules said.

"You wouldn't believe the full-court press these guys have put on you," Adara said.

Rashid glanced around the corner. "I'd suggest you wait five minutes. Elena, Jules, if I come out from behind the dumpster and wave you toward the car, you'll know everything is fine. If I don't, assume there's trouble. If I open fire, you'll know there's trouble. Then you two will take off, running low and fast in S-curves, toward our car. There, you'll get down behind the tires. If you receive incoming fire, Adara will return it from this corner. In the meantime, I'm going to circle around the store and come up on their flank. If I run, I can make it in three or four minutes."

Elena nodded, and he took off. Elena looked at her watch and they waited.

Two minutes later, Rashid opened up with staccato, noise-suppressed bursts from the far corner, and two men behind the dumpster ran to its other side.

Adara stepped out from behind the building and cut them in two with her H&K 9mm MP7.

"Both of you go!" she shouted to Jules and Elena.

They ran, zigzagging hard at a low angle, Elena working the slide on her

12-gauge Ithaca pump as fast as she knew how as the men poured out of the passenger side of the SUV. The pattern was so spread out, the double-0 pellets so numerous—each the size of a .22 round—she hit men with every blast. Crouched down behind one of the van's tires, Jules shot at men's ankles, hitting one of them in the foot. He went down, howling.

Elena circled around, and the screams were silenced by the pop of her 10mm Glock.

Finally, there was silence.

At their van, Elena and Jules took the backseat. Adara got behind the wheel, while Rashid climbed in on the other side. Starting the car, she drove around the far corner of the Safeway.

"Who were those men behind the Safeway?" Jules asked.

"They weren't CIA or FBI," Elena said.

"I heard one of them shout '*Yarhamuk Allah*' when his comrade was shot," Rashid said. "Allah have mercy on you."

"I heard one of them scream, '*Astaghfiru lillah!*'" Adara said. "I seek forgiveness from Allah."

"Yeah," Elena said, "but the guys in the vans back in the front lot were Agency or Bureau."

"Did we just gun down half the CIA, FBI, ISIS, and al Qaeda?" Jules asked.

"We're up against a global alliance," Rashid said. "That's for sure."

"Someone wants us dead really bad," Jules said.

"Yeah, and I'm afraid this van's also made," Adara said, "which is why we have to get to the other one parked down a dark street three blocks over. We need to get in it and get the hell out of here."

"What do we do after that?" Jules asked.

"Rashid and I," Adara said, "were told to protect you. I have an address for a safe house."

"And you've done great," Elena said. "I have another idea though."

"I hope it's not who I think it is," Jules said.

"I have a friend who'll put us all up," Elena said, nodding.

"We're in for it now," Jules said to Rashid and Adara.

PART IX

When the deal goes down,
And you're lookin' to score,
When the shit hits the fan,
When the firestorms roar,
When there's blood all around,
When there's nuclear war,

You'll be rockin' the apocalypse
Rockin' the apocalypse,
You'll be rock-rock-rock-rock-rockin' the
  apocalypse.

—Sister Cassandra, "Rockin' the Apocalypse"

1

Shouts of *"Al mawt li Amreeka!"* or "Death to America!" rocked the farmhouse.

Later that night, Hasad assembled the men in the living room. When he purchased the old sprawling four-story, ten-room farmhouse, he'd also bought the previous occupants' furniture. The old couple had been devout Baptists, and walls were covered with religious paintings and crucifixes. When they'd first gotten there, Hasad ordered the men not to defile, deface, remove, or destroy the Christian décor. He viewed the artwork as protective coloration. He also wanted the men to get used to the world they were about to enter. They were no longer in Pakistan, but in the land of the Great Satan. When one of them rebelled, saying that tolerance of infidel religious symbols and relics violated Allah's law and then ripped the crucifix off the wall, Hasad's newly recruited adjutant, Fahad, had hammered him so hard the man hadn't just hit the floor, he'd bounced. Twice. Hasad was surprised that Sergeant Fahad hadn't broken his jaw.

He was pleased he'd picked Fahad. With Fahad and Hamzi running things at the nuclear power plant, there would be no insubordination.

The men sat on straight-back chairs, worn-out couches, and thread-bare armchairs. Most of them were now drinking Styrofoam cups of black coffee. They did not seem to care that the caffeine might keep them awake.

His experience with ISIS/TTP was that they recruited men as much for their religiosity as their special ops background, so he had no faith in this group's professional skills. Still, he had to work with them. To that end, it was important to give them confidence in their mission, the unshakable belief that they would succeed no matter what the odds.

"We know quite a bit about American nuclear power plants," Hasad began. "We've had agents working in U.S. nuclear plants for over two decades. Some of you might have heard of Sharif Ewan? He was a young man who got jobs in a half dozen U.S. nuclear plants despite being on the FBI's watch list. He proved how easy it was for us to find jobs in U.S. nuclear facilities. He had access to every department of these plants even though he railed at his fellow employees, denouncing them as 'infidels.' Ironically, no one in the plants turned him in. Nobody. Management didn't, and neither did the workers. Sharif Ewan proved how easy it is for us to infiltrate U.S. nuclear power plants. We will now prove how easy it is to breach their security and destroy them."

"Placing a number of our people at these sites," Hamzi said, "we made sure they were disciplined jihadists, that they blended in with those around them. We had them emulate their fellow workers' lifestyle and manners, most of whom didn't even know our agents were of the true faith.

"Since that time, we have succeeded in placing two highly skilled, deep-cover agents in the Hudson River Nuclear Power Station, otherwise known as HRNPS. They have each been there over ten years. In two weeks, I will take a dozen of you into the HRNPS in the dead of night. You will cut through the fence, sneak in the same way Sister Megan Rice did at the Y-12 nuclear site, and help us melt down its reactors and set fire to its spent fuel rods. We will kill millions of infidels and render the surrounding area, including New York City, uninhabitable for ten thousand years!"

Cries of *"Jazak Allahu Khair!"* (May Allah reward you) and *"Bismillah!"* (In the name of Allah) spontaneously erupted across the living room, some of the young men ecstatically rising to their feet.

Hasad motioned them to remain seated.

"That is only the beginning. On that same day, we will hit two other U.S. cities with Hiroshima-style bombs, nuking them off the face of the earth."

The applause, shouting, and foot stomping were deafening, utterly out of control. Fahad had to slap one man and force several of them back into their chairs before Hasad could continue.

"We are going after three targets. Jamil will take three of you out west, where you will do some truly spectacular, top-secret work. Jamil will prep you for it thoroughly. I will take Hamzi, Fahad, and the rest of you up to the HRNPS, which is only ninety-five miles north of Manhattan Island. Two days before you melt it down and raze it to the ground, I will leave for my own assignment. I will be taking out one of the most important cities in America and will be handling that one alone."

Shouts of *"Al mawt li Amreeka!"* or "Death to America!" rocked the farmhouse convulsively.

"Let them get it out of their systems," Hasad said to Fahad. "I want them confident, even arrogant."

"They're taking on a hard job," Fahad acknowledged.

"Three hard jobs," Hasad said, "so let them blow off some steam."

"If they start to break the furniture," Fahad said, "I'll step in."

"Good," Hasad said. "We have two weeks to go, and we'll need every minute of it and every ounce of their energy and strength."

2

"Like I've been rode hard and put up wet."
—Jules Meredith

Elena drove the big SUV through a labyrinth of dark Virginia country roads, high into the steep, wooded Blue Ridge Mountains.

"I can't see the hand in front of my face," Rashid said.

"You got any idea where we're going?" Adara asked.

"We're seeing an old friend of Jules and mine," Elena said.

"Mostly Elena's friend," Jules said.

"At least, he used to be," Elena added.

"You did dump him pretty hard," Jules said.

"This guy's pissed off at you?" Rashid asked.

"To say the least," Jules said.

"But he's supposed to help us?" Adara asked. "Why?"

"I'll give him my killer smile," Elena said.

Elena flashed Adara her "killer smile."

"You look like a mako shark eyeing a mackerel," Adara said. "Jules, you sure this is going to work?"

"It better," Jules said. "We need him. Jamie can hack into any computer system on earth."

"That could be helpful," Adara admitted.

"He also has more money than Vladimir Putin," Elena said.

"And we're going to need a lot of money if we're going to get through this in one piece," Jules said.

"Do I know this guy?" Rashid asked.

"John C. Jameson?" Jules said. "Sure. He invents and builds the encryption and antihacking systems that most governments, intelligence agencies, and defense contractors use worldwide in their computer networks."

"When it comes to Internet and computer security, Jamie's the gold standard," Elena said.

"I read about him," Adara said. "The crazy recluse who lives in a hidden mountain redoubt surrounded by nothing but computers, guns, and fine wines. He never sees anybody."

"Oh, he saw Elena," Jules said with a malicious laugh. "He's never recovered from the experience—Post-Traumatic Elena Syndrome."

"What was the attraction?" Adara asked.

"Pelvic," Jules said.

"You're shitting me," Adara said.

"He had a thing for me," Elena admitted.

"But Elena pissed him off?" Adara asked.

"He was mad enough to murder the earth," Jules said.

"Can you get him to help us?" Adara asked. "For old times' sake?"

"Depends how mad he is," Jules said. "How mad is he, Elena?"

"Pretty mad," Elena acknowledged.

"On a scale of one to ten," Jules asked.

"A twenty-eight," Elena said.

"This isn't going to work, is it?" Rashid said.

"I have faith in Elena," Jules said. "I've seen her in action."

"What's she like?" Adara asked.

"Wicked as sin, proud as Satan," Jules said.

"That's why he'll help us?" Adara asked.

"That—and my killer smile," Elena said.

Elena flashed them the grin again. It did resemble a mako shark's.

"I thought powerful men liked pliant women," Adara said.

Elena shrugged. "So I'll wilt like a lily."

"Yeah, right," Jules said.

"He'll know," Adara pointed out, "we're wanted for capital crimes. It's all over the news."

"And the people who want us are some of his best customers," Rashid added.

Elena looked back at Rashid and Adara and shrugged. "I'll make him an offer he can't refuse."

Elena continued up the winding mountain switchbacks until the road dead-ended. The SUV was facing a heavy twelve-foot cyclone fence topped with coiled razor wire and multiple surveillance cameras and motion detectors. A computerized lock with a digitized punch code controlled the gate. Elena exited the car and punched in the same code she'd used when she and Jamie were together. The gate swung open.

She and her friends entered the compound. They were facing concrete steps—so steep and vertiginous they looked as if they touched the stars. But they only led to the mountain summit, on which was perched a fortress-like mansion.

"There must be a thousand steps," Rashid said.

"Nope, 663," Elena said.

"And we'll be monitored every step of the way," Jules added.

"He's a dead shot with a .300 caliber, bolt-action Winchester mag," Elena said.

"It's a sniper rifle," Jules explained.

"He has one on a tripod facing down these steps in the event of unwelcome intruders," Elena said, "such as nosy reporters."

"He just shoots around them, scaring them back down the mountain," Jules said, "which is why Elena and I will lead the way. He knows us."

"I can't guarantee he won't take a few potshots at me," Elena said as she and Jules started up the mountain.

Three steps up, a rifle shot blew a baseball-sized chunk of concrete out of the steps two feet to Elena's right.

Reluctantly, hesitatingly, Adara and Rashid took up the rear.

"Just his way of saying 'good to see you,'" Elena said.

"I would hate to see him really antisocial," Adara said.

"Oh, you'll see that, too," Jules said.

They continued up the steps with Rashid counting them out one by one until Adara slapped him in the back of the head. After the first hundred, all the breath had run out of him anyway, and he was heaving and wheezing. Then the sky cracked open and rain poured down on them. Still, they continued upward.

As they neared the summit, Elena began counting out the last two dozen concrete steps. They were now facing the mansion's massive stone porch and its heavy oak door with a huge brass knocker in the shape of a rhinoceros head.

"Can you stop a minute?" Adara said, panting. "My pulse is ringing in my ears."

She sat on the porch's floor.

"Mine's hammering in the high hundreds," Rashid said, sitting down next to her.

"Lazy sluts," Elena said.

She bounded up the porch steps and banged the knocker hard.

The door opened a couple of inches.

"As I live and barely breathe," John C. Jameson said and stepped outside onto the porch.

He was big—six two, over 220. Decked out in a short black karate gi, he looked fit. His eyes were brown, his hair the same color but lighter. Pressed against his right thigh, he had a nickel-plated .45 magnum semiautomatic Desert Eagle—the most powerful semiautomatic pistol made.

"Hi Jamie," Elena said, using his old nickname. "The prodigal girlfriend returns."

Jules noticed the magnum was cocked but not locked.

"Let us in," Elena said. "We need to talk."

"I don't see why."

"For old times' sake," Elena said.

"That's a joke, right?" Jameson said.

"Come on, Jamie. It's me, Jules. We're soaked to the bone."

"We got nowhere else to go," Elena said.

"You can go to hell," Jamie said.

"We just came from there," Jules said.

"I know," Jamie said. "You're all over the news."

"Then you know you have to let us in," Jules said.

"Do the words 'aiding and abetting' mean anything to you?" Jamie asked.

" 'Life without hope of parole'?"

"It's not what you think," Elena said.

"Thirteen agents dead in a mall parking lot?" Jamie asked.

"They dealt the play," Elena said.

"Too bad you didn't leave anyone alive to testify to it," Jamie said.

"We can testify to it," Jules said.

"Not to me. I've had some ring time with you two in case you forgot." He stared at Elena a long angry moment.

"You're a hard man, Jamie," Elena said.

"Only in the heart."

"But you're going to help us, right?" Jules asked.

"With every survival instinct in my brain blinking red?"

"Please," Elena said. Her eyes looked like they were tearing but maybe it was just some rain drizzling down her face from her hair.

Jamie shook his head. "You got a lot of chutzpah, coming up here like this, like you care, like we're long-lost buddies."

"I do care," Elena said. "I never stopped caring, and if you don't help, they're going to kill us."

"It'll improve your character," Jamie said.

"Just listen to us," Adara said, pushing her way to the top of the stairs between Jamie and Elena. "You don't like what you hear, we're out of here, like somebody fired a gun. I swear."

Jameson let out a long exasperated sigh. Slowly, reluctantly, he opened the door and let them in.

Their shoes were soaked, so they took them off by the door. Elena led them through the vestibule. Along the walls were glass-enclosed bookcases filled with pre-Columbian statuary. They then entered the living room. The size of a basketball court, it had a twenty-foot ceiling and black shag carpeting so thick the fibers reached their ankles. The furniture was polished blond oak and white, overstuffed leather. Tables were everywhere, most of them overflowing with computer monitors and keyboards. Three ninety-six-inch HD flat-screen TVs were hung on the interior brick walls.

Jamie brought out a stack of thick white bath towels and several terry cloth bathrobes. They discreetly slipped out of their wet clothes and slipped on the bathrobes. They then sat on big stuffed leather armchairs in front of a huge fieldstone fireplace. In its massive, fire-blackened maw, oak logs blazed. The four guests pulled the chairs as close to the hearth as they could get. They needed the heat to dry their clothes and skin.

Elena brought them glasses and bottles of Rémy and Saint-Emilion to warm their insides and a couple of coolers filled with iced Heinekens.

Jameson sat on a stuffed leather armchair. His feet were up on a hassock. They all sipped drinks and listened to Elena explain their situation.

"Now," Elena concluded, "you have heard just about everything."

"In nut-cracking, skull-crushing detail," Jameson said.

"Do you understand our problem?" Elena said.

"You're saying that ISIS—which is famous for decapitating its enemies and stringing their heads from lamp posts and electrical towers—has joined forces with Pakistan's biggest terrorist group, and with the help of the Saudis' American ambassador, Shaiq ibn Ishaq, and the ISI's General Jari ibn Hamza, it is now in possession of nuclear weapons."

"Exactly," Adara said.

"Now they're sending teams armed with nukes to the U.S.," Jameson said. "They're going to incinerate a couple of major cities and at least one nuclear site."

"And that's just round one," Elena said.

"And their reason?" Jamie asked.

"To drag the U.S. into a full-scale, all-out war against *Dar al-Islam,* starting initially in the Mideast," Elena said.

"They say they 'yearn for the End of Days,'" Jules said.

"They aren't very tightly wrapped," Adara explained.

"Correct," Elena said.

"And you say since the president of the United States is in the pocket of Shaiq," Jameson continued, "he will not go against him?"

"He will not acknowledge this coming cataclysm," Jules said.

"He's blinded by Shaiq's money," Elena said.

"And his own avarice," Jules added.

"Instead," Jameson said, "Shaiq, the president, and his pet snake, Conrad, see you as the threat."

"So much so that Shaiq and the president each sent a team of shooters after us," Elena said.

"Whom you unceremoniously dispatched in that D.C. mall parking lot," Jameson said.

Elena and Jules stared at him, quiet.

"What do you think?" Adara finally asked, breaking the silence.

"That you four want to kick the hellgate off its hinges and hope I'll help you," Jameson said.

"Shaiq and General Jari want to do that," Rashid said. "These women just want to stop them."

"Who says you guys are needed?" Jameson asked. "These nuclear installations already have security forces in place."

"You're talking low-wage, part-time rent-a-cops who couldn't deter a team of cheerleaders," Elena said.

"High school cheerleaders," Jules said.

"Hasad's last e-mail said that ISIS and TTP had people working in the plant," Elena said. "They'll have insiders helping them every step of the way."

"You claim they can infiltrate these plants at will?" Jameson said.

"Piece of cake," Jules said.

"So what do you want from me?" Jameson asked.

"You created the best computer security systems in the world—systems designed to resist every possible hack attack known to God and man," Elena said. "Your firm installed those systems for half the nations on the planet—systems that protect their military establishments, their energy grids, their telecommunications networks, their intelligence agencies."

"Which means," Jules said, "you know how to circumvent your own systems and how to penetrate them."

Jameson stared at them, silent.

"Come on," Elena said. "You don't trust these assholes any more than I do. I can't believe you didn't install back doors into those systems just in case you ever wanted in."

Jameson's face remained expressionless, empty of any affect or connotation.

"We need Jari's plans for the attack," Jules said, "and we need to know what Shaiq has on President Caldwell."

"Should I throw in the combination to the Fort Knox vault as well?" Jameson asked.

"You could throw in some operating capital," Elena said.

"For what?" Jameson asked.

"Somebody has to stop these bastards," Elena said.

"And how do you plan on doing that?" Jamie asked.

"You don't want to know," Elena said. "All of it's illegal."

"You guys are full of good news," Jameson said.

"'Good news' is our middle name," Jules said.

"Will you recognize these terrorists when you see them?" Jameson asked.

"Sure," Elena said. "They'll be wearing robes, riding camels and reading the Koran."

"And when you find them?" Jameson asked.

"We'll kill them," Elena said.

"Think of it as bridging the cultural divide," Jules said.

"And no one in Washington can help you?" Jameson asked.

"Looking for that D.C. daisy chain to do anything," Jules said, "is like looking for cherries in an El Paso whorehouse."

"Say all this is true. You really think Caldwell and his cronies would conceal evidence of an impending terrorist attack on the U.S.?" Jamie asked.

"It's happened before," Elena said. "If Caldwell and Conrad are anything like Bush and Cheney, they are probably hoping for it. You know what Bush-Cheney did the summer before 9/11? They had the CIA's top anti-terrorist officials pounding on the table and yelling at them, 'The terrorists are coming here. We're going to be struck hard, and they're going to kill a lot of people.' One of the CIA's major antiterrorism officials told them, 'The roof has fallen in!' Yet the Bush people did nothing."

"And then, when 9/11 hit, Bush and Cheney benefited from it," Jules said. "The attack even got them reelected."

"And got them the Patriot Act," Elena said.

"They almost pulled off a hostile takeover of Iraq's oil industry," Jameson said.

"It'll be worse this time," Jules argued. "General Tommy Franks, who led the Iraq invasion, told me once in an interview that after the first nuclear terrorist strike, our Congress will rip the constitution to shreds and hand the country over to a military despot."

"It's not impossible," Jamie had to agree. "The Roman senate gave Caesar Augustus total power in the name of stability and peace."

"Of course, they got neither," Elena pointed out.

"They got two or three centuries of conquest and empire," Jules said.

"'Perpetual war for perpetual peace,'" Elena said.

"'The savage wars of peace,'" Jules added.

Jameson stared at them a long moment. "I guess the question now is, how are you guys feeling?"

"Like I've been rode hard and put up wet," Jules said.

"My stomach's starting to think my throat's been cut," Elena said.

"We've been up for forty-eight hours," Adara explained.

"And in the same clothes," Rashid said.

"You smell like it," Jameson said. "Why don't you take four of the rear bedrooms—any ones you want—and clean up. They each have a bathroom, towels, and toiletries. The refrigerator's full of beer and deli stuff. You're safe here."

"But not for long," Elena said. "Caldwell and his crew have been on us like white on rice, like cold on ice."

"Like stink on shit," Jules said.

"You're full of good news," Jamie said.

"I'm not going to piss in your pocket and tell you it's raining," Elena said. "Help us, and you could get hurt."

"I could get hurt getting oral sex," Jamie said.

"Just so you aren't getting it in Leavenworth," Jules said.

"Then I better come up with a game changer," Jamie said evenly.

"If you don't," Elena said, "Caldwell and buddies change it for all of us."

"Let me start by getting you that intel you asked about," Jamie said.

"That would be a great start," Elena said.

"Among other things," Jules said, "I hear the head in Leavenworth is really bad."

PART X

Therefore shall [Babylon's] plagues come in one day, death, and mourning, and famine; and she shall be utterly burned with fire. And the kings of the earth shall bewail her, saying, Alas, alas that great city Babylon, that mighty city! And the merchants of the earth shall weep and mourn over her; for no man buyeth their merchandise any more...

—Revelation 18:8–11

1

I'm sick of playing hostage to their fortunes.
—President George Caldwell

The president and William Conrad sat in the Oval Office on overstuffed chairs upholstered in black silk. Between them was an end table of Western Red Cedar, on which sat a liter bottle of Rémy Martin Napoléon 1738 Accord Royal Cognac.

"Thirteen dead shooters in a D.C. mall?" the president asked. "All of them head shots and two women did all that?" the president asked, unable to get his head around it.

"Yes, and we were supposed to ambush *them,* not the other way around."

"What happened?" the president asked.

"Our guys never saw it coming," Conrad said.

"Where did you find these clowns?"

"They weren't clowns," Conrad said. "They were our best."

"Then Elena's even better at this shit than we'd imagined," the president said.

"And now she's split," Director Conrad said.

"And taken that New York reporter, Jules Meredith, with her?" the president asked.

"It seems so," Conrad said, "but we can't find hide nor hair of either of them."

"We have no clues at all?"

"Like they vanished into the void."

"But not before Meredith leaked that piece to The Huffington Post," Caldwell said.

"She quoted an unnamed CIA source as saying that Pakistani agents told us about an ISIS/TTP alliance, which is preparing nuclear strikes against the U.S."

"She connected me financially to Shaiq ibn Ishaq," Caldwell said. "But Meredith doesn't have any proof to back that claim up, does she?"

"No," Conrad said. "But she knows which rocks to look under."

"Any minute, Meredith could be back online, exposing our offshore, tax-free accounts, further connecting us to Shaiq."

"We have to take them off the board," Conrad said.

"We tried before," the president said. "All we got were thirteen dead shooters."

"For us, their disappearance is the difference between freedom and prison."

"I don't know," the president said.

"Suppose they put you in a cell with an eight-hundred-pound, muscle-bound, tattoo-freak psychopath?"

"I'd have to reconsider my position on gay marriage," the president said.

"Then there it is," Conrad said. "We have to find those women—fast."

"When you do," the president asked, "can I call in a napalm strike?"

"I'm ready to nuke the bitches," Conrad said.

"Let's do it," the president said. "I'm sick of playing hostage to their fortunes."

"I'm talking war to the knife, sir," Conrad said.

"Then let's blow up their fucking shit," the president said.

2

Eyes empty as void, unreadable as God.

When Elena came out of the bathroom into the bedroom, she had towels wrapped around her hair and her body. Jameson was waiting for her with a plate full of ham and Swiss on rye and a half dozen Heinekens in a bucket of ice. He opened a bottle for her, then took a swig of his own.

"I still have a lot of your clothes here," Jamie said. "I gave Jules and Adara some of them. I gave Rashid some of mine."

"Thanks." She began eating a sandwich.

"What's your take on Caldwell?" Jameson asked.

"This country's about to go up in flames," she said, drinking a beer, "and all he's probably thinking about is how to make another dirty buck off the Saudis."

"I had some business dealings with him before he took office," Jamie said. "We used to say 'he'd take the dimes off a dead man's eyes and put back nickels.'"

"The Caldwell I know'd suck blood from a bat," Elena said.

After a long moment, Jameson said, "Maybe he's the guy you ought to waste."

"He can't die. He reanimates himself every night in his coffin."

"What about the terrorists?" Jamie asked. "Do you have a plan for stopping them?"

"Sure. Hunt them down and kill them."

"Some plan."

"Right now it's the only plan," Elena said.

"Caldwell doesn't even care about terrorist attacks on U.S. soil?" Jamie asked.

"Caldwell can't afford to care," Elena said. "If he looks into these terrorist groups too deeply, he'll find Shaiq's checkbook."

"What about the nuclear industry?" Jamie asked. "They won't help?"

"They're corporations, and like someone once said, corporations have neither bodies to be punished nor souls to be condemned. Therefore, they do what they like."

"The nuclear power industry doesn't even care about attacks on their own power plants?" Jamie asked.

"It costs them too much money to protect those sites, so why should they care?" Elena asked. "Anyway, if a nuclear site goes up in flames, the company that owns it doesn't pay for it. They just declare bankruptcy, and the principals go onto their next money-making scheme. The taxpayers get stuck with the bill."

"That's cold," Jamie said.

"It'll get even colder for you if Caldwell's bloodhounds catch us," Elena said, moving in close, staring at him intently. "So you can't be seen helping us. You need deniability."

"No way you're doing this without me."

"Cross that line, there's no going back."

"I'm never going back. I'm not letting you get away again."

"We're offering you plausible deniability. You can say we held a gun to your head. Even if you help us, you can still walk away."

"Never happen."

"You don't know me. If you did, you wouldn't even like me. I don't like me much myself."

"But I do like you. I love you. I've never stopped loving you."

"You don't know what I do. You don't live in my world. You're just a tourist."

"I'm a tourist who's not going away."

"But these guys we're going up against, they're no ordinary psychopaths. They hate life and would just as soon be dead. They see themselves as half-dead already."

"So let's finish the job for them."

With the towel still wrapped around her head, Elena roughly dried her hair. Dropping the towel on the bed, she shook her hair loose. All the time she kept her eyes focused on Jameson's. Placing her hands around the back of his neck, she pressed her hips tightly against his and kissed him.

"All this talk about death and destruction is getting you hot," she said, releasing him from the kiss.

Still staring hard into Jamie's eyes, she finished drying her body with the covering towel and dropped it on the bed.

"It's been a long time," he said.

"Too long."

Again, Elena put her hands around his head and pulled his lips onto hers, her tongue probing his mouth, circling his teeth and lips, darting in and out, around and around. One hand dexterously untied his black belt and reached beneath his karate gi. He groaned, and his body sagged.

"'The wind in the air, the sea on the rock,'" she said softly.

"'And the way of a man with a maid,'" he whispered hoarsely, finishing the quote.

Pulling off his gi, Elena pushed him onto the bed, kissing him again long and hard.

"I'm sorry for what I did," Elena said, her words hoarse. "I'll never leave you again."

Lazily, languorously she worked her way down his chest and stomach with her lips and tongue, assiduously exploring his navel, then continuing down his abdomen.

"Anything you want," she said, pausing to look up. "I don't care what. I will do *anything* for you . . . *to you.*"

All the while, her wide, expressionless, unblinking eyes remained locked on his—eyes empty as the void, unreadable as God, fathomless as the abyss.

3

"What's life worth without a little violence and terror?"
—Adara Nasira

Jules sat in Jameson's living room with Adara and Rashid. They were staring wordlessly into the fireplace's blazing maw.

"Elena and Jamie have known each other a long time?" Adara finally asked, breaking the silence.

"Ten years, at least," Jules said. "She was with the CIA's bin Laden Unit on the Afghan-Pakistan border, and Jamie, who was a Marine Corps captain, was assigned to assist her. She also ran some of the Agency's assassination ops in that region and was responsible for eliminating some very important al Qaeda leaders. In return, Osama ordered her eliminated, so she and Jamie saw some very hairy shit. They did capture her in the end. She was held hostage in the Pakistani desert country for five weeks. Imprisoned in a scorchingly hot spider hole, overrun with rats, scorpions, and tarantulas, abused day and night in every conceivable way, she still never gave them a single name or location. Jamie led the raid that got her out. The doctors said another week in that hole would have killed her."

"Jamie did all that?" Adara asked.

"And took four bullets in the shoulders and legs doing it," Jules said.

"How did he go from black ops to earning cybersecurity billions?" Rashid asked.

"By the end of his second tour," Jules said, "he'd burned out on the war—felt the whole thing was a hopeless waste. He resigned his commission and came home. But he didn't return empty-handed. He and Elena had worked closely with some cyberanalysts in Afghanistan, and he'd learned a lot about hacking encryption systems. He had an intuitive understanding of how to design unbreachable security systems—and then how to hack them. Once he was home, Elena hooked him up with some private contractors, and after he learned the business end of the security industry, it was just a skip and a jump to setting up his own firm and developing his own new, improved security programs. His systems were so revolutionary they changed cybersecurity forever. They're the best, most bulletproof, most sophisticated made. He peddles them to everyone, particularly foreign intelligence services."

"And after Elena returned to D.C., they began seeing one another again?" Adara asked.

"For four or five years," Jules said. "In many respects, they were a good match, but then one day Elena stumbled across an ISIS/al Qaeda/TTP consortium, bankrolled with Saudi money and run by Pakistan's ISI. She believed nukes were involved, and she completely dedicated herself to it, 24/7. She also suspected that the opposition had a mole in the Agency and that she was being monitored and followed. She feared something horrible was about to happen. She couldn't tell Jamie about her work—it was completely classified—and she was paranoid as hell about it. She especially feared he'd get hurt if they continued to see each other. She'd been abducted in Pakistan and knew what it was like. So she stopped seeing him. Unfortunately, she couldn't tell him why. She couldn't even give him a plausible lie. He knew her too well—better than almost anyone. It was as if he was her secret sharer, her alter ego, her second self."

"And he was smart," Rashid said.

"Infuriatingly smart," Jules said. "He'd have recognized the deception in a nanosec."

"How many people know they were seeing each other?" Adara asked.

"Only me," Jules said. "They're both almost pathologically closemouthed, and since they were in the same business, they did not publicize personal relationships. When they broke up, they did so in secret and in silence."

"'The course of true love never did run smooth,'" Adara said.

"You just wrote my epitaph," Jules said. "In their case, however, the breakup was hardly poetic. They'd fallen in love, but suddenly Elena was trapped in a world so lethal, love could not exist. She was up against people willing to burn, rape, torture, and kill."

"And nuke the earth," Adara said.

"Correct," Jules said.

"But now she and Jamie are back," Rashid said.

"So it seems," Jules said.

"And we just happened to need him," Adara said.

"That, too," Jules conceded.

"You seem to know her pretty well," Rashid said. It was a statement, not a question.

"I've known her a long time."

"How long?" Adara asked.

"Pretty much forever," Jules said.

*F*orever *might have been an exaggeration, but Jules had known Elena since the seventh grade—long before Elena became a CIA superstar. In fact, she'd been the child of crime—the one-quarter-Mexican daughter of a Southwest Texas meth manufacturer.*

Meth's essential ingredient is ephedrine, which her father purchased in bulk from illegal Mexican dealers and trucked north over eighteen hundred miles of porous desert border country. Three times a year, Elena's father would drive Elena down to Mexico to get the "eph." They took a camping trailer with them, which they used to haul a ton or more of the ephedrine back over the border. Her father would then spend the next four months in the southwest desert country, camped out next to abandoned shacks, in which he cooked meth for his brutal consortium of Hells Angels distributors.

Elena was a skinny kid with her father's dark hair and dark eyes. She also possessed an affinity for violence that sometimes shocked her teachers, even her father. Not that she was angry or mean. For the most part, she was amazingly even-tempered, never resorting to force unless seriously provoked. But when assaulted, she responded with overwhelming ferocity.

Born with a vertiginously high IQ, she was surprisingly disciplined and was one of the school's most gifted students. The teachers liked her and encouraged her. They also liked that she had a burning sense of injustice and did not tolerate bullies. She was especially quick to defend the more vulnerable pupils—special ed students, obese children, slow learners, those who were unusually short or simply odd-looking or -acting. To some extent, she was the only law and order on that ethnically mixed, routinely violent school yard.

Jules's father was an army sergeant stationed at Fort Bliss in El Paso, and her mother was a nurse. They moved to El Paso just as Jules was entering the seventh grade, and middle school had proven a difficult transition for her. She had gone to a relatively small grade school in Idaho, and was now sent to a junior high nearest the base that had nearly two thousand students entering seventh grade. Most of them were Mexican and many of them were gang affiliated, and life for the vulnerable, the timid, the unprotected was hellish.

The first day, Jules came home with a black eye and a bloody nose. She told her parents she'd slipped on the curb. The second day she came home with two black eyes and skinned knees. The next day during Jules's third lunch period, six fat, tattooed, gangbanger girls in dirty jeans and even dirtier T-shirts assaulted her behind the school. Knocking Jules on her back, two of them held her down while the biggest of the three pounded her head on a concrete curb, demanding her lunch money.

Elena, who was standing nearby, had finally had enough. The dark-haired, dark-eyed girl yanked the two of them to their feet by their long black hair and banged their craniums together so hard the whack! *cracked like a rifle shot, and the two girls collapsed, unconscious. Elena knocked the third attacker to her knees, then finished her off with a forehead kick.*

The rest of Jules's tormenters fled.

Elena reached down and helped Jules up.

"Let me know if those girls give you any more shit."

Jules and her parents viewed Elena as a hero, a savior, but the school's attitude was less adulatory. According to school rules, all participants were equally responsible. Because Elena had given one of the girls a concussion, their parents contacted the authorities and pressed to have Elena prosecuted. The lawsuit, which the girls' parents brought against the school for its failure to protect the three gangbangers from Elena, made the principal anxious to punish and expel the girl.

Moreover, Elena's father had been killed in a run-down, abandoned desert shack the month before, where he'd been cooking methamphetamine. The explosion had blown the shack a half-mile in every direction, and the DEA had only been able to identify him by his teeth.

That Elena now no longer had a home to go to made the school even more determined to send her to a correctional facility.

Jules's parents did not have much money, but they did have a profound sense of right and wrong. They were not about to let Elena go to a reform school for protecting their daughter from a cadre of psychopaths who, among other things, had been banging her head on the sidewalk. They bailed Elena out of jail, hired the best El Paso lawyer they could find, and fought the case tooth and nail. By the time Elena was acquitted, she was already living with them.

The next year, when Jules's younger sister, Sandy, entered the school, she was also untouchable. All she had to do was tell the other kids she was a close friend of Elena Moreno, and any would-be attackers faded away, parting before her like the Red Sea.

Soon Elena, Jules, and Sandy were inseparable.

get the sense," Adara said, "you and Elena are pretty good friends."

"We have a lot of history," Jules said.

"The Agency must have frowned on that—a top non-official cover spook being best friends with a *New York Journal-World* investigative reporter," Adara said.

"We were careful not to advertise it. Jules isn't my birth name, and since we weren't related by blood, and we don't share a last name, we were able to keep our friendship private. No one had any reason to connect us."

"But you said you knew her since when?" Rashid asked.

"Junior high in El Paso, Texas."

"What was El Paso like?" Adara asked.

"Boring."

"What did you do for fun?" Rashid asked.

"After school, Elena, my sister, Sandy, and I would take off into the desert on my motorcycle and hunt jackrabbits and diamondbacks with her dad's 12-gauge Winchester pump."

"Bag any big game?" Rashid asked.

"One time Elena killed a wild pig."

"No shit?" Rashid asked.

"No shit," Jules said.

No shit, indeed. Jules and Sandy had been in a dried-up desert arroyo when they'd stumbled on a litter of piglets. Unfortunately, their mother—a two-hundred-pound feral sow who was maybe ninety feet up the ravine—was highly protective of her offspring and charged.

The beast's whistling screams scared the girls almost as much as her crazed eyes and curved tusks. Knowing that they couldn't outrun the animal and armed only with a .22 Colt Woodsman pistol, Jules stood her ground. Taking aim, she began firing.

Elena, who had warned them to stay out of the barranca, was on its rim with her late father's ancient 12-gauge Winchester pump. When she saw the attack, she dropped twenty feet onto the canyon floor. Fracturing her left ankle, she still managed to stand on her right leg. Pushing her two friends behind her, she raised the shotgun. Taking aim at the charging sow—now less than sixty feet away—Elena pumped round after round of 12-gauge double-ought buck into the shrieking beast. In the canyon's close confines, the shots were shockingly, painfully loud, but they had no discernible effect on the big pig. The shot pattern was so spread out the blasts didn't even slow her down. Only with the sixth and final shell did the pattern tighten up enough for the round to break the pig's right shoulder. Dropping, skidding across the dirt, she stopped less than four feet from Elena's torn sneakers. Screeching loud enough to wake the damned, the trembling beast rose on three legs, stared at the girls with blood in her eyes, and began stumbling toward them.

This time, Jules pushed Elena aside and placed the .22 Woodsman directly in front of the sow's face and put a round in her right eye.

At the same time, Sandy was also on top of the dying pig. Her Buck Omni Hunter 12pt knife in both fists, she drove the blade repeatedly into the animal's skull.

Elena stared at her two friends.

"You didn't run," Elena said.

"Neither did you," Sandy said.

"I'm impressed," Elena said.

Refined in gunfire, bonded in the wild pig's blood, the three girls from that moment on were friends for life.

Elena and Jameson returned to the living room. Jameson was back in his black gi and leather sandals. Elena's dark hair was in a ponytail. She wore a maroon T-shirt, Adidas running shoes, and black Levis, which she'd appropriated from Jameson's closet.

"You aren't going to believe it," Elena said, "but guess who just joined the cause?"

"The same guy who an hour ago was going to throw us off the mountain?" Jules asked.

"The same," Elena said.

"What changed your mind?" Rashid said.

Jameson came up behind her, smiling. "Hey, I couldn't let you losers have all the fun."

"Yeah, after all," Adara said, "what's life worth without a little violence and terror?"

"You got me," Jules said.

Jamie allowed them a self-deprecating shrug.

"Then there is the subject of money," Elena said. "If we're to counter a series of Saudi-funded nuclear attacks, we're going to need some instant cash."

"One of the perks of Jamie's megawealth is instant cash," Jules said.

"How much instant cash can you come up with," Elena said, "without attracting undue attention?"

"How much do you need to finance this operation?" Jamie asked.

"A mill?" Elena said.

"I have more than that here in the house," Jameson said. "What else?"

"Weapons, ammunition, wheels?" Rashid asked.

"Done."

"Liquor, drugs, underage sex slaves?" Rashid asked.

"Why not?" Jamie said.

"Are you sure you're spoken for?" Adara asked.

4

"Can we shoot the women on sight?"
—Shaiq ibn Ishaq

The president, Shaiq, and Conrad sat in the president's private study. They were wearing white shirts, loose ties, and slacks. Dimly lit with brass table lamps, the study was all dark wood and leather. The walls were lined with books, whose shelves were interspersed with Rembrandt and Rubens prints. The president had personally ordered it swept for bugs and had even patted Conrad and Shaiq down as soon as they'd shut the door. Conrad and the president had allowed Shaiq to do the same to them.

Conrad recycled the events of the last seventy-two hours for the two men.

"Those two women killed thirteen of your best men?" the president asked, after Conrad had finished.

"Two other people appear to have helped them, but then escaped undetected," Conrad said.

"I'd have paid anything to have seen her eliminated," Shaiq said. "She's been digging up dirt on me for over a decade."

"Me, too," the president said, "and we have no idea where and how she gets her information."

"She's found shit on me," Conrad said, "I didn't even know about."

"They both think you're financing nuclear strikes against the U.S.," the president said to Shaiq.

"Can you imagine anything loonier than that?" Shaiq said, laughing.

"When Elena presented her crazy ideas at a meeting," the president said, "I immediately revoked her security clearance and had Conrad relieve her of her ID."

"If she went public," Conrad said, "we promised to put her in the penitentiary."

"Jules took that story to *The Journal-World*," Shaiq said. "Her main source was obviously Elena. I killed that, but then Jules shotgunned it to every major news outlet, and The Huffington Post ran with it. The other outlets followed suit, and now the whole planet thinks I have ISIS on speed dial."

"Don't you?" the president said. He was only half-joking.

Shaiq shot him an irate look. "Not funny. My people have more to fear from them than you do."

"Point taken," the president said. "Those women, however, have hurt us badly—each of us in this room."

"You must have some sort of backup plan," Shaiq said, "some way to stop them."

"We have a full-court press out there," Conrad said. "All-points bulletins, surveillance of their best-known hangouts, cell phone and computer searches, known credit cards, biometric facial matches from surveillance cameras. If they enter a 7-Eleven, we can spot them."

"The problem is they've dropped off the map," the president said. "They found some place where they don't need gas, food, money, anything."

"Neither of them have vacation cabins," Conrad said. "I doubt they have friends who are willing to harbor treasonous fugitives."

"And risk life in prison for harboring treasonous fugitives," the president said.

"Very few people have friends like that," Conrad said.

"With that much surveillance, we will eventually catch them," the president said. "It's only a matter of time. The problem then is, what we do with them?"

"Can we shoot the women on sight?" Shaiq said.

"We tried that," Conrad said.

"After Jules's articles linked you and me, Shaiq," the president agreed, "we can't simply gun them down."

"I can," Shaiq said.

Both men stared at him in silence.

"In my country, we are less squeamish about exterminating such vermin," Shaiq said. "I think this matter is best left to me."

"I hope your people are better than the ones we sent," Caldwell said.

"Send me a file on their most likely whereabouts, all and any known associates. Photos might help. I already have another crew in place."

The president turned to Conrad. "Give him anything he needs."

"Got it," Conrad said.

Shaiq rose wearily from his overstuffed leather chair. Conrad and the president walked him to the door.

5

"You're hotter than a two-dollar pistol."
—Rashid al-Rahman

Adara and Rashid lay atop a king-sized bed in one of Jamie's back rooms. The lights were out, and all Rashid could see was the red, burning tip of her Turkish cigarette.

"You really want to go through with this?" Rashid asked her softly.

"What else can we do?" Adara asked.

"It sounds crazy."

"We were crazy to get into this whole damn business," Adara said.

"We were even crazier to get involved with Hasad," Rashid said.

"So what's kept us with him?" Adara asked.

"He pays better than anyone else," Rashid said.

Adara nodded her agreement. "And I always dreamed of that one big score, the one that would set me up for life."

"And let you walk away clean," Rashid said.

"With Hasad, we each had a better chance at that than with anyone else," Adara said.

"And this could be it," Rashid said. "Hasad's offered to set us up for life."

"If we see this through to the bitter end," Adara said.

"'Bitter' is the operative word," Rashid said.

"He also said if we back out, we'd die a thousand times."

"You believe him?" Rashid asked.

"I believe the part about dying a thousand times," Adara said.

"But do you think he'd pay off—big money?" Rashid said. "Like he promised?"

Her silence spoke volumes. "Something tells me he's in deeper shit than we are," Adara finally said.

"And if he goes down," Rashid asked, "where does that leave us?"

"In hell."

"You want to run for it?" Rashid asked.

"I don't know," Adara said. "I'm starting to think this thing with Elena, Jules, and Jamie has a chance."

"You may be right," Rashid said. "Jamie sure as hell has the money, and you've seen the way he looks at Elena. He'd do anything for her."

"I never had a man look at me that way."

"Hasad seems to feel the same way about her," Rashid said.

"What's she got that I don't have?" Adara asked. "Sex? I got sex."

"You're hotter than a two-dollar pistol," Rashid said, "but you don't have billionaires risking their lives and their fortunes for you."

"Maybe she's got moves I don't know about," Adara said, nodding. "You know, in bed."

Rashid turned and stared at her in blank astonishment. "You kidding? If pussy were bullets, you could kill France."

"Maybe, but whatever it is with Jamie," Adara said, "money's no object—not when it comes to Elena."

"You think he's our pot of gold at the rainbow's end?" Rashid asked.

"I trust him to pay off more than Hasad," Adara said.

"You think if we can help Elena beat this thing," Rashid said, "Jamie will pay off?"

"Like we'd robbed Fort Knox," Adara said.

"One thing's for sure," Rashid said, nodding, "Hasad's ordered us to look after those two until they're safe. If we cut out now and if Hasad survives and if he finds us . . ."

"I wouldn't want to be us," Adara said.

"I'm starting to think this is the score we've been looking for," Rashid said.

"And I'm not crossing Hasad," Adara said.

"That's a lock," Rashid said.

Adara put out her cigarette in the bedside ashtray.

Rashid stared at her in the dark a long hard minute. "Can the dying man get a last fuck?" he asked.

"You back my hand when this goes down," Adara said, "you get me out of this alive and help me find that big fucking pot of gold, you can have anything you want."

"But will you love me in the morning? Rashid asked.

"Morning, night, daylight as well."

"Then fuck me dead," Rashid said.

"That, too," Adara said, pulling off her jeans and climbing on top of him.

Rashid slowly began unbuttoning her blouse.

PART XI

For the great day of His wrath is come; and who shall be able to stand?

—Revelation 6:17

1

They were on their way.

Hasad watched the eight dark commercial vans parked behind the big barn. They were filled with men dressed in jeans, T-shirts, and running shoes. Guns, ammunitions, MREs, first aid kits, money belts, water bottles—everything they needed to get them through the next few days—were packed and sealed in plastic boxes and bins.

Hasad had dragged the men through three long weeks of planning and training exercises. A lot of it was done in the huge empty barn with sentries stationed on all sides, often at night. They were in one of the least populated counties east of the Mississippi, so they were far away from prying eyes. They were also seasoned soldiers, some of the most brutal killers in the Mideast.

Their drill included endless map work and chalkboard exercises, in which Hasad hammered them relentlessly on their itinerary, tactics, and strategy. He instructed them on how they would enter the nuclear power plant, how they would work with the trusted insiders—two men who had each worked at the HRNPS for over a decade—perfect sleeper agents. They were recognized in their communities, never went near a mosque, and when they went to services at all, they went to a Catholic church.

One of them was passing for Italian.

Each session began and finished with physical training—push-ups, pull-ups, crunches, and jumping jacks, with Fahad barking out the time.

Hasad went to the head of the line and climbed into the lead vehicle.

He was already sick of the op and eager to get it over with.

At last, they were on their way.

2

"Think of it as boudoir patriotism."
—Elena Moreno

Elena Moreno woke early. Finding the bed empty, she got up, went to a chest of drawers. Grabbing a pair of gym trunks and a T-shirt, she put them on, followed by her sneakers. She went to the kitchen and found Jules in sweat clothes in the kitchen, making Arabian mocha in a demi-litre French press.

"Jamie with you?" Jules asked, pouring her a cup.

"I don't know where he is," Elena said.

Elena and Jules left Rashid and Adara asleep in the living room and went looking for Jamie. They found him in his office—a large sprawling work area with a half dozen desks, a big conference table with a dozen swivel armchairs, and two leather couches. Flat spaces were everywhere, and they held every kind of computer imaginable—laptops, desk models, notebooks. Smartphones of every make and description were also scattered around the room. On one desk was an open box of burners.

Still dressed in a black karate gi, Jamie was sitting at his desk behind an HP Z840 desktop computer, staring into a twenty-one-inch flat-screen monitor. A white porcelain coffee carafe and a matching mug were at his elbow. The mug was half-full of old, cold black coffee. His hollow eyes were streaked with red, his face drawn and haggard. He'd been up all night.

Elena stood behind him and placed a cup of fresh-brewed French roast next to his computer. She began rubbing his temples, neck, and shoulder muscles.

"You poor baby," she said softly in his ear, "you've been up all night. Are you getting anywhere?"

"It's not that tough. It's a Beijing rip-off of a security program I designed four or five years ago. I've just got in."

"They didn't add any safeguards?" Elena asked. "No additional encryption?"

"The Chinese pirate so much stuff that in this case they were in too big of a hurry. They unthinkingly lifted the entire system, even the encryption program and its back door. They never learned or understood what was in it."

"Okay," Jules said, "but now you're in. Are you having any trouble cracking the encryption?"

"Of course not," Jamie said. "I designed and built the system myself and wrote its code directly."

"What kind of security do Shaiq and Jari have?" Jules asked. "Air gap?"

"The distances separating these two are so great they preclude the use of an air gap," Jamie said.

"Also, air gap switches are overrated," Elena said to Jules. "For their computers to connect to each other within a building, they have to have Bluetooth systems. But we have a software that can switch off Bluetooth, then access the computer's contents through the dormant Bluetooth."

"Shaiq and Jari," Jamie said, "have something much more impenetrable— a single dedicated line and server system between them that goes directly and exclusively through their router."

"Couldn't they communicate through couriers and stay off the Internet?" Jules asked. "Give each other flash drives?"

"Sure," Jamie said. "Then I wouldn't be able to get in period."

"Staying off the Internet kept bin Laden free all those years," Elena said. "He communicated solely through letters and flash drives."

"Fortunately for us, Shaiq and Jari need instant access to each other," Jamie said. "They don't have time to swap flash drives."

"True, but Islamabad and Riyadh are just a few hours apart by air courier," Jules said.

"Correct," Jamie said, "but then you have to trust your couriers, which they apparently didn't."

"Bin Laden was eventually betrayed by his messenger," Elena said.

"But did you install a back door when you fabricated the program?" Jules asked Jamie.

"Of course," Jamie said. "Since I wrote the computer code myself, I even made the back door an organic part of it. The entrance is so intrinsic to the program it's not visible to anyone scanning for it."

"No chance the ISI could have located it?" Elena asked.

"I buried it so deep God Himself couldn't have found it," Jamie said.

"But you can," Jules said.

"Yes, and my back door allows me to access their hard drives. That's more difficult, but at some point we may have to go in there."

"Now I'm curious," Jules said. "How does a back door work? Do you just shout 'open sesame' and walk in?"

"Almost. I gave myself secret access to all the root passwords, the user-names, and the three IP addresses."

"Three IPs?" Jules asked. "I understand that Prince Shaiq and General Jari each have an IP address, but who's the third IP address for?"

"Since it's a line and a dedicated server, the machine governing the data transfers has an IP," Jamie said.

"Can you also probe the illegal offshore tax-free bank accounts he set up for President Caldwell?" Jules asked.

"That's a cakewalk," Jamie said. "One of my Chinese surrogate companies set up those computer systems, and Shaiq's and Jari's banks don't allow dedicated lines for those financial transactions. Shaiq and the president have to go through the Internet. Even without back doors, I'll slip through his and the bank's roadblocks and firewalls at will."

"How long will it take you to get in?" Jules asked.

"Bingo! What Jung called 'synchronicity.' We're in."

"What do we do now?" Elena asked.

"Every parcel of data is called a packet. We capture each of them, decode their raw information, then analyze it, all of which our 'packet-sniffer' is about to do—message after message after message."

Suddenly, Jamie fell silent. Staring quizzically at the table, he shut his eyes and began rubbing his temples.

Elena went to him and gave him a neck rub. "What's wrong?" she asked.

"It's all laid out, and we can get into his hard drive. There's one problem though. If Shaiq is on the computer while we're doing it, he may very well be able to detect our presence. At that point, he'd know his computer is being breached, and he'd shut down all communications. We have to hope he's not on it."

"Would it help if we could distract him?" Elena asked.

Jamie and Jules stared at her.

"You know how to get Shaiq away from his computer?" Jules asked.

"Uh-huh."

"Oh my God," Jamie said. "You haven't . . . ?"

Elena treated them to a faint ghost of a smile. "Let me borrow one of your encrypted sat-phones," she said to Jamie.

"That one on that table will reroute and sat-bounce your call all over hell's creation—here to the Rapture," Jamie said. "The NSA won't even be able to intercept it." He pointed to a portable phone on the work table next to him.

Walking over, Elena picked it up and punched in a brief, cryptic text. She came back a half-minute later. "Done. He's being distracted," Elena said. "In five minutes, you'll be able to enter and copy his hard drive files with a vengeance."

"We have to be absolutely sure he's not at his computer screen," Jamie agreed.

"Wouldn't matter," Elena said. "He won't be able to see straight for the next two hours."

"Why?" Jules asked.

"Why do you think?" Elena asked back.

"You say you have one of his mistresses working for you?" Jamie asked in blank disbelief.

"His most accomplished courtesan," Elena said. "Who do you think got her the job in the first place?"

"You evil bitch," Jules said, stunned. "You pimped a high-priced call girl on Prince Shaiq?"

"With whom he's fallen madly, devastatingly into . . . *lust*," Elena said.

"There are laws against that, you know," Jules said.

"Think of it as boudoir patriotism," Elena said.

"But you procured a whore," Jamie said, stunned.

"Think of her as our whore," Elena said. "Anyway, she comes by it honestly."

"She's an honest whore?" Jamie asked.

"Prince Shaiq doesn't know it, but he signed off on the stoning death of her favorite niece. His mistress raised the young girl like a daughter, and she'll do anything to avenge her."

"You still pimped her," Jamie said.

"True, but Shaiq claims she's hotter than all of hell's furnaces with their doors flung open," Elena said.

"You probably taught her yourself," Jamie said to Elena, shaking his head in dismay.

"That would be a trade secret," Elena said, smiling.

Exhaling slowly and deeply, he began accessing the contents of Prince Shaiq's hard drive.

3

"I have a lot to atone for."
—Sam Mazini

Saif al-Mazini—known to his fellow workers as Sam Mazini—pulled up into the parking lot of the Hudson River Nuclear Power Station in his white Toyota Prius. A tall, lanky man with short dark hair and a mustache, he was wearing a tan suit, a pale-yellow shirt, and brown Florsheim wing tips. Fellow worker and security guard James J. Robinson pulled into the space next to his in his dirty black Jeep Grand Cherokee. Robinson was wearing gray sneakers, faded Levis, and a gray athletic T-shirt. His hair and beard were unkempt and disheveled. When he turned off the ignition, black smoke belched out of his exhaust pipe.

"You know among the diesel SUVs, your model Jeep Grand Cherokee CRD is one of the worst CO_2 polluters on the road?" Sam said as Robinson climbed out of his Cherokee.

"What does a guinea bastard like you know about good patriotic American cars?" Robinson said, giving him the finger. "I want your opinion, I'll ask you how to make clam sauce, fry garlic, or boil linguine."

Though he was born in Yemen, everyone assumed Mazini was an Italian name.

"Yeah?" Sam said. "Well, it's better than boiling the planet with greenhouse gases."

"Tell it to those girls you bang at the strip club," Robinson said. "They got pollutants, too—STDs NIH never even heard of."

"I kill those diseases with garlic."

"By breathing your stinking garlic breath on them?"

"I was told what was natural couldn't hurt me," Sam said, grinning.

"Were all those shots of 151 you were throwing back last night 'natural'? What were they? Some kind of new nature beverage?"

A heavy drinker, compulsive gambler, chain-smoker, recreational drug enthusiast, and notorious womanizer, Sam liked to nonetheless act as if he were also a Greenpeace fanatic. The slightest hint of climate change denial could throw him into paroxysms of fake liberal rage, as if greenhouse gases were the End Time incarnate.

"I was hoping it would disinfect all the impurities I pick up around here."

That Sam espoused Greenpeace and a natural diet while working in a nuclear power plant was an irony not lost on anyone.

"A bunch of the guys are going to the casino after work, thinking of getting a poker game together," Robinson said. "You in, or is gambling too unnatural for you?"

"I learned the game at church socials. Father O'Doole taught me personally when I was an altar boy."

"Let's hope that's all he taught you."

"Are you suggesting I was his catamite?"

"In a word, yes."

"I'll admit I was his altar boy," Sam said.

"Then you probably corrupted him," Robinson said.

"Oh, you think my flesh is weak?"

"For a man who constantly espouses natural living, you're the most unnatural sonofabitch I know."

"Which is why I attend Mass faithfully. I have much to atone for."

"I heard the last holy father, who took your last confession, ran out of the booth, screaming into the night."

"He said I was 'sired by Satan.'"

"Then you're on for tonight?"

"Have you ever known me to say no?"

"Never!" Robinson roared.

He slapped Sam on the back, and the two men headed toward the plant.

4

"Do you want me to *un*neglect him?"
—Malika al-Mansour

Malika al-Mansour, Shaiq's *femme de la nuit,* sat on his long black office couch in his palatial penthouse office. Her sensuous sloe eyes focused unwaveringly on her client. Flinging her long black hair over her right shoulder, she crossed her legs. She was wearing a short, low-cut black negligee with matching fish-net stockings, garters, and spike heels. Her dress hiked up to her thigh, and her legs were crossed, the top leg bouncing up and down impatiently.

She watched him working at his desk computer. He was still dressed in a black business suit. He'd been away in D.C. for two months, and she had frequently visited him there. Now, however, his work here in Riyadh had backed up, and his desk was piled high with papers. His eyes were red with fatigue.

Getting up from the couch, she walked over to him, seated herself on the edge of his massive mahogany desk, and crossed her legs again. Her already short negligee was now hiked up over her hips. Staring out the windows at the bright full moon, she absently studied the cloudless star-filled midnight sky. Viewed from eighty-seven stories up, the Arabian Sea was filled with what looked to be a thousand yachts, tankers, tugboats, barges, and dhows. Still, Shaiq's eyes were buried in his computer monitor, ignoring both her and the spectacular, panoramic view.

"I need you, Shaiq," Malika said. "It's been over a week."

"I really can't. It's after midnight, and I have work to finish. You can see that. I have a big day tomorrow. I'm exhausted."

"Just one kiss," she said, "and I'll leave you alone. I'll just sit on the couch and worship you from afar."

Shaking his head, he sighed deeply. "Just one."

She pulled his chair away from his desk and eased herself onto his lap. Her tongue went deep in his mouth, probing and palpating his teeth and lips, even as she rubbed his chest, stomach, abdomen, luridly, lasciviously working her way down, all the way down.

"Why, I don't think you're tired at all," Malika said. "At least, part of you isn't tired—a very big part. In fact, he feels abandoned and neglected. Do you want me to *un*neglect him?"

Shaiq let out a long, slow, gasping groan and gave her a weak nod, his pupils dilating.

"I think I should take you to the couch."

Shaiq was now incapable of objecting.

She dragged him like a dog to the long suede sofa.

PART XII

Those that I fight I do not hate,
Those that I guard I do not love. . . .

—William Butler Yeats, "An Irish Airman
Foresees His Death"

1

"In short, we should act like mindless, moronic Americans."
—Hamzi Udeen

Ever since they'd left the safe house and Hasad's crew, Jamil and Adman had scanned the highway for surveillance vehicles and searched the sky for choppers.

"A van full of Arab men might well attract attention," Jamil explained to Adman back at the safe house.

"Or we could get pulled over for a routine traffic stop," Adman said, "have car trouble—any number of things could draw attention to us."

"Our cover story is we are innocent tourists," Jamil said. "That's why we're all wearing country-western T-shirts. We are fans of American music, and we're in the U.S. to enjoy the blues, bluegrass, rock and roll, and country music."

"Our papers are bulletproof," Adman said.

"We should be able to pull it off," Jamil said.

All of them were dressed like rednecks and rockers—Wrangler jeans and a variety of rock and roll/country music T-shirts blazoned with the logos and likenesses of Hank "A Country Boy Can Survive" Williams, Jr., Bruce "I Answer to Only One Boss" Springsteen, and Toby "I Love This Bar" Keith. The two men in the front seat—Jamil and Fahad—favored western-cut shirts and cowboy hats. At every stop, Jamil kept a weather eye out for country-music-and-culture regalia with which to adorn the van and his men—miniature plastic guitar keychains; fake Elvis driver's licenses; bumper stickers with "I-Aint-Giving-Up-My-Beer-Can-Till-You-Pry-My-Cold-Dead-Fingers-Off-It!" on them; Confederate flags; and posters of a young, buxom, scantily clad Tanya Tucker, her booty and boobs boasting beaucoup décolletage.

Per Jamil's orders, all of them had close-cut hair and were clean shaven. Jamil had even outlawed mustaches. He had brought two Norelco electric razors and insisted the men shave twice daily. He did not want them looking like bearded terrorists.

Taking I-95 to Petersburg, Virginia, Jamil ignored the turnoff for the National Museum of the Civil War Soldier—featuring its famous Battle of the Crater exhibit—and hooked a left onto I-85. Following it all the way to Durham, North Carolina, he turned onto I-40, which he would take straight through to California.

Initially, Jamil had wanted to put as much mileage on the van at a time as possible, stopping only for take-out food, coffee, and restrooms. During these stops, he let the men out one at a time so as not to attract too much attention.

On the way to Nashville, however, he decided to reinforce the men's cover story. Spotting a fifty-foot-high neon sign of a cowboy in a Stetson with a bucket of spare ribs under one arm and chawing on a rack of baby backs with both hands, Jamil quickly pulled in and parked. Above the restaurant itself was a neon sign emblazoned with the words, DONNY'S DOWN-HOME BARBEQUE!!!

Explaining to the men in the van that they were to pose as infidel tourists, Jamil said they should eat pork, drink beer, laugh, sing, smoke, and swear.

"In short, we should act like mindless, moronic Americans."

When Dawad, however, pointed out to him that "Islamic law strictly forbids both drinking and the eating of pork," Jamil stared at him with cold eyes.

"We only eat it to convince the infidels that we are like them!" he said.

"It's still pork," Dawada countered.

"It's also *Darura*," Jamil said.

"The Islamic law of necessity," Adman explained. "If the act is necessary for righteous survival, then one is allowed to commit it—as long as it does no harm—even if it violates Islamic law."

The men grudgingly agreed.

The hostess sat them at a big circular table, and Jamil ordered for everyone: baby back pork ribs, pulled pork, beef brisket, and fried chicken, all of it drenched in Donny's Down-Home Bar-B-Que Dressing. Quickly warming to their role—that of redneck Americans—they ravenously devoured colossal plates of coleslaw, macaroni salad, potato salad, and baked beans from the all-you-can-eat buffet. Much to everyone's surprise, the men found they loved the greasy food. Jamil watched in astonishment as they demolished mountains of pork and beef, pausing only to pound down multiple schooners of Pabst Blue Ribbon draft.

A five-piece country music band came on. Except for Adman, Jamil's men spoke little English, but they were able to repeat a few lyrics from some of the songs. One they especially seemed to like. It was called "Achy, Breaky

Heart," and they enthusiastically bellowed out the chorus along with the crowd:

> Don't tell my heart
> My achy breaky heart
> I just don't think he'd understand.

Ordering more pork ribs, they then chanted at the top of their lungs:

> "Darura! Darura! Darura!"

After chanting, they threw back shots of Jack Daniel's backed by more pitchers of Pabst draft and roared out more country music choruses:

> She's actin' single,
> I'm drinkin' doubles.

More shots, more pitchers, and they were hollering in badly mangled English:

> Jose Cuervo
> You are a friend of mine
> I like to drink you with
> A little salt and lime.

Near the evening's end, Hamzi muttered in Jamil's ear:
"This country truly is the Great Satan."
Jamil could only shake his head.

2

"They told me I was a bipolar castrato-psychopath!!!"
—Elias Edito

Whenever Elias felt anxious, cleaning his guns and listening to Sister Cassandra's melodic voice soothed his soul. Tonight he needed both. As he oiled and swabbed out his .50 caliber Barrett M82 rifle down in his gun room, he listened to the Good Sister's haunting rendition of "End of Days." It seemed to Elias a harbinger of things to come and a tragic summation of his own life and times.

> *I have seen the end,*
> *(The end-time, my son).*
> *And I have heard the cryin'*
> *Faced the dyin' all around.*
> *And I have felt the fire*
> *For all time to come.*
>
> *In the darkness*
> *In the thunder*
> *In the blaze*
>
> *I have felt the rumble*
> *Felt it tumblin' down.*
> *And I have heard the thunder*
> *Seen the wonder to come.*
> *And I have smelled the blood tide*
> *In the flood tide I was drowned.*
>
> *In the fury*
> *In the flood*
> *In the fray*

End of days
End of days
End of days

Just as Cassandra wrapped up the first chorus, Elias finished wiping off the Barrett. He was pleased with the big gun. He planned to get a lot of use out of it. Built to take out planes, choppers, armored personnel carriers—even tanks—it was also accurate enough to kill people over two thousand yards, though he had other weapons that could do that. Using a Barrett on a human being was like swatting a fly with a drop forge.

Tonight, however, Elias couldn't focus. He had a lot to do, a lot to think about, and his mind was wandering. Pulled away from his work by Sister Cassandra's melancholy ballad, he could not concentrate on the weaponry, and he finally let himself go with the sad song.

Oh, I have seen the madness,
(The madness, my son).
And I have known the darkness,
(The darkness to come).
I was broken on a rack,
On a rack of the sun.

I have seen the end.
(Please, say it ain't the end.)
I have witnessed the end.
(Don't let it be the end.)
I have prayed for the end.
(Lord, it can't be the end.)

In the wrath
In the rage
In the flames

In the violence
In the hate
In the pain

End of days
End of days
End of days

End of days
End of days
End of days

End of days
End of days
End of days

Through an act of will, Elias begrudgingly dragged himself back to the job at hand. He began digging a sizable assortment of weapons, ammunition, and equipment out of the big safe—his 9mm Glock and the MP7 machine gun, which he could conceal under a coat. He had a 7.62 NATO assault rifle in the power plant's watch tower, so he didn't need to bring one of those. He also assembled a dozen magazines for preloading, as well as sniper scopes, noise suppressors, and a Ka-Bar combat knife.

All of these weapons would be smuggled into his guntower the night of the attack.

He then dug out a heavy steel grenade box with a padlock on it.

Why the hell not?

But then his mind began wandering again, and he was recalling, once more, how it all began. . . .

His AA meetings had not been going well. When he tried to explain to the other members about his Iraq nightmares and the hundreds of firefights he'd survived, to say nothing of the more than two hundred men, women, and children he'd killed, a number of the people raised their hands to protest. Some of the complaints were insulting.

A slender white-haired woman in dark slacks and a white sweater was especially irate. She looked about eighty but attacked him with the energy of an eighteen-year-old.

"Listen, Elias," she began, "why don't you think about the families of those men and women you killed. Think about the lives you cut short—men and women who'll never see their kids grow up, who may never have kids because of you. If you thought more about other people and less about yourself, you wouldn't have to drink. And you wouldn't have gone off to that idiotic war in the first place."

Man, she had a mouth on her. Elias wondered what she was like when she was young and had all of her strength and energy. He wouldn't have minded getting her in his gun sights.

Most of the comments were along those lines. Nobody wanted to hear about his war troubles. They were so hostile about the conflict that he didn't dare tell them the real truth was he didn't feel guilty or sorry. He felt rage and hate over the way he'd been treated. That U.S. political leaders could lie to their own people, bullshit them into a war fought for oil—then cut and run when the tsunami of oil money didn't materialize—filled him with a lust for revenge that he could not contain.

Finally, there was that last night at AA when the meeting leader—a nice man in a blue blazer, Levis, and a white T-shirt—took him aside after the group broke up. He told Elias that the members had asked him to tell Elias they wanted him out of the group. His angry obsession with Iraq wasn't help-ing them with their own drinking problems. In fact, he made them want to hit a bar and get smashed.

The man gave him a list of phone numbers he could call if he wanted to en-roll in another session somewhere else. He also advised him to "put a lid on the Iraq shit."

Instead, for the first time in a year, Elias went to a bar near his house, where he ran into Sam Mazini from work. They had a couple of drinks, and he told Sam about getting kicked out of AA because they disapproved of his participa-tion in the Iraq War. They didn't want to hear about all the Iraqis he'd shot to hell and gone. They didn't want to listen to his complaints and his anger over it.

A couple of vets on stools next to him overheard and started sending down shots. They were wearing VFW hats and dirty factory clothes. They'd just gotten off the 3:00–11:00 shift at the Honda plant. One of them—a friendly older man with a pale gray beard and a 101st Airborne Screaming Eagles tat on his forearm—said:

"I hate creeps like that who piss on those of us who fought, when they have no idea what it's like. When I came back from Desert Storm, I got treated the same way. Man, you should never feel bad—not even for one second—about your service. I don't care what you did. Drinks are on us tonight. You're with friends now."

Unfortunately, Elias did not feel friendly. As the night progressed, he got unfriendlier and unfriendler. As he later explained to Mazini, "You know the worst part is that when I got home, my mother confided to me that my real father had been an Iraqi. She had conceived me during a secret adulterous fling. My legal father—her husband—never guessed, and she tried to keep it a secret. He had just died though, so she didn't have to hide it from him anymore.

"She told me she was opposed to me going to Iraq because I might end up killing some of my own flesh and blood. Sam, I killed so many hajjis over there that I probably did. Whatever the case, that's how I feel."

"It just takes time," Sam said. "You'll get past that."

"Not really. Truth is I don't see any point to even living. I got me some serious ordnance at home in my safe. My favorite is the Barrett M82 .50 caliber. It's an antitransport weapon. I'm thinking about going home, putting that barrel in my mouth, and springing the trigger. Maybe with my big toe, like Hemingway did. Or strapping on a half dozen grenades and yanking the pin. Then it's 'adios, motherfuckers!' No shit. I don't see any reason not to."

"I can give you a reason," Sam said without missing a beat. "The guys you ought to kill are the ones who sent you overseas to waste strangers you had no grievance with and who wished you no harm. Elias, you have to turn your hostility away from the innocent—including yourself—and turn it toward those who have hurt you and those around you."

Mazini's words shook Elias to his soul.

"But how?" he asked.

"If you're really interested, I can help you on that front. It'll take balls though—more than you can imagine—but then I suppose those are something you have plenty of."

The truth was, Elias didn't. When his tour ended and he was taking the long ride back to the Baghdad airport, his personnel carrier hit an improvised explosive device (IED). The blast had robbed him of cojones, after which the marines cashiered him and he took a job working security at the Hudson River Nuclear Power Station for $18.50 an hour and no benefits.

He planned to apprise Mazini of that fact in a few nights.

But not now.

That night they got bombed instead. Elias was never a good drunk, and on that occasion he was a maniac. A couple more shots and he turned to the vets, who were setting them up, and said, "You want to know something? I loved the Iraqi people a hell of a lot more than I love these imbeciles here. Allah never sent me ten thousand miles to kill strangers who meant me no harm. Mohammed never ordered me to shoot women and children. I want to take up arms against the sons of bitches who sent me over there. I want to kill a bunch of those assholes in Washington. In fact, I've had enough of killing brown-skinned people for Christ, Mom's apple pie and the American flag." Pausing, Elias took a deep breath and roared: "I want to start . . . acing assholes for Allah and killing cocksuckers for the Prophet! . . . All those idiots who sent me over there to murder all those innocent Iraqis? I want to empty a whole trainload of whip-ass on those imbeciles." Then he thundered, "So when I come back and I see a shrink about my PTSD, instead of helping me, he takes away my Valium and replaces it with lithium, telling me I'm not only castrated, I'm bipolar. Bi-fucking-polar? Lithium? Lithium? Lithium's for sissy bitches and sissy creeps. They canned my ass, threw me out of the service for *bi-fucking-polar disorder and no-fucking-balls, then took my sniper rifle away, and why—?*

"Why—?

"*Because I was a bipolar castrato? No, they then told me it was because I was also a bipolar castrato-psychopath!!!*"

"*Psychopath?*"

"*Yeah, Sam, that's right. They said, 'Only a psychopath could kill as many A-rabs as you blew away and laugh about it afterward.'*"

Standing up, Elias bent over backward and shook his pelvis at the two vets, like a drunken, demented stripper. "Bite on this, assholes!" he roared at the top of his lungs.

All hell suddenly busted loose—a real broken-bottle barroom brawl with stools, teeth, and glasses flying. Unfortunately for the regulars, Elias was a lifelong martial arts student. Nor was Mazini any slouch. The two of them took some lumps, but Elias broke one man's nose, shattered three teeth, and blackened at least two eyes, and Mazini landed an assortment of crotch kicks and karate chops.

Elias's outburst would have been the end of his job at the plant. The company was very strict about personnel losing it in bars. But Mazini covered everyone's expenses and bills and settled all the complaints out of court, so there were no charges. The payoffs and legal fees cost him a small fortune, but he never asked Elias for a dime. He only wanted one favor in return.

"*I checked your record online. Elias, you have a big-time drinking problem, and you've had a lot of drunk and disorderly charges in your past. When you drink hard liquor, you not only pick fights and scream obscenities at strangers, you're a menace to everything around you. You're filled with hate and rage over Iraq, and that I understand. Believe it or not, you can do something about that, and I can help you. But not if you hammer down all that hard liquor. You have to promise me, no more hard booze.*"

Elias had made that promise, and three years later, he had still been good to his word.

He'd gotten so absorbed in his reminiscences and in fieldstripping, cleaning, and reassembling his weapons, he'd lost track of time.

Hell, the sun's even coming up.

God, Elias felt good. The day of reckoning was indeed at hand. It seemed like he'd waited his whole life for it to come.

He was settling up for the Iraq War once and for all—for what it had done to him, to his family, and not least of all to his virility.

Payback's a bitch, and I'm finally getting mine.

The bill had, at last, come due, and the deal was going down.

3

"You should never pity the truly stupid."
—General Jari ibn Hamza

The Saudi ambassador to the U.S., Shaiq ibn Ishaq, sat at his desk. His private security team had just swept the room for bugs and left. Shaiq finally reached General Jari. They were on encrypted phones, talking on a scrambled, dedicated line; therefore, they could speak freely.

"So we're fine with the CIA director—President Caldwell, too," General Jari said. "But we still have those two women on our trail."

"Do they have evidence of what we're doing?" Shaiq asked.

"The CIA agent, Elena," General Jari said, "she used to run the Pakistan desk. She probably knows more about your dealings with us than you know yourself."

"And who knows which way she's going to jump?" Shaiq asked.

"If she somehow learned what we're doing and got it to Caldwell, can you imagine his reaction?" the general asked.

"Intemperate," Shaiq said.

"To say the least," General Jari said. "And Conrad?"

"His paranoia is already on terminal alert."

"He'd go into anaphylactic shock," the general said.

"Then keep an adrenaline syringe handy," Shaiq said. "As long as those two women are alive, they could destroy everything we've worked for."

"And if Conrad and President Caldwell find out about our coming attacks?" General Jari asked.

"We'll lie to them, of course," Shaiq suggested.

"They'll eat it up," the general said. "They love lies."

"Their lives are built on lies," Shaiq said.

"And they positively eat betrayal," the general said. "Illusions are all America has," he continued. "It's the only thing holding their ignorant world together."

"Still, we can't let them find out what we're doing," Shaiq said.

"True, though my reading on President Caldwell is that if push came to shove, he'd let us set those nukes off."

"If it were a choice between having us expose his illegal offshore tax havens and having us incinerate a few U.S. cities," Shaiq agreed, "he'd let their cities fry."

The general laughed long and hard over the phone. "Ah, my friend, you restoreth my soul. Caldwell and Conrad really are that dumb, aren't they?"

"What choice do they have? We've got them between the hammer and the anvil."

"With the clock running out," General Jari said.

"If they didn't so richly deserve it, I'd almost feel sorry for them."

"You should never pity the truly stupid."

"The suicidally stupid," Shaiq said.

"Too stupid to live," General Jari said.

"Not even when they go down—go down hard?" Shaiq asked.

"Think of it as evolution in action," the general said. "By destroying them, we strengthen the species."

"Then we kill them all?" Shaiq asked.

"We rid the earth of their shadows," Jari said.

"Yes, but it's a shame about the Agency bitch," Shaiq said.

"Why?" the general asked. "She's been trying to destroy us for years."

"I know, but—"

"But what?" General Jari asked.

"She has the most outrageously arrogant derriere I've ever seen on a woman," Shaiq said, shaking his head sadly.

Again, the general howled hilariously. "Thanks so much. It was a joy talking to you."

"Always," Shaiq said.

"We've waited a long time for this moment."

"Over fourteen hundred years," Shaiq said.

"Just so," the general agreed.

"Then *Maa Shaa Allah*." As Allah has willed.

"*Ya Allah*." Oh Allah.

4

That night Sam returned from the casino $1,133 richer but sick at heart. He'd played the role of a corrupt infidel for so long—drinking, doping, whoring, gambling, cracking filthy jokes, and attending Mass like a pious Roman Catholic—it had become a way of life. True, it was a ruse, sanctioned by fatwa and designed to deflect suspicion away from his jihadist mission, but still he should have felt some remorse over his decade of irredeemable, irremediable sin.

But he didn't. Nor did he feel the sacred rage of this holy cause smoldering in his soul. Yes, he would kill many infidels when he melted down the Hudson River Nuclear Power Station, but he would not do it with hatred in his heart. In truth, he did not revile those around him. He'd lived too long among them for that. Nor did he love those for whom he would commit these acts.

His feelings brought to mind a poem he'd once read by a poet named Yeats titled "An Irish Airman Foresees His Death." Part of it went:

> *I know that I shall meet my fate,*
> *Somewhere among the clouds above;*
> *Those that I fight I do not hate,*
> *Those that I guard I do not love . . .*
> *Nor law, nor duty bade me fight,*
> *Nor public men, nor cheering crowds,*
> *A lonely impulse of delight*
> *Drove to this tumult in the clouds;*
> *I balanced all, brought all to mind,*
> *The years to come seemed waste of breath,*
> *A waste of breath the years behind*
> *In balance with this life, this death.*

Was that true of him? If so, what had driven him down this road toward the most horrendous martyrdom in history? It had not been fanaticism or even religiosity. He had never burned with jihadist fever. At the madrassa, he had not been the most committed, most devout student. He was recruited and taken to Purdue University, the engineering college in the States, because the tests indicated he had an unusually retentive memory, a talent for languages, and an aptitude for mathematics. Also, during the martial arts training, his instructors noted that he exhibited exceptional ruthlessness.

Nowhere had he tested high for piety.

In plain truth, he was like the poem's Irish airman: those he fought he did not hate, and those he guarded he did not love.

So why was he doing it?

Sam, aka Saif, did not know.

In times of stress, he liked to lock himself in his bedroom, turn off the lights, and pray, hoping against hope for some epiphany from Allah that would convince him he was on the right path. Now more than ever, he needed a sign. In nothing but a white robe, he turned off the bedroom lights, dropped to his knees, and began fingering his *subha* prayer beads.

Prayer beads had been used in Catholic, Hindu, Persian, Buddhist, and Islamic religions for over a thousand years, and before that the faithful had used their fingertips and knuckles. A mnemonic device, the *subha* beads assisted the righteous in the counting of their invocations, in the alleviation of stress, or, as the name *subha* implied, "in the glorification of Allah."

The beads themselves were most often made of glass or plastic, the connecting cord of nylon or cotton string. Sam's beads were shiny obsidian spheres, and the cord was finely strung silk. The necklace was composed of ninety-nine beads, divided by thin white ivory disks. A larger leader-bead signified the first recitation, and a tassel represented the finish.

Sam's traditional prayer was the *dhikr,* the rote recitation of Allah's ninety-nine names. Tonight, however, he chose to offer up the *subha* itself, the prayerful exultation of God. Beginning with thirty-three incantations of "*Subhannallah*" (Praise be to Allah), he followed those with thirty-three reiterations of "*Alhamdillah*" (Glory be to Allah), finishing with thirty-three recitations of "*Allahu Akbar*" (Allah is great).

Sam chose the *dhikr* because it was ordered by Mohammed himself in the holy hadith, in which he urged his daughter, Fatima, to remember Allah by invoking these prayers. If she did so, Mohammed told her she would have "all her sins forgiven, even if they were as vast as the froth on the sea's face."

When Sam finished his ninety-ninth prayer, he removed his white robe and took the small leather box out from under his bed. In it was an assortment of whips. He took out the black leather cat-o'-nine-tails, the one with

214 | ROBERT GLEASON

hooked steel tips. He then began the flagellation ceremony, slowly, brutally flogging his back till blood flowed and tears ran down his cheeks.

He had so much to atone for: drunkenness, drugging, philandering, gambling, blaspheming Allah's name. Of course, he knew why he did it—to protect the secrecy of his mission—so his base behavior was pardonable.

But the pleasure he took in his debaucheries and his indifference to his sins could never be forgiven.

He looked forward to dying for Allah.

He accelerated his flogging, accelerating it, accelerating it—

Until—

Until—

In a moment of unbearable anguish and agony, it came to him—the revelation he'd been looking for but never received. First he heard it: a basso profundo voice, booming out of the heavens like a thunderclap:

"*DIE!!!*"

Then he saw it—brighter than ten thousand suns, more ear-shattering than a supernova detonating in its death throes, more horrific than hell itself, hotter than all the fires of the inferno rolled up into one. Its blast wave slammed into his tortured soul like a stellar tsunami, like a comet stopped—so hard the End Time had to be at hand. He could sense Allah was calling him, promising that the American infidels' Day of Reckoning was finally at hand.

Swept away by the epiphany's juggernaut power, by a force he could neither fathom nor resist, by an arousal so overwhelmingly libidinous, he—

He—

He—

He—

He climaxed violently, his whole being plummeting-spiraling into a bottomless abyss of illimitable oblivion. When he came to and his vision returned, he was staring at a billion-trillion blindingly bright, giant red stars, all in the midst of their supernova death throes, a hell-hot universe of everlasting pain and infinite annihilation.

Then Sam's consciousness faded again, flickered once, twice, three times, and was gone.

PART XIII

Feel the flash.
Now the blast.
Now the bomb.
Hiroshima's gone . . .

—Sister Cassandra, "Hiroshima Girl"

1

Their scars, their bars,
Their hell, their jail?
Who wants their bloody arms,
Their crucifixion nails?
　　　—Sister Cassandra, "Hiroshima Girl"

Elias could not believe the Day of Reckoning was so close. One of the only things that calmed his nerves was listening to Sister Cassandra and her band, the End Time. They were the patron poets of a new musical genre currently sweeping the world, apocalyptic rock. He picked up the remote and hit his DVD player. He always kept his DVD of "Sister Cassandra Live" in it. She had performed a three-hour show in Madison Square Garden featuring her greatest hits, and her music company had recorded it live. Elias must have watched it a thousand times.

"Some of you want to know what the end is going to be like," Cassandra said to her faithful followers as she stepped out onto the stage.

Their ovation was an apocalypse all by itself.

"You have heard my revelations. But don't take my visions as gospel. It's all happened before: the pica-flash, the fireball's rise, the blast wave, the firestorms, the black rain, the rivers of blood and fire.

"Scroll back—1945. Hiroshima. Can you dig it, amigos?"

Her band, the End Time, gave Cassandra her opening organ chords, and in a rasping Janis Joplin contralto, she began to sing.

See the bird in the sky
In the sky so blue.
Do you ever wonder why,
As she slowly glides by,
She's in love with you.
She's in love with you.

While Cassandra sang, on the six overhead movie screens—visible throughout the amphitheater—was projected the mating rituals of two bald eagles in upward flight, twisting and turning around one another, over and over and over again. In endless pursuit, in rising vertical rolls, they performed their seductive dance of courtship and foreplay, mating and procreation.

> *See the picture in my hand.*
> *Portrait of my man*
> *See him there on the right.*
> *He's holding me tight.*
> *That long ago night.*
> *See him holding me tight.*
> *That Hiroshima night.*

The eagles dissolved into a framed, close-up photograph of a young, innocent-looking Japanese woman in a white silk kimono with lowered eyes and shy demeanor. Her lover stood next to her and wore an army uniform.

Flames licked, scorched, and smoked the edges of the montage, sizzling, smoking, igniting the film's edges until the two lovers burst into a fireball, shrouded in white mushrooming smoke.

> *Feel the flash*
> *Now the blast*
> *Now the bomb*
> *Hiroshima's gone.*

The orchestra went full instrumental—woodwinds, strings, brass, percussion—then softened to a delicate diminuendo. Cassandra's spotlight dimmed.

On the overhead screens, a Japanese girl stood nude, disfigured by yellowish keloid burn scars.

A *hibakushu*—a Hiroshima maiden.

The frame of the tortured teen froze on the screen, and a woman's voice described her ordeal.

While the camera moved in slowly, the young girl spoke:

Almost every building was destroyed and in flames. There were people whose skin was peeling, leaving their bodies red and raw. They were screaming pitifully, and others already were dead. The street was so covered with the dead and the seriously injured that we couldn't get through. To the west, I saw the flames coming nearer. I found myself on the riverbank. People suffering from burns were jumping into the river screaming, "The heat! The heat!" They were too weak to swim and with a last cry for help, they drowned. Soon the river was no longer a river of clear, flowing water but a choked stream of floating corpses.

Cassandra was once more in the spotlight, the musing rising in volume and amplitude.

> *Had me a man.*
> *I knew he was mine.*
> *He swore to love me*
> *Till the end of time.*
> *He got time—eternity.*
> *And my scars*
> *For a dowry.*

The young, horribly ravaged Japanese woman was still visible, but now naked, full figure. She spoke:

The people were walking toward me as if in a daze, their skin blackened. They held their arms bent forward and their skin—not only on their hands, but on their faces and bodies, too—hung down. Wherever I went, I met these people along the road, like walking ghosts. They didn't look like people of this world. They had a special way of walking—very slowly. I myself was one of them.

Cassandra painfully wailed the chorus:

> *Feel the flash.*
> *Now the blast.*
> *Now the bomb.*
>
> *Hiroshima's gone.*
> *Hiroshima's gone.*
> *Hiroshima's gone.*

A nuclear fireball blazed, then dissolved into another shot of a young, hideously cicatriced Hiroshima maiden.

Who wants this woman.
Her face a mass of scars?
Who wants this little boy,
Who has no arms?
Who wants this blind girl?
She has no . . . eyes!

Screaming the word "eyes" at the top of her lungs, Cassandra softened and modulated her voice as she slowed and segued into the bridge:

Who wants their broken limbs,
So torn, worn, frail?
Who wants their empty eyes,
So vacant, bleak, and pale?
Who wants their desperate dreams,
Dreams destined now to fail?
Their scars, their bars,
Their hell, their jail?
Who wants their bloody arms,
Their crucifixion nails?

The spotlights faded, and Cassandra vanished into darkness. This time, the screens filled with several pair of rising, soaring eagles, each duo twisting and turning around each other, again and again and again, in their eternal ascent, then drifting languorously apart.

See the bird in the sky,
In the sky so blue.
Do you ever wonder why,
As she slowly glides by,
She's in love with you.
She's in love with you.

More massive fireballs, engulfed mushrooming smoke, exploded on screen, seeming to cover everything—the entire planet, life itself.

See the picture in my hand.
Portrait of my man.
See him there on the right.
He's holding me tight.

That long-ago night.
See him holding me tight.
That Hiroshima night.

Then Cassandra wailed:

Feel the flash.
Now the blast.
Now the bomb.

Hiroshima's gone.
Hiroshima's gone.
Hiroshima's gone.

Hiroshima's gone.
Hiroshima's gone.
Hiroshima's gone.

Hiroshima's gone.
Hiroshima's gone.
Hiroshima's gone.

The spotlights and music dimmed. Cassandra faded into darkness, her body racking with convulsive sobs, and after a while, all was still.

Except for Elias, who was also racked by uncontrollable sobs.

What had happened to him over there in Iraq? What had he lost?

His soul?

His sanity?

And his balls?

Everything?

But now, he said to himself, *it's going to be all right. You're gonna get back something of your own.*

He still had a few hours before work. He decided to clean his guns again.

2

The sin that ye do by two and two, ye must pay for one by one.
—Rudyard Kipling, "Tomlinson"

Hasad caught I-95 near Petersburg, Virginia. He drove the van in a pounding rain up through Richmond, stopping only at off-ramp gas station, restrooms, and fast-food restaurants. In Arlington, he had his adjutants, Hamzi and Fahad, stash the men in an out-of-the-way hotel, while he made a quick trip into D.C. to once more appraise the Capitol Building.

He planned on handling that part of the operation last.

By himself.

Changing into a polo shirt, blue denim jacket, jeans, sneakers, and sunglasses, Hasad caught the Washington Metro in Crystal City, Virginia. Taking the train to the Capitol South stop, he got out and walked to First Street NE and East Capitol Street, the closest he could get to the building without a pass. He then found a nearby restaurant with a window view of the Capitol dome. Seated at an outdoor table, he ordered a cheeseburger and coffee while he reviewed his plan of attack.

Pakistan intelligence services—ISI—had first asked him to devise and present them with a plan for attacking three U.S. cities with terrorist nukes. The general's orders were to develop a plan that would inflict maximum damage on the Americans, and Hasad had worked on it and prepared for it for almost four years. It consisted of three nuclear strikes, two of which would be incomprehensibly devastating and would cripple the U.S. economy for decades to come. The third strike would obliterate all three branches of the U.S. government.

Only one attack could accomplish that feat. Every year in January, the president, the U.S. House of Representatives, the Senate, the Supreme Court, the Joint Chiefs, and the president's cabinet officers met in the congressional chamber of the Capitol Building for the president's State of the Union address.

In fact, this year the president would give a second State of the Union address: on July Fourth.

So there it was.

If a man were able to get a nuclear device close enough to that meeting, he could vaporize the U.S. government.

It was harder than it appeared, however. Hasad had traveled to D.C. and studied the security at the last two addresses. His five-kiloton HEU-fueled nuke had a blast radius of a third of a mile, but the security perimeter around the Capitol dome stretched well beyond that radius and was formidable. He did not see how he could get a vehicle carrying the bomb within six hundred yards of the congressional chamber, and he had to get at least that close. The Capitol Building was a veritable fortress.

Originally, it had been constructed out of sandstone, but over the subsequent decades the sandstone had eroded, and the government had replaced much of the crumbling rock with white marble. This upgraded marble-and-rock exterior was formidable enough to withstand a nuclear explosion detonated outside the bomb's blast perimeter.

Was there any way to circumvent or slip through those defenses?

Hasad had studied ancient Greek history and literature in college, and he had been obsessed with the subject all his life. The Odyssey, *in particular, haunted him—so much so that he'd come to identify with its crafty, ever-resourceful antihero, Odysseus, the man responsible for razing Troy and massacring every man, woman, and child within its walls. Hasad had once even visited the ruins of Troy in southern Turkey, sat on the remains of its amphitheater and reread his favorite passages from the* Odyssey.

A high, heavily walled city, Troy had successfully resisted a bloody ten-year siege—until Odysseus conceived of the Trojan horse. A victory offering to the city, this hollow towering wooden equine hid twenty-nine silent soldiers in its belly.

After drunkenly celebrating their victory over the Greeks, the exhausted Trojans slept like the dead. The Greeks—who, during the day, had pretended to sail home—surreptitiously returned that night. The warriors in the horses' belly then crept out through a secret, ingeniously concealed trapdoor and opened the city gates. The marauding army outside the walls poured into the city and murdered the Trojans in their inebriated slumber, burning Troy to the ground.

Hasad smiled. He, too, had a Trojan horse in place—a vehicle that could not be searched and that would be driven directly to the front entrance of the Capitol Building. He even had a man working for the car's owner as a chauffeur-bodyguard. He had gotten the man the job almost three years ago when he had begun preparing for the operation. Hasad had worked with him many times all over the Mideast. The man had told Hasad repeatedly he was sick of the fighting and wanted to die a glorious martyr so he could ascend to Allah's paradise and spend all eternity consuming seventy-two virgins. The man would be willing—indeed, eager—to immolate himself in the fireball's blaze.

The man's desire to die for the jihad was a well-established fact. On two different ops, Hasad had had to stop him physically from strapping on a suicide vest and blowing up himself, infidels, and half his own platoon.

His man was in charge of the limo's maintenance—as well as acting as its chauffeur—and he'd arranged to have the trunk's bottom and the rear axis heavily reinforced. Soon he would plant the nuclear device in the limo's trunk. The moment they reached the entrance to the building, Hasad's man would trigger the bomb electronically. Such a circuit would be impossible to jam. Moreover, the bomb had a backup detonating system. If necessary, a second man a mile or so away could set it off with a two-way radio detonator.

Even better, the vehicle carrying the concealed nuke was Shaiq ibn Ishaq's gold-plated limo. Since it was property of the Saudi ambassador, neither the FBI nor the Secret Service had a legal right to search it.

Therefore, Shaiq would be one of the bomb's first victims.

And General Jari? If Elena and Jules did not expose him for the treasonous bastard he was, Hasad would hunt him down himself.

And make him curse the day his mother had given him birth.

Even so, Hasad was not pleased with his new role. Like it or not, he was now the backup man, wielding the two-way radio detonator. He didn't like being part of the mission, but he did like his overall plan. He felt the op was one of his more . . . creative. Among other things, he had no doubt the chauffeur-bodyguard would carry out his end. His only fear was that the man was too devoted, too fanatical, too eager to reach paradise and violate his seventy-two virgins.

He might detonate the trunk's A-bomb before the limo reached the Capitol Building.

Hasad looked out the restaurant window, sipped his coffee, and stared wistfully at the Capitol Building. What were those lines Elena had loved to quote? Kipling?

"The sin that ye do by two and two, ye must pay for one by one."

That was it. Elena had always been hard-nosed when it came to good and bad, right and wrong. As in the Kipling poem, she had wanted evildoers to pay for their transgressions—one by one by one. Remembering that, he began to recognize how quixotic his dream of winning her back had been. He was a terrorist in the employ of Pakistan's ISI. She ran the CIA's Pakistan desk. She made her living killing men like him. What had possessed him to think she might leave the Agency and run off with him—one of the most feared and hunted men on earth?

Well, better men than he had said love was a dangerous delusion.

Still, he could settle up with Shaiq, then the general.

And America.

That country had been asking for it for seventy years—seventy years of peddling the Arms of Armageddon worldwide—and now he was determined to see to it that America got a taste of what she had been so merrily retailing.

Yes, the sin that ye do by two and two, ye do pay for one by one.

H e had only one regret. He was sorry he would miss the melting down of the Hudson River Nuclear Power Station.

Oh well, he thought with rare amusement, *you never get it all in this life.*

PART XIV

*I sing thee Bomb Death's extravagance, Death's
  jubilee,
Gem of Death's supremest blue . . . O Bomb I love
  you*

—Gregory Corso, "Bomb"

1

He hoped and prayed his men wouldn't beg to visit Graceland.
—Jamil Masoud

Starting out well before sunup, Jamil was hell-bent on making up any time lost at Donny's Down-Home Barbeque. The men were begging for pit stops, but he kept moving. He had promises to keep.

Just past dawn, the big van reached Dandridge and entered Tennessee. At Dixie Lee Junction, he decided to circumvent Nashville. The men weren't happy with that decision. In fact, they were openly irate. They were not only over their hangovers and demanding food, they said they wanted to listen to more country music and eat more barbeque—this time on Nashville's Music Row and in Printer's Alley.

To their chagrin, Jamil disdainfully ignored their pleas.

Moreover, at the one gas and restroom stop, Adman spotted a copy of *The Memphis Flyer* and picked it up. He and Jamil both read English, and Adman quickly spotted that on that very day Memphis was hosting both THE ELVIS AARON PRESLEY MUSIC FESTIVAL and THE WORLD'S BEST BARBEQUE COOK-OFF!

The big tent boasted countless blues bands and barbeque stands. Over three hundred barbeque vendors in all promised to cook more than three tons of pork, to say nothing of brisket, steak, beef ribs, and smoked chicken. They were competing for that much-coveted culinary prize—winner of the Whole Pig Cook-Off Championship

What the hell, Jamil thought.

Maybe he could pick up more souvenirs and T-shirts. It could help their cover, if they got pulled over.

Jamil turned off I-40 and onto the Memphis cutoff.

He hoped and prayed his men wouldn't learn that Elvis had lived here and beg him to visit Graceland.

2

"If a thing's worth doing, it's worth doing right."
—Elias Edito

Sam and Elias had been hanging out for months now. Since Elias was in security, he and his colleagues frequently discussed the different ways terrorists could circumvent the guards and melt down the plant. It was part of his job to worry about such things, and he'd developed a macabre fascination with these "intrusion-meltdown scenarios" as they were called in the antiterrorism textbooks.

And now he had a real expert with whom he could share his obsession.

Elias loved listening to Mazini as he explained at length and in detail how easy it would be for well-organized, well-funded terrorists—after breaking into the plant—to quickly incinerate the plant's fuel rods and spent waste, turning the entire Tri-State area into a radioactive death trap.

One day when he met Mazini at a coffee shop, Mazini shared some of these speculations with his newfound friend. Since nuclear power operations were his specialty, Mazini was a bottomless trove of technological minutiae.

Elias poured more coffee. "Is the spent fuel really as lethal as I've heard?" Elias asked.

Sam nodded. "Radioactive iodine hits the thyroid like a heat-seeking missile. Cesium attacks the soft tissues. Strontium builds up in the bones and teeth and is long-lived. It'll spend a full thirty years poisoning you."

"I read that the stuff is radioactive for 100,000 years."

"Depends on the isotope. Plutonium-239 has a half-life of twenty-four thousand years. Cesium-135 can last 2.3 million years."

"Maybe we shouldn't have closed the Yucca Mountain central storage site," Elias said.

"Maybe, but the truth is, in the long run, no site is safe. Eventually everything leaks, and security deteriorates. Also the longer the stuff is stored, the more valuable to nuclear terrorists it becomes."

"Why?" Elias said.

"After a few hundred years, the oxides and compounds disintegrate, and the pure nuclear bomb-fuel is all that's left. What used to be a storage tunnel in a mountain for nuclear waste is now a plutonium bomb-fuel mine. Nuclear traffickers will burrow into those mountain tunnels like miners to steal all that plutonium-239."

"These Americans are evil," Elias said. "We ought to melt this plant right down to the ground."

"I couldn't agree more," Mazini said, "but we would have to do it right."

"Absolutely. If a thing's worth doing, it's worth doing right."

"So?" Mazini asked. "Would you want to do it right? If I put together a team of guys—stone pros, who wanted to teach America the error of its ways—would you help us?"

"In a fucking heartbeat."

And now it was about to happen.

3

Like moon-mad dogs baying their brains out in hydrophobic rage.

The event was even bigger than Jamil had ever imagined. Memphis was holding its festivities on King Street in Elvis Aaron Presley Park. He and his men arrived there on the first night of the festivities and found themselves in a throng of over 100,000 drunken, barbeque-reeking rednecks. Girls in killer cutoffs, tight halter tops, or even tighter T-shirts adorned with renderings of Elvis in his myriad incarnations—Teen Idol Elvis, "Love Me Tender" Elvis, "Hound Dog" Elvis, "Jailhouse Rock" Elvis, "King Creole" Elvis, "GI Blues" Elvis, Hawaii Elvis, Tuxedo Elvis, Black Leather Elvis, Karate Elvis, Vegas Elvis, Fat Elvis, Skinny Elvis, Dead Elvis. Many of them stood behind stands, hawking Elvis barbeque and Elvis brew.

Men everywhere were attired in boots or sneakers, dirty-scruffy jeans, and the ubiquitous Elvis T-shirts, most of them with the sleeves cut off. Their baseball caps featured more ludicrous likenesses of the King.

Everyone had a beer in one hand and food in the other. Barbeque stands were up and down the streets and all over the park. Mexican fast food, however, was also popular, and many of the celebrants were stuffing their mouths with burritos or tacos. Stands also peddled mashed potatoes with burnt-bacon gravy and fried peanut butter and banana sandwiches—two of Elvis's favorite foods.

Jamil had never seen so many people in one spot outside of Mecca's holy hajj. But there the pilgrims were gracefully arrayed in white robes and behaved with dignity and decorum. These pilgrims pounded down plastic quart containers of draft beer like they were straight shots. They attacked the ribs, fried chicken and pulled pork like feral wolves on a kill.

His own group immediately got into the spirit. Loading their Styrofoam plates with ribs, chicken, and pulled pork, juggling quart cups of beer, they worked their way through the mob toward the bandstand.

It was easy to spot. They only had to follow the earsplitting, skull-crushing din of the band.

Jamil was oblivious to the music. If he could just get his men out of Memphis in one piece, he'd be happy. The prospects did not look good.

Fake Elvises were performing on bandstands all over the park as well as up and down the nearby streets. The festival's headliner on the main stage was a top Las Vegas Elvis impersonator. He was hammering through Elvis's long litany of hits—"Heartbreak Hotel," "Don't Be Cruel," "Return to Sender," "Marie's the Name," "Promised Land." In full Vegas regalia, he was bringing down the house with a raucous rendition of "Trouble."

Jamil's men instantly turned into bombs and exploded as the sneering, leg-shaking, karate-punching, arm-trembling Elvis doppelganger snarled the song's opening lyrics.

> *If you lookin' for trouble*
> *You came to the right place.*
> *If you lookin' for trouble.*
> *Just look right in my face.*

Jamil had now lost control of both his men and his sanity. What had happened to them? These previously devout young boys were now beer-chugging, dope-smoking, pork-gobbling, music-screaming, woman-lusting louts. That America could corrupt his committed young men so quickly and thoroughly proved, for once and for all, that it was indeed Gehenna on earth, the Great Satan's own lewd, lascivious lair.

Jamil surreptitiously fingered his prayer beads, silently muttering, "*Astaghfirullah . . . Astaghfirullah . . . Astaghfirullah*" nonstop, meaning, "I seek refuge in Allah . . . I seek refuge in Allah . . . I seek refuge in Allah," while his men hammered beers, devoured pig, gyrated their rear ends, pumped their crotches, vibrated their legs, wave-trembled their arms, sneered, leered and howlingly mispronounced the words to "Trouble," "Suspicious Minds," "All Shook Up," and "Jailhouse Rock," which they could not even remotely understand, like moon-mad dogs baying their brains out in hydrophobic rage.

4

___

They were going to make the Great Satan pay.

Sam and Elias went out night after night after night. Elias shared his most secret fantasies with Sam. He identified powerfully, almost irresistibly, with Charles Whitman, an ex-marine who one afternoon in 1966 had climbed to the observation deck of the University of Texas clock tower in Austin. There, for ninety minutes, with a Remington 700 6mm rifle and a .30 caliber M1 carbine, he shot people, mostly students, killing fourteen and wounding thirty-two. Elias had the same, almost erotically murderous urge, to enter one of the nuclear power plant's guard towers and to gun down plant employees until the authorities finally killed him.

"I want to do it so badly," Elias had told Sam, "I sometimes fear if I don't, I'll lose my mind."

"You're kidding," Sam said.

"Not in the least," Elias said. "I'd like to go up in one of those gun towers and smoke every one of these sickos working here."

"You really want to shoot them?" Sam asked, amazed.

"I want to do them so bad my dick hurts," Elias said.

That night, Sam had put an arm around Elias's shoulders. "I understand. I really do."

Elias felt he'd found the brother he never knew he had.

They also shared a passion for the great singer-songwriter Sister Cassandra and the End Time. When they hung out at Sam's house, they would play her CDs over and over again, blasting her music into the night, full force.

One of their favorites was "First Strike."

It'll be a First Strike (Boom!)
For world peace.
A final fatal blow
To our sworn enemy.
Our last true chance
To finally be set free.

To save the planet earth
Oh, our country 'tis of thee.

Then came the soft melodic bridge:

When the dust has settled,
When the thermonuclear dust comes down,
When the fallout drifts slowly,
Slowly to the ground.
Will anyone be around?
Will anyone be around?

Then back to more hard, hammering, earth-shattering rock:

A levitating fireball
And all our pain will cease.
Blast waves, firestorms,
War'll no longer be.
We'll finally kill them all,
The godless enemy!
We'll save the human race,
O sweet land of liberty!

One time after an intense night of beer and Sister Cassandra's apocalyptic rock, Sam confided to Elias his own fantasy: "I think all the time about melting down the HRNPS. Maybe we could somehow combine our two dreams."

"You help me, I'll help you?" Elias said.

"Exactly," Sam agreed.

It turned into a fantasy game for the two friends. They evaluated the different ways they could wreak havoc on the HRNPS. They began by evaluating the plant's various vulnerabilities. Since Mazini was the chief reactor operator, he was a genuine expert in these matters, and he quickly convinced Elias that America's nuclear plants were utterly vulnerable to terrorist attacks. In a sense, they were terrorist strikes waiting to happen.

"Why doesn't the U.S. government protect these sites against well-organized, heavy-duty assaults?" Elias asked.

"The Nuclear Regulatory Commission—otherwise known as the NRC—runs the whole show. It has the last word on everything, but it's in the pockets of the nuclear industry."

"Which means the NRC doesn't want to spend additional money on nuclear security?" Elias asked. "All the NRC wants to do is to generate revenue for the nuclear power companies."

"You got it," Mazini said. "Neither entity wants to spend the money necessary to protect the plants and the surrounding population. Particularly when it comes to securing spent fuel. It would cost too much to cover all the nuclear waste pools with domes of reinforced concrete. That's why we keep them in sheet-metal sheds."

"Why doesn't the NRC force the nuclear industry to protect their facilities with in-depth defenses?" Elias asked.

"The Supreme Court has ruled that terrorist attacks are a national security problem and that private industry is not required to protect the nuclear plants against such assaults. Nor is the nuclear industry responsible for losses sustained by such strikes."

"Why doesn't the federal government bring the troops in then," Elias said, "and build up perimeter defenses until HRNPS looked like a fortress?" Elias asked.

"The NRC, Congress, and the courts have ruled that creating and maintaining such defenses would cost too much and would be too intrusive to the operations of the plant."

"What's the real reason they don't want our troops defending nuclear plants?" Elias asked.

"Taxpayers wouldn't want to pick up the tab, and the expense of such troop deployments and in-depth perimeter defenses would bankrupt the nuclear industry," Mazini said. "Also, once our war colleges analyzed our nuclear installation defenses, they'd come to the same conclusions I have: nuclear power is militarily indefensible—unless you're willing to send costs soaring out of our solar system and into the Outer Dark."

"Does the nuclear industry know how indefensible their plants are?"

"Of course. How could they not? They just don't want anyone else to know," Mazini said.

"So there is no way to protect any of our nuclear installations against trained, committed, organized terrorists?"

"One way, and one way only: shut them all down."

And so it went. On and on into the night, they'd sit and plan—plan, scheme, connive, and dream.

And now the time had finally arrived.

All their scheming and dreaming was coming to fruition.

They were going to make the Great Satan pay.

And always, through all their planning, scheming, conniving, and dreaming, the Good Sister was there for them—inspiring them, beguiling them, wailing to them of the End Time to come.

It'll be a First Strike (Boom!)
For World Peace.
A final fatal blow
To our sworn enemy.
Our last true chance
To finally be set free.
To save the planet earth
O our country 'tis of thee.

PART XV

"I'm not sure anyone can defend nuclear plants like these. After all, we aren't trying to rob Fort Knox. All we want to do is burn up a highly flammable firetrap. You can't defend the facility if all the arsonist wants to do is set it aflame—and if he's willing to die to do it."

—Hasad ibn Ghazi

1

"We're going to do to this plant what that tsunami did to Fukushima."

—Hamzi Udeen

The next day, Hasad was again behind the wheel, with his crew packed
like lemmings in the back of the Ford Transit-350 Passenger Van. Just
outside of Arlington, they got back on I-95 and then stayed on it through
East Baltimore and East Philadelphia, taking it all the way through New
Brunswick and Elizabeth to Newark, NJ. Catching the Lincoln Tunnel just
outside of Hoboken, they crossed under the Hudson River and entered Manhattan. Hasad immediately turned off onto the West Side Highway, which
carried them uptown, where it became the Henry Hudson Parkway. They
stayed on the HHP until they reached Route 9, then Route 9W, which they
stayed on until the Kingston exit. After which a succession of city streets
followed by county roads brought them to another safe house—this one a
massive four-story clapboard farmhouse with jutting gables and gingerbread
trim. Hasad entered its adjacent barn.

Parking inside, Hasad got out first, turned on the lights, and shut the
barn's huge sliding door.

He then let the men get out, use the barn lavatory, and grab some coffee
and sandwiches. He then had them return to the big barn.

"This is your headquarters," Hasad told the assembled team. "I'm going
to go over plans and operations with you. I know we've been over this before in Virginia. Consider this a refresher course. We're going to go over it
one last time. Then I must take off to complete an attack of my own—one
even more devastating than this strike. Hamzi, who accompanied me on a
similar strike overseas, will ably lead your assault here. You will follow his
orders exactly and explicitly."

Hasad looked out over the sixteen assembled men. Like himself, they
were all dressed in Levis, T-shirts, and sneakers. Hamzi was handing each
of the men tan manila envelopes filled with eight-by-ten glossies of the
HRNPS, taken both inside the main buildings and outside of them.

"I want to again stress the importance of what you will be doing," Hasad

242 | ROBERT GLEASON

said. "This will not be an isolated mission but the beginning of a series of global nuclear power plant strikes."

"We're giving them the ultimate nightmare from hell," Hamzi said.

"We're making America pay for its crimes against humanity, its nuclear crimes," Hasad said. "The first of our attacks will be here on the HRNPS. We will use shaped charges to shatter the spent rods, driving them into contact with each other. We're going to blast and burn off the spent rods' one-millimeter protective covering, boil the water away, and expose the spent rods to air. When the nuclear waste interacts with the air, those rods will turn to flame, and those thousands of tons of waste will go critical. We will render almost 50,000 square miles off the East Coast uninhabitable and kill twenty million people minimum. The damage we will inflict on the HRNPS will dwarf that of Chernobyl, which stored relatively little spent fuel and which was largely a fuel-rod meltdown, not a spent-fuel conflagration."

"I know some of our people are already working at the plant," Fahad said. "Tell us how the rest of us will get in."

"On an isolated stretch of highway at night, you'll cut through the fence and walk to these buildings through the woods," Hasad said. "Now you do have to be alert to sensors—not that it matters that much if you do set one off. Deer and raccoon trigger so many that the guards typically ignore them."

"It's not that tough," Hamzi said. "We told you how an eighty-two-year-old nun with a heart condition broke into a nuclear weapons plant, a place that was far more closely guarded than this power plant. If she can do it, we can do it."

"So we're all in the plant," Hasad said. "Here is a master shot of the Auxilary Building's interior. Here are the three emergency diesel generators." Hasad pointed them out. "Saif Mazini—known to his colleagues as Sam—will mark those pumps and generators with duct taped X's. You will then mine them all with C-4—the residual heat removal pumps, the auxiliary pumps, all the coolant pumps, and the emergency diesel generators."

"In an Auxiliary Building storage closet, Saif has hidden a seabag filled with C-4," Hamzi said. "Saif's also secreted more guns and shaped charges in one of the locked storage closets. You'll have keys to it and to the other storage closets. Here it is on the screen. Hamzi can also direct you to it, and you have a glossy in your manila envelope showing you its location."

Hamzi pointed them out to his men. He then showed them close-up slides of each pump and handed them eight-by-ten glossies of each of the slides.

"After we have secured the building, Faiz, Mahmud, Fahad, Ghurayn, Gohar, you will tape C-4 to the pumps," Hasad said. "Back in the control room, Saif will sit at the big board and lift the HEU fuel rods out of the coolant, then lock them in place. Fahad, you will mine the controls with C-4 while Hamzi is mining the reactor coolant pump adjacent to the reactor. When the HEU fuel rods catch fire, Saif will exit the control room, remotely blowing up the pumps and computers after all of us leave the building."

"By this time, won't the U.S. military and the state police be storming the compound?" Fahad asked. "Hamzi told me they have bases nearby."

Hasad treated them to a rare smile. "We will have a skilled marksman in the main gun tower. Their trip to the Hudson River Nuclear Power Station will not be . . . *uneventful*."

Laughter filled the barn.

"Inside the Turbine Building are the main feed pumps and the condensate pumps," Hamzi said. "The circulation pumps are between the Turbine Building and the cooling tower. After we detonate those pumps with RPGs and blow out the bottoms of the massive overhead water tanks—which will deluge the plant with tens of millions of gallons of water—the reactors and storage pools will quickly run out of circulating coolant and boil away the water still surrounding them."

"Excellent," Hasad said. "Now Elias will man the front gun tower that night. He will drop a line down and one of the men will lash an ordnance bag to it."

"Correct," Fahad said. "Amir here will assist."

Amir raised his hand. "It will contain a Barrett M82 with a night scope and a daylight scope, an MP7, and a 9mm Glock, as well as grenades and preloaded magazines for all the weapons."

"Sirens will be blaring," Hamzi said, "sprinklers will be set off. Blinding, burning smoke will fill the plant. Bombs will be going off. Water will be pouring out of the tanks in torrents."

"You will need nose-and-mouth gas masks and after the lights go out maybe even night goggles," Hasad said.

"The plant will smoke and burn for a long, long time to come," Hamzi said.

"The Americans may never put it out," Fahad said.

"Especially when the spent fuel starts to burn," Hasad said. "The plant stores almost two tons of spent fuel, the bulk of it in pools. That's ten times the amount of toxic radioactivity contained in the HEU fuel rods. We're going to blow everything to hell and gone with shaped depth-charges, then finish them off with a dozen or so Russian-made phosphorous charges."

"The phosphorous is really that devastating?" Fahad asked.

"You clearly never fought the Russian army in Chechnya," Hasad said.

"Ask the Chechens, who were on the receiving end of those bombs. Our phosphorous charges will burn those spent rods down to their raw, radio-active core."

"Phosphorous sucks the air right out of water," Hamzi said. "It's also self-feeding. It'll burn in outer space."

Fahad stared at them, astonished. "I don't believe how vulnerable these plants are," he finally said. "It's as if they're begging us to burn these nuclear plants down to the ground."

"I'm surprised they don't pay us to do it," Hamzi said, agreeing.

"Well, America is paying us, sort of," Hasad said.

Fahad looked confused.

"Ever heard of petrodollars?" Hasad asked.

"The operative word is 'dollars,'" Hamzi said.

There was a long moment of silence.

"This is going to work, isn't it?" Fahad said.

"We're going to do to this plant what the tsunami did to Fukushima," Hamzi said.

"But ours will be a tsunami of C-4, RPGs, and shaped charges," Hasad said.

"You are so confident, my friend," Hamzi said facetiously. "You act as if you've done this before."

"You all saw the news footage of the terrorist assault on that Pakistani nuclear site a while back," Hasad said. "That was one of my operations."

"Nor was that our only other Pakistani nuclear assault," Hamzi said. "I must say, however, it is a relief to be attacking the infidels' installations in-stead of Pakistan's."

"It's very cathartic," Fahad agreed.

"Still, those last Pakistani nuclear attacks were excellent practice," Hasad said.

"And one of them got us the bomb-grade HEU," Hamzi said, "with which we fabricated our new nuclear weapons."

"The raids were exceedingly instructive, and thanks to lessons learned, we will set the HRNPS's waste aflame, after which it will spew radioactive death for tens of thousands of years."

2

_____

He was going to arrive on time after all.

Starting out at dawn, Jamil and his crew crossed the mighty Mississippi over the massive arch bridge connecting Memphis, Tennessee, with West Memphis, Arkansas. Named after Hernando de Soto, the explorer, in part because his body was reputedly interred in the big river, it was six lanes wide and 5,954 meters long. Jamil rolled over the great waterway in less than four minutes.

Slipping back onto I-40, they followed the path of the old Beale Wagon Road. Built over 150 years ago by the U.S. Army, it originally used camels as pack animals for the highway's construction. Lieutenant Edward Fitzgerald finished the job in 1859, linking California to the east with the country's first major thoroughfare. Spanning the thousand-mile stretch between the Arkansas–Mississipi River crossing and California, the road was eventually replaced by Route 66 and later I-40.

Jamil was making good time, but he was still concerned he might not reach the Sandia nuclear weapons lab on the edge of San Francisco within thirty-six hours. Rounding Little Rock and then North Little Rock, Jamil rocketed past Conway, then Russellville, then Fort Smith, where 140 years earlier Judge Isaac Charles Parker had hanged outlaws and renegades by the score. Once, after lining up six prisoners on the long plank trap, he solemnly announced, "May God have mercy on your souls," and with a single yank on the trapdoor's lever, his hangman sent their earthly souls plummeting into the everlasting night.

At Fort Smith, he ignored the old fort—now a museum—and he stopped only for gas, a quart of 20-weight, and nothing else. The men didn't even get a restroom break. He told them to tie a knot in it or piss in their beer cans.

He had miles to cover and highway to burn.

In Oklahoma, he barreled through Elk City, Clinton, Henryetta and Roland, stopping in Oklahoma City again for gas with no restroom break. Blasting out of OKC like a bat out of hell, he hit the Texas panhandle and made no stops at all until Amarillo.

New Mexico was a blur. Gallup, Santa Rosa, Albuquerque, more Indian reservations that he could not name or remember.

Into Arizona, thundering past the Grand Canyon's South Rim—no, he wouldn't let them stop to gawk—past Flagstaff, Williams, and the Navajo Nation, the largest Indian reservation in the world.

He could not believe it. He was smoking into California less than a dozen hours later.

He was going to arrive on time after all.

3

"All we want to do is incinerate a highly flammable firetrap."
—Hasad ibn Ghazi

Hasad stood on the bridge of a thirty-five-foot trawler with Fahad and Saif al-Mazini, aka Sam Mazini. The anchored boat rocked in the river's chop, and Hasad carefully gripped the rail. They were all dressed in shorts, T-shirts, and running shoes. The cloudless summer sky was a brilliant blue—the perfect weather for an afternoon on the Hudson.

Mazini had bought the trawler three years earlier when Hasad had first approached him about the operation. Hasad had wanted it as a possible getaway boat. Now, standing on the bridge and holding the rail, Hasad stared in silence at the Hudson River Nuclear Power Station, ninety-five miles up-river from Times Square.

"Why are you so sure you can get us into the plant?" Fahad asked Mazini.

"I work the midnight shift, and my boss is a drunk. By eight o'clock, he'll be in his office with the door shut, chugging vodka out of his Evian bottle. By ten fifteen, his head will be on his desk and he'll be sound asleep."

"He doesn't care about getting caught drunk?" Fahad asked.

"I warned him the company'll can his ass," Mazini said. "The idiot said, 'The company can go fuck itself.'"

"Sounds to me like he needs an attitude adjustment," Fahad observed.

"Too late for that," Mazini said. "He's six weeks from retirement and just wants out. He's also battling metastasized prostate and bowel cancer, which he blames on the job. He plans on suing the plant before he dies."

"So you just blow the cooling pumps?" Fahad asked. "That's it?"

"That's part of it," Mazani said. "Since I operate the reactor, I can melt the fuel rods down from inside the control room. That way we can accelerate the process."

"We're really going to do it?" Fahad whispered, astonished.

"Balls out, pedal to the metal," Mazini said.

"Same plan as Pakistan," Hasad said. "We'll have guns, silencers, ammo, and explosives. We'll be wearing guard uniforms or white coveralls with matching lab coats. You'll all have impeccable credentials—badges and IDs.

We'll also have ordnance stashed in storage closets. First we mine the cooling pumps with C-4, then Mazini'll hightail it to the control room. After Mazini gets the fuel rods out of the coolant, he'll go outside and blow the pumps remotely."

Fahad stared at Mazini, amazed. "How the hell did you get to be a reactor operator?"

Mazini shrugged. "It doesn't take much. I've been there fifteen years, but all you really need is a high school diploma and three years' experience, one year of which has to be at the current plant. You need three months' actual experience in the control room. You have to pass two or three bullshit exams. That's it."

"What do we do about security guards?" Fahad asked.

"They're nothing. The major leagues are holding their all-star game on July Fourth, and all the security guards will be crowded around the rec room TVs."

"You're kidding," Fahad said.

"It's always like that, for any ball game," Mazini said. "Look at it this way: security work at a nuclear plant is one of the most boring, uneventful, low-paying jobs in the world. Nothing happens. Nothing. You have nothing to worry about."

"He's right," Hasad said. "What we're doing is unprecedented. They have no plan for it, and we're going to catch them with their pants down."

"And if someone stumbles onto us," Mazini said, "we'll all have silenced pistols in our bags."

"And?" Fahad said.

"We kill them all," Hasad said.

"I read that at Fukushima they had auxiliary pumps and emergency diesel generators," Fahad said.

"Yes," Hasad said. "We will blow them up as well."

"We'll be a tsunami of fire," Fahad said, smiling.

"We leave no turn unstoned," Mazini said.

Only Hasad got his joke.

"How is it possible?" Fahad asked. "Seriously. We're going to render most of three states unlivable for at least twenty million people, and we're up against almost no resistance."

"I'm not sure anyone can defend plants like these," Hasad said. "After all, we aren't trying to rob Fort Knox. All we want to do is incinerate a highly flammable firetrap. You can't defend it if all the arsonist wants to do is set it aflame—and if he's willing to die to do it."

Hasad looked at his watch.

"I have to run. I've got a charter plane to catch. I have to be back in my D.C. hotel in three hours. I have a big day tomorrow."

PART XVI

And when ye shall hear of wars and rumours of wars, be ye not troubled: for such things must needs be; but the end shall not be yet. For nation shall rise against nation, and kingdom against kingdom: and there shall be earthquakes in divers places, and there shall be famines and troubles: these are the beginnings of sorrows ...

—Mark XIII: 7-8

1

"That's not much of a plan."
—John C. Jameson

After twenty-three straight hours at the computer, Jamie walked into the kitchen, got a mug of coffee, and sat down at the dining-room table. He was in gray gym shorts and a white T-shirt. His hair was unwashed and uncombed, his face grizzled. He wearily stared into his coffee, then took a drink.

Everyone else was up, sitting in the living room, watching the news, reading the papers, and also having coffee. They joined him at the dining-room table.

"Learn anything?"

"Shaiq and General Jari are skeptical of everyone and everything, including each other," Jamie said. "You can see it in their private e-mails. They pretend to trust each other, but that's a façade. They can't stand each other."

"But they're working together," Elena said.

"They have common interests." Jamie drank more coffee. "They're trying to keep close tabs on Hasad ibn Ghazi, who's the strategic and tactical planner behind this operation. They had to coerce him into accepting the final phase of the job, and they know how much he hates them. All this, of course, helps us, because they make him account for his actions in triplicate. So I know where he and his people are headed. Therefore, I also know where their targets are."

"Are you sure?" Elena asked.

Jamie gave them a hint of a smile. "Why else would Hasad send his people to the Hudson River Nuclear Power Station just outside of New York City? You think his men are going there for a seminar on nuclear power?"

"Oh, shit," Jules said.

"You mean Hasad won't be going with them?" Elena asked.

"No, after a day or two he's leaving them at the plant and heading south to D.C.," Jamie said.

"How do you know he's hitting D.C.?" Elena asked.

"He's registered at the Capitol Needle Hotel—a full suite," Jamie said. "You know, the new needle tower?"

There was a heavy silence.

"Any idea when all this goes down?" Jules finally asked.

"That's the tricky part," Jamie said. "Hasad, Shaiq, and Jari talk like it's next week. That doesn't sound right though. Hasad's team has been in place for several days and is ready to rock."

"Also tonight the president is holding a special Fourth of July State of the Union address," Elena pointed out. "If Hasad hates Shaiq, Caldwell, and these guys as much as you say he does, Jamie, what better time to wreak vengeance on them at the Capitol Building?"

"He wouldn't get his final payment," Jamie said.

"If Hasad hates them as much as we think he does," Elena said, nodding thoughtfully, "his revenge will be the payment."

"You used to know Hasad," Jamie said to Adara. "Is that plausible?"

"He sure as shit doesn't like people messing with him," Adara said, "and he doesn't need the final payment."

"He looks to have about $30 million in offshore accounts," Jamie said, glancing at his computer.

"In the black ops world, he's always been high end, top of the line," Adara said, "the best at what he does."

"You think he'd try to take out Shaiq and Caldwell with their own bomb?" Jamie asked.

"Shit, yeah," Rashid said.

"You may be right," Jamie said. "Those guys gave him cause. They bragged in their e-mails about how they threatened to kill his sister and fuck him out of his last payment."

"We've got to tell the feds," Jules said. "Jamie, you can get to them. You have copies of what you've hacked, and you have great connections with the Bureau. You've done a hell of a lot of work for them."

"Sure, but we've got no real smoking-gun evidence," Jamie said. "None of these guys implicated Shaiq and Caldwell and Jari in these coming attacks. All I have is Hasad arranging for lodgings at these locations, and for himself in D.C. I also have Shaiq and Jari bragging about how they fucked Hasad over."

"Nothing else?" Adara asked.

"Oh, I do have President Caldwell's and Shaiq's offshore tax-free black-hole bank accounts. Shaiq has practically made that bastard a billionaire."

"We might be able to do something with that," Elena said.

"I doubt it," Jules said. "Jamie broke about a million laws invading Shaiq's and Caldwell's privacy."

"Everything he learned," Elena said, "is 'fruit of the forbidden tree,' as lawyers say, and inadmissible in court. Jamie'd probably end up doing time."

"I also examined the way they're set up," Jamie said. "It looks to me like our president could deny knowing anything about them. He could probably get away with it."

"Just shoot me now," Jules said.

"It gets worse," Jamie said. "I found e-mail, text, and phone metadata confirming that Elena's been communicating with Hasad."

"You mean Rashid," Elena said.

"I found time lags in those e-mails. Rashid was sending them to Hasad, who then bounced them to you, using Rashid's server."

"Why?" Elena asked.

"You were running the Agency's Pakistan desk," Jamie said. "Why was he doing you such a spectacular favor?"

"He wants his baby girl back in his life," Jules said, laughing. "The motherfucker's still in love—after all these years."

"Couldn't be anything else," Adara said.

"That's right," Jamie said, "and while I can't prove the president, Shaiq, and Jari are connected with Hasad's coming attacks, I can connect you to him. In fact, after Hasad launched his assaults, you'd most likely be viewed as a coconspirator."

"If Elena and I called the FBI," Jules said, "and told them what we know, they'd still think we were involved in the coming attacks."

"They'd say we'd gotten cold feet," Elena said, "and were now chickening out. That we hoped to curry favor with the feds by ratting out our coterrorists, thought it might help clear our names."

"Let me try," Jamie said. "Anything else you want me to do?"

"And then there's those eleven feds we killed."

"So what do you want to do?" Jamie asked the two women.

"You said you know where Hasad is staying in D.C.?" Elena asked.

"He's due to check into the Capitol Needle Hotel today," Jamie said.

"It's on East Capitol Street about a mile and a half due east from the Capitol Building," Jules said. "I wrote a piece on that building once."

"I read it," Jamie said, nodding. "You called it 'a monument to hubris.'"

"'And predatory greed,'" Jules said. "The condos are perfect squares, seventy-five feet on edge. The hotel is made up of suites offering a 360-degree view of D.C. It's a hundred stories high and less than ninety feet across."

"Its western view includes the Capitol Building itself," Jamie said.

"So Hasad has a gorgeous room," Elena said.

"My money's on Hasad nuking the State of the Union address tonight," Jamie said.

"Since his fellow terrorists plan on melting down the Hudson River nuke plant," Jules said, "that's where I'm heading."

"Hasad will want simultaneous strikes," Elena agreed.

"It's how the terrorists did it on 9/11 and during the African embassy attacks," Jules said.

"And what will you do up there, Jules?" Jamie asked.

"I have a sister, Sandy Meredith," Jules said.

"Do you trust her?" Jamie asked.

"With anything," Jules said.

"I trust her as much as anyone I've ever known," Elena said. "And I've known her since she was ten."

"What's she do?" Jamie asked.

"She's a TV news reporter," Elena said. "Her specialty is helicopter news broadcasts—particularly superdangerous war stories. She does a lot of work for MTN News."

"She gets the shots no one else can get," Jules said, "and she's covered every war on the planet for the last eighteen years."

"So have you," Elena said, "for the print media."

"What do you plan on doing up there?" Jamie asked Jules.

"If Hasad's men try something," Jules said, "maybe Sandy and I can spot them, and Sandy can alert the authorities. At the very least she can cover it for the news."

"That's not much of a plan," Jamie said.

"It's better than hanging around down here doing nothing," Jules said.

"Jamie, you said you thought there was a third attack scheduled," Elena said.

"Couldn't get anything on it," Jamie said. "If there's another team, I'm not sure Hasad has anything to do with it."

"I better take off now," Jules said. "Jamie, you always had a lot of cool motorcycles, if memory serves."

"A bunch."

"Good, I'm biking it up to the HRNPS. I can make it in five or six hours if I go flat out."

"I got a better idea," Jamie said. "Rashid, you and Adara will drive Jules to meet her sister. Then you'll cut across to the Greenwich Harborside Marina in Connecticut, where I have a power launch. Head up the coast to the

Crestview Cove, where Jules and her sister can meet with you after they cover their story. It's less than forty miles from the power plant. You'll have extra cans of gas, rations, weapons, whatever at the dock. We'll all rendezvous later down the coast. Prepare it for a long trip. If these guys melt down that power plant and the nukes start going off, the sea will be your best chance of escape. Elena, I know what you're planning, and I'm going to try to talk you out of it. What you're thinking is suicide. In fact, you and I will want to hit the water as well if and when this goes down. I have a second really fast boat we can use. We can rendezvous later with Jules and her people somewhere along the coast."

Jules, Adara, and Rashid went to their rooms to pack a bag.

Jamie turned to look at Elena. She didn't look happy. Her face was an angry mask of obstinacy.

Still, he had to try.

He didn't want her going anywhere near the Capitol Building.

2

Kid, Sandy said to herself, *sounds like we're going to war.*

Sandy Meredith's cell phone rang eight times before she had the strength to roll over and answer it. She'd been up in her news chopper covering a hurricane that had ravaged Long Island's Southampton coast for nearly seventy-two straight hours, and she'd never been so tired in her life. Fumbling blindly for the cell, she finally pulled off her night mask and picked it up.

"This better be the end of the world," she rasped irritably.

"Pretty close," the voice said.

Sandy froze. She knew who it was.

"Goddamn you to hell," Sandy said, careful not to use the woman's name. "I hope you don't need something."

"Oh, do I ever."

"Not from me. You're all over the news, kid."

"Which is why I'm calling you on one of your throwaway burner phones," Jules said, "so no one can tap into our call."

"Maybe," Sandy said, "but you're still in a whole world of hurt. You and your friends are burning up the news media worldwide, and people are screaming for your blood."

"None of what they say is true."

"Tell that to the thirteen men you guys smoked. The attorney general is even bringing treason charges against your friends. They still can't identify a couple of them, but they will. They claim you're also plotting nuclear strikes on the U.S. and that the FBI is authorized to shoot you on sight. They're ready to gun you down like Dillinger."

"I've got the story of a lifetime for you," Jules said.

That stopped her cold. Her sister could smell a real story ten thousand miles away, and she knew Jules wouldn't shit her. Her news instincts fought her survival instincts.

"What do you need?" she asked cautiously.

"I need a fully tricked-out news chopper ready to roll by midnight tonight."

Shit, Jules did have a story. She couldn't believe it.

"Do you have any idea what you're asking?"

"Yes."

"Do you know what I have to go through to get an unscheduled spur-of-the-moment chopper all to myself on such short notice?"

"Yes."

"The lies I'd have to make up."

"Sandy, you may have to steal one."

"Yeah, right. Steal a news chopper?"

"Complete with a fully integrated electronic news-gathering system, which can transmit, receive, and record live AV. Oh, and we'll need at least two really great cameras."

Christ, now she was interested.

Sandy picked up a pad off her night table and began jotting down notes.

"We'll need audio, a video switcher, in-cabin monitors, a microwave transmitter, and a minicam as well," Jules added.

"We're using R44 Newscopters now."

"Any good?" Jules asked.

"The best—six cylinder, fuel injection, a forty-eight-gallon fuel tank, a 350-mile range, and an operating altitude of over fourteen thousand feet. I've covered wars in them."

"We also need two really good cams—a nose-mounted, gyro-stabilized HD and a tail-mounted microcam," Jules said.

"We got them," Sandy said, "but you'll have to run them off a laptop. Do you still know how?"

"Does a shark shit in the sea?" Jules asked.

"You really want to pull a Grand Theft Chopper?" Sandy asked.

"I'll bring a piece. We'll say I kidnapped you at gunpoint."

"They're already indicting you for treason and thirteen counts of murder one. What's a little kidnap time, right?"

"Just tell me where the helipad is," Jules said.

Sandy gave her the pad's location and their time of takeoff.

"Sis," Jules said, "we're going to rock the world news like it's never been rocked before."

"Just as long as it isn't the Jailhouse Rock."

"You'll be 'the cutest little jailbird I ever did see.'"

"Then I'll see you on the women's rec yard at Atlanta Fed," Sandy said.

"We'll rock that joint, too," Jules said.

"Over and out."

Kid, Sandy said to herself, *sounds like we're going to war.*

Then she laughed. Turning on the light, she glanced in the side mirror and saw that she was smiling reflexively. She could not help herself. She could not express how much she loved Jules.

Jules was the only person she knew who was crazier than she was.

Except maybe Elena.

PART XVII

When churchyards yawn and hell itself breathes
out Contagion to this world...

—*Hamlet* III, ii, 380

1

"For America to believe we would never use their nuclear weapons technology against them—which they so arrogantly sold us—is pathologically stupid, suicidally . . . naive."
—Jamil Masoud

It was a long hair-raising drive, but Jamil and his crew—Adman, Bahram, Dawad, and Hanif—had finally made it. Just east of San Francisco, they stood on a hill overlooking the Edward Teller Nuclear Weapons Laboratory. Like himself, Jamil's men had on a clean change of clothes—Levi's, country music T-shirts emblazoned with the likenesses of Elvis, Willie, Waylon, and Taylor Swift, and running shoes. They were freshly shaved, and their recently lightened hair was cut short.

Below was the Teller Lab, an assortment of over a hundred gray concrete-block buildings, sheet-steel storages sheds, warehouses, and crisscrossing rail tracks, all converging on the main train station. The facility encompassed an area the size of a small town. Near the entrance stood four huge, nine-story limestone buildings. They were the lab's main office buildings. Two concentric wire-topped cyclone fences surrounded the facility.

At the edge of the sally port, which all the visitors and employees had to pass through, stood a vast sprawling parking lot packed with thousands of cars. Twenty yards into the facility was the Visitors Center—a long rectangular one-story building with high wall-length windows. Beyond the Visitors Center and in front of the massive eight-story Administration Building was a large grassy park filled with clumps of pine, spruce, and oak, small colorful gardens, park benches, and drinking fountains. Near the entrance were also gift shops, the Edward Teller Museum, and restrooms made of cement blocks. Statues of nuclear scientists were also scattered throughout the park, as were popcorn, hotdog, and soft drink stands. There was also a statue of President Truman, who oversaw the completion of the first atomic bomb and the beginning of the hydrogen bomb program. Towering above the other buildings and monuments was a statue of Edward Teller himself, carved out of gray New Hampshire granite. A brass plaque was affixed to its five-foot-high gray granite base. Inscribed on it was:

1908–2003

"I WAS THE ONLY ADVOCATE FOR THE HYDROGEN
BOMB, AND THAT, I THINK, IS MY CONTRIBUTION."

To the east, north, and south, the lab was surrounded by high wooded hills. Due west through an open valley lay San Francisco.

"There, my friends," Jamil said, "we see before us one of the world's great weapons labs. And that lab deserves our respect. We owe those scientists down there a lot. For the last seventy years, for instance, they've worked tirelessly on the miniaturization of nuclear weapons so they could shrink them down until they could be squeezed onto the tips of cruise missiles."

"Nonetheless, we will blow them all to Gehenna and gone," Hanif said.

"Tomorrow at 5:00 P.M., give or take a few minutes," Jamil said.

"Good," Bahram said. "Burn the infidels."

"They are generous in a perverse kind of way," Hanif said.

"Arrogant is the more accurate word," Adman said. "They think they are smarter and better than us. That's why they invited our best scientists over here and taught them how to build these wicked weapons."

"The word you're looking for is greedy," Jamil said. "Americans sell anything to anyone."

"What was it Lenin said about capitalists?" Adman said. "They would sell him the rope he would use to hang them?"

"They sold us everything we need to make our own nuclear bombs," Jamil said, "with which to incinerate them."

"For money," Adman said.

"And not just us, they did the same for India," Hanif said, "our most implacable enemy." They were all Pakistani.

"And Iran," Jamil said, "another one of our nemeses. Even now, the U.S. is trying to sell nuclear power reactors to our patron and closest ally, the Saudis."

"Which will soon be turned into a nuclear bomb-fuel factory," Adman said. "All they need to do is construct a low-tech nuclear bomb-fuel reprocessor with which to extract the bomb-grade plutonium from the spent fuel rods."

"Which our friends can build out of the equipment from an old dairy farm or old winery," Jamil said.

"These infidels are insane," Dawad said. "They deserve anything they get."

"Indeed," Jamil said. "For America to believe we would never use their nuclear weapons technology against them—which they so arrogantly sold us—is pathologically stupid, suicidally . . . naive."

AND INTO THE FIRE | 263

"Tomorrow," Adman agreed, "we will teach them the error of their ways."

"You assume they are educable," Jamil said, "which is a fact not in evidence."

"They've had these weapons close to eighty years," Adman said, nodding his head sadly, "and still haven't learned anything, have they?"

"As Napoleon said of the pre-Revolution Bourbons," Jamil quoted, "'They learned nothing; they forgot nothing.'"

They were silent a long moment.

"Who would invent such demonic devices?" Hanif asked.

"Fiends from hell," Adman said.

"Then this place is . . . *what*?" Dawad asked.

"The infernal . . . *pit*," Hanif said.

"I am glad we are vaporizing it," Dawad said.

"I am, too," Jamil admitted. "Still, I feel a modicum of regret. We would not be the atomic weapons power that we are today if not for the people here in the Teller Lab."

"Who was Edward Teller?" Bahram asked.

"The craziest of them all," Jamil said. "He thought you could stop surreptitiously smuggled nuclear bombs with a *Star Wars* space shield."

"He was clearly mad," Adman said.

"Madder than mad," Bahram said.

"What else did he do?" Hanif asked.

"He worked on the atom bomb," Jamil said. "His claim to fame, though, was creating and running the hydrogen bomb program, advocating the expansion of nuclear weapons systems, opposing all nuclear peace treaties of any sort, and most famously proposing the 'Star Wars' space-based missile defense system."

"He sounds Satanic," Adman said.

"His critics thought so," Jamil said.

"What's under those two big black shrouds?" Bahram asked, studying them through his binoculars. Each of the shrouds was draped over a large object.

"The Saudi Kingdom," Jamil said, "in honor of the 175-year anniversary of the California Republic, is presenting the Teller Lab with a statue of the great grizzly bear on the state flag, except their version of the grizzly is rearing up on his hind legs. Under the other tarp is another Saudi gift—a replica of the famous cannon that the Bear Flag rebels commandeered at the Old Spanish Fort and then spiked. In this case, it's a poor excuse for a replica. It's actually an old 155mm howitzer with a ten-foot barrel. The stupid Americans can't tell the difference between a twentieth-century artillery piece and a 175-year-old relic."

"Don't tell me that's the bomb we worked so hard on?" Bahram asked, astonished. "That's where it ended up?"

"You got it," Jamil said.

"We turned that cannon down there into a nuke?" Hanif asked.

"Why not?" Jamil asked. "That is essentially how the Hiroshima bomb was made. A bunch of bomb-grade rings of highly enriched uranium placed edge-wise and parallel to each other in a howitzer barrel. Our howitzer nuke is the same. The ends of the barrel are tamped shut. One group of HEU rings is backed with extra-high explosive. That group of rings is six feet from its target HEU. The explosive-backed HEU—the so-called bullet—will blast into the target. Scientists called it 'the gun-barrel bomb' because the HEU is housed in a howitzer 'gun barrel.'"

"You're shitting me," Hanif said, amazed. "We're giving America an atom bomb as a Mexican War anniversary present?"

"It'll be an anniversary they'll never forget," Jamil said, nodding. "It'll make 9/11 look like a Ramadan prayer meeting."

"I wish Osama were here to see it," Dawad said.

"He'd laugh his ass off," Adman said.

"We'll laugh extra hard for him," Hanif said.

"They'll be having a grand old time honoring the grand old Bear Flag. The flag itself will be up and flapping in the breeze in all its glory. The governor of California, the secretary of energy, San Francisco's mayor, a bunch of nuclear power officials, and a mob of tourists and plant employees will be in attendance. When the officials pull the black velvet shrouds off the two statues, the local high school band will play 'Stars and Stripes Forever,' and a half dozen men with old rifles, wearing what will presumably be Bear Flag Revolt uniforms, will fire a five-round volley salute."

"What part do we play?" Dawad asked sleepily.

"We'll be up here on the far edge of this hill with a remote detonator," Jamil said. "We'll have earplugs, very dark glasses, plain white clothes, white gym shoes, and lots of iodine tablets. Also heavy layers of fifty SPF sunscreen. When we hit the remote, we will instantly race down the opposite side of this hill."

"I may be too tired to race down any hills," Dawad said.

"Your work will pay off. The days and nights we were driving here," Jamil said, "then working our asses off, installing the detonator and welding the tamps shut. The last seventy-two hours we worked around the clock, no breaks."

"So we were loading that cannon onto the limber," Dawad said, "so the delivery crew could haul it here and roll it up next to the bear statue."

"I have to admit," Hanif said, "I'm amazed."

"Oh, it'll be even more amazing after the bomb goes off," Jamil said. "All those wildfires due east of here have changed the wind patterns. Prevailing winds tomorrow are predicted to blow to the west, straight toward San Francisco. Those winds will blanket the city of St. Francis with shockingly toxic radioactivity."

"Will it really be that bad?" Dawad asked.

"Know why no one has ever ground-tested a nuclear weapon?" Jamil asked. "Set one off that's flush on the ground? The sheer quantity of fallout would be so prodigious, so inconceivably lethal it would kill over time almost every living thing in a radius of a hundred miles. Even worse, that kill zone would remain lethal to human beings for at least tens of thousands of years."

"So the City on the Bay is going to eat a trillion tons of radioactive dirt," Dawad said.

"We're burying it alive in eternally toxic shit," Jamil said.

2

The tape would not attract attention.

D ressed in his blue officer's uniform, Elias passed through the three detectors—metal first, then explosives, then the radiation detector. As usual, he cut through the Administration Building—the most direct route to his work site. As a tower guard, he attracted no troublesome attention.

Elias had had no difficulty finding duplicate work clothes and counterfeit IDs for the men. Plant security would find distinguishing between the attackers and their fellow workers almost impossible—at least at first glance. When they cut through the cyclone fence that night and sneaked into the plant, they would look exactly like the real guards and technicians.

For the guard impersonators, Elias had obtained blue pants and matching jackets, white shirts, black shoes, and plastic-encased IDs to be strung around the neck in clear cardholders. For his fake techs, he'd gotten white coveralls and white lab coats. Such clothing was widely available and used in many industries. The difference was that his men would have shoulder-slung silenced MP5 Personal Defense Weapons under their jackets and coats.

The lobby was sixty feet by eighty feet with a twenty-foot-high ceiling. Elias briefly noted the rear wall. At least two dozen computer screens were mounted on it. Surveillance cameras, indoors and out, dutifully recorded the plant's daily activities and transmitted the footage to those rack-mounted wall monitors.

A half dozen uniformed guards sat on stools at a long row of high black desks. They greeted guests and studied the bank of computer monitors on the desktop before them.

They waved Elias through with terse "Hi's" as he walked through a maze of hallways following the exit signs to the building's rear doors.

Exiting the rear of the building, he saw the two white concrete-and-steel reactor containment domes. Flanking the one on the left was the Auxiliary Building, which housed most of the plant's backup equipment. Once inside the Auxiliary Building, he waved to Mazini, who was marking the emergency pumps and generators for demolition with Xs fashioned out of duct tape. Plant foremen frequently marked equipment in that manner for repair. The tape would not attract attention.

The overhead coolant tanks were so gargantuan, so glaringly visible that they required no such signage.

3

"You don't want twenty thousand fuel rods burning up on you."
—John Selke

Mazini passed through the Administration Building and entered the courtyard. The main control center—a big gray structure made of concrete blocks—was dead ahead.

Entering the Control Building, Mazini went down the hall, took two turns, and reached the control room. When he entered, he went straight to the coffee station. As his two operators waved to him, Mazini toasted them with a cup of coffee and waved back. They immediately regaled him with shouts of "Hey wop" and "Yo dago." He encouraged their mistaken belief—in fact, laughed right along with them—since he did not want them to know his grandfather had been Pakistani. No one in the firm ever traced his ancestry back to Pakistan, the homeland of his grandfather, and he liked it that way. He even peppered his diction with Italianisms and periodically cooked ravioli, manicotti, and lasagna at home and brought it frozen for his fellow workers to reheat in the microwave.

Mazini entered the big windowless bunker that was the control room. He remembered the first day he entered it, shocked by its sheer size—fifty by a hundred feet, filled with endless arrays of computers, monitors, panels, alarms, and blinking lights. It had taken him a few years before he had learned enough to run it, and he always stayed in awe of it. A world unto itself, it was the nerve center of the facility. Its computers controlled the plant's water circulation; turbine, steam, and electrical generators; the condensate-feedwater loop; reactor and storage coolant systems; pumps; the reactors' control rods; and the emergency support systems. It even monitored the plant's key installations and areas on the computer screens along the north wall.

In the control room, Mazini was responsible for the cooling of twenty thousand fuel rods and well over two tons of spent fuel. Tonight, he would set them all ablaze and kill everyone in the plant, to say nothing of the millions of people living within a hundred-mile radius. He would turn the Tri-State area, including New York City, into a charnal house of nuclear annihilation and a permanently toxic waste dump.

He felt no remorse over the violence to come. He knew in his soul that he was bringing a sort of rough justice to the people at the Hudson River Nuclear Power Station, at least to those who were in charge of the plant—an operation that Mazini viewed as morally monstrous as anything in the history of the Free Enterprise System.

As for those friends and colleagues who would die tonight? How much feeling did they have for those innocent men, women, and children in Iraq who only sought to protect their land from the Infidel Invaders?

Mazini walked over to the horizontal bench board, whose panels controlled the operating equipment. On the wall above that bench board was a colored mimic panel, which showed the status of the valves—whether they were open, closed, or in midposition. It also depicted the state of the pumps—whether they were running or not. Directly in front of Mazini were the middle panels of meters and computer monitors, which alerted him to the operating conditions.

His main job was to manage the reactors' radioactivity and to filter, then pump fifty million gallons of Hudson River water per hour—or fifteen thousand gallons a second—into the plant to cool the reactors' fuel rods and the station's nuclear waste. The water, which the fuel rods boiled, was turned to steam, which powered the twin turbines, located in the huge one-hundred-foot-high Turbine Building. Those dynamos generated the plant's electrical energy.

"How did the three-to-eleven shift go?" Mazini asked the man he was relieving.

"The fuel rods are running a little hot," John Selke, the previous shift operator, said. He was a tall, handsome engineer in a white lab coat and matching pants. A former all-state basketball player, he had a ready grin and a love of sports. He was captain of the HRNPS sixteen-man softball team. A dead pull hitter, he could hammer those oversize balls almost four hundred feet. No one knew where all the power came from.

"They usually do," Mazini said with a shrug.

"Still, you should watch the coolant pumps," Selke said. "I marked them for inspection later in this shift."

"I'll ask a millwright to look at them," Mazini said.

"The problem might be electrical," Selke pointed out.

"If the millwrights can't find anything," Mazini said, "I'll ask electrical to inspect them."

"Do that," Selke said. "You don't want twenty thousand fuel rods burning up on you."

Oh yeah? Mazini thought sardonically. *Maybe* you *don't.*

4

The nuclear storage casks looked like cement corn silos.

Elias exited the Auxiliary Building. On his way to the primary gun tower, he called Mazini on his cell.

"You're marking all the backup pumps and emergency generators for the men. Are you squared away?"

"I'm on it."

"Good."

Elias clicked off. He was walking past the two dozen concrete-and-steel dry nuclear storage casks. Situated out in the open, in plain sight, they were painted industrial gray and looked like cement corn silos.

Turning right, he headed toward two twelve-foot-high parallel wire-topped cyclone fences. Between them, seventy-five yards from the front gate, was a gun tower. A five-story concrete blockhouse, it had a thick steel door facing the inside of the plant. The interior security fence abutted the tower.

At the front door, Elias punched in his code, and the tower bull buzzed him in.

Entering the tower, he walked up to the heavy steel spiral stairs and began his long climb up to the tower house, where he would relieve the evening guard.

It was eleven at night and the man had put in a twelve-hour shift.

Elias would now begin his.

PART XVIII

Now the brother shall betray the brother to death, and the father the son; and children shall rise up against their parents, and shall cause them to be put to death.... For in those days shall be afflic- tion, such as was not from the beginning of the creation which God created unto this time, neither shall be ... and the powers that are in heaven shall be shaken.

—Mark 13:12,19

1

"This whole government was built by slaves."
—George Caldwell, Jr.

Shaiq was in his legendary gold limo with the First Lady and her queru-lous children. Her two kids had not wanted to attend the address, and they constantly treated their mother and Shaiq to tirades about how un-happy they were.

"Hey, Mom," the girl, Judy Caldwell, asked, "what's the big deal about this boring speech and this boring Capitol Building anyway?"

The Caldwells' blond-haired eight-year-old daughter, Judy wore a blue and white dress with thin blue stripes and black shoes. She sat directly across from Shaiq. Next to her was seated her seven-year-old brother, George, Jr. Red-haired and freckled, he wore a black suit and a white shirt with no tie. He fussed continually with the collar and looked miserable.

"Children, the ambassador here knows more about Washington, D.C., than anyone I've ever met, including most of our senators and congressmen." Emily Caldwell gripped Shaiq's hand with both of her own. "Please, tell the children a little about this building where their father will be speaking to-night and why the speech is important."

"Of course," Shaiq said with a superior smile. "This building is the capi-tol of your nation's capital. Finished in 1800, the city's four quadrants meet at this edifice, and here the streets begin their numbering. So in a sense, it is the district's nerve center. Its white granite and marble façade and its mas-sive dome make the capitol visible to the people here for miles around. At night, when lit up, it appears from a distance as a pale, almost alabaster pres-ence, a luminous symbol of everything America is and everything she will eventually be."

Eight-year-old Judy stared at him with wide, innocent, light blue eyes and said, "My teacher says we forced black slaves to build it."

"And when they didn't work hard enough," George said, "we whipped them."

"Your teacher was right," Shaiq said. "Some of the workers were freed slaves, but many of them weren't."

"What's that ugly thing on the dome's top?" Judy asked.

"It's a huge cast-iron statue called Freedom. It weighs almost eight tons," Shaiq said.

"Why's it so ugly?" George wanted to know.

"Its name is 'the Statue of Freedom,' and it's not ugly," Shaiq countered. "The sculptor's depicting Freedom as a woman warrior in the style of the ancient Romans and Greeks. She wears a Chilton, or toga, and her helmet is topped with an eagle. In one hand she grips the sheathed sword of battle and in the other the laurel wreath of victory. Her war is over now. The Statue of Liberty could be viewed as her protégé, what Freedom can evolve into after the wars are over."

"It was also made by slaves," Judy announced.

"This whole government was built by slaves," George said.

"And we whipped them if they didn't work hard enough," Judy said, nodding vigorously.

Their mother cleared her throat. "White people built lots of things, too, children. Now Mr. Ambassador, tell them where we'll be seated and where their father will speak."

"We will sit in the gallery—" Shaiq started to say.

"What's a gallery?" Judy asked. Now she was starting to fidget.

"A big balcony," Shaiq said.

"It was also built by slaves," George said knowingly.

"And did we whip them, too?" Judy asked.

"Children," their mother said. "Let the ambassador tell you about the House chamber. Try not to interrupt."

"It has many, many seats. Those on the floor run in a semicircle, and the representatives have 448 permanent seats. The senators have a hundred. The rest are for visitors. Tonight, we will be visitors."

"Mr. Ambassador," Judy interrupted, "does your country have slaves?"

Rolling back her eyes, the First Lady stared at the ambassador.

"And do you also whip them?" George asked.

The First Lady looked ready to explode.

2

"An eighty-two-year-old nun with a heart condition broke into the Y-12 nuclear storage facility, and it took several hours to detect her. We'll be fine."

—Hamzi Udeen

A lone man in a blue security guard's uniform hid in the thick trees watching the highway. The last security jeep had just driven past, making its hourly rounds. He and his men had an hour to cut through the two chainlink fences and tie the rent back into place with thin strands of aluminum wire in an attempt to conceal the fence tears from passing guard patrols. They then had to sneak into the wooded grounds beyond the double fences. The lone man dog-trotted back up the twisting dirt road toward the big Chevy van parked deep in the trees. Filled with his fourteen men, it was concealed from the highway by the dense woods.

Hamzi tapped on the rear window. The door swung open, and the men began climbing out. They wore either the white lab coats of the techs or the guards' blue security uniforms. They all had professionally counterfeited plant IDs and badges with conforming IDs in their wallets. Their short hair was colored brown, gray, or blond. Hamzi had made them each shave three times.

Under their coats and security-guard jackets were slung the short, silenced MP5 submachine guns along with silenced 9mm pistols holstered inside their pants. They kept extra magazines and other ordnance in their backpacks. Several of them carried duffel bags filled with shaped charges, rocket grenade launchers, and other weapons.

"We're on a special investigation," Hamzi said to them in a voice just above a whisper, "if anyone asks."

"They'll probably think we work here," Amir said.

"And if they don't," Fahad said, "we can kill them."

Amir nodded. "But we should be okay. We're indistinguishable from the over eleven hundred employees working here. The turnover's huge. No one knows who's who."

"Okay," Hamzi said. "One last time. Amir, you and your team are taking

276 | ROBERT GLEASON

out the silos—dry and wet. Fahad, your men are helping Mazini with the Reactor Containment Building and the Auxiliary Building. Elias and Mazini will have marked the pumps and generators with duct taped Xs. Fahad and I will tape C-4 to the pumps, intake pipes, and emergency generators. As soon as the attack commences, Amir will blow holes in the bottoms and lower sides of the tanks with RPGs. Elias has stashed the launchers in a maintenance storage closet in the Auxiliary Building. It's to your right—one hundred feet from the front door. A taped X will be on that, too.

"Now, you have Mazini's number programmed into your cell phones. You have maps and photos in your belt bags. I will point the buildings out to you. Everyone got it?

"We're at a blind spot in the fence. The perimeter is too enormous for effective surveillance and the cameras never work. Neither do the motion detectors. They get hundreds of false alarms nightly—deer, coyotes, raccoons, stray dogs and cats. Hell, an eighty-two-year-old nun with a heart condition broke into the Y-12 nuclear storage facility, and it took several hours to detect her. We'll be fine."

They fast-walked up the dirt road to the highway. Checking to see that no one was around, they jogged across the road. Hamzi got a pair of twelve-inch Tekton bolt cutters out from under his belt and quickly clipped a large L-shaped tear in the chain-link fence.

3

If you're going to greet the Reaper tonight, you might as well meet him with a grin on.
—Elias Edito

Elias was on the gun tower's steel catwalk. Six stories aboveground, it circumscribed the tower room and afforded him a commanding view of the entire Hudson River Nuclear Power Station. More important, however, he could also stare up Highway 9, the two-lane road in front of the plant that ran due east, to where it crossed Highway 12. North of the intersection, on Highway 12, was a New York National Guard base. Ten miles south of the junction was a state police station. In case of attack, those two forces would be the first responders.

Elias could see the intersection of H-9 and H-12 clearly. It was a moonlit, windless, cloudless night. The crossroads was well lit and 234 yards away. He knew the precise distance because he'd measured it on his pedometer and had adjusted one of his rifle scopes for that exact range. Elias felt good.

When he finally saw a man step out of the nearby trees, it was 9:45 P.M. He was wearing a plant security guard uniform and had a heavy navy-blue seabag over his shoulder. Elias hung his Northern pulley hoist on the top catwalk rail, wound the line through it, then dropped it down to the man approaching the tower. Lashing the big seabag to the rope, the man jogged back to the tree line. Elias quickly pulled the heavy bag up to the catwalk, dragged it into the tower room, and shut the steel door behind him.

The room was twelve feet by twelve feet with a ten-foot-high ceiling. It had steel floors, low steel walls, and bullet-resistant Lexan windows. If the guards had to fire their rifles, they were expected to do so from the catwalk. Were anyone to return fire, the guards were under orders to take refuge in the tower room and to call in the National Guard and the state police. Plant security was not trained or equipped to confront serious opposition.

The furnishings weren't much. He spent a good deal of his time at the small desk, on which he wrote out his nightly reports. Since a guard was expected to observe the plant and its grounds at all times, the bathroom facilities were exposed. Even seated on the toilet, Elias could see out the Lexan windows. At night, the post was essentially dark, so no one could see in. There were panel heaters for winter and an air conditioner for summer, which was currently broken. In the middle was a steel swivel stool on which the guards could sit. To his left was the locked, gray, metal gun box, six feet long, rectangular in shape. The tower bulls universally referred to it as "the coffin." Some of the tower guards brought blankets and slept on the gun box—particularly those who also worked day jobs. It was strictly forbidden, but no one could check on the officer without getting buzzed in first. It was almost impossible to catch them.

Nothing ever happened at the facility anyway. Why would anyone want to break into a power plant? Plant personnel said that all the time, usually with a laugh. Elias smiled grimly at the thought.

He opened up the gun box and took out the AR-15 7.62mm NATO semiautomatic assault rifle and a dozen magazines. For anything under three hundred yards, it would do. He placed it on the floor. He removed the 12-gauge Remington pump shotgun along with five ten-round boxes of double-ought buck. He laid the boxes of shells down alongside the AR-15.

He lifted the big canvas seabag onto the gun bin. He dragged out the Barrett M82 .50 caliber heavy vehicle sniper rifle and a dozen preloaded magazines. It was a de facto antitank, antiaircraft weapon. Then he dug out a 9mm Glock in a nylon holster plus silencer and magazines, as well as a Ka-Bar combat knife in a nylon belt sheath. Those last three were his evacuation weapons. Next to it he placed more magazines, grenades, and boxes of phosphorus rounds on the floor. Digging around in the bag, he finally found the file with which he would carve firing grooves onto the rails.

At the bag's bottom, he found the olive-drab army surplus ammo box. It was secured with a combination lock. Lifting it onto the desk, he opened it. Inside was a liter bottle of a 101-proof Wild Turkey and two six-packs of half quart Colt 45 in cans.

If you're going to greet the Reaper tonight, you might as well meet him with a grin on.

Almost immediately, Elias spotted Fahad's men on the plant grounds below. They had broken up into two-to-three-man groups, which were spread out along the main roadway over an area of around 150 yards. Dressed in white tech clothes and guards' uniforms, their presence in no way looked out of place. He did not see how they would attract undue attention.

The men had earpieces and part of his assignment was to advise them of any approaching trouble.

"So far so good," he said softly. "The guards haven't reported anything. They're probably asleep by now."

Two groups were now moving casually toward the Auxiliary Building. Four more men were heading toward the two Reactor Containment Buildings on the right of the Auxiliary Building. Two more men strolled past the Turbine Building and went into the huge sheet-steel shed, housing the belowground spent fuel rod storage pools. Behind and to the right was the even larger sheet-steel warehouse-sized shed containing the aboveground nuclear waste storage ponds, which two more men were approaching. The final group continued on to the dry casks, containing partially cooled spent rods. Those eight silos were on an aboveground concrete platform. They were out in the open.

4

"We get the chance to film a group of heavily armed terrorists turn a nuclear power plant into a raging volcano of radioactive fire."

—Jules Meredith

Jules sat in the jump seat of an AS350 AStar news chopper that was parked at a small helipad eight miles south of the Hudson River nuclear plant. Her friend, colleague, and sister, Sandy Meredith, stood next to the chopper staring up at her. She was dressed, like Jules, in blue jeans and a T-shirt. Sandy wore a Windbreaker instead of a black hooded sweatshirt. They both wore baseball caps—Jules the Yankees, Sandy the Mets. Jules, however, wore hers on under her hood and also sported wrap-around shades.

An independent producer-reporter who worked primarily for MTN, the world's largest cable news network, Sandy specialized in filming impossible-to-get segments, particularly combat footage. The two sisters had covered wars all over the world but mostly in the Mideast—Iran, Iraq, Syria, Lebanon, Pakistan, Yemen, Gaza, Israel, and Afghanistan. They'd flown in thousands of news and military choppers during their journalism careers, sometimes with Elena.

"You know I could go to prison for this," Sandy said with a wry smile as she swung up into the cockpit and dropped down into the pilot's seat.

"I have a 9mm Wilson," Jules said. "We'll tell them I held it on you the whole time."

"And my own reason for going along with you—other than another opportunity to lie to the police, abet an international terrorist, and face certain death or life in prison—is . . . ?"

"If we fail, we get the chance to film a group of heavily armed terrorists turn a nuclear power plant into a raging volcano of radioactive fire," Jules explained.

"And this is also where I get the chance to have a squadron of Phantom jets blast forty or fifty heat-seeking missiles up my ass, blowing me straight into hell and gone with flames shooting out of every gaping orifice of my body?"

"If we get there in time, we can transmit out footage to the military and the state police. We can stop these guys."

"We could alert the authorities now," Sandy said.

"Won't work. Jamie tried to convince the FBI and failed."

"The FBI didn't believe Jamie?" Sandy asked, shocked. "He built their whole antiterrorist computer system."

"They think *we're* the terrorists. *We're* the only ones they want to catch and kill."

"Jamie couldn't even convince his friend at the Bureau?"

"He said it was like talking to an Easter Island statue."

"I can't believe that," Sandy said again, still incredulous.

"He described their response as 'a black hole of skepticism,' and he was talking to an old friend way the fuck up the food chain."

"Okay," Sandy said, "suppose the feds are wrong. Suppose the terrorists do hit this place and melt it down. What happens then?"

"HRNPS will spew fallout, soot, fiery debris, poison, and nuclear death all over the Northeast, fatally irradiating a minimum of twenty million people, transmogrifying the Tri-State area into a terminally toxic waste dump for maybe a hundred thousand years."

"In other words, I also get to die from radiation sickness?"

"Not if the terrorists kill us first."

"I like it," Sandy said, giving her sister an insidious grin. "In the immortal words of Gary Gilmore, 'Let's do it.'"

She started the big Lycoming LTS101 turboshaft engine and the three-blade Starflex rotor began turning. Sandy gradually opened the throttle, cranking up the RPMs. After she lifted the left-hand control lever and the chopper pitched forward, she partially depressed the left pedal with her foot. Lifting the control lever higher and pushing the left pedal again, the chopper rose. Even as she adjusted the vertical stick protruding between her legs, she continued to work the control lever and pedals. Slowly, the chopper leveled out. Heading due north, she eased the stick left, heading northwest toward the Hudson River Nuclear Power Station.

PART XIX

And I looked, and behold a pale horse: and his name that sat on him was Death, and Hell followed with him.

—Revelation 6:8

1

Hamzi shot him in the face between his two pressed hands.

Mazini sat in front of the big board in the control room. He'd spent the last half hour lifting fuel rods out of their coolant and locking them into place. Soon they would catch fire, and all hell would break loose.

Inside the bunker-like control room, he heard the door buzzer. Someone wanted to enter. Mazini got up and buzzed him in. It was Hamzi, dressed in the white lab clothes of a tech. Mazini's two assistant operators were also approaching, returning from their dinner break. Hamzi walked up to Raymond first, reaching out as if to shake hands.

"Raymond," Mazini began, "meet—"

As Raymond leaned toward Hamzi, smiling, Hamzi removed a silenced Glock from under his white lab coat and shot him an inch and a half above the left eye. The other assistant, recognizing what was happening, immediately pressed both hands against his face and shouted, "No, God, no!"

Hamzi shot him in the face between his two pressed hands. When the hands dropped, Mazini saw he'd hit the man squarely in the center of his face, giving him a bloody gaping hole where his nose had been.

Mazini felt a twinge of regret for the dead men, but only for a second. Hell was about to break out in the HRNPS sooner than he expected. The three men from the Auxiliary Building—also dressed in white tech attire—were coming through the side door, guns cocked, locked, and pressed against their legs. They had already mined the pumps and generators in that other building.

Soon hard, sharp, muffled shots were popping all around the No. 1 Containment Building. Finally, the men in his building gave him the thumbs-ups and he headed for the front door. Their mission was also accomplished, and it was time to move on.

They exited the front and side doors in small groups in an attempt to appear inconspicuous—to blend in with the night shift. Hamzi had the remote detonator under his coat along with his own Glock, stuffed under his front waistband. Up in his gun tower, Elias, acting as the chief coordinator, would soon give him the signal, and Hamzi would press the hot button.

2

Heartbreak dead ahead.

Hunched aerodynamically over the handle bars, blasting up I-95 on Jamie's Kawasaki Ninja H2, Elena Moreno was riding the fastest commercially made street bike in the world. In an ebony leather jacket, matching pants, and a jet-black helmet with a darkly tinted windscreen, she looked like a kill-crazed ninja. All she could feel was the gale-force wind hammering her helmet, windscreen, and shoulders. All she could hear was its roar in her ears and the thunder roll of her blood.

Shifting into fourth, she cranked the throttle up, up, up. Hazarding a glance at the speedometer, she saw it was now well over 100, then 110, then 120, then 130 mph. Keeping her eyes on the center line and the vehicles ahead, she struggled to stay focused. She had to do this full throttle—screw the fuzz, the highway, the cars, the bomb, death itself. Elena was now doing 160 on a crowded D.C. interstate. Lurching in and out of traffic, passing speeding automobiles like they were roadkill, she heard only the blare of their angry horns, her tires screaming, the engine howling, the wind's roar, and the wild wailing of her soul.

Fuck 'em all but six and save them for pallbearers.

One heart-stopping, nerve-fraying, hair-frying turn and she was rocketing north up I-395. Her supercharged ninja bike—with its 210-horsepower engine—was barely five hundred pounds and had a max speed that easily topped 200 mph. With the power and torque of a race car and one-fifth the weight, it could go from 0 to 65 mph in two and a half seconds.

If the rider could hold on.

And, oh, Elena could hold on.

Slowing to 80 mph, she swung onto Pennsylvania Avenue, burning rubber all the way. Angling north onto Fourth Street, she spotted the Capitol Needle Hotel—a towering, ultrathin hotel edifice of glass and steel—on East Capitol Street. According to Jamie, on the penthouse floor, with a 360-degree view of D.C., her old college boyfriend, Hasad ibn Ghazi, was waiting with a nuclear detonator in his hand.

Heartbreak dead ahead.

Slowing, she turned into the hotel entrance. Limos were lined up, drivers helping their affluent employers out of the vehicles while hotel workers rounded up their bags.

Elena went straight to the head of the limo line, jumped free of the bike, and yanked off her helmet. With her short, platinum-bleached hair, Ray-Ban Aviator sunglasses and raccoon eye makeup—a style Jules derided as "hooker couture"—she was not recognizable as the violent fugitive whose photo was now adorning every newspaper and TV screen worldwide.

And anyway, when she shook hands with the uniformed doorman and he glimpsed the five folded $100 bills in his fist, he was instantly oblivious to her face. All he saw was the currency.

"Leave it here up front," Elena said. "I'll be back in ten minutes."

"I'll attend to it personally," he said, surreptitiously pocketing the cash.

"More where that came from," Elena whispered sweetly, kissing his cheek.

She entered the big automatic glass doors and crossed the palatial lobby toward the penthouse elevator.

3

One by one, Fahad dropped them into the cooling pools.

By the time Fahad—dressed in white laboratory clothes—entered the vast, sprawling sheet-steel shed housing the belowground spent fuel pool, the last of the sharp silenced pops had died away and the building was pacified. A duffel bag bulging with a dozen Krakatoa shaped charges hung from his shoulder. The platform overlooking the sunken pool was a dozen feet above the ground. Fahad took the steel steps two at a time to the catwalk encircling it and overlooking the two silo-sized ponds.

This one was at least twenty feet across. Its exterior walls were reinforced concrete, four and a half feet thick and twenty-five feet deep. A dozen feet of water covered the hundreds of spent fuel assemblies, each of which held over two hundred spent fuel rods.

He took the first of the Krakatoa charges out of his bag. The size of Coke cans, they were each painted a dark gray and had thick, heavy lead slugs duct taped around the armor-piercing end of their copper-plated noses. The extra weight would assure that the charge—after dropping through a dozen feet of H_2O—would reach the spent fuel assemblies with the business end pointed into them. Then when the charge exploded and the copper plate metamorphosed into a sharply pointed armor-piercing artillery shell, it would blast through the spent fuel assemblies and protective cladding with unstoppable kinetic energy.

At the bottom of the bag, Fahad had a dozen phosphorous incendiary charges as well. They would guarantee the assemblies were set aflame.

The first of the Krakatoa charges was preconnected with twenty feet of insulated copper wire affixed to the charge. When he hooked it up to his detonator and pressed the button, the explosion would sympathetically detonate the pool's other impact-fused charges.

He began removing charges from their seabag. One by one, Fahad dropped them into the cooling pools.

4

"The Divine Hand of Manifest Destiny."
—Governor Walter G. Arnett

In the late afternoon, Jamil and his two friends stood at the top of a hill. At its base a mile or so away was the Teller Lab. They studied it through binoculars. The two Saudi gifts to the lab were still concealed by the black velvet shrouds.

The five men were tired but pleased.

The lab's park area was packed with almost a thousand people seated in grandstands, many of them employees who were able to leave their job for a few hours. This was California, and most of the crowd was dressed in shorts, T-shirts, and sandals. The overflow stood under trees or sat on blankets on the grass. The weather was bright, sunny, and close to a hundred degrees. On a small grandstand behind the podium, two dozen dignitaries were seated. The men wore summer suits of soft gray, pale green, and powder blue. The governor—the Honorable Walter G. Arnett—looked particularly distinguished in his gray goatee and mustache, white linen suit, red tie, and a Panama hat of bleached straw. The women were decked out in summer dresses and heels. Even under the three big beach-style umbrellas—two at the ends of the grandstand and one in back—the dignitaries sweated profusely. Several cooled themselves with fans.

At the podium, Secretary of Energy Harold Reeves was just finishing his speech. Dressed in a light-blue seersucker suit, he was so hot he'd been forced to loosen his tie and fan himself continuously. He'd just finished extolling the work of the employees and was now thanking them for "their irreplaceable labor on the front lines of geopolitical deterrence."

The local radio station was broadcasting the speeches in the lab's park, and Jamil and his friends could hear them on their black Sony ICF-38 radio.

"The Edward Teller Lab keeps the peace," Reeves thundered, "by fearlessly forging the nuclear sword. Americans will sleep safe in their beds tonight because you are extending and expanding our nuclear might."

After the energy secretary finished, the managing director of the lab,

Howard Roseman, went to the podium. A balding man with a bulging paunch, he was dressed in a light-weight lemon-colored suit, a yellow shirt, and green tie. Summoning all the hype and hyperbole at his command, he went on to extoll the governor for his work in the aerospace industry before taking office, as well as the nearly twenty years he'd spent working for Hardrock Enterprises International, the world's nuclear contractor.

Tall, craggy, rugged-looking, Governor Arnett stood, took off his hat, placed it on his chair, and went to the podium. Raising the adjustable mike until it was at mouth level, he began with the usual pro forma acknowledgments. After thanking the various personages, including the energy secretary, San Francisco's mayor, and the lab's directors and employees, he addressed the lab's purpose, its raison d'etre:

"Why are we celebrating this glorious day at the world's foremost research center for nuclear arms? The same reason our close friend and ally, Shaiq ibn Ishaq, the dear and trusted Saudi ambassador to the United States, is honoring the lab with two magnificent gifts. He is donating them to the lab as symbols of his nation's love for the American people and out of respect for those hard at work at the Edward Teller Nuclear Weapons Laboratory, who are so resolutely defending the free world.

"We are also here to honor the great patriot who, 175 years ago, shed so much blood and treasure to set California free, to throw off the yoke of Mexican oppression. We are here to honor the great James K. Polk, one of our country's most audaciously farseeing presidents, a man who envisioned an America whose amber waves of grain and whose purple mountains' majesty would stretch across the fruited plain from sea to shining sea, a man who recognized the Divine Hand of Manifest Destiny and who grasped it, who refused to be a doormat for Mexican aggression, and who stood up to the Mexican tyrant on our southern border.

"We are here to honor the other great American patriots who also struggled to free California—those intrepid heroes of the great Bear Flag Revolt, to whom we Californians owe so much; Captain John Fremont—author, explorer, man of war; James Sutter, who—"

Suddenly, the energy secretary came to the podium, took the governor's arm, and interrupted.

"Governor, if I may interrupt for a moment. As we all know, the president has assembled the Senate, Congress, the cabinet, and most of the country's military and political leadership for a message of overwhelming national security importance. In the interests of national security and all those assembled, we are going to pipe his speech in over our loudspeaker system. Here now is the president of the United States. . . ."

5

They were about to pulverize those silos with some very heavy ordnance.

When Amir entered the massive sheet-steel shed, which housed the vertical aboveground spent fuel pool, he was relieved to see his men had already disposed of the six techs working inside. They were dragging their bloody bodies into a corner.

After his men sequestered the bodies, Amir ordered them to leave.

He and Mustafa now had the building to themselves, which was just as well. When they finished with the big concrete storage silos, no one was going to want to be near them.

The silo sat on its own concrete-and-steel platform at opposite ends of the sprawling warehouse-sized structure. The sheet-steel shed was over eighty feet high and seventy-five yards across—longer than a football field. It may have been the biggest single room Amir had ever entered, and his team would need at least that much space. They were supposed to be at least seventy-five yards from the Krakatoa charges when they went off.

His men now dragged the shoulder-launched FGM-148 Javelin out of their seabag, unfolded its tripod, and bolted the TOW missile launcher onto its mount. They loaded a nineteen-pound tandem warhead into the launcher's breech and locked it in. Its two consecutive warheads would strike the Krakatoa within nanoseconds of each other. The precursor charge in the first warhead would hit the Krakatoa, driving it into the wall of the pool silo, while the second, even more powerful shaped charge would almost instantaneously blast into both the Krakatoa and the precursor, its own detonation exponentially increasing their destructiveness. The synergist, force-multiplying combination of the three charges would shatter the thick concrete-and-steel silo wall with such shaped, sharply pointed explosive force that it would crater the cask with almost indescribable violence.

They looked up at each other and nodded. This could be rough going.

They were about to pulverize those silos with some very heavy ordnance.

6

"The snake in our blissful Eden."
—President George Caldwell

With studied insouciance, the broadcaster, Linda Rodriguez—an attractive Hispanic reporter with large dark eyes—tossed a long twisting coil of gleaming black hair over her front shoulder. She was elegantly attired in an ebony evening dress. Linda wore no jewelry except for the single strand of Tahitian black pearls adorning her throat. She was introducing the president from the anchor booth:

"Here he comes, President George Caldwell, entering the hall of Congress. A dozen steps behind him—and fashionably late—is the Saudi ambassador to the United States, Prince Shaiq ibn Ishaq. He is escorting the president's wife and two children; they are headed for the presidential box."

Linda's blond-haired tuxedoed co-anchor, Brad Williams, laughed. "The ambassador is reputedly the richest man in the world, and he brought the president's family here in style. Did you see their arrival on East Capitol Street?"

"How could anyone miss it? They showed up in Ambassador Shaiq ibn Ishaq's gold limo."

"The most expensive limo money can buy," Williams said. "I heard the sultan of Brunei has one like it. Cost him $14 million. Wonder who got his first?"

"Knowing the ambassador, it was probably him."

"Here, let's look at some earlier footage of the ambassador," Brad Williams said, "when he was riding up to the Capitol Building in it." Footage of the ambassador's gold limo appeared on national television, heading toward the Capitol Building. "Get that footage up on the screen. There he is. There's the footage now."

"The president's people tell us Shaiq is President Caldwell's closest friend in Washington," Linda said. "I guess that's why he's got the First Lady and the president's two kids with him."

An earlier clip of Ambassador Shaiq ibn Ishaq's gold limo was now on television sets around the country. The limo was stuck in a paralyzing traffic jam half a block from the Capitol Building. The ambassador, the children, and the First Lady were helped out by black-suited Secret Service agents with cuff mikes and sunglasses.

"It's nice to know that even the super-rich get stuck in the traffic," Linda said with a high, tinkling laugh.

"Just like the rest of us," Brad agreed. "On the other hand, they did arrive here in a Rolls-Royce Silver Spur stretch limo plated with twenty-four-karat gold. That's not how the rest of us drive to these events."

"I'll say," Linda concurred. "Look at that limo! How's that for big bucks?"

"If you got it, flaunt it!" Brad shouted, laughing.

"Something tells me no Secret Service agents are searching that car with crowbars and monkey wrenches," Linda said. "Scratch that thing, and the ambassador's lawyers will own you."

"Let's cut back to the chamber. Linda, can you give us a little background on State of the Union addresses?"

"Sure, Brad. Article two, section three of the Constitution requires that the president of the United States give 'from time to time information on the State of the Union.' Now there's nothing in the Constitution dictating when the president must deliver such a speech. Tradition has typically determined the timing of the speech, its form, and indeed the place where it was delivered. In fact, for over a hundred years, it wasn't delivered at all but handed up to Congress in written form. FDR was the first president to deliver one at night."

"So President Caldwell's decision to deliver a State of the Union address on July Fourth does not violate the Constitution?" Brad asked.

"Not in the least. All the Constitution requires is that these speeches are to be given 'from time to time.' Now the four hundred plus House and Senate members are in their seats. Here come the House Speaker and the Senate majority leader escorting the president into the House chamber."

"As we all know, the vice president is recovering from an appendectomy in the Bethesda Naval Hospital."

"I'm sure, though, that he's watching us on TV," Linda said, waving at the camera. "Hi there, Mr. VP."

"Hi, indeed," Brad said. "Here comes the president, entering the chamber. The sergeant at arms is announcing his presence."

"Mr. Speaker, the president of the United States!" the sergeant's voice roared.

Amid cheers and applause, the president worked his way toward the Speaker's rostrum, where he would address the audience.

"No copies of his speech have been circulated," Brad said, "so he doesn't have to stop and sign them for any adoring onlookers."

"Just so. A few handshakes and that's it. Now he's there at the rostrum."

The Speaker began introducing the president.

"Members of Congress, I have the high privilege and distinct honor of presenting to you, the president of the United States."

The president took over the rostrum.

After the usual litany of greetings and thank you's, shout-outs, and hand waves, President Caldwell began his speech.

"Some of you may wonder why we are interrupting your wonderful Fourth of July celebrations for this State of the Union address. It is because the Ship of State is in grave peril. At this very moment, tyrants abroad—just as in the day of our Founding Fathers—threaten our way of life. You know them by their myriad names and acronyms—al Qaeda, ISIS, ISIL, Daesh, Hamas, Hezbollah, Iran. These entities are the very incarnation of evil, yet some at home would tell you otherwise. They see no reason why we can't all just get along. They think people such as these are like anyone else. 'We're all the same underneath. You just have to get to know these people. See it from their point of view. Put yourself in their position. Walk a moon in their moccasins.'

"People like this don't believe evil exists. Our Founding Fathers had suffered the brutal tyranny of George the Third, and they knew better. Today, a lot of our people have come to doubt their wisdom though. Easy times, easy living have made us soft, complacent. We smirk and sneer at the very mention of evil. Evil's a fantasy, we say, conjured up by fire-breathing, pulpit-pounding preachers, by demagogic politicians to scare the good people of the world for partisan gain and financial profit. Well, I'm here to tell you that evil not only exists, America today is surrounded by it on all sides as well as facing enemies within, all of whom wish to acquire nuclear weapons or expand their current nuclear arsenals. And make no mistake about it, if allowed to continue unchecked, our enemies will use those weapons to raze this land, incinerate our shining city on the Hill. Our brothers and sisters in Saudi Arabia and Israel have battled the demon face-to-face, eyeball-to-eyeball, and they can tell you about him chapter and verse. They have extended the olive branch and the hand of friendship only to have them slapped away. They have dealt with al Qaeda, ISIS, and Iran close-up and in far more perilous proximity than we have. They have learned after much pain and rejection that all such enemies understand is eye for an eye, tooth for a tooth, brute force for brute force. They have learned the wisdom of the great Roman Renatus, who wrote: *Si vis pacem, para bellum*. If you seek peace, prepare for war. Be a good friend, but a merciless, implacable foe. Offer peace, but if it is spurned or even merely ignored, let your wrath know no bounds.

"Let the word go forth that we have great institutions like the Edward Teller Nuclear Weapons Lab, which is celebrating its seventy-fifth anniversary this very day, an event our energy secretary is happily attending. We have such nuclear weapons facilities for the very reason that if the world's evildoers choose the wicked road, if they slap away our hand of friendship, if they persist in their craven terrorism and extremist violence, if they continue to test and push us and, heaven forbid, if they even *think* of attacking America here on our own shores, that hand of friendship, which we so generously extend, will clench into a fiery fist of nuclear rage."

The last line was greeted with a mixture of shocked silence, confused consternation, and scattered bursts of hysterical applause.

"But just as our enemies abroad shall learn firsthand our righteous wrath, so the enemy on our shores will suffer our retribution, too. Let me be crystal clear about that. Ruthless as we shall be with the foe abroad, we shall be doubly so with the vipers at our breast. Those here, who would see the flag of our Fathers muddied, sullied, trampled on, and burned; those who would see this once-proud people dragged weeping to their knees—against them our fury will know no stint or limit.

"God is fair, God is just, but His patience is not perpetual, and His forbearance is not forever. I swear to you now"—and here President Caldwell put his hand over his heart—"the God who doth not spare our foe abroad shall not forgive the devil in our midst, the snake in our blissful Eden."

7

Enemies he would cheerfully castrate if he could.
—Governor Walter G. Arnett

A cross the continent at the Edward Teller Nuclear Weapons Laboratory, California's governor sat down with other distinguished guests in a small grandstand behind the podium. He and the others present watched the president's Fourth of July State of the Union address, which was being televised live and projected onto huge screens erected off to the sides of the grandstand. Governor Arnett, an ardent conservative, was particularly pleased with the commander in chief's oratory, especially the part about showing no mercy to America's enemies at home. When Governor Arnett was president, that was a policy he would happily embrace. He also had a whole host of enemies at home whom he would love to settle up with when the time came.

Enemies he would cheerfully castrate if he could.

But now the president was pausing for a glass of water, and Governor Arnett could feel a dramatic announcement coming on:

"And now in keeping with my comments on the enemy within," President Caldwell said, "I would like to begin my policy of 'no quarter given' here and now. I am placing a bounty on the heads of Elena Moreno and Julie "Jules" Meredith of $20 million each. Their photos are being flashed on the screen now and have been e-mailed to the news services."

Close-up head shots of Elena and Jules appeared on the television screen and President Caldwell's voice-over continued:

"I have ordered our attorney general and the FBI to bring these women back alive, if possible. I have informed them, however, that these women must be considered armed, extremely dangerous and quite possibly in possession of portable terrorist nukes. They have already killed thirteen federal agents. We have reason to believe they are working with ISIS and are obsessed with committing an act of nuclear martyrdom. Our agents must prepare for the probability that they are wearing suicide vests and carrying nuclear detonators. Anyone who comes upon these two women must assume the worst. Therefore, the FBI and the U.S. military are authorized to shoot them and their accomplices on sight."

Now that's *the kind of action I could get behind,* the governor thought to himself.

8

The 7.62mm cartridges tore through the canvas duffel bag at 650 rounds per minute.

Dressed in white boating garb and deck shoes, Adara and Rashid let themselves through the high green iron gate of the Crestview Boat Basin with Jamie's plastic, magnetic key. A tall, rawboned, redheaded security guard in a light-blue uniform and a shoulder-slung M16 met them as they opened the door. Jamie had cleared the way, and they were on the guest list.

The guard led them down the walkway, into the enclosed cove, and onto the concrete pier. Rashid had a heavy duffel bag slung over his shoulder, and when the guard offered to carry it for him, he politely declined.

"Thanks, but it's not a problem," Rashid said.

High, green, cement walls surrounded most of the yacht basin, and for good reason. The marina of choice for Greenwich's ultrarich, it contained at least a hundred of the world's most expensive boats. Adara immediately fixated on an Oceanic 70M, two M60 SeaFalcons, one SF60, a fifty-five-meter Sovereign, and at least three M57 Eidos; and they were only a handful of the first ones she noticed. All the vessels were a scintillating alabaster and not one under fifty meters in length or with fewer than three decks. Sensuous young women in string bikinis—with drinks in hand and hips swaying to blaring music—adorned most of them.

Adara immediately spotted their own craft—a Tanga II. Over sixty meters in length, it was part of the 105 series. Built by Overmarine, it was arguably the fastest yacht on the high seas. It featured two standard MTU diesel engines and a Lycoming gas turbine linked to a central booster. Together, they gave her almost eight thousand horsepower and a top speed of forty-six knots.

Jamie had told them it was fully stocked and that his captain, Roberto Guttierez, a former Mexican drug smuggler, could be relied on if things got rough. Jamie had once paid a king's ransom to a Mexican justice minister to free him from prison, where the Juarez judiciary had sent him for the twenty-year-old murder of a cartel drug lord. Jamie felt it was worth the seven-figure bribe, however. Roberto's loyalty to his boss was absolute, and

Jamie valued such things. When Jamie had briefly outlined for Roberto what he needed, the man immediately agreed. Roberto would take them all to Central America until this thing was over.

Attired in a light-blue shirt with epaulettes, matching pants, and a captain's hat, Roberto waited for them on the dock. His black, sweeping mustache made Adara feel like she was boarding a pirate ship.

"We have plenty of gas, food, liquor, everything," Roberto said without preamble. "And we're ready to push off."

"Ordnance?" Rashid asked.

"But of course," Roberto said with a modest, palms-up gesture.

After Roberto retired to the pilothouse, Rashid went out onto the bow with the duffel bag, and Adara retreated to the stern. The redheaded security guard was undoing the bowline. He tossed it to Rashid, while the other man—a barefoot boater in a T-shirt and cutoffs—threw the stern line to Adara.

Rashid stayed on the bow with his duffel bag, even as they pulled out of the harbor. He was soon glad he had. While they were heading out to sea, an open-deck, thirty-foot coast guard patrol boat approached them on their starboard.

One of its three uniformed officers, standing on the boat's bow, shouted at Rashid through a bullhorn:

"We're pulling up alongside. We have to board. We're inspecting all craft leaving this marina. There's been a reported theft."

A fellow officer joined him on the bow. "What's in your duffel bag, sir?"

"Why nothing, Captain," Rashid said, giving them his most innocent smile.

Reaching inside, he quickly locked the M60 machine gun's ammo belt into the gun's loading port. Raising the bag up to his right hip, he opened fire on the boat's three-man crew, two of whom were on the bow. The 7.62mm cartridges tore through the canvas duffel bag at 650 rounds per minute. The duffel bag burst into flames just as nearly two hundred rounds slammed into the three coast guard officers at twenty-eight hundred feet per second, morphing them into hemorrhaging, bullet-ripped wrecks. Shaking his weapon free of the blazing shroud, Rashid continued to fire unabated, refusing to stop until he'd blasted away most of the hull's waterline.

By the time the Tanga II had passed the coast guard boat, the patrol boat was listing hard-port and starting to submerge. Roberto turned out to sea and up the coast at high speed. When Rashid glanced back one last time in her direction, she was gone.

9

The fuel assemblies were laid bare, their exposed rods blindingly ablaze.

Hamzi stood outside under the hot sun in front of the dry-cask silos. He was sure the ringing and banging in his ears would never stop. Even with earplugs, the roar of the shoulder-fired FGM-148 Javelin missile launchers and exploding Krakatoa shaped charges was beyond bearing.

For the last twenty minutes, Hamzi had watched the six men under him blasting nineteen-pound tandem warheads into Krakatoa charges duct-taped to the sides of the dry casks with tripod-mounted FGM-148 Javelin TOW missile launchers from seventy-five yards away. The copper plates in the shaped charges' tips, on detonation, were transformed into sharply pointed antitank shells that pierced and blasted through the concrete and steel with tightly focused force.

After they had finally succeeded in blowing a hole in the silos' sides, he'd watched them shove Krakatoa charges into the smoking, gaping rents and pour missile after missile, tandem warhead after tandem warhead into each of the new Krakatoas, which had been freshly placed in those openings. For the coup de grace, they had shoved and taped three Krakatoa charges into each of the twisted, jagged craters. Those final blasts had knocked everyone to their knees and their TOW launchers to the ground.

After the flames, smoke, and dust partially cleared, Hamzi watched the six men shove a final round of shaped incendiary phosphorus charges into the vast, deep, fire-flickering holes. These last blasts would do it.

Dry-cask security depended on two faulty assumptions: that the terrorists would not destroy dry casks en masse, and that they would not, at the end of the attack, hammer the shattered casks with shaped incendiary charges. Hamzi and his men had proved those assumptions wrong. Now Hamzi could see the fuel assemblies were laid bare, their exposed rods blindingly ablaze.

10

"Fire in the hole!"
—Elias Edito

At the moment, Elias had his hands full. While coordinating the major explosions, he also had to keep an eye out for approaching military units, state trooper vehicles, or intrusive plant guards. The last duty was important. Someone had hit an alarm, and consequently, he'd spent the last half hour taking out approaching guards with his silenced M110 7.62mm assault rifle. Between the noise and flash suppressors, the men he killed didn't even know what hit them. There was nothing to see or hear. Furthermore, he'd taken them all out with head shots, which had frightened the surviving guards even more. Their comrades dropped dead as doornails right in front of them, and they couldn't tell where the rounds were coming from.

Still the plant security kept coming. Even now a half dozen security personnel with assault rifles were rounding the corner of the Visitors Center and quick-jogging past it toward the Auxiliary Building.

Elias had walked that pathway two weeks earlier with a pedometer and written down the precise distance of each visible landmark along the way, so he had the opposition bracketed. When the men reached the edge of the Auxiliary Building, they would be 175 yards away.

Elias raised the 7.62. Contrary to much rumor and disbelief, noise suppressors have virtually no effect on the weapon's accuracy, and he had already locked the KAC noise suppressor's yoke onto the barrel's gas block. Adjusting the Leupold 3.5-10×30mm Sniper Scope to 175 yards, Elias rounded the catwalk. He now faced the roadway—Main Street, as it was known in the plant. Kneeling on the catwalk, he wrapped the shoulder strap around his arm and rested the barrel in the bottom rail groove, which he'd cut with a crosscut file earlier in his shift. He sighted in on the piece of roadway aligned with the Auxiliary Building's far edge.

Since it was only prudent to assume they wore vests, he aimed for their heads. First number one, then two, three, four, and five went down. Number six, however, had begun running in S curves, and Elias missed him. Aiming at his thighs, he shot his right leg out from under him. The man fell, screaming, sprawled on his side, clutching his shattered femur. Elias had a clear shot at the back of his head. A 7.62 coup de grace to his nape ended his howls.

Elias turned to look at the Auxiliary Building, Reactor Containment Building, nuclear waste storage sheds, and dry fuel silos. The men had done well. Smoke was pouring out the buildings' windows and doors; the spent fuel pools and the dry casks were ferociously ablaze.

Hamzi and Fahad were a hundred or so feet away from the Auxiliary and Reactor Containment Buildings. They had both wired and wireless detonators. Elias inserted his earplugs, turned on his sleeve microphone, and shouted:

"*Bismillah!*" In the name of Allah, let us begin. Followed by, "*Alhamdu-lillah w Ashokrulillah!*" Praise be to Allah for granting us these gifts. Then Elias screamed in English, "Fire in the hole!"

At which point Hamzi and Fahad hit all four detonators.

The reactor containment dome muffled the control room blasts, but the Auxiliary Building shook with multiple detonations, which coalesced into a single convulsive roar that rocked the plant like the crack of doom. Elias, who was 150 yards away, could feel the ground and the six-story-high gun tower shake beneath his feet.

All the while the FGM-148 Javelin TOW missiles with their double warheads and the Krakatoa charges continued to thunder in the storage shed, which housed the aboveground spent fuel storage pools. Almost directly in front of him, less than 250 feet away, he could see that Hamzi's men had also fired the final rounds of shaped charges into the dry-cask storage silos. When the dense, fog-like haze in front of those silos cleared, Elias could see through his binoculars that the dry-cask storage silos were ripped open with cavernous craters, their fuel assemblies grotesquely exposed, filling up with smoke and flames.

Now Klaxons were whooping through the plant, and in the far distance, maybe a half mile away, sirens of the National Guard and state police screamed as they raced toward the plant.

Meanwhile, overhead fire extinguishers were spraying and hosing down the interior of the plant's various buildings. At the same time, the colossal H_2O tanks—both overhead and at ground level—were deluging the grounds, computers, heavy equipment and work areas with tens of millions of gallons of water.

Elias stared out over the destruction in awe. Against his will, he had to drag himself away from the spectacle and back into his tower room. There, he picked his Barrett M82 up off the blanket-covered storage bin and rested the barrel on his shoulder. Exiting the tower room, he rounded the catwalk till he faced the incoming choppers, APCs, and cop cars approaching the crossroads on Highway 12. Kneeling down, he rested the barrel of his M82 in one of the notches he'd carved in the steel railing two hours before. The vehicles would have to slow down when they reached that ninety-degree turn at the intersection 237 yards up the road. He'd measured that distance on his car's odometer, and he had sighted in his Leupold Mark 4 Scope at that range. Its ten-round box magazine was filled with Raufoss Mk 211 Mod 0 rounds, his favorite brand of armor-piercing incendiary ammunition (API). He'd be ready for them when they slowed at that junction.

Then he saw a news chopper sweeping over the tree line maybe three-fourths of a mile away. He smiled to himself. He had no problem with a little publicity. If he was going to die tonight, why not go out in a blaze of televised glory?

He went into the tower room and turned on the two-way radio. He adjusted the frequency until he got the news chopper.

"Hi guys," he said cheerfully, waving at them. "Welcome to hell."

"This isn't the gun tower, is it?" a woman's voice shouted, incredulous.

He could see her in the chopper, studying him through a pair of binoculars. She had obviously seen him waving, and she was now waving back at him.

"Sure is, but don't be afraid. I won't hurt you. Promise. It's lonely up here, and I'd love the company. Also my superiors would love the PR. Get those cameras rolling. Focus on the smoking building and spent fuel silos. This whole place is going up in flames."

Then he lifted the liter bottle of Wild Turkey 101, held it up to the chopper in toast, and said, "Here's looking at you, kids." Taking a long hard chug from its neck, he bellowed into the two-way at the top of his lungs: "There'll be a hot time in the old town tonight!"

PART XX

Babylon the great is fallen, is fallen, and is become the habitation of devils, and the hold of every foul spirit, and a cage of every unclean and hateful bird.... For thy merchants were the great men of the earth; for by thy sorceries were all nations deceived. And in her was found the blood of prophets, and of saints, and of all that were slain upon the earth.

—Revelation 18:1–24

1

He was going to teach them all a painful lesson in nuclear humility.

Hasad stood on the eastern side of his hotel suite in Washington, D.C.'s premier hotel, the Capitol Needle. A soaring needle tower, with a square base ninety-six feet on edge and ninety-six stories high, it was sometimes known as Needle 96 and was far and away the tallest building in D.C. This, its George Washington suite, had a 360-degree view of D.C. and a 180-degree view of the Capitol Building.

At the moment, Hasad stood staring through a high-powered Zhumell 20×80mm tripod binoculars at the most embarrassingly ostentatious limousine in the world. The Saudi Ambassador, Shaiq ibn Ishaq, the president's family, and the group's bodyguards had exited the limo a half hour earlier, and, Hasad estimated, should be entering the congressional chamber about now. Glancing at one of his dozen TV monitors, he saw they were already in the hall, entering the president's box. The TV camera moved in for a close-up of the smiling, hand-waving ambassador, the photogenically smiling First Lady, and her two clearly bored kids.

Hasad and the chauffeur had concealed an HEU bomb in the false bottom of the trunk. He had also installed a two-way remote radio detonator in the bomb's triggering system. Setting it off would not be all that difficult. He glanced at the handheld detonator on the dining-room table. It looked like a black outsized TV remote with a six-inch antenna. All Hasad had to do to set the bomb off was press the red button. He did not even have to point it.

To avoid accidental detonation, he'd programmed the trigger to release on receipt of his 5MHz SSB transmission—a frequency so seldom used as to be almost nonexistent. He'd also removed some of the extra-high explosive from in back of the "HEU bullet." He didn't want too big a blast—one that might topple the tower, in which he was now ensconced. . . .

He wondered what Elena would think of all this. In truth, he was sick of both America's arrogant ignorance and the Mideast's maddeningly moronic vendettas. He'd told her he despised them all and had long ago declared a pox on both their houses.

Furthermore, he was still bitter after his last mission. His Pakistani handlers had withheld his final payment and had threatened him unless he agreed to execute this insanely dangerous mission, which he had never agreed to and for which he had never contracted.

And, of course, they had foolishly stated they would kill him, too.

They had finally crossed the line with him.

As for America, it was a country of lunatics who capriciously invaded and destroyed Third World nations, then argued that they had to destroy them to save them. By the same demented illogic, they justified their eternal development of newer, wickeder weapons of thermonuclear destruction, saying they needed them to save the "Free World."

Before it was over, he had told Elena, he was going to teach them all a painful lesson in nuclear humility. Afterward, he would grab his tens of millions of dollars in offshore, tax-free, black-hole accounts and go to ground—his blood-ground—pulling the hole in after him.

In his final e-mail to Elena, he had told her that her career would be shot when he was finished and that he wanted her to come with him. She could bring Jules, too. Hell, Jules was like a sister to him. But Elena had to make up her mind then and there. He said when he was gone, he was gone. No one would ever find him. Elvis would finally leave the building. Forever.

She had to send him a note, though, a signal, and he would arrange to meet her. She could stay with him and live a life of peace and luxury. They would have everything they had dreamed of back in college two decades ago, and most of all he would have the woman he'd torched it for all those years.

The only person he'd ever loved.

But she never got back to him.

The pounding on the door snapped him out of his reverie.

What the fuck was that?

Ignoring the commotion, he turned back to the street below. The cars were like a parking lot down there, as if locked in concrete. Shaiq's limo was hopelessly quagmired on East Capitol Street right across from the Capitol Building entrance. Moreover, its two deflated tires and raised hood guaranteed it would be on that spot for some time to come. Hasad had plenty of time to incinerate everyone in the Capitol Building. The president was still at the rostrum, blathering away. One of Hasad's ten TV monitors showed the congressmen, senators, and now the Saudi ambassador and First Family hanging breathlessly on his every word.

The hammering in the hallway was now aggravating and unrelenting, so he went to the door and looked through the peephole. All he saw was a thumb.

Fuck it.

He grabbed a Colt Mark IV .45 automatic from under his belt in the small of his back. Holding the gun slightly behind his right leg, he opened the door. To his never-ending surprise, he was staring at Elena herself, bigger than life, in a black leather jacket and pants, a matching motorcycle helmet in the crook of her left arm, her hair short and platinum-bleached, a witches' coven's worth of crow-black makeup encircling her eyes, and big Super Dark Black Gascan wraparound biker shades atop her head.

And a smile like the end of the rainbow.

"Hey there, sailor," she said, "long time no fuck."

2

"I'M GIVING YOU THE STORY OF A LIFETIME!"
—Elias Edito

Jules was up in the news chopper with Sandy at the controls, attempting to interview Elias over her radio and broadcast his comments live over the MTN global cable TV network.

"Can you tell us who you are and why you're attempting to melt down the HRNPS?"

"My name is Elias, and we aren't attempting anything. We *are* melting it the fuck down."

"What's your role in this, Elias?" Jules asked.

He walked out onto the catwalk to answer her. "See those two dozen dead guards down there—their bodies strewn all over the plant grounds? That's why I'm here."

"How were you able to get into the tower?" Jules asked.

"How do you think I did it—levitation? I climbed up. I've worked here for fifteen years."

"Elias, you've killed an awful lot of people today. Don't you think it's time to quit?"

Shit. He was upending the big whiskey bottle again.

"Hell, no! Those two dozen men down there are nothing. I was a Marine Corps sniper for old Uncle Sam. Chris Kyle's got nothing on me! In Iraq and Afghanistan, I shot the living shit out of over three hundred hajjis. I killed everything that walked, ran, or crawled—men, women, children, dogs, goats, cats, rats, eight to eighty, blind, crippled, or crazy, long as they didn't fly or have webbed feet."

After taking another gigantic chug out of the whiskey bottle's neck, he washed it down with a half-quart can of what looked to be Colt 45.

His explosive laughter shook her headset like a level-9 earthquake.

"But why kill these people here?" Jules asked.

"'Cause I hate nuclear power?" His derisive laughter echoed through the night.

"Apparently, all the murder and mayhem and the talk about Iraq's unhinged him," Sandy whispered to Jules, her hand over her mike.

"Maybe this interview isn't such a good idea," Jules whispered back.

"That's about as plain as the balls on a tall dog," Sandy whispered back.

But now Jules couldn't shut him up.

"See all the flames and the smoke? My friends down there have blown up and incinerated every piece of radioactive shit that will burn."

"But you've done that," Jules said. "Why not stop now? You could end it all here."

"There's no fun in that! Anyway, what's the point of having a skill if you don't use it? The goddamn U.S. Marine Corps taught me how to shoot. Now it's time to pay the piper, and I'm going to pipe our country a tune it'll never forget. I'm going to pipe it right up America the Beautiful's beautiful fucking ass. And I don't mean by shooting a bunch of diaper-headed . . . *dune coons*. I'm going to shoot me some . . . *righteously white Americans*. How do you like it so far, ladies?"

Again his idiot laughter ululated in their headsets.

"Elias," Jules said softly, placatingly, still hoping to calm him down, "remember we're on international television. People all over the world, children included, are tuning in."

"So?"

"You could watch the . . . obscenities a bit."

"Are you shitting me?" he whooped into her headset, roaring with rage like a gored water buffalo. "Five seconds in the minds of our Washington elite—and all those other brain-damaged, bed-wetting bastards, who sent me over there—are fouler than all the filthy language ever spoken or written since Homer and Gilgamesh, paintings, carvings, and monument inscriptions included."

"But you made your point. Do you really intend to—"

"We aren't intending to do anything. See all that smoke and fire down there? My friends have set aflame some of the most poisonous crap on earth. That shit is instantly, everlastingly, intergalactically toxic, and those men are standing right next to it. What do you think they intend to do?"

"Well maybe they intend to—"

"*Are you a complete idiot?*" His insane laughter exploded in her ears like a volcanic eruption. "*What do they intend to do? They intend to fucking . . . DIE!!*"

"Elias," Jules said, her voice genuinely sad, "that's just awful."

"Yeah, but look on the bright side, girls."

"What possible bright side could all this death and destruction have?" Jules asked.

"I'M GIVING YOU THE STORY OF A LIFETIME!"

Again, his hilarious howls rang through the night.

Actually, Jules had to admit, he was right. He was giving them the story of a hundred lifetimes. He even began adding background music to go with it as Sister Cassandra and her band, the End Time, began to blare. . . .

Elias was pumping her music up into their radio, full volume, through the plant's loudspeaker system, and Sandy, in turn, was now broadcasting it globally over MTN, the world's largest news network. The Good Sister's signature anthem, "Rockin' the Apocalypse," was blasting into Jules's headset and on TV sets everywhere even as Sandy televised the fiery inferno that was now the Hudson River Nuclear Power Station.

> *When the deal goes down,*
> *And you're lookin' to score.*
> *When the shit hits the fan,*
> *When the firestorms roar,*
> *When there's blood all around,*
> *When there's nuclear war,*
>
> *You'll be rockin' the apocalypse*
> *Rockin' the apocalypse,*
> *You'll be rock-rock-rock-rock-rockin' the apocalypse.*

Elias thundered over the deafening music at the top of his lungs:

"ISIS and al Qaeda got nothing on me. I'm a lean, mean killing machine. *How do you like it so far, ladies? I'm murdering morons for Mohammed and acing assholes for the one true God!*" Elias's psychotic laughter reverberated through Jules's headset like a rolling howitzer barrage.

"But why?" Jules asked, hoping against hope to talk him down. "This doesn't have to happen."

"It sure as hell does. Over there I found out who the real bad guys were. Like Pogo said: I met the enemy and guess what? *He . . . is . . . fucking . . . us!* And then my mother told me I was a bastard and that my real old man was Iraqi and that I probably blasted some of my own relatives into Muslim hell. Well, know what I said to that one? *Too bad for them, old lady!! Tell it to somebody who gives a shit!!*"

Again, his hideous howls rang dementedly in Jules's headset. He turned the Good Sister up to skull-cracking levels:

> *When there's no more prayers,*
> *When it's too late for cryin',*
> *When there's flames all around,*
> *And the missiles are flyin',*
> *When you're all out of time,*
> *When you're all out of dyin',*
>
> *You'll be rockin' the apocalypse,*
> *Rockin' the apocalypse,*
> *You're rock-rock-rock-rock-rockin' the apocalypse.*

"Wait, wait," Elias screamed. "Here's the bridge! Don't you love the bridge?"

> *When the last lie is told,*
> *When the last word is said,*
> *When the heart grows cold,*
> *When the world is dead,*
> *You'll hammer hard and bold,*
> *You'll hammer straight ahead.*

"But Elias," Jules asked, yelling frantically above the music, "there has to be some way to stop this. Sure, our country has made mistakes, but melting down the HRNPS will kill hundreds of thousands of people—"

"Millions of people, if I have my way."

"But, it doesn't have to be. We can—"

Elias cranked up the decibels, drowning Jules out with more of the Good Sister:

> *You'll get your ass pumpin',*
> *When it all comes down.*
> *You go out jumpin'*
> *When the bombs hit the ground.*
> *No point in cryin',*
> *When there's dyin' all around.*
> *You go out with a bang,*
> *With a hell-fired sound.*

When you're rockin' the apocalypse,
Rockin' the apocalypse,
When you're rock-rock-rock-rock-rockin' the apocalypse.

When you're rockin' the apocalypse,
Rockin' the apocalypse,
When you're rock-rock-rock-rock-rockin' the apocalypse.

PART XXI

And I beheld when he had opened the sixth seal, and, lo, there was a great earthquake; and the sun became black, and the moon became as blood; and the stars of heaven fell unto the earth. And the heaven departed as a scroll when it is rolled up; and every mountain and island were moved. And the kings of the earth, and the great men, and the rich men hid themselves in the dens and in the mountains; and said to the mountains and rocks, fall on us, and hide us from the face of Him that sitteth on the throne.

—Revelation 6:12–16

1

"You know, kid, I always loved you. I hope it is you who punches my ticket."

—Hasad ibn Ghazi

Elena entered Hasad's suite, still in jet-black leathers, holding a matching helmet in her left arm along her side. Hasad stared at her, speechless. Her right hand was empty, her jacket unzipped. He opened it and removed the 9mm Beretta tucked under her leather pants. He stuck it under the waistband of his black Levis. He then removed another one shoved under her pants beneath her jacket in the small of her back. He checked her boots as well; none were there.

"I see you're well armed," Hasad said.

She followed him into the suite. From the room's center, she took in the all-embracing 360-degree view of D.C.—including the 180-degree western view of the Capitol Building one mile away. Beyond that lay the District's monuments and museums and its many legendary structures and edifices— the National Mall, the Washington Monument, the Vietnam Memorial, the Lincoln Memorial, the great Georgetown School of International Studies, the Mayflower Hotel, the Watergate, and, of course, the Potomac River.

"Room with a view," Elena said.

"Nothing but the best," he said, staring at her, curious.

Elena glanced around the suite, which occupied the needle tower's entire floor. It was over ninety feet across. A huge white leather semicircular couch faced the Capitol dome. Each end was flanked by a pair of leather armchairs and footstools. Glass-and-steel end tables with brass lamps sat in between the couch and the chairs. A circular glass coffee table fifteen feet in diameter stood in front of the couch on a stainless steel base. Elena thought it matched the couch's curvature so perfectly it had probably been custom-built to fit into it. Near the kitchen area was a large glass dining table with stainless steel armchairs with white leather seats and backs. A few very good black marble replicas of Michelangelo's *David, Moses,* and the *Pieta* stood along the sides of the room. At opposite ends of the big room, two flat-screen TVs were on stands—each a good hundred inches across. In front of them were more stuffed leather chairs, couches, and more glass tables.

And that was only half the suite.

Elena, however, focused solely on the bank of computers, monitors, two-way radios, and receivers on wheeled carts and folding tables in the room's center. Also the tripod binoculars pointed at the street in front of the Capitol Building.

Then she saw the remote detonator on the dining-room table.

Oh shit, this is control and command.

She looked at Hasad, revealing no emotion or expression, but he knew she knew. She could tell from the small smile forming at the right corner of his mouth.

"Elena, I love you like life itself, but I must say you've arrived at a very inopportune time."

"I can see I'm interrupting something. Care to tell me what?"

Suddenly one of the monitors caught her eye. On the screen was a master shot of two ivory-white domes, surrounded by concrete buildings and gray steel sheds—

And—

And—

Those were nuclear power plant containment domes.

Shit, those are HRNPS's containment domes.

And smoke is pouring out of two of the plant's buildings.

She forced herself to look at the adjacent monitor. It looked like some kind of crudely transmitted ceremony at the Teller Lab—maybe sent via an iPhone. She recognized the energy secretary and the governor of California sitting behind the podium.

Jamie had hacked into a lot of communications from Hasad to the general and to Ambassador Shaiq. He had picked up hints about something happening at the Hudson River Nuclear Power Station and something going on in D.C. Something called Operation Trojan Horse. She and Jamie just couldn't figure out what the Trojan horse was. Hasad had the Teller Lab on a monitor, so something was clearly happening there.

Maybe Hasad wasn't running that one.

If so, he'd have had no reason to discuss it with anyone.

Elena could barely take her eyes off the two monitors. It was like watching a bullet-train wreck or a nineteen-spiral car crash. She had to drag herself over to the third monitor. It was a great, gaudy gold limo—only it was stuck in traffic. The hood was up, and the driver was bent down staring at the two collapsed tires. She suspected someone had put an ice pick in them.

Angry drivers were milling about pissed off at the jam. She knew the car's owner. Everyone did. It was the Saudi ambassador's Golden Chariot, as he gloatingly called it.

"You sonofabitch," she said, turning to Hasad.

She went over to the high-powered tripod binoculars. They were state of the art. She'd used the same model several times in Islamabad and twice in Peshawar: a Vixen BT125-A Binocular with a Lanthanum Wide 1.25-inch eyepiece, a fork mount, and a tripod. It had a wide-angle range and at the same time offered highly detailed depth perception. With its 34x magnification, if the Capitol Building was two thousand yards away, through the binocular it would look to be less than sixty yards.

Elena looked through them. It was as she figured. They were focused on the gold limo, hopelessly mired, the hood up, its two front tires flat.

Oh fuck.

Looking back at Hasad, he was now—

—crossing the suite toward the remote radio detonator on the glass dining-room table near his left hand.

The receiver-trigger would be in the nuke. The nuke in—

in—

in—

In the Trojan horse.

In Shaiq's garishly grotesque limo.

His Golden Chariot.

So that was it.

She pulled a 10mm semiautomatic Glock out from under the black scarf in her black polymer helmet, still cradled in her arm. Pointing it at Hasad, she said:

"Locked, cocked, and ready to rock."

"Why you little bitch," Hasad said, turning to her, smiling and shaking his head, "you had a gun in your fucking hat. You were always smarter than I was."

"And always will be. So don't touch the detonator. Don't even look at it. You can walk out of here. I promise."

"No-can-do, Elena. These people are just too bad. Always thought I could work for anyone, but I was wrong. These guys are going down."

"Maybe, but if I have to, I'll end you first—here and now. Keep you from killing all those innocent people down there."

"I took some explosive out of the nuke. It'll yield a kiloton or two—enough to wipe out every asshole in that State of the Union address. It won't burn down the whole city, though."

"There'd still be a lot of undeserving dead when it was over."

"True, but how else can I get Caldwell, Shaiq, and his bunch off the board? When this is over, they're planning a military takeover with them in charge. Is that what you want?"

Hasad was right. She and Jules had suspected it all along. All this was a nuclear Reichstag fire—the phony terrorist plot to blow up the German parliament, which Hitler himself had fabricated to force marital law on Germany and declare himself *Führer*.

Hasad was right twice. It was the only way to get them all—and to stop Caldwell and his gang.

Still, she couldn't let him do it.

She just couldn't.

She began inching closer to him.

He saw what she was doing.

"You know, kid," Hasad said, "I always loved you. I hope it is you who punches my ticket."

"Really?" Elena said with a sardonic half smile.

"You're the only thing I ever loved. No shit. You and that crazy friend of yours, Jules. I've torched it for you my whole life long."

"Then let's bolt on out of here. Forget these bastards. There's a beautiful world out there. Let's go. You can still find some of it."

"Never happen, kid. The shit ends here."

"Nothing's worth this."

"You got no idea how bad these guys are, do you? Who do you think paid me to set this up? Shaiq and Jari with Caldwell's ignorant complicity."

She and Jamie had imagined as much.

"Caldwell and Shaiq just never figured you'd do it to them?" Elena asked.

"That I'd shove the nuke straight up their constipated assholes with the rest of their shit? Then blow them off the face of the earth?"

Elena had to smile. "I like it. I really do. But you reach for that detonator, I'll shoot you where you stand."

"Maybe, but the driver actually detonates the bomb. I'm just a failsafe system—backup in case he can't do it. Unfortunately, I'm afraid now he didn't."

Elena raised the Glock with both hands, sighting it on his face.

"Doesn't matter. You go for that detonator, I'm putting a 10mm 180 grain Hydra-Shok hollow point right between your eyes. It'll hit your cerebellum at a thousand feet per second, shorting out your somatic nervous system on impact. Before you can think or blink—let alone touch a detonator—you'll be deader than Kelsey's nuts."

"You're forty feet from me, and you aren't that good with a pistol. I know. I taught you how to shoot back in Texas. Remember?"

"You want to bet a Hydra-Shok on it?"

"Too late."

"Don't. Please."

"You know I always loved you, Elena."

"I love you, too."

"Then maybe I'll see you on the other side."

He reached for the detonator, and the Glock jumped in her fist. Before he could touch it, a bloody smoking hole materialized in the upper bridge of his nose, and his head snapped back. His legs buckled. He crumpled like a puppet unstrung he dropped to his knees inert and fell on his side. The penthouse floor was filling with blood from the massive opening in the back of his head before she could reach him.

Somehow his eyes remained locked on hers, their expression quizzical, asking a mute question.

How did you do it?

Elena bent over him until their faces were only inches apart.

"Remember how you get into Carnegie Hall?" The light was fading from his eyes, but still she got it in. "Practice, practice, practice."

Grabbing the detonator, she placed it on the floor, bent over it with her left hand shielding her eyes, and fired three rounds into it.

It happened anyway.

Eleven seconds later.

She knew what it was, even with her back turned.

The limo driver had pushed the red button after all.

The big suite's 180-degree windows dazzled with the brilliance of a thousand suns, but she knew not to look at it.

She did notice that the monitors went blank, and the suite's lights went out, too.

Lights were going out citywide.

Since she was barely a mile from the epicenter, she heard no sound. Like Hiroshima's silent flash, it was too loud to register on human eardrums unless listeners were miles away. Nor did she turn to watch. She knew not to stare into the thermal blaze, thereby searing her retinas forever.

She put on her helmet and shoved the Glock under her waistband. As she ran toward the door, the needle tower began rocking violently, destabilized by the blast wave.

Bad news, Hasad. That was more than a one- or two-kiloton yield.

Somehow, she kept her footing, and made it out the door, lurching and stumbling like a drunken sailor on a rolling deck, bouncing off the hallway walls.

She went straight for the stairs, the skinny skyscraper swinging convulsively, a weak reed whipsawed by wild winds. Slamming off the hallway walls, she leaped down the fire stairs five at a time, desperate to escape the tottering tower before it went down.

2

And then the Apaches were no more.

Jules and Sandy were closer to the plant now—less than a half mile away—and Jules could see everything with agonizing clarity. The bases of the two white containment domes were seething with a pale, dense, infernal haze. The windows and doors in their adjacent buildings were filled with flames, while coils of black radioactive smoke writhed out of those openings high into the starry, moonlit sky.

Jules had the camera/transmission control laptop on her knees. The HD nose-cam was ready to roll, the video-assist monitor already on. She eased the joystick gently toward twelve o'clock. The blazing, smoking sheds and block-houses promptly appeared on the small video-assist monitor, confirming that the camera was zeroed in on them.

"Check your three o'clock!" Elias warned them.

Glancing over her shoulder, Jules saw an interminable queue of two dozen state cop cars and SWAT vans on Highway 9 with flashing rack lights on top. Coming toward them from the other direction on the same road toward the intersection of Highways 9 and 12 was a caravan of over a dozen Armored Personnel Carriers. At that intersection they would have to turn onto Highway 12, which ran in front of the HRNPS, to reach the plant.

The lead APC and the lead cop car, however, had rushed to the crossroads, each anxious to block the other and get their people to the plant first. Both drivers had pulled into the middle of the intersection, each refusing to yield. The two men got out and began yelling at each other. Jules wondered if there was going to be a fight.

The first half dozen of the National Guard's APCs were M1097 HMMWV troop carriers, otherwise known as Humvees. They were sixteen feet long, weighed three tons, and were rated for payloads of two and a half tons. The soldiers sat in long-bed canvas-covered cargo carriers. The tarpaulins were desert tan, the sides and end-curtains rolled up in case the troops needed to engage the enemy. Another dozen troop transports followed the line of Humvees. They appeared to be old army trucks with rolled-up tarps above the cargo beds which also contained soldiers.

They were all stopped stock-still, bumper to bumper.

Suddenly the sniper in the tower was back on: "Hey ladies, you checked out the traffic jam at the junction crossroads?"

"Roger that," Jules said.

"Get cameras on both of them."

Jules swung the tail-cam around till it was locked on the intersection's traffic jam. Through her handheld minicam, though, Jules fixed on Elias as well. She could see him, kneeling, sighting in some kind of big rifle, which he balanced on the middle rail.

"That's some cannon you got," Jules said.

"Barrett M82," he said.

"What's the matter?" Jules said. "You couldn't get a 155 Howitzer?"

"I could but it stretches the holster."

Again, the hysterical howls.

Again, the upturned whiskey bottle.

"Very funny," Jules said. "But do we really have to do this?"

"Is a pig's pussy pork?" he roared into their headsets. "Does the pope shit in the woods? You bet your butt *we* gotta do this. You just keep that camera on those cop cars and personnel carriers. You're going to love me in the day-light."

"Why will we love you, Elias?" Sandy asked, dumbfounded.

"'Cause I'm gonna make you both rich and famous. I'm gonna make you two . . . *rock stars!!*"

A state cop car, rack lights coruscating brilliantly, and an APC were still stuck in the intersection, their front bumpers touching. Now two long lines of vehicles stretching up and down Highway 9 were jammed end to end, frozen in place.

"Oh no," Jules said.

A blazing .50 caliber incendiary round hit the state cop engine like a fire-bomb out of hell. The phosphorus and friction sparks combined to ignite first the gasoline vapor in the engine, then the fuel line, then the gas tank, resulting in a series of three explosions—*whomp! whomp!! WHOMP!!!* With the third blast, the cop car turned into one stupendous reddish-yellow fire-ball levitating fifteen feet in the air, lifting the vehicle right along with it, the entire conflagration billowing black noxious smoke. Moreover, the cars were jammed so tightly together that the inferno, which had been the first car, was blowing up other vehicles, turning each of them into a floating globe of flame, which, through sympathetic detonation, blew up the police car nearest it. One after another, the cop cars began exploding into fire-balls, all the way down the line. Rack lights, bumpers, tires, side mirrors, steering wheels, Smokey Bear hats, Maglites, shotguns, pistols, handcuffs, engine hoods were flying in all directions at once.

Elias fired an incendiary round into the hood of an APC. Its engine vapor, gas lines, and fuel tanks were blowing so hard that the final *WHUMP!!!* and swelling fireball lifted the APC ten feet into the air, bursting its uniformed, helmeted, fully armed guardsmen straight through the sheet of flames that had been the canvas top once covering the carrier bed. That exploding APC ignited another, which ignited the one jammed up against its bumper, which set fire from the one next to it, straight down the road.

Highway 9 was now a seamless concatenation of blazing wrecks a quarter mile long.

"Hey ladies, check your six," Elias shouted. "Look what's coming now."

Jules scanned the night sky with her binoculars. Over the small woods a mile or so behind them were six army choppers. Jules focused, then zoomed the tail-cam in on them. The women could see them close-up on the video-assist's twelve-inch screen.

"Sandy," Jules whispered, her hand over the mike, "Elias is in the deep shit now."

"He's got six AH-64E Apache helicopters on his ass," Sandy said. "I wonder if he knows what he's in for."

Jules and Sandy did. A four-blade attack chopper with twin-turboshaft engines driving the rotor, nose-mounted target acquisition, and night vision systems, it had a 30mm M230 chain gun mounted beneath the main fuselage right between the landing gear. Capable of firing AGM-114 laser-guided Hellfire missiles and Hydra-70 rockets, the gunner could slave the chopper's chain gun to his mounted helmet display so that when he stared at a target, the big gun automatically sighted in on it.

The two women had seen the U.S. deploy Apaches in over a dozen military theaters, including hundreds of firefights in Iraq and Afghanistan. They'd witnessed the Israelis employ them against Hezbollah in 2006 in Lebanon and later against Hamas in Gaza, even using their Hellfire missiles to assassinate Hamas's leaders, and then again in Syria against ISIS and Assad. They'd watched the Saudis flying them in Operation Scorched Earth, in which the choppers launched air strikes against Houthi rebels, driving them out of Saudi Arabia, then following and attacking the rebels in their home bases in Yemen. The Apaches flew air cover for the Egyptian government as well in its attempt to take the Sinai Peninsula back from armed extremists, and the women had been there, too.

Greece, Singapore, Japan, the Arab Emirates, Kuwait, Korea, Taiwan, the

326 | ROBERT GLEASON

U.K.—the U.S. had sold that attack helicopter to a dozen countries, and Jules had seen them all over the world.

Yes, Elias was in for a whole world of pain.

But apparently no one told Elias about it. Sighting the Barrett in on the lead chopper, he sent a .50 caliber incendiary round streaking across the black sky.

More phosphorus rounds hit home, more, more, and the choppers too began exploding one at a time into massive blood-orange fireballs. The last survivor had gotten close enough to Jules and her sister that they felt its shock waves rock their chopper.

And then the Apaches were no more.

3

"I was told 'no loose ends.'"
—Jamil Masoud

Jamil and his four men stood at the top of the hill overlooking the Edward Teller Nuclear Weapons Laboratory just outside of San Francisco.

Then he heard a beep on his cell and saw the text: *Trojan horse has landed.*

He clicked off the iPhone, with which he'd been transmitting the celebration to Hasad.

"Let's do it," he said to the men, ordering them down the hill. Putting on a pair of Locs Super Dark sunglasses with maximum UVB/UVA blockage, he and his men started down the far side of the green, sloping, tree-lined hill. Stopping long enough to raise the remote radio detonator just above the hill's crest, Jamil pointed it toward the great Bear Flag Revolt cannon, in which he and the bomb maker had encased their Hiroshima-style nuke.

He pressed the red button.

Jamil thought he was physically and psychologically prepared to handle the explosion's force, but the sheer inconceivable power of it caught him and his men by surprise. The outer reach of its blast wave knocked him and his men off their feet and sent them somersaulting down the hill.

When Jamil finally picked himself up, he saw he was all right. He'd positioned most of his body just below the summit. His men, however, had lingered too long atop the hill. With their Super Dark sunglasses, they'd hoped to catch a passing glance of the blast. The thermal pulse had burned their exposed arms and faces a painful crimson. The fireball was rising, its heat almost preternaturally intense. Still he had to look. He was pretty sure his sunglasses would allow him to sneak a peek, not at the thermal flash but at the fireball now floating over the hill.

He was wrong. Its brightness was blinding.

That close up, the explosion's decibel volume was far beyond any human being's auditory range. So the men walked to their parked black van in silence, zombielike, a dull stopped-up ringing in their ears. Jamil went to the passenger side to unlock the door and let them in.

Hesitating for a second, he said, "Just one thing."

Instead of taking a key from his pocket, he removed a snub-nosed Ruger .44 mag—a Super Blackhawk—from his belt clip and shot all of them in rapid succession, the first one in the throat, the next in his right cheekbone near the nose, the third in the left eye, the fourth in the forehead.

"Sorry guys," he said softly. "I was told 'no loose ends.'"

Ordinarily, he wore earplugs when he fired the magnum. Not today. Thanks to the bomb, the gun's loudness was not a problem.

A couple of hundred people in summer clothes, many badly burned, were racing across the street, fleeing the scene. All were deafened and/or blinded by the bomb, and all of them ignored or failed to notice the murders. No one seemed to care. "Caring" belonged to another life, another world. All anyone wanted now was to escape.

In the parking space in front of him was an ebony Jeep Wrangler all-terrain vehicle with a 3.6-liter engine, skid plates, a Garmin navigation system, blacked-out trim, heavy-duty bumpers, tow hooks, a winch, and a Torx tool kit for stripping off the roof, doors, and bumper cap ends. It could go almost five hundred miles on a single tank of gas.

Putting on the shades, he hazarded a quick sideways glance at the gray billowing mushroom floating high above the hill and the huge orange-crimson fireball rising under it. Even at a mile-and-a half away, the incendiary sphere was blisteringly hot.

He slipped in behind the wheel and turned the ignition. Laying rubber, he peeled up the street toward the dense traffic. Cutting to his right, he passed the line of jammed cars, driving over sidewalks and lawns.

4

Like a planet-killing comet strike.

Low in the saddle, leaning over her handlebars, Elena was back on her Kawasaki Ninja H2, gunning it up Second Avenue. Sliding around a stalled car, she whipped wildly around a wrecked one, then jumped a curb to avoid an overturned bus.

She was tearing through the D.C. night with no street or window lights in sight. When the bomb went off, all the power for the street and building lights had gone out all at once, but that was no matter. Fires were erupting everywhere, illuminating D.C. like high noon in Death Valley.

Suddenly, a big red Cadillac Escalade swerved up onto the sidewalk in front of her, flattening a fire hydrant, flipping over, and cutting Elena off. An arcing blast of H_2O geysered straight up a hundred feet in the air. Elena skidded to an abrupt stop. Behind her stood a wall of fire, over two hundred feet high, where the buildings surrounding the Capitol Building had once been, and spontaneous conflagrations were combusting all around her. The air must have been 150 degrees, and the D.C. fire department was going need every ounce of the water that hydrant could have supplied.

You can forget about that one, boys, Elena thought grimly.

Hot as it was, however, Elena didn't take her leathers off. Gas mains under the street and gas jets in the buildings were exploding all over the place, their fiery blasts breaking up pavement and blowing out office windows. Flying chunks of concrete, masonry, and glass shards continually ripped her leathers and rang off her helmet. Many of the survivors, wandering and crawling around the sidewalk and street, looked to her as if they had been blown to pieces with buckshot.

Unable to negotiate the wreckage-strewn streets, Elena attempted to climb the curb and walk her bike up the sidewalk. Second Avenue's sidewalks, however, were also impassable. Even now, the upturned Cadillac SUV blocked her. Walking her bike around the Caddie, she worked her way up the street for several more blocks. Shoving and dragging the Kawasaki around the smoking remains of burnt-out cars, past torn, bloodied, spread-eagled casualties, and over piles of masonry that had been blown out of the walls of shattered buildings, she was now dizzy and light-headed from hypoxia, the smoke-filled air nauseatingly unbreathable.

Stay focused. Get your ass out of here.

Like Lot's wife, however, who could not refrain from looking back, Elena had to bear witness to the hellworld around her. The sidewalk and street were littered with hideously disfigured people, their bodies charred and bleeding, seared by thermal blast burns and machine-gunned by flying glass.

Fires were igniting everywhere, and she was choking on the smoke. The fireball that had consumed the Capitol Building had started to die and descend, but its mushroom cloud was still swelling and levitating, casting a black deathlike pall on those sections of the city unilluminated by fire.

She pushed her bike past a sobbing high-school-age girl in sandals, shorts, and what had been a tank top. She'd removed the shirt and thrown it away, but Elena still knew it had been a tank top. The burns on her body mimicked the lines of the shoulder straps. Elena knew darker shades absorbed heat more intensively than lighter colors. On this tank top's front had been darkly emblazoned:

Washington Nationals

Black as charcoal, those letters were now seared into the girl's breasts.

All around her thousands upon thousands of the walking dead stumbled blindly through the night, many having lost their vision to the initial flash. The horribly scorched held their arms above their agonizingly charred bodies to avoid touching their inflamed torsos. Radically dehydrated from their burns, they staggered up the sidewalks and streets, sobbing, *"Water. Water. Water."*

And then she heard a tearing, groaning, deafening howl, as if some stupendously powerful Godzilla, gone mad with feral suffering, was bellowing an earsplitting, skull-exploding roar of primordial rage. She turned to face it and then saw that a soaring glass-and-steel tube, less than a hundred feet across and a thousand feet tall, was starting to go down. It was the Capitol Needle—the hotel she'd just visited—ripping loose from of its steel-rod and -plate moorings. Angling out over the city, it hung there for a seeming eternity, then began its torturous descent. Slowly, slowly, breaking free, it finally began to fall. Dropping, dropping, dropping, faster, faster, faster, it plummeted until its earth-cracking crash knocked Elena to her knees, smashing and devastating the world around her, shaking her to her soul, like a planet-killing comet strike.

Landing less than half a block from her, Elena saw and felt the whole thing.

This is Death City, kid. It's like Hasad said: Get the fuck out of Dodge.

Pulling herself to her feet, she finally pushed her big Kawasaki off the sidewalk, swung on, and was once again back on H Street.

But now the congestion was starting to lighten up. This was the government district, and the area was packed with unlit government office buildings. Since it was dark, all the workers had gone home. The traffic and wrecked vehicles slowed her down, but it was far less crowded than it would have been had Hasad nuked the Capitol Building at noon. The farther she got from that area, the fewer cars she encountered.

Soon she was once again twisting crazily in and out of traffic at 90 mph, tires smoking and engine screaming like damned souls in hell. Next a screeching left onto Massachusetts Ave, then a savage skid around Columbus Circle. Cutting in and out of traffic at 95 mph, she hammered past that grand old granite edifice, Union Station.

No time for sightseeing, girl.

Skidding onto K Street NW, then First Street NW, then back onto K, she was westbound and down, tires shrieking around Washington Circle. Rocketing up K at 115 mph, slipping in and out of honking cars, she finally spotted her destination. Grinding the breaks frantically, she careened into 3000 K, the Washington Harbour, at a full slide.

Still she stayed on the bike, banging down the stone steps at 40 mph, bouncing on and off the seat like a drunken bull-buster fighting the clock for a hard, hot eight. Circling round the plaza's big circular fountain, she washboarded up and down more steps, cutting through the open-air tables at Tony and Joe's Seafood Place, onto the Potomac riverwalk, right up to the boat marina.

At which point she saw Jamie standing there on the walkway, waiting for her—just like he said he would—in pristine white pants, a white polo shirt, white boating shoes, a white New York Yankees baseball cap, and dark Armani sunglasses. He was drinking a bottle of Heineken and looking like he'd just stepped out of central casting for *The Great Gatsby.*

He was waiting for her in front of his 2006 MTI 40 Series offshore catamaran—the one with two Mercury 575 horsepower engines. It was the same boat Sonny Crockett had piloted to Cuba in the film *Miami Vice.* It could outrun anything on the sea.

Pandemonium reigned on the river walkway. Hundreds of people were milling and crowding about hysterically, begging boat owners for a ride.

"Ready?" Jamie asked.

"We are so fucking out of here," Elena said.

Swinging off the bike, Elena let it fall where it stood. Following Jamie, she jumped onto the boat without looking back. Jamie was already seated and at the wheel. His four armed guards in jeans, T-shirts and wraparound shades and with MP9s slung under their sport coats stood guard in front of the catamaran. After Elena boarded, the guards cast them off, then headed for their own power launch.

Taking the seat next to him, Elena pulled an icy bottle of Heineken out of the red cooler on the deck beside her. A church key was in the cooler with it. Cracking it open, she took a long pull.

Jamie was already bouncing them up the Potomac toward the sea.

Flat out, pedal to the metal.

5

She wondered if he had made it.
—Jules Meredith

Time to get the hell out of here," Elias shouted into Jules's and Sandy's headsets.

Thick, dark, oily smoke was billowing out of the burnt-out choppers and the twisted remains of the armored personnel vehicles.

A dense white soot-filled smog engulfed the HRNPS. Fire, however, did illuminate some portions of the plant. At least four of the buildings—including the spent fuel warehouses—were ferociously aflame. The dry-cask spent-fuel silos—which were in the open and plainly visible—blazed fiercely, proving once and for all that dry casks were not as safe as the nuclear industry had so tenaciously and deceptively proclaimed.

"Any last words for our viewers?" Jules asked.

"Yeah," Elias said, "head upwind, if you want to avoid radiation poisoning. The three of us have been lucky in that a hard wind's been blowing off the Hudson River sweeping the shit south. We're still breathing in some of it though."

Sandy swung north, heading straight into the headwind.

"This is where the cowgirls ride away," she yelled into her radio.

"Then I'll see your souls in hell," Elias shouted back, his mad laughter convulsing their headsets.

Somehow Sister Cassandra's "Mission Apocalypse" continued to pound at their eardrums.

Where do we flee when the End's at hand?
Where do we run when it's our last stand?
Who has our back when the End times land?

When the mission's apocalypse
The mission's apocalypse
The mission's apocalypse

334 | ROBERT GLEASON

Then came the bridge:

> *Oh, who has the deal when we're too scared to cry?*
> *How does it end? Will the whole world fry?*
> *What do we do? Must everyone die?*
>
> *When the mission's apocalypse*
> *The mission's apocalypse*
> *The mission's apocalypse*
>
> *When the mission's apocalypse*
> *The mission's apocalypse*
> *The mission's apocalypse*

All the while, Jules was duct taping the ventilation holes, door frames, and windshield edges—even as she and her sister gulped down iodine tablets.

But as they fled the plant and its toxic soot-heavy smoke, the reactors were also generating incalculable quantities of hydrogen gas inside their containment domes. The burning of the fuel rods' zirconium cladding was filling the two concrete-and-steel hemispheres with intensely flammable H_2, as if inflating a pair of Hindenburg dirigibles. The gas was so light it instantly shot up to the top and stayed there. As the amount increased, however, and the gas expanded, the hydrogen levels inside the domes dropped lower and lower, closer and closer to the fires below, finally reaching the now nakedly exposed, incendiary fuel rods below. When the gas finally touched the flames, the explosion was almost beyond comprehension.

At first, Jules thought Elias had set off a pair of nukes. The twin fireballs blasted the concrete dome casing several miles in all directions. Even though the chopper was now two miles away, several shards hammered its rear cabin. The other pieces rocketed past like artillery rounds, thankfully circumventing their helicopter.

Jules glance one last time at HRNPS and saw two gargantuan globes of scintillating fire rising above a pair of disintegrated domes, ascending high over the obliterated nuclear plant and riding the thermal down-river drafts toward New York City.

With excruciating lassitude, the debris began falling to earth, barely missing the rotor and the blades but pummeling everything else. Looking back through her Vortex Viper HD 12×50 binoculars, Jules could see that most of the HRNPS was gone, and the guard tower, where Elias had stationed himself, was a shattered wreck.

She wondered if he had made it.

But then all at once, Sandy was yelling at her:

"You won't believe it, Jules, but Rashid and Adara are on the radio. They've got some big oceangoing boat and are twenty minutes from here on the Connecticut coast. They're in a cove with a big empty beach. We're setting down there, then boarding the craft."

"What about Elena and Jamie?" Jules asked.

"We're meeting them along the Jersey shore in the morning."

"And then?" Jules asked.

"We're all Belize-bound."

"Lord knows what happens then," Jules said.

"Whatever it is," Sandy said, "it's got to be better than what's happening here."

"Copy that."

By some perverse miracle, the final refrain of "Mission Apocalpyse" was suddenly thundering out of the rubble of the gun tower, Elias's audio system eerily and inexplicably intact.

Who do we turn to when it's time to die?
How do we stop the children's cries?
Where do we hide when the End is nigh?

Oh, what do we do when the bill comes due?
Where do we flee when humanity's through?
Where do we run when it all comes down?
How do we die when the End rolls 'round?

When the mission's apocalypse
The mission's apocalypse
The mission's apocalypse

When the mission's apocalypse
The mission's apocalypse
The mission's apocalypse

When the mission's apocalypse
The mission's apocalypse
The mission's apocalypse

Sandy banked east and headed for the Connecticut coast.

EPILOGUE

When the dust has settled,
When the thermonuclear
Dust comes down,
When the fallout drifts slowly,
Slowly to the ground.
Will anyone be around?
Will anyone be around?

—Sister Cassandra, "When the Dust Has Settled"

1

We kept the faith.
—Jules Meredith

The three nuclear attacks had been so singularly horrific that many leaders in the U.S. and abroad sought a war against Islam, some even arguing for nuclear strikes. Fortunately, the American vice president, James C. Hoffman, who had been undergoing minor surgery at the Bethesda Naval Hospital at the time of the State of the Union attack, survived. After taking office, he resisted these demands for nuclear retribution on the grounds that no one at that time knew who the real state sponsors of the attack were. He refused to nuke entire populations out of a lust for revenge.

So the apocalyptic land war in the Mideast—which, according to General Jari's Islamist texts would commence in Dabiq and in al-Amaq in northern Syria and would end in the West's final obliteration—did not materialize. Furthermore, had Jari claimed credit for the attacks, it had become clear that he would have only elicited the thermonuclear destruction of his homeland as well as much of the Mideast. He would not provoke the land-fought Armageddon, from which he had mistakenly believed his people would emerge victorious. Even the most fanatical extremists saw no percentage in provoking the vaporization of entire Islamic states. Consequently, no one in the jihadist movement claimed credit for the attacks. Staring into the nuclear abyss, General Jari and the terrorists . . . blinked.

Hoffman's peacemaking efforts cost him a second term as president, but he did prevent a Middle Eastern Götterdämmerung.

As the months wore on and it became clear no one could prove that a foreign power had sponsored the attacks, people wanted scapegoats. The news media was quick to blame Elena Moreno and Jules Meredith. Many of the country's talking heads even claimed to have "absolute proof" that the two women had engineered the nuclear assaults. Moreover, before President Caldwell, William Conrad, and Ambassador Shaiq were killed, they and General Jari had fabricated incriminating e-mails and text messages from the women to Hasad ibn Ghazi—a known global terrorist—in which Elena and Jules allegedly helped him plan the three strikes. The evidence seemed irrefutable.

There were also the five incontestable communications between Elena and Hasad, confirming at the very least that Elena had somehow been his friend—a fact she'd illegally concealed from the Agency. And, of course, witnesses eventually came forward, testifying that the two had dated in college.

The women's subsequent actions also made them appear guilty. Among other things, they'd fled. Their reasoning was simple. They refused to submit to a star-chamber tribunal packed with hanging judges who would have tried them on trumped-up charges, then convicted and sentenced them under the Patriot Act's antiterrorist statutes. They would have undoubtedly faced life without parole in a Guantanamo-type hellhole or lethal injection in some federal pen. Free, they could still work to prove their innocence.

Jules's sister, Sandy—under indictment for aiding and abetting her mass-murdering sister—also joined them abroad.

First, Jamie took the three women to Belize, which, long ago, he had effectively bought and now owned. Then he flew to Sweden—where he personally convinced the Swedish prime minister that the women could not get a fair trial in the U.S. and that they were innocent. Once they were granted asylum by the Swedish government, they settled down in Stockholm.

Jamie and his three friends eventually moved to an old castle-fortress perched on a mountaintop, previously owned by Sweden's prime minister. He hired a small army of private contractors to fortify and defend it. The world press was rife with rumors and news reports that a CIA/Navy SEAL abduction attempt was likely, and Elena, in particular, saw to it they were militarily prepared for such a contingency.

They had been in the castle a little more than a year when Hasad's Swiss banker called them. Hasad had $23 million in a Swiss bank in gold bullion in a numbered account, the banker said. In the event of his death, he had told the banker to notify Elena Moreno and explain that she was his sole beneficiary. The bankers had spent a full year confirming that Hasad was dead.

"Oh yes," the bankers told her on the phone, "there is one other item—a small padded envelope, which is only to be opened in private by Elena Moreno."

Jamie arranged to have the money deposited in an account under Elena's name and have armed, certified couriers deliver the envelope in person to her at the castle.

The package contained a flash drive. Being one of the world's top computer experts, Jamie made multiple copies of it. He and the two women then examined its contents on a desktop computer with a forty-inch monitor.

The USB stick held detailed evidence proving that Shaiq and Jari had conspired to inflict three nuclear strikes on the U.S. Shaiq had also planned to blackmail President George Caldwell by threatening to expose his illegal financial dealings. Hasad had evidence on the flash drive that Caldwell had accepted Saudi bribes and hidden them in offshore tax havens. Hasad had the locations and account numbers of those clandestine accounts on the thumb drive. Hasad also had evidence that Shaiq—in order to eventually blackmail Caldwell and Conrad—had counterfeited e-mails allegedly proving that Caldwell had knowledge of the impending attacks and failed to notify the FBI, the CIA, or the National Security Council. Shaiq had intended to use those manufactured e-mails to terrify Caldwell into secretly handing over to Shaiq the reins of American power. He would then force Caldwell to use the nukings to frighten the U.S. Congress into tearing up the Constitution and giving Caldwell martial power. After Caldwell declared martial law, Shaiq would become the power behind the throne—the absolute dictator of the United States.

On the flash drive, Hasad also provided them with both written and voice-recorded testimony exonerating the women of any wrongdoing. Hasad apologized to the world for ever having "gotten involved with such an appalling gang of psychopaths."

He concluded with a bizarre coda that would become world famous:

I've done a lot of bad things in my life, but I've never believed humanity, as a whole, was bad. Except when it comes to things nuclear. I've watched the Bomb summon forth the wickedest hubris in the human soul. Like the serpent in Eden, its dark power told us that we could become as gods. We, too, could grasp the Luciferian flame, wage war on the planet, and lay waste to the stars.

As you know, Elena, back in college I was fascinated by the Greeks—Homer, Aeschylus, Thucydides. Remember that speech I used to recite to you from Aeschylus' *Agamemnon*? I used to tell you it summarized everything we would ever need to know about humankind.

We learn nothing save through suffering.
The pain of memory falls drop by drop
Upon the heart in sleep.

Against our will comes wisdom.
The grace of the gods is forced on us.

Maybe in the end, that's why I did what I did. Your country created nuclear weapons and peddled their technology worldwide to anyone and everyone who wanted it, no matter how dangerous the purchasers. If your people saw and felt firsthand, on their bones and blood, the horror and agony atom bombs and nuclear meltdowns visit on living, breathing flesh, if they realized the consequences of their nuclear trafficking and how easily feasible such strikes were, maybe, just maybe, they'd awaken from their blind avarice, their fatalistic denial . . . and see that the light at the tunnel's end need not be the fireball's blaze.

It took Europe, Japan, and Russia two world wars to purge them of their war-lust. Maybe the U.S. needed these nuclear attacks before they were cured of their nuclear insanity.

At least, that's how I eventually came to justify what I did. On the other hand, maybe you knew me better. That night after I'd laid out those three football players who had assaulted you and Jules, with those socks filled with batteries, you had kidded me about it, calling me your "Fourth Horseman of the Apocalypse." Maybe you were right. Maybe that was always my destiny: the Fourth Horseman, "whose name was Death and hell followed with him."

One thing's for sure—I certainly brought hell to your homeland.

Still, I hope some good comes out of it.

He'd certainly shown Americans the consequences of their nuclear profligacy—"on their bones and blood." A uniquely severe El Niño had exacerbated those prevailing westerly winds, and they were blowing especially hard the night of the HRNPS attack as well as during the weeks that followed. Lifting the plant's nuclear dust and debris high into the air, the winds carried and deposited endless tons of it onto the heavily populated Tri-State area, but they mostly carried the fallout out to sea.

Still, the Tri-State area had been caught unprepared. For decades, critics had derided the nuclear plant's "evacuation plan" as "a fantasy document." The meltdown's true "zone of lethality" was everything within a radius of a hundred miles, and in reality no one knew how to evacuate and provide for the zone's twenty million inhabitants. So FEMA's first serious plan was to supply those affected with duct tape, iodine tablets, water, food, flashlights, portable radios, batteries, and medicine. When FEMA proved incapable of quick, timely house-to-house deliveries, the supplies were simply deposited in central storage sites, and the citizens were invited to brave the endless deluge of radioactive fallout and pick them up.

FEMA advised everyone within a hundred miles of HRNPS to duct tape the edges of their windows and doors, then to stay indoors. Almost no one was sufficiently provisioned to do that for long. Many ultimately fled their homes, took to the highway in their cars. Some even left on bicycles or on foot. Too often, they found their journeys fraught with violence, robbery, hunger, toxic fallout, disease, and death.

On the other hand, staying home was no panacea. Looting, injuries, illness, and death were pandemic. Millions eventually contracted radiation sickness.

The Edward Teller Nuclear Weapons Laboratory was outside San Francisco, and the City on the Bay suffered even worse than New York's Tri-State area. Unbeknownst to the bombers, some six hundred yards south of the cannon bomb was a boxcar filled with long steel storage containers. They were packed with bomb-grade HEU in the form of flat-bottomed rings, vertically aligned. These rings essentially had the same size, shape, and upright positioning as the HEU rings in the first atom bomb and as those rings inside the Bear Flag cannon-barrel atom bomb. The rings' steel storage boxes were twelve feet long and a foot across, and they functioned as a kind of Hiroshima gun barrel. Moreover, the long rectangular steel boxes were encased in a concrete container. When the A-bomb blew, its shockwave struck the ends of the HEU containers, slamming the rings one into the other with the power of the stars, telescoping them like colliding boxcars in a high-speed train wreck. Unfortunately, the storage rings' steel and concrete containment system served to compress and exponentially increase the explosion's power.

The rings did not achieve supercriticality, but there were so many tons of bomb-grade HEU in those containers that the detonation's yield was a thousand times that of the Hiroshima bomb.

The two combined blasts lifted billions of tons of radioactive debris into the air. Unfortunately, a hot, powerful wind, generated in part by a million-acre wildfire to the east, carried the poisonous debris through the mountain pass straight toward San Francisco. The state of California, which had long suffered a record-setting drought, was about to experience a record-setting rainstorm. Most Californians were grateful for the much-needed precipitation.

Not the citizens of San Francisco.

Not now.

The monstrous cloud of radioactive fallout appeared over San Francisco just as the deluge commenced, turning the torrential downpour into a filthy, pitch-black rainstorm of radioactive death. Its toxicity was total. Such black rain constituted the most lethal form fallout could take.

San Francisco was rendered an uninhabitable wasteland for decades to come. For over a year, evacuation of that city proved to be impossible, and the death toll soared.

The San Francisco and New York disasters were expected to eventually cost millions of lives and over $100 trillion.

Then there was Washington, D.C. True to his word, Hasad had removed some of the extra-high explosive from the bomb's trigger. The bomb, however, was still more potent than he had expected. He had reduced its yield not to a single kiloton but closer to four kilotons, which was enough to set fire to most of the city. Obliterating many of D.C.'s most famous landmarks, it razed the White House and flattened the Capitol Building. It toppled the Washington Monument and leveled the Lincoln Memorial. It also burned K Street—the lobbying capital of the world—down to the ground.

The deaths ran over a million.

Many nations had drunk the nuclear power Kool-Aid, and they had built such plants by the hundreds. Some nations, however, had grown increasingly skeptical of nuclear power's unsustainable costs and myriad dangers. The U.S., for instance, had closed Indian Point, which had been a mere thirty miles from New York City. A terrorist strike against Indian Point would have contaminated New York for all time.

Canada, too, had become increasingly aware of nuclear power's hazards, particularly the threat of terrorist strikes. To avoid a panic, their leaders kept their operations secret, but they built several Chernobyl-style containment shells in prefabricated sections. They quickly transported the segmented shells to the devastated New York plant. There, outfitted in hazmat suits, crews of spectacularly brave Canadian technicians cobbled the pieces of the dome together. It covered the ravaged reactor like a sarcophagus.

The first shell was a solid, impermeable, but temporary structure, capable of preventing the radiation's spread for at least two years—long enough for a permanent concrete-and-steel shroud to be installed over the hastily built dome.

Some nuclear pollution had reached New York City—enough that the EPA had to raise their previous toxicity standards in order to declare the city's new increased toxicity levels as marginally acceptable. Pregnant women were temporarily evacuated, but most people remained in their homes, sheltering in place. That state of affairs did not last long, however. Soon people drifted out of their residences and returned to work. Within six weeks, most of the city's citizens were back on the job, and the city was chugging along as it always had.

Notoriously resilient, most New Yorkers refused to be cowed by the plant's meltdown. Throughout the entire ordeal, the major networks had continued to broadcast out of New York, the newspapers had continued to publish, and it was said thereafter that nothing short of a direct nuclear hit could force New Yorkers to abandon the Big Apple.

Still, the damage to the U.S. was catastrophic in both human and financial terms. Globally, the three nuclear strikes created an economic depression that wreaked inconceivable havoc, ultimately bankrupting many of the planet's corporations, to say nothing of ordinary citizens. At times, it seemed as if the world would never recover.

The good news was that any and all naiveté over nuclear weapons and nuclear power had come to an end. The people of the world had always hated nuclear power and nuclear bombs, and the industry had survived only because a handful of politically rich plutocrats reaped fortunes off these taxpayer-financed enterprises and had bought off the politicians.

Those days would come to an end.

It took a few more nuclear terrorist strikes for antinuclear rage to reach a global tipping point, but eventually, over the years, it did come to pass. Now the hatred of things nuclear was visceral, ubiquitous, and unyielding. People took to the streets with an unprecedented rage. After the riots began, it took less than a year to ban nuclear power and nuclear weapons. Even nuclear reactors and nuclear fuel were universally outlawed. Any person caught violating the antinuclear law, including any corporate head or political leader responsible for the violation of those laws, was subject to life in prison without parole.

A heavily armed global force was given almost unlimited military and political power to enforce the new antinuclear laws.

An international tribunal was empowered to indict, convict, and sentence offenders.

Elena also discovered that Hasad had left a diary on his flash drive—a memoir of sorts. It did not make for pretty reading. His life had been a nightmare horror show. When, at age two, George H. W. Bush's Baghdad bombing killed his parents, he was thrown into Iraq's orphanage system. There, he learned to fight for survival—with no quarter given. Fearless,

346 | ROBERT GLEASON

possessing an intuitive affinity for violence, he was, while still in his teens, recruited into Saddam Hussein's Republican Guard, where he was soon dragooned into its Special Forces. He became especially adept at assassinations.

After the toppling of Saddam and Iraq, he fought for a variety of groups, including al Qaeda, ISIS, and Pakistan's ISI. He was more interested in money than ideology, however, and he eventually began selling his services to the highest bidder.

His only reprieve from this life of unremitting violence was the nine months he spent in the U.S., hanging out with Jules and Elena. The ISI had sent him there to learn to "speak like an American" in anticipation of future undercover operations in the U.S. However, hanging out with the two women, he learned something else. He confessed they were the only two people he had ever loved.

Obsessed with his narrative, Jules wrote his biography, entitling it *Gunman*. A global megabestseller and international blockbuster movie, it made Jules millions.

It even changed many people's opinion of Hasad. As catastrophic as his attacks were, he had achieved something all the antinuclear people and peace protesters had failed to accomplish in close to a century of effort.

Hasad ibn Ghazi had, Jules wrote, eradicated "all things nuclear."

In her next book, she then set out to write the story of her and her best friend, Elena Moreno. It was the hardest, most painful thing she would ever do.

She wrote of their hardscrabble childhood in the West Texas border country desert, Elena's gangster father, her own family's struggles, college, and of Elena's falling in love with a murderous undercover terrorist named Hasad ibn Ghazi. She wrote of her years as a journalist; the wars she'd covered, often with her sister, Sandy; Elena's two decades as a CIA NOC, later as head of the Pakistan desk. Jules wrote of Elena's mad passionate fling with Jamie, which he could never forget; and of Hasad returning to the States; the terrorist attacks; Elena's race through D.C.'s fiery streets to kill Hasad; Jules's chopper coverage of the flaming, smoking inferno that had been the Hudson River Nuclear Power Station. She wrote of then fleeing the country; of Jamie's devoted, unswerving support of them both despite the U.S. government's and the media's persecution; the endless death threats; the loyalty of the Swedish prime minister and government, to the point that Sweden was expelled from the EU for refusing to extradite the four fugitives. Jules wrote of their never-ending fears of a CIA abduction and danger of them languishing forever in supermaxes or dying by lethal injection. At last, however, thanks to the posthumous intervention of a violent, mass-murdering, nuclear psychopath, Hasad ibn Ghazi, she and her friends were vindicated, redeemed, and lauded by the same media and the same governments that had previously screamed for their blood.

Jules, of course, had to find a title for the book. One thing that had always haunted her was the idiocy of Caldwell and the gang of nuclear power zealots with whom he had surrounded himself. He was always raving about how nuclear power was the hope of the future and how nuclear power would turn our nuclear weapons into nuclear plowshares, saving humanity from the Damocles sword of nuclear war. Once, when Jules and Elena had been watching the president speak on TV, they heard him proclaim in one of his loonier moments:

"Thanks to nuclear power, we can finally jump out of the nuclear frying pan!"

"Yeah," Elena had muttered to Jules, "and into the fire."

Jules titled her book:

And Into the Fire.

And so their odyssey came to an end. The four friends found their Ithaca. Sweden was now their home. None of them wanted to return to the United States. There was too much blood under the bridge.

Yes, writing that story was the hardest, most painful thing Jules Meredith would ever do. But finally the ordeal was over, the story told. At the book's conclusion, Jules tried to sum up what it had all meant, what their journey had come down to, what any life comes down to in the end. It all was an almost impossible task, but still she tried. Leaning on St. Paul's last letter, she wrote:

> *In the end we did all any of us can do: We ran our race. We finished the course. We kept the faith.*
> *Yes, <u>we kept the faith.</u>*

And with those final words, Jules Meredith ended her book.

AFTERWORD

Once when I was a young New York book editor, I commissioned an alien invasion novel. It was to be very violent. In fact, at one point, in order to subdue humankind, the aliens were to push an asteroid into our orbit and slam our planet into it. The consequences of the asteroid strike were earth-shattering in the extreme. I was twenty-nine at the time and had never heard of anything so horrendous. Almost no one had back then. The magnitude of the destruction so consumed me that I asked the authors to also do a synopsis for a second novel about an asteroid colliding with our planet.

Eventually the authors, Larry Niven and Jerry Pournelle, turned the premise into two books. The collision novel was *Lucifer's Hammer,* a number two *New York Times* bestseller, and the alien invasion novel became *Footfall,* a number one *New York Times* bestselling novel.

However, when the authors sat down to write *Lucifer's Hammer,* they made one important change. They substituted a comet for the incoming asteroid, which made the impact even more disastrous. Among other things, comets can hit harder than asteroids. Their velocities are often two to three times higher, and they're frequently much larger—up to sixty miles across. Their hard rocky nuclei are bound together by ice, and their orbits are often erratic, making their strikes harder to predict. Since they possess dazzlingly luminous comas and tails, they are scintillatingly radiant.

In the novel, our comet swung a little too close to the sun, which melted the binding ice. The nucleus broke up into two Mount Everests of rock, which then rocketed toward the earth at something like forty miles per second. One mountain hit the Atlantic Ocean, one the Pacific. Each of the masses passed through the earth's atmosphere and the two oceans in mere seconds, hitting the oceans' floors largely undegraded, almost without slowing down. Their momentum—mass times velocity—was beyond comprehension, generating mile-high tsunamis, which inundated most of America's East and West Coasts. Each of the strikes cracked the earth's mantle, liberating zillions of tons of magma—the molten iron from the earth's core—which, in turn, vaporized zillions of tons of seawater, which came down in the temperate regions as saltwater rain, thereby destroying the topsoil for thousands of years to come, and in the polar regions as ice and snow, thus inaugurating a new Ice Age.

The comet destroyed civilization pretty much . . . forever.

Lucifer's Hammer was and remains the most overpowering novel I've ever read. It haunted me while I edited it, and it still haunts me to this day.

About five years later, I began writing professionally, and in the back of my mind I always wanted to tackle an end-of-the-world novel. In fact, while my first novel was on submission and I had a few months to kill, I attempted a nuclear Armageddon novel. The year was 1982, it was during the Cold War, so I had the U.S. and Russia hit each other with all the nukes at their disposal.

I even composed a two-hundred-page treatment. I did not take the next step, however—the writing of the novel—because I could never make the scenario work. The problem with an all-out Russian–U.S. nuclear exchange scenario was that it was a mutual suicide pact. I could find no plausible motive for either side to willfully self-destruct.

Instead, I wrote a sequel to my unwritten end-of-the-world novel, titling it *Wrath of God.* It did well, both critically and commercially, despite the outrageousness of its plot. Rosie O'Donnell, the redoubtable stand-up comic and talk show host, once asked me to describe that plot. I said in a single breath, as rapidly as I could, like an insane tobacco auctioneer desperate for bids:

"George-S.-Patton-'Stonewall'-Jackson-Amelia-Earhart-and-a-dinosaur-fight-Tamerlane-and-the-Great-Islamic-Horde-in-the-late-twenty-first-century-in-the-southwestern-desert-after-a-nuclear-apocalypse."

"Smoke a lot of crack, don't you, Bob?" Rosie responded.

While *Wrath of God* was a lot of fun, I still wanted to write a big end-of-the-world novel in which I dramatized in great detail the obliteration of humankind. After all, every one of our religions and mythologies has had a Genesis myth and an End Time myth, and the End Time myths are invariably the more interesting. It's in our blood. We want to know what humanity's grand finale will be like. But I still didn't have a plausible plot—not for a nuclear apocalypse.

Then the world changed. In 1991, we witnessed the breakup of the old USSR. Overnight, their centralized security system collapsed, and security at their nuclear bomb-fuel storage sites evaporated. The guards simply walked off the job. Fissile nuclear bomb fuel was there for the taking. Russell Seitz called Russia during this period, "The yard sale at the end of history."

For some time, I'd studied the technology of nuclear weapons. I'd learned that once in possession of bomb-grade highly enriched uranium (HEU), the fabrication of a crude but powerful Hiroshima-style terrorist nuke was surprisingly simple. I learned, for instance, that if a terrorist placed a grapefruit-sized chunk of bomb-grade HEU on the ground and then dropped an identical chunk onto it from a height of six feet, the impact could achieve half the Hiroshima yield. If he put two smaller chunks into a piece of cannon barrel—an old Civil War cannon barrel would do—tamped off the ends, and blasted one into the other with extra-high explosive, a terrorist could conceivably achieve the Hiroshima yield. As Luis Avarez, who designed the Hiroshima bomb's triggering mechanism said, a couple of high school kids could do it.

I'd then read a book by Herman Kahn called *Thinking About the Unthinkable.* Kahn created a lot of nuclear scenarios in which various countries suffered different kinds of nuclear attacks; he then analyzed what the nation's response options were. One of his scenarios was called Catalytic Nuclear War, in which "a small vengeful power" nuked other nations but created the illusion that one or more of the great powers was guilty of the attacks. Example? Pakistan could surreptitiously nuke China but would deceive the Chinese into believing India did it. China would then retaliate against India with nukes, and India would nuke China in response.

Some experts have said that catalytic nuclear war is our most frighteningly plausible scenario for a global nuclear Götterdämmerung. I used Kahn's concept as the basis for my novel *End of Days.*

Still, I needed an antagonist with a plausible motive for launching these attacks and fomenting a nuclear End Time.

Once again, reality intervened. During the 1990s, Sunni Islamist terrorists launched a series of bombing attacks on Americans—on the World Trade Center in 1993; on the U.S. Air Force living quarters in Khobar, Saudi Arabia, in 1996; on two U.S. African embassies in 1998; on the USS *Cole* in 2000; and again on 9/11/01 when they flattened both of the World Trade Centers and wiped out part of the Pentagon in a series of kamikaze-style airliner crashes. Al Qaeda—which executed the last three attacks—was a cult, bent on launching nuclear attacks against the United States. A dozen years after 9/11, its spin-off organization, ISIS, would announce that they sought a Middle Eastern Armageddon.

Now I had my villains.

My research, however, was time and labor intensive. While many people, including every American president in my lifetime, talked publicly about how frightened they were of nuclear terrorism, when I combed the major newspapers, magazines, and Web sites, I found almost nothing of substance on the subject. Nor was anyone writing books about how such attacks would be planned, equipped, and executed. Studying an almost nonexistent subject was a long, arduous, tortuous challenge.

End of Days took me almost fifteen years to write—largely because the research was so difficult. True, I did other things in between. I was and still am a full-time book editor, and I also co-authored a series of five Aztec novels, started by the late Gary Jennings, the number-one *New York Times* bestselling author of *Aztec* and *Aztec Autumn*. But I put at least ten of those years into *End of Days*, and when it was finished, I'd done so much research I felt another book needed to be written. Most of the factual information I'd collected over that period did not exist in book form. I felt I needed to get it all down for those who were interested in the subject.

But were I to put all that information into a book, how would I organize it and what would I emphasize? One fact jumped out at me right away. I'd tracked down a couple of scientific reports—one from the Oak Ridge National Laboratory, the other from the Sandia National Laboratories. They both proved that terrorists would have a shockingly easy time building a fissile nuclear bomb-fuel reprocessor. With the equipment from an old dairy or an old winery, a half dozen nuclear technicians could build a fissile nuclear bomb-fuel reprocessor in just six months. In as little as a month—according to Oak Ridge—they could extract enough plutonium from the spent fuel rods to power the Nagasaki bomb.

In other words, a nuclear reactor—with the addition of a low-tech, easy-to-build fissile nuclear bomb-fuel reprocessor—was a fissile nuclear bomb-fuel factory.

But then, given the fact that these reactors were so potentially dangerous, why were we selling them worldwide to anyone with the money to pay for them? In fact, if the nation didn't have the money, the U.S. would often give it to them in the form of a federally guaranteed loan.

President Eisenhower started this global nuclear proliferation movement. Back in 1953, he had established Atoms for Peace, in which he declared all nations had an inalienable right to nuclear power (assuming that the U.N.'s atomic energy agency did not catch them using their nuclear technology for military purposes). Under Atoms for Peace, the U.S. began purveying nuclear reactors globally, knowing full well that with the addition of a low-tech fissile bomb-fuel reprocessor, the spent fuel rods could be converted to bomb-grade plutonium. As a further gesture of good will, Eisenhower even released many of the most deeply classified scientific-engineering secrets to nuclear weapons production.

Eisenhower claimed that proliferating nuclear fuel and nuclear reactors to the nations of earth would make the world a safer place, saying, "Who can doubt, if the entire body of the world's scientists and engineers had adequate amounts of fissionable material with which to test and develop their ideas, that this capability would be rapidly transformed into universal, efficient, and economic usage?"

Eisenhower said this even after the USSR had warned him that the global proliferation of nuclear power reactors would ultimately result in the global proliferation of fissile nuclear bomb-fuel factories. As I have pointed out, extracting bomb-grade plutonium from rods was a low-tech, straightforward operation. If the U.S. wanted to stop the proliferation of fissile nuclear bomb-fuel, the USSR told him, it had to block the proliferation not only of nuclear power reactors, but of all reactors. The facts were irrefutable, but Eisenhower ignored them. Instead, he made the U.S. the world's number-one nuclear proliferator. He sold Pakistan its first nuclear reactor and established the protocols that allowed Iran to purchase their first one as well. In other words, the U.S. sold both these nuclear rogues their first reactors.

So what was Eisenhower's motivation? I would argue that his reverence for free-trade, free-market capitalism trumped all national security concerns and made him almost criminally indifferent to the dangers of nuclear proliferation. It is certainly true that the USSR's prediction was right, and Eisenhower's utopian belief in the benefits of nuclear reactor proliferation was wrong. In the years following Eisenhower's Atoms for Peace speech at the U.N., nuclear power was the Trojan horse inside of which the nuclear rogues hid and developed their fissile nuclear bomb-fuel manufacturing programs.

But nuclear power was only part of the nuclear proliferaton/terrorism problem. Another energy industry was throwing money at the nuclear proliferators. When the nineteen hijackers flattened the Twin Towers, wiped out part of the Pentagon, and attempted to crash an airliner into the White House, the world quickly discovered that fifteen of the hijackers had been Saudis. Even worse, a number of important oil-rich Saudi royals had helped to bankroll some of the hijackers' preparations. As former Secretary of State Hillary Clinton would later say, wealthy Saudis were the premier financiers of Sunni-sponsored terror—that is, al Qaeda/ISIS-style terror—globally.

So where did all those Saudi petrodollars come from?

The U.S. was easily the world's biggest consumer of oil products. With 5 percent of the world's population, America consumed 25 percent of its hydrocarbon energy. So by that logic, the U.S. oil industry was also helping to back al Qaeda and eventually ISIS, which Saudi seed money had also helped to create.

The U.S. had always been in denial about the Saudis' support of terrorism. In Robert Baer's book *Sleeping with the Devil,* he wrote that when he was a CIA station chief in the Mideast, Saudi allegiance to the U.S. went unquestioned. Critical CIA investigations into the Saudi royals were discouraged, and he never even heard CIA officials seriously evaluate a possible Saudi terrorist threat. In his second book, *The Devil We Know,* Baer described the Bush administration's willful disregard for the Saudis' financing of terrorists and their nuclear sponsors.

Nor had anything changed since 9/11. U.S. politicians and defense contractors were still selling the Saudis hundreds of billions in high-tech weaponry. The Obama administration had single-handedly sold the Saudis over $100 billion worth of cutting-edge weaponry.

The facts regarding America's corrupt alliance with the Saudis were painful to contemplate:

- Saudi Arabia was one of only three nations, pre-9/11, that recognized Afghanistan's ruling Taliban as a legitimate government.
- Fifteen of the nineteen 9/11 hijackers were Saudis, but the Bush team did not demand instant access to their files in Riyadh or the right to immediately interrogate their friends, family, and associates in the Saudi Kingdom. Nor did the Bush administration punish the Saudis for their refusal to cooperate with U.S. agents for their willful obstruction of U.S. justice.
- Craig Unger documented in *House of Bush House of Saud* that the two Bush presidents and their close associates pocketed a total of $1.475 billion in Saudi paychecks, donations, and investments. In fact, Unger left out several lucrative payments—since he could not obtain precise figures—so he may have understated the total.
- The U.S. government blacked out twenty-eight pages on the Saudis' 9/11 participation in the official Congressional Report on 9/11. Members of the Senate Intelligence Committee in both parties characterized those deletions as a cover-up. Over a dozen years would pass before Barack Obama would eventually declassify those unredacted pages.
- After leaving the Senate, former senators Bob Graham and Bob Kerrey filed affidavits in court stating that serious evidence of Saudi involvement in 9/11 had not been pursued. Graham had been chair of the Senate Select Committee on Intelligence and had held that

position on 9/11. He'd also chaired the Congressional Joint Inquiry into 9/11. Kerrey had served on the official 9/11 Commission. They both had detailed knowledge about what the Bush team had hidden from the American public.

- Senator Graham was especially concerned about evidence that exposed high-level Saudi involvement in 9/11 that the FBI had concealed from the 9/11 Commission. In one instance, a rich Saudi couple in a well-to-do gated Sarasota community had walked away from their lavishly affluent house. They abandoned their opulent furnishings as well: three expensive automobiles, leaving dirty diapers in a bathroom, the running toy-filled pool, food in the refrigerator, mail on the table, and clothes in the closet. They fled to Riyadh, Saudi Arabia . . . two weeks before 9/11. The friends they left behind included three of the 9/11 pilots. Mohamed Atta, who had lived nearby, was one of them. Phone records, photographic evidence the security guards had gathered when their car went through the gate, and the guards' questioning of the passengers—all of it established the Saudi family's personal relationship with the three 9/11 pilots. They had phoned and visited the couple on a number of occasions. Furthermore, the house's owner was a wealthy Saudi financier closely connected to the ruling Saudi family, *but Bush's FBI had concealed all this information from the 9/11 Commission.*

- Two days after 9/11, the White House ordered 160 important Saudis flown out of the U.S. before the FBI's counterterrorism experts could debrief them. Many of these 160 passengers had clear connections to the bin Laden family; two dozen of them were relatives of bin Laden. They flew out of Washington, New York, Los Angeles, Chicago, Houston, Boston, Detroit, Atlanta, Dallas, Denver, San Francisco, Cincinnati, Newark, and Tampa. The Tampa flight—at the White House's request—was airborne at a time when all other private flights in the U.S. were grounded due to 9/11. Fifteen of the Saudis, who flew out of Lexington, Kentucky, left the U.S. in style. Craig Unger reported that their Boeing 727 came equipped with "a master bedroom suite furnished with a large upholstered double bed, a couch, nightstand, and credenza. The master bathroom had a gold-plated sink, double illuminated mirrors, and a bidet. There were brass, gold, and crystal fixtures. The main lounge had a 52-inch projection TV. The plane boasted a six-place conference room and dining room with a mahogany table that had controls for up and down movement."

Dan Grossi, a former Tampa police officer, and Manuel Perez, a retired FBI agent, accompanied the passengers on the flight. Perez now says: "The White House, the FAA, and the FBI all said the flight didn't happen." Grossi confirmed that Craig Unger's account of the Tampa flight in *House of Bush House of Saud* was accurate. However, when *The St. Petersburg Times* attempted to cover the story thirty-three months later, they reported: "The FAA is still not talking about the flights, referring all questions to the FBI, which isn't answering anything either. Nor is the 9/11 Commission."

The 9/11 Commission ignored the Tampa flight, which was authorized by the White House when all U.S. private flights were still grounded.

Furthermore, the Tampa International Airport said "its records indicated that no member of its [security] force screened the Lear [jet's] passengers."

Two days after 9/11, they were flying out of the country.

The contrast between the Bush administration's treatment of Saudi suspects and those of other Mideast countries was extreme. Unlike those Saudis, who were sneaked out of the U.S. after 9/11, other Middle Easterners—clearly not connected to bin Laden and al Qaeda—were herded up and incarcerated in Guantanamo Bay and INS facilities often for years on end. Colonel Douglas Macgregor, who retired from the U.S. Army in June 2004, reports: "We ended up incarcerating over 46,000 people, less than 10 percent of whom deserved to be incarcerated."

In *After: How America Confronted the September 12 Era*, Steve Brill reported:

"In the hours and days immediately following [the September 11] attacks, attorney General John Ashcroft . . . directed that FBI and INS agents question anyone they could find with a Muslim-sounding name . . . in some areas . . . they simply looked for names in the phone book . . . Anyone who could be held, even on a minor violation of law or immigration rules, was held under a three-pronged strategy, fashioned by Ashcroft and a close circle of Justice Department deputies including criminal division chief Michael Chertoff, that was intended to exert maximum pressure on these detainees."

Years After 9/11, al Qaeda Funders Still Operated with Impunity

Douglas Farah reported in *The Washington Post* that a full twenty-seven months after 9/11, Saudi charities backing bin Laden—and supposedly shut down—still operated worldwide with impunity.

Governments around the globe ignored sanctions designed to halt the flood of cash to al Qaeda, "allowing the terrorist network to retain formidable financial resources. . . ."

Businessmen and charities labeled by the U.N. as al Qaeda funders were allowed to run huge global operations and travel unchecked. The General Accounting Office reported U.S. law enforcement was equally in the dark and that the FBI still did not "systematically collect or analyze" data on al Qaeda's fund-raisers. "The Justice and Treasury departments had fallen more than a year behind in developing plans to attack terrorist financial mechanisms, such as the use of diamonds and gold to hide assets." The Council on Foreign Relations reported that over six months after 9/11, "Saudi Arabia . . . ha[d] yet to demand personal accountability" from its more prominent financiers of terrorism.

- Crown Prince Abdullah of Saudi Arabia told the Saudi people on national television that "Zionism is behind [9/11]," and Saudi Interior Minister Prince Nayef blamed the rash of al Qaeda attacks on the Israelis—beginning with the Riyadh bombing on May 12, 2003—explaining that "Al-Qaida is backed by Israel and Zionism."
- Saudi antipathy toward America forced the U.S. government to urge U.S. citizens to leave Saudi Arabia thirty-two months after 9/11. The largest Western contractor in Saudi Arabia, BAE Systems, had to offer substantial bonuses to its Western employees to stem their exodus from Saudi Arabia, and *The Washington Post* reported that "97 percent of Saudis view[ed] the United States in a negative light."

Feeding D.C.'s Greed

The Saudi royals always knew how the Washington, D.C. game was played: feed the greed of America's political power brokers. Saddam Hussein, on the other hand, had never adopted those economic tactics. He had never sent charming, free-spending, politically astute emissaries to our nation's capital—such as the ones the Saudis deployed. Had Saddam sent officials to D.C. who lavished massive financial emoluments on Washington's political elite, the U.S. would have probably erected monuments to him instead of hanging him.

The Saudis also underwrote the proliferation of nuclear weapons technology, including the equipment and expertise needed to manufacture fissile nuclear bomb-fuel. They bankrolled Pakistan's nuclear weapons program and its director, A. Q. Khan, often described as "the Father of Pakistan's atom bomb." Khan eventually became the world's most prolific purveyor of black-market nuclear weapons technology in history, offering it to rogue states everywhere—Libya, Iran, Iraq, North Korea, Syria, even, some believe, Pakistan's arch-enemy, India. Reporters would one day baptize Khan "the Johnny Appleseed of Nuclear Proliferation."

Another fact of Saudi life, which was seldom publicized in America's mainstream media, was its religiously inspired savagery. Long before ISIS was born, Wahhabism, Saudi Arabia's state religion, had institutionalized all of that terrorist group's worst abuses—the demonization of art, science, mathematics, archeology, music, journalism, democracy, women, and all non-Wahhabist peoples. The American media pilloried ISIS for its barbaric brand of justice—its amputation of heads, hands, feet, even eyes; its stonings; its interminable floggings, during which they administer as many as a thousand lashes; its subjugation and sequestration of women. Saudi Arabia, however, routinely brutalized its people in the same ugly way in public view and in plain sight.

Riyadh's Deera Square is known in the Kingdom as "Chop Chop Square" for its endless beheadings and amputations. Sometimes after a person has his head cut off, the Saudis crucify the body, placing the head in a plastic bag and hoisting it over the body where it appears to float, almost preternaturally abeyant. They display these crucified headless corpses in public for as long as four days. For example, the Saudi secret police arrested Ali Mohammed al-Nimr—the nephew of Sheikh Nimr al-Nimr, a renowned Shiite cleric, whom the Saudi authorities had recently killed. After torturing and beheading him, his body was crucified and publicly displayed. His crime was attending a peaceful prodemocracy rally.

During one New Year's celebration, the Saudi monarchy decapitated forty-seven people in thirteen cities in a single day. After those horrific executions, the Algerian journalist, Kamel Daoud, made the inevitable connection, calling Saudi Arabia "an ISIS that has made it."

Yet the U.S. media was and still is embarrassingly silent about this incessant procession of atrocities that Saudis call a judicial system.

U.S. officials also turn a blind eye to these horrors. Treating the Saudis as allies, all but drowning them in oil money, Pentagon's central goal is to maximize high-tech arms sales to the Kingdom. The standard rationalization has always been that since they have vast oil deposits, the U.S. has to curry favor with them regardless of their support of terrorism; hence, we arm them to the teeth. Saddam Hussein, however, also had prodigious oil reserves, and we executed him. The more direct explanation is that the Saudis know how to play the United States. They understand that the weakness of America's power elite is money and that they have always had a small, fanatical army of Saudi billionaires eager to invest in firms friendly to U.S. politicians and in the campaigns of the politicians themselves—often secretly via partisan think tanks and unregulated trade organizations.

Nor was the Obama administration immune to Saudi influence and entreaties. He and his people have attempted to sell the Saudis nuclear power plants, which would be a never-ending nightmare of apocalyptic proportions. (Source: http://www.nti.org/gsn/article/us-nuclear-marketers-visited-saudi-arabia-trade-talks-under-way/). As we have seen, with the addition of a low-tech fissile bomb-fuel reprocessor, a nuclear power reactor can be converted into a fissile bomb-fuel factory.

Obama's Nuclear Collusion

After the Fukushima nuclear disaster, President Barack Obama asked the NRC to determine whether U.S. nuclear power plants were safe and secure. His sudden faith in the NRC's truthfulness contradicted his earlier skepticism. Four years earlier, he had denounced them as a captive of the industry they were assigned to watch over, but after taking office, he quickly climbed into bed with the commissioners.

The reasons are obvious: his first chief of staff, Rahm Emanuel, had been an investment banker whose firm was instrumental in raising the $8.2 billion for the corporate merger that produced Exelon. Obama's number one political advisor, David Axelrod, was a paid advisor to Exelon, and that firm eventually became the largest nuclear power company in the U.S. His energy secretary, Stephen Chu, was one of academe's most committed nuclear power advocates. Even after the meltdown of Fukushima Daiichi—a nuclear power plant that regulatory misfeasance had turned into a fiscal and medical nightmare—Dr. Chu announced that federal regulators should not postpone construction of new U.S. nuclear power plants because of Fukushima . . . despite the NRC's corrupt, collusive track record. As for Obama, the nuclear lobby had deposited huge sums in his campaign coffers for years—up to $395,000, which was a lot for a fledgling senator with two years' senatorial experience. In return, *The New York Times* reported:

> "[Exelon] was chosen as one of only six electric utilities nation-wide for the maximum $200 million stimulus grant from the Energy Department. And when the Treasury Department granted loans for renewable energy projects, Exelon landed a commitment for up to $646 million."
>
> Obama and his advisors were to the nuclear industry what the George W. Bush and his oil-rich entourage had been to the petroleum industry.

The deeper I got into my research, the angrier I became. Everyone said a nuclear terrorist attack was their single worst nightmare, but no one had analyzed that possibility in any detail, gathered any factual information on how it might be conducted, or written any serious articles on it, let alone books. No one was even discussing the subject, not in any depth.

To make matters worse, in 2007, nuclear terrorists fired a warning round over humanity's bow, which should have been the shot heard round the world but which the U.S. essentially ignored. For decades, the Saudis had bankrolled the Pakistani Taliban—known as Tehrik-e-Taliban Pakistan (TTP)—and that funding finally began to generate acts of genuine nuclear terrorism. The first wave of assaults commenced when the TTP struck that country's own nuclear installations. These attacks were so impressively professional that some experts believe that the SSG, Pakistan army's elite commando unit, trained these al Qaeda/Taliban teams.

These nuclear terrorist attacks included:

- A 2007 raid on a nuclear missile base south of the Pakistani capital, in which the terrorists killed eight people.
- In August 2008, terrorists entered and blew up parts of a Wah Cantonment facility, which was believed to be a nuclear weapons assembly plant.
- In December 2008, suicide bombers next attacked Pakistan's Kamra air base—which was thought to be a nuclear weapons storage facility.
- In October 2009, terrorists disguised in army uniforms breached the Pakistan Army General Headquarters in Rawalpindi. In this ruthlessly professional, painstakingly planned assault, nine soldiers and nine militants were killed along with two civilians, even as the militants took forty-two hostages.
- In Bara in 2010, terrorists blew a hole in the military base's wall and

entered, killing six soldiers and wounding fifteen before twenty-five of their own fighters were killed.

- In 2011, in one of their most daring and meticulously organized raids, ten black-clad terrorists stormed and occupied Karachi's Mehran naval air base, which is only fifteen miles from a reputed nuclear weapons storage site near Masroor. They not only knew the locations of the base's surveillance cameras, they knew how to neutralize them. In this operation, fifteen attackers killed eighteen military personnel and wounded sixteen. They also set fire to several state-of-the-art warplanes with rocket-propelled grenades.

Nor did the TTP limit itself to nuclear sites.

- In 2012, militants assaulted a military base near Wazirabad in Punjab, killing seven security personnel.
- In August 2012, dozens of terrorists attacked an army installation, again near Wazirabad, killing eight soldiers. The press reported that they decapitated several of them.
- On February 2, 2013, *The New York Times* reported that TTP militants killed nine Pakistani soldiers and four government-hired mercenaries—possibly more—in an assault on an army base in the Khyber Pakhtunkhwa province. The militants were equipped with military machine guns and rockets; they also murdered ten civilians. A spokesman for the terrorists said they were avenging the drone assassinations of two Tehrik-e-Taliban leaders.

Similar attacks continue to this day.

Moreover, the Pakistani military heavily protected the bases these terrorists assaulted. Not so in the U.S. rent-a-cops secured U.S. nuclear weapons labs, our fissile nuclear bomb-fuel sites, and our nuclear power plants; and according to the Supreme Court, they did not have to defend these sites against serious 9/11-style terrorist attacks by a dozen or more heavily armed intruders. For the kind of superbly organized, rigorously trained terrorists who detonated portions of Pakistan's nuclear bases with such effectiveness, blowing up America's nuclear sites—especially its nuclear power plants—would be a day at the beach.

Slowly, the basic elements of my nonfiction book on nuclear terrorism came together. It also took years out of my life, but I eventually finished it. I called it: *The Nuclear Terrorist: His Financial Backers and Political Patrons in the U.S. and Abroad.*

As if to confirm my descriptions of how poorly secured U.S. nuclear installations are, in 2012 Sister Megan Rice, an eighty-two-year-old nun with a heart condition, broke into the Y-12 fissile nuclear bomb-fuel storage site. Along with two late-middle-aged men, she reached the main storage building, which contained 100,000 tons of bomb-grade highly enriched uranium. Spray-painting peace slogans on its walls, they sat on a curb and sang peace songs. Only after Sister Megan and the men spent several hours in Y-12 did security guards accidentally spot and arrest them.

Instead of pinning a medal on Sister Megan and her two friends for exposing the ludicrous lack of security at our nuclear sites, the Obama administration tried and convicted them as nuclear terrorists. All three were given lengthy sentences. Sister Megan was to do her time in a federal lockup in Brooklyn, New York. Since I live in Manhattan, I wrote a letter to her. I began visiting her on a weekly basis.

Sister Megan is perhaps the nicest, sweetest person I've ever met. I felt immediately as if I had known her a long, long time, and in a sense I had. I'd written a character very much like her in *End of Days*. Sister Cassandra, one of the novel's main characters, is an antinuclear activist-nun who is always in and out of prisons. Long before I met Sister Megan, I'd imagined her. After all my work on nuclear issues, it was as if I'd been looking for her my whole life.

Ironically, I also have a long prison history. I grew up near a maximum security facility in Michigan City, IN, and some of my earliest memories were staring at its high white walls in something resembling awe. The town had a sizable community of corrections workers and ex-convicts who settled down there after they were released. Prison people were scattered all over the city, so the penitentiary seemed to be everywhere.

In high school during the summers, I played eight or nine tennis tournaments inside the walls. Since the prison had a single tennis court, only one or two of us could play on the court at a time. The other three or four players had time to kill, so we'd walk the rec yard and talk to the inmates. We frequently played basketball with them, almost like we were cons ourselves. In those days, prisons—even a hard-nosed lockup like my hometown maximum security facility—were a lot more relaxed than they are today.

The Most Frightening Father Any of Us Kids Had Ever Heard Of

Back when I was playing those tennis tournaments on "the Big Yard," my family had two highly memorable neighbors. One was the prison doctor-psychiatrist; the other was the prison torturer. (Yes, they had a prison torturer.) After a tennis match, I'd memorize and write down the serial numbers of the inmates, then give them to the doctor-psychiatrist. He'd pull their file jackets and let my old friend, Jerry Gibbs, and me read them. They all contained the prisoners' pre-Miranda police confessions, their conviction records, and often lengthy psychiatric interviews.

Jacob Bronowski once wrote that "violence wears the face of fallen angels." He also called violence "the sphinx by the fireside," and many of the prisoners gave that impression. They were intensely ingratiating—soft voices, soft eyes—but we soon learned from their file jackets that they'd all done terrible things. The most ingratiating of the inmates and the prison's best tennis player was an axe murderer.

Jerry and I would then tell my neighbor, the torturer, about the men we played and who they were. He'd nod and explain to us, in his unforgettable words, "I've beaten the mortal piss out of all of them."

He was a huge man—six three, biceps like cannonballs, over three hundred pounds, much of it hard fat—and very scary.

"I can whip any man in the Indiana State Prison," he used to brag, "young or old, big or small, white or colored. I take them into a sub-basement cell, put on the kid gloves, take off the cuffs, and cuddle with them for a half hour. I never leave a mark on them."

He smiled a lot, but the smile never reached his eyes. In fact, he had the deadest eyes my friends and I had ever seen on a human being. We also knew his son, and we agreed unanimously that his old man was the most frightening father we had ever heard of, let alone seen. My friends and I all went to bed every night and prayed to God, thanking him for not having made that monster our father.

After graduating from high school, I worked seven years, on and off, in the steel mills in Gary, Indiana, getting through college, and one of the mini-mills I worked in signed parole papers for convicts. Half the workers there were ex-offenders, so one way or another I got to know a lot of convicts and ex-convicts growing up.

Even when I moved to New York, prisons seemed to follow me. My first year as an acquiring editor, I happened to publish a couple of very good ex-con writers, Nathan C. Heard and Malcolm Braly. (At the International

Association of Poets, Essayists and Novelists (PEN) we still give the annual Malcolm Braly Award for the best book, fiction or nonfiction, written by an inmate.) As a book editor, I've had to travel a lot, and these two authors encouraged me to visit the local prisons during my trips. I'd talk to inmates about getting free books from publishers, organizing book classes, and writing, both commercially and for pleasure. Over the decades, I've published a score or more of inmates and ex-cons. When New York City learned of the work I'd done in prisons, they named a day after me. Atlanta presented me with a similar award.

So I began visiting Sister Megan each week. The living area in which she and her fellow women inmates served their time was cramped, congested, and shockingly inhumane. The facility housed approximately 115 of them in sixty bunk beds in a space the size of a high school basketball court. The bunks were so close together the women could touch the prisoner in the bed next to them. For the 115 women, there were six sinks, six showers and six toilets, several of which were often broken; all of them were enclosed inside the same small area where the women slept. The women had no access to an outdoor exercise yard, and they had no mess hall. They received food trays through a hole in the wall. Most of them had to eat off the trays, sitting on beds. For a recreation area, they had a room with a TV and some chairs. They had no educational opportunities, and the counselor could only give them approximately ten minutes a week to schedule visitors' appointments. They had no real guidance or career counseling. A number of the women were doing life. This would be their home until they died. It was to be Sister Megan's home until she died or was released.

Sister Megan and her fellow prisoners were warehoused and locked away like forgotten furniture in a storage attic.

The women's prison was so horrendous I suspected that the administration would not allow journalists inside for fear they would expose the conditions to the media. (I later discovered my suspicions were correct. A *New Yorker* writer had not been allowed to interview Sister Megan in the prison.) Still, I managed to help a reporter, Linda Stasi, get into the jail. She wrote an electrifying, full-page-with-no-ads exposé on Sister Megan's disgraceful incarceration in *The New York Daily News*.

Linda, *The Daily News*, and I tweeted and e-mailed everyone we could. We asked them to read the linked newspaper piece, forward it to other people—do something, anything to get Sister Megan and her two friends released. We also argued that the Federal Bureau of Corrections need to improve conditions in the prison—or better yet, shut it down.

Approximately ten days after Linda's newspaper piece hit the stands, eight federal judges—all of them women—descended on the facility; they spent an entire day inspecting the living conditions and interviewing the women prisoners. Within another ten days, Sister Megan's conviction was denounced by the federal appeals court as a grotesque miscarriage of justice and overturned. She and her two friends were instantly released.

> Sister Megan's shameful imprisonment summarizes everything that's wrong with Washington, D.C.'s policies toward nuclear weapons and the management of our country's nuclear facilities.

As frightening as the subject matter was, however, the nonfiction book was not without hope. I did offer answers on how to deal with the nuclear terrorist threat. One of them I thought was obvious. Generals Sherman and Sheridan defeated America's Plains Indians in large part by depriving them of their sustenance—the buffalo. They waged a war of extinction against the great herds, and by 1900, there were fewer than a thousand bison in North America. We can question the ethics of Sherman and Sheridan's strategy—and I certainly do—but we cannot question its efficacy. To defeat Middle Eastern terrorism, the U.S. would have to do the same thing: deprive it of its sustenance—in this case, its financial sustenance. We could purge the Middle East's terrorists of their life's blood by freeing the world of oil. Do that, and in three years Saudi Arabia would be Somalia, Iran would become Afghanistan, and if Saddam Hussein were still alive, he'd be invading his neighbors on a dromedary, waving a scimitar.

After the book was published, I did several months of radio and TV. The History Channel had me host and star in the two-hour special on man-made catastrophes. Part of my assignment was to also speak for a half hour on nuclear terrorism.

A Harvard instructor began asking me to come up and speak on nuclear terrorism. The first time I visited there, I talked about how insecure the world's nuclear sites were, particularly fissile nuclear bomb-fuel sites, and how culpable so many Saudi terrorist financiers and American politicians were. As I spoke, however, I also began to envision a possible novel on the subject. Instead of a nuclear apocalyptic epic, this would be a nuclear terrorism thriller. In midspeech, I could suddenly see it all: I not only had my Pakistani nuclear terrorists, I also had my Saudi and American supervillains—witty, sophisticated, erudite, politically powerful billionaire-plutocrats, funding the terrorists and pulling the other characters' strings like pernicious puppet masters from the pit of hell. I also knew where my fissile nuclear bomb-fuel was, and I knew how to steal it. I had some U.S. nuclear sites my terrorists could easily destroy, as well as any number of cities I could incinerate with my horrifyingly lethal, Hiroshima-style terrorist nukes. Heroes? Over the years I'd known some very courageous war correspondents and undercover intelligence officers who could serve as my heroes. Two women, in particular, came immediately to mind. The two I was thinking of would do anything to pull our so-called republic back from the nuclear terrorist's abyss.

The plot and characterization for the book hit me as if I were Paul, traveling the road to Damascus, instead of an author talking to a classroom full of Harvard students.

My old friend William Burroughs once defined *Naked Lunch* as that "frozen moment when everyone sees what is on the end of every fork." Standing there in front of those Harvard students, I had my "frozen moment" when I could glimpse the nightmare horror that was truly "on the end of every fork."

I was still seeing it the next day on the train ride from Harvard back to New York. *What the hell,* I finally said to myself, sitting there in that Acela Express car, *You've done your research. You've written your nonfiction book. Why not write the novel?*

I decided to call it *And Into the Fire.*

Getting out my laptop, I began to type.

Since Auschwitz we know what man is capable of. Since Hiroshima we know what is at stake.
   —Viktor Frankl, *Man's Search for Meaning*